C000260774

THE LAST MAD S

MARK HODKINSON

The Last Mad Surge of Youth

POMONA

A Pomona Book
P - 0 1 7

Published by Pomona Books 2009
PO Box 50, Hebden Bridge, West Yorkshire HX7 8WA, England, UK
Telephone 01422 846900 · e-mail admin@pomonauk.co.uk

www.pomonauk.co.uk

1

Copyright © Mark Hodkinson 2009

Mark Hodkinson has asserted his right under the Copyright, Designs
and Patents Act 1988 to be identified as author of this work.

All rights reserved. Without limiting the rights under copyright reserved above,
no part of this publication may be reproduced, stored in or introduced into a retrieval
system, or transmitted, in any form or by any means (electronic, mechanical, photocopying, recording or otherwise) without the prior written permission of both the
copyright owner and the above publisher of this book. It is written in the
stars above. The gods decree. You'll be right here by my side.

A CIP catalogue record for this book
is available from the British Library

ISBN 978-1-904590-20-0

Set in Linotype Granjon by Christian Brett
Printed and bound in England by
CPI Cox & Wyman, Reading, RG1 8EX

PRAISE FOR PREVIOUS BOOKS:

'Hodkinson writes quite beautifully, which means that those
of us with lesser gifts are given a glimpse into his soul.
It is a richly rewarding place to be.'
– Richard Whitehead, *The Times*

'Hodkinson has a light touch and a modest, self-effacing style.
He is a fine writer.'
– Andrew Baker, *The Daily Telegraph*

'His prose is never less than first-rate.'
– Tom Boncza-Tomaszewski, *The Independent on Sunday*

'A respected writer.'
– Fabienne Williams, *The Observer*

'He writes with economy and elegance, self-deprecating
but never self-pitying'
– Tom Dart, *The Times*

'Hodkinson can weave magic out of the mundane.'
– *Daily Mail*

'A deft writer, poignant and funny at different times.'
– Harry Pearson, *The Guardian*

'The stuff of extraordinary fictions, given fine telling from
Hodkinson's evocative prose.'
– *Big Issue*

'Sharply written and frequently deeply moving. Hodkinson's
reflections are peculiarly profound.'
– *The Independent*

www.markhodkinson.com

1980

The library was almost empty. Carey shielded his eyes from sunlight piercing the high windows. When he lowered his hand, he could see dust slowly turning inside the beams of light. Good, the photocopier was free: no one from the tenants' association clunking coins, jabbing in leaflets, carrier bags all over the place. He pulled the artwork from a plastic wallet. The cover of the tape was a mill chimney standing tall above lines of jagged roofs. He had photocopied the original picture repeatedly until he was happy with the degeneration, the white taking on a greyish hue and the harsh lines softening or breaking up. The track-listing had been done on a typewriter, the words stuck down with glue and a space left to drop in the band's name later; they hadn't thought of one yet.

"I was hoping the machine would burn out," he told Barrett afterwards.

"How come?"

"I love that scorching effect you get. It overheated once and it looked brilliant, this sepia colour fading to black."

They decided on Group Hex.

"I love the letter X," said Carey.

"Why?"

"Just do. Must be something about the shape."

The tape was their debut 'album' recorded on Carey's Aiwa cassette recorder. The C90 contained a single track on each side: *Factory Workers* and *Alienation*. They had strummed unplugged and out-of-tune electric guitars while the television, radio and vacuum cleaner were on in the background, re-creating, they hoped, the cacophony of the factories and mills around them. Barrett hadn't sung but groaned and yelped, with passion. Twenty copies, individually numbered, were run off by placing two recorders next to each other.

"The deterioration in sound quality adds to the post-industrial authenticity," said Barrett.

"That's precisely what I was going to say."

Carey had hand-coloured the cassettes using paint he found in the garage — the packaging was at least as important as the music. At first he did it conventionally but then stippled them, dabbing the brush against the plastic, careful not to get any on the tape itself.

*

2009

The sunbathers on all sides were loose-limbed, stretched out and serene. Barrett was crabby, running red. Mad at the heat, the sand, the Spanish: everything everywhere.

"It doesn't suit you," said Esther.

"What?"

"The grumbling."

It didn't suit him being told his grumbling didn't suit him but he was determined to maintain grace.

"I know. You're right. There'll be no more."

He gave a mock salute.

They didn't speak for a few minutes. When he next heard his wife's voice it was dry and shallow as if it had blown across the bay. Maybe he'd been asleep.

"Why don't you dip your feet in? Seawater's supposed to be good for you," she said.

Everyone knows that, he thought, resisting the urge to answer sarcastically. He remembered jeering shortly after they had first met, 'Where's the egg?' when she had told him something similarly obvious.

'What egg?'

'The one you've just crawled out of.'

Her face dropped, and something inside him.

'Sorry,' he said.

He knew the word formed a pitiful transaction, like handing a plaster to someone he'd just shot. He vowed that he wouldn't bruise her again so easily but sometimes it was a job to resist.

3

The tide was coming in. Water lapped beneath him. He surrendered his feet. It was unexpectedly cold and the muscles in his throat tensed. Checking Esther wasn't looking, he tucked his feet back under the lounger, slipping on leather sandals. Sand fastened itself to his wet toes.

Holly was singing as she dug with a plastic spade. The same song. Over and over again. Words mixed up. Out of tune and out of season. Little doggie carry Mary on a dustee road.

"Can't you just dig?"

His daughter squinted as she turned to face him.

"I *am* digging."

"You're making a lot of noise while you're doing it."

"I didn't know."

"Well, you are."

She carried on, unperturbed. A second later she asked if he had any shells to decorate the castle walls.

"No."

*

They had always met up at Carey's house, from being little kids. It was usually too mad at Barrett's, too much going on — rowing and shouting, doors slamming, his dad wanting some peace and quiet if you don't mind, thank you very much. Before the music, they had produced their own magazine, a cross between *Mad* and *Monty Python*, running to about ten issues, which they passed around their class at school. At Carey's the felt tips stayed where they had been put but at Barrett's they were scattered everywhere, dried up, ends squashed, lids missing, sometimes thrown in the bin.

"Well, they were in the bloody way."

4

The band was another project. After the 'sonic dissonance' of their debut ('It was crucial we captured the pre-tutored, unfettered version of the band for posterity,'—quote from their interview with *Laughing Boy* fanzine) they began forming songs with at least a vague structure which they might possibly be able to play more than once. Most of these skeletal numbers were based around two or three strummed strings of a guitar, rather than the routine six. Conventional playing, the type learned from Bert Weedon books and *Play-in-a-Day* pamphlets, was viewed as repugnant. Enthusiasm and energy was the mantra and they scoffed at anyone spending hours learning to play *properly* – they mimed being sick after saying the word.

"When you get good on an instrument you become a slave to the conventional."

"Definitely," agreed Carey. "Proficiency is a disease."

Their sole lyrical theme was atomic annihilation; to even consider anything else felt timorous and dim-witted—the world was seconds away from striking midnight. They soon realised a synthesiser was needed on songs like *Neutron Bomb* and *Last Person on Earth* to add ghostly trails of sound evoking a nuclear winter. At first Carey was apprehensive about augmenting the gang of two.

"That's the challenge, bringing others in and getting it all mixed up," said Barrett. "Duos are boring. We don't want to end up like Simon and fucking Garfunkel, droning on about nothing."

They agreed on another edict: no auditions.

"Your audition is who you are, how you live your life," said Barrett.

"Totally."

Barrett had someone in mind, a kid new to their school.

★

Thinking about it, where *were* the shells, the driftwood and the rock pools? Why wasn't it like it used to be? Barrett realised he was getting mixed up with holidays in Devon where he'd gone as a kid. His mind drifted back to caravans smelling of Calor gas and damp. Sleeping in pullout beds secreted in the walls. Seagulls clomping on the roof. His mum asking that the door be left open to get rid of the mustiness, let some air in. Rain falling in the night, tapping on the tin roof and making patterns on the windows. The sun coming back in the morning, everything golden again.

His thoughts were fractured by cars revving up on the road behind. He cursed. They had to cross this busy dual carriageway every morning by footbridge to get to the beach. He usually stopped and watched the vehicles charging past, drivers honking their horns, cutting each other up. He mused on where all these ill-mannered bastards were heading and imagined them listening to soft rock, singing along to saxophone solos.

He sat deeper into the lounger. A wave of pain ran across his chest; this had happened intermittently over the previous weeks. He gulped at the air and wondered whether he should walk into town and buy another bottle of vodka. That would sort him out, see him right. He shuddered.

"What is it?" asked Esther.

"A wasp or something landed on my arm."

"You're sweating."

He ran fingers across his forehead. He was soaked. Esther stood over him.

"Are you sure you're okay?"

"Fine. A bit tired, that's all."

She smelled sweet. It was only perfume or soap but it reminded him of something.

★

Barrett liked the look of Jason Fisher straight away. He was skinny with caved-in cheeks and ratty hair. He had arrived at their school a few weeks before they were all due to leave. His family had moved back to the area when his dad left the army.

Word got through to Barrett that Fisher had taken a few mates home one dinner time and demonstrated his synthesiser, wiring it up to a Watkins Copycat to make it repeat and echo.

'It sounded like something off *Dr Who*,' one kid told him.

A few days later they were in their once-a-week music lesson when Mr Bacon (known as Crispy) appealed for a volunteer to stand at the front and illustrate breathing techniques while singing. He kept asking and asking, sitting forward in his chair.

"Come on, I only need one of you."

No one moved.

"Don't be shy."

Bacon wore clothes similar to a school uniform and had the haircut, slightly grown out, that barbers gave kids when they went in with their mums. It made him look as if he hadn't left the building since childhood. He asked again. Everyone was getting uneasy. He pushed up his glasses with the back of his hand, loosening his collar.

"What is it with you lot? Why won't you have a go?"

Debbie Green volunteered. Fisher muttered that she was a mug. Bacon heard and ran at him, knocking over a chair. He dragged him to the front, jabbing fingers into his chest, pushing him on the shoulder.

"Mug did you say? Mug? Who's a mug now Fisher, hey?"

7

He poked him repeatedly as if goading him to strike back so he could deliver a punch and release the fury. Fisher rocked on his feet, stumbling against the blackboard.

*

The heat intensified. Barrett fell asleep and when he awoke didn't know if he'd been out for seconds or hours. He heard himself gasp. His fists were clenched. Esther was reading a book with her back against a large rock while Holly worked on her model village, moulding sand. Barrett was overwhelmed with affection for them and wanted to draw closer. He made a small movement as if to rise but it was less than half-hearted, more a thought that had almost come to life. Still, he rallied. He had a lot to live for: Esther, Holly, his music (regardless of how well it sold or was critically received). And he was fundamentally a healthy person. A few weeks off the booze, a month or two possibly, and he'd be fit again, strong.

"Est, have you got a pen?"

"There's one in my bag."

While she looked for it he took out a piece of paper from the back pocket of his trousers. It was a print-out of a list of questions from a music website. Rupert Green, his manager, had cut and pasted it into an e-mail sent to him before they left for Spain:

'Hi John, here's that short interview I told you about. I don't know a lot about the site but it claims to get lots of hits. At least it'll get your brain working. Stir that soup! I've left gaps after their questions so you can fill in your

replies. I'm sure (if you ask nicely) Esther will
type up the stuff on her laptop. There's no mad
rush to get it back to me. Have a great holiday.
Relax! All my love to Est and Hol.
    Rupe.'

Esther looked across.

"What is it?" she asked.

"The website thing I've got to do for Rupert."

He had mentioned the questionnaire over the previous days,
complaining that Green was 'out of order' expecting him to
take work on holiday. Secretly, he had longed for the moment
when he could revert to his old persona as he summoned replies:
witty, informed, cocksure. It might have been a love letter or a
set of rediscovered holiday snaps.

*

"Why is she a mug, Fisher? What makes her a mug and you
so special? What is it? Come on, tell us. We all want to know.
What's so special about you?"

He didn't reply but looked directly into Bacon's eyes, not
with menace or defiance but blankly as if he knew that only by
meeting his gaze could he defuse his temper. Bacon shook him
fiercely.

"Do I have to shake it out of you? Do I?"

He gave up and shoved Fisher away, looking at his hands and
frowning as if they were covered in shit, wiping them on his
trousers.

"Get out, get out of my sight."

Fisher was told to wait outside until the end of the lesson.

When the rest filed out later, he was still there. Barrett was impressed with his defiance, for not running off home and crying to his mum and dad.

★

Remind us, just how successful have you been in terms of record sales? Go on, show off!

Hey, don't ask that. I'm a shy northern lad. Okay then: three UK number one singles with Killing Stars, six in the top ten. Worldwide album sales of, er, a few million. Two solo UK number one singles, five (or is it six?) top tens, tons of albums sold. Sorry, can't remember how I've done elsewhere. It's about the music anyway, not the sales. So they say.

Tell us about Group Hex.

We were a bunch of zealots, spreading the gospel of musical and cultural fundamentalism. That was the aim, anyway. They were my bedroom band (actually 'front room band' or 'room above a working men's club band' to be precise) — and spawned the behemoth that became Killing Stars.

How do you view punk all these years on?

I sometimes wonder whether it has done me any good banging on about punk so much. It dates me, locks me into a particular time frame. In strict terms we were post-punk or new wave anyway which, for me, had a more artistic and cerebral slant. All the same, punk was the wake-up call. We thought we were going to change the world but

that's not possible really. It's a dream I suppose and
if you don't have a dream ... I know much of what I
believed in then still matters, even more so in some
ways. It's ironic because I'm now on an independent
label where there's a real do-it-yourself ethos. I've
come back round to punk in a way.

★

Fisher left school without taking any exams.

"Can't be arsed," he said. "It's a farce, man."

He began working at a scrap yard, wearing huge boots and
an over-sized greatcoat with the collar turned up. He had given
Barrett his phone number, telling him to 'give me a tinkle' and
arrange a visit to his *gaff* — a terraced house left to him by his
grandad.

Barrett and Carey called round. They were intrigued, they'd
never heard of a sixteen-year-old kid having his own house
before.

"Everyone should have their private space," said Fisher.
"There was no way I could live with my dum and mad anymore. They were doing my swede in."

The house was done out with a false chipboard pillar in the
front room, painted pink and orange. Heavy, velvety drapes
hung at the windows. On the walls were pictures of Victorian
street scenes in chunky gold frames. There was barely any
furniture, so visitors had to sit on scraggy cushions strewn
across the floorboards.

"Tell me all about this group of yours, then," said Fisher.

Carey told him that the social and political philosophy was as
important as the music. In short (and he could make notes if he

11

wanted): educate yourself, celebrate yourself, banish ego, do something, speak out. And, of course: fight capitalism. Fisher listened, nodding his head while fiddling with rolling papers and shreds of tobacco. When Carey used the word 'project' Fisher held up his hand.

"I like that word: *project*. Do you know what I say? Zero tolerance for apathy. It's what this fucking town needs, people willing to shake things up. It shouldn't be music for its own sake. Anyone can do that. It's about using this that matters."

He banged his forehead with his knuckles. Carey winced. After his speech, Fisher stopped abruptly and trilled:

"Anyone for a brew?"

He made the word 'brew' last for about four seconds.

*

Tell us about your new album.
Well, it's called Godspace and I think it's the most achieved record I've ever released. It's taken me years to properly learn about space and tension in music. I wanted to create something that stood up to repeated listens, which you found more in every time you returned to it.

Will it sell trillions?
Absolutely not. It's all rigged, who gets to sell loads and who doesn't. It's about money: m-o-n-e-y. Those that spend the most on marketing and advertising (and bribing!) have most success, simple. I can't complain, I had my turn at being a rock god (ouch) and had a great

time, thank you very much, but I'm much happier doing
the current stuff.

**Anything vital that you'd like to impart to our sub-
scribers?**
Always wash your hands, say your prayers and dare to be
different. It's done me okay. And, lest I forget, please
buy my new album. It will enrich your life massively,
probably.

★

Fisher's house became the band's headquarters. Most nights,
Barrett and Carey went there straight from college where they
had started A Levels, picking up fish and chips on the way.
They talked late into the evenings, curtains open, darkness
falling over the room. Fisher would light the gas fire and switch
on the lamp on top of the broken television. Barrett and Carey
were often sleepy but he carried on talking regardless. They
found him easy to be around. He was eager to listen and counsel, though his responses were often anodyne; he believed most
problems were related to the weather or time of year:

"We'll all feel a lot better when it stops raining and summer
comes round again."

His language was peculiar too:

"Forgive me please, for I must defect to the uppermost part of
the house."

"You mean you're off upstairs?"

"Indeed, that I am."

They began going out at weekends, drinking in town centre pubs. The first time, they agreed to meet at The Flying Horse. Fisher was early, smiling broadly at the bar and waving a pint glass as a greeting. He was dressed in a suit; no one under thirty wore a suit unless they had a job interview. They drank the first pints quickly as if they were water. The place began filling up. Giggling girls, their perfume sharp and sickly, ordered Cinzano and lemonade before ambushing tables, bags at their feet, puffing on cigarettes. Lads entered in streams, following the leader, sniffing out beer, passing heavy glasses along the row to swill down in greedy mouthfuls. They seemed oblivious to the cold, their thin white shirts unbuttoned, sleeves rolled up.

"Look at them, what wankers," said Fisher cheerfully. "It's like a fucking cattle market in here."

The three of them scoffed and imagined the record collections of the people around them.

"It's like punk never happened," said Fisher. "Where's the individuality, the expression? Where's the poetry? They all look the fucking same."

He made the sound of sheep baaing.

Four pints later:

"Let's go to a club."

Barrett and Carey weren't sure.

"It'll be disco crap."

"Come on, there'll be more of this lot to laugh at," said Fisher.

They trooped out into the night. The streets were swarming with people, everyone shouting, everyone pissed, taxis swerving to avoid them. A burger van was parked close to the club entrance and two or three waited while the vendor, a scrawny bloke in National Health glasses, pulled steaming onions from a vat of hot water and placed them on muffins. A couple meandered by, hardly able to walk, holding each other upright.

A queue had formed outside the club. Bouncers flirted with the girls, smiling, holding back their shoulders. Barrett announced that he couldn't be bothered waiting. Carey agreed. Fisher said he'd go in on his own, no problem.

"You two go and get yourself a candle wax hand-warmer."

"A what?"

"It's what I call a kebab."

After nearly two months of talking and scheming and sneering they had still not heard Fisher play synthesiser or even seen it. It didn't matter. They liked who he was, how he lived his life. He was in.

*

As he finished the questionnaire, Barrett remembered. Most years, when his family made their way to Devon, they stopped off at the same pub somewhere near Taunton. The beer garden was swathed in plum trees and the fruit was often juicy ripe, buzzed by bees and wasps. Barrett and his brother David would mess about, lying on their backs, eyes closed, sniffing the air, happy that their mum and dad were in holiday mood and getting along for once. They'd find the odd plum that had burst, forming luscious lips on either side of the tear. That was it: Esther's scent was vaguely reminiscent of that same sweet smell.

He was relieved that he could recall the garden, the fruit and those nights in the caravan. He still thought like a poet.

*

The three of them finally began working on material at Fisher's house. Carey noticed that Barrett's guitar playing was soon impressive. He could tune up by ear and was making chord shapes, picking out catchy lead runs too. Carey thought it but didn't say: he was definitely on his way to a diseased state.

Barrett contributed most of the lyrics and hummed outlines of tunes but said he'd rather concentrate on guitar than sing. Paul Schofield — Scoffer — a kid off the Bluebell estate, volunteered for the role. Fisher had told him about the band when he'd called at the scrap yard with his dad looking for engine parts. They said they didn't care whether he could sing (he couldn't and neither could he shout in time) or how he looked (glasses, slightly overweight): wanting to do it was enough, being committed. Others soon offered themselves as drummers, bassists or guitarists although most had been playing for just a few weeks. This was all cool, said Barrett, because Group Hex was a 'floating zoo', a phrase they began issuing routinely.

They quickly realised they were forming their own kingdom made up of kids who had never been in gangs before: the quiet ones who had kept their heads down at school, read books (Salinger, Camus and Satre mainly) and were now buying records and listening to John Peel on Radio One. Several didn't actually make it to a practice but seemed happy enough to have talked about the idea, imagining themselves to be in a band.

As part of their 'umbrella agenda' — everything had to be categorised — Carey started work on a fanzine, *Word Hex*. He was the natural choice as editor because he'd told everyone that, should the group not make it, his long-term plan was to become a novelist.

"What you going to write about in your books?" asked Fisher.

"You lot, stuff about growing up around here."

"Too fucking right. You make sure the mundane gets its beautiful due."

"Did you make that up?"

"Nah, nicked it. Can't remember where from."

★

They left the beach and returned to the villa. After showering and changing, the three of them sauntered through the resort to a restaurant. While they waited to be served, Holly played with some children in a courtyard at the side of the main room. Barrett was talking quickly. The waiter arrived with the wine list.

"I think we'll have a bottle of Rioja. Yep, we will," said Barrett.

Esther smiled tightly. She didn't want to say anything and risk spoiling the mood. He was on holiday; everyone had a drink on holiday. And this was different anyway, drinking while you were talking, while you were with people. She locked into his eyes. She loved him like this, telling stories, animated, alive. She stared at the hard line that formed from the corner of his eyes to his mouth when he made certain expressions; the strong and masculine nose; the way he sat, open, hands at his side, drawing her in, wanting to tell her something funny or vital or incisive, wanting that from her too. She reached for his hand across the table.

★

Carey was permitted use of *the* school duplicator for the fanzine. He typed the articles on waxy paper that smelled of charcoal and had to be hand-fed into the machine. The subject matter was vetted by the school's community officer whose job was to support local nursery groups, pensioners' clubs and, now, teenagers peddling insurrection. He noticed the swear words:

"Look lads, I don't want to impinge on what you're doing and it's fantastic that you're not out on the streets mugging old ladies, but could you spread your 'fucks' out a bit? If they're all in one place we might get a few complaints."

The fanzine's opening statement was an excerpt from a poem written by someone called Stevie D that had been included on a compilation LP of home-recorded material. He had spoken the words while speeding up and slowing down a jazz track on a record player:

> 'Life is what you make it
> Music is anything you want
> You don't have to be able to play
> You don't have to have something to say
> Just do it
> Fucking do it.'

A few days after they had put *Word Hex* on sale in local shops, a lad knocked at Carey's door.

"Hello, I'm Stevie D."

Shit, thought Carey, they had probably breached all kinds of copyright laws.

"I've just bought your magazine," said Stevie, flashing a mile-wide smile. "It's really good. I thought I'd drop by and say hello."

Carey liked that he called it a magazine and not a fanzine, it sounded more substantial.

"We're not in trouble for printing a bit of your poem, are we?"

"No way. I'm flattered. It's good to know it inspired you."

He told Carey he lived in Matthews Street, about a mile across town, and they spent several minutes saying they couldn't believe the coincidence of living so close to one another, being into the same things, and never having met before. Stevie wore a combat jacket with a thin shoelace around his wrist. He was lean with fine cheekbones, his hair thick and spiked as if simultaneously not thought-about but also meticulously arranged, a happy accident.

*

Barrett told Esther it was refreshing being out in public and no longer harangued by fans.

"It's quite nice doing ordinary things with ordinary Joes like your good self," he teased. "Before, I always had to have someone to clear the way, keeping people at a distance."

He remembered something:

"I once made a special effort to meet some normal people. What a bad idea that was."

He explained that he'd asked the record company to organise competitions with local radio stations, where winners could meet him before shows. After two of these meet-and-greets (known, he told her, in the industry as 'shake-and-fakes'), the idea was dropped.

"Why?" she asked.

"I couldn't cope with all those ugly mugs gawping at me and having to make small talk. Yuk!"

"You cruel thing. What did the label say?"

"They took the piss because that was supposed to be my

thing, man of the people and all that. They were telling me it was those very people who bought the records."

"They were, weren't they?"

"Sort of, but they weren't the people who *first* did."

★

Group Hex became regular visitors to the flat Stevie D shared with his girlfriend, Julie. It had polished floorboards, lines of beads hanging from doorframes and the woodwork was painted red and green. Julie had etched a mystical symbol in the centre of the longest wall and visitors felt like they had entered a small temple.

The main room was lined with cassette tapes. Alongside the regulation punk and new wave was obscure stuff: Neu!, Ladies WC, Faust, Henry Cow, The Fugs, The Eyes, Zodiac, Red Crayola, The Residents, Can. Dotted around were Stevie's lyrics and articles, destined for fanzines and leaflets — essays on feminism, religion, gender stereotyping, racism, vegetarianism. He was also working on his next record, an EP for a French label.

Stevie was unlike anyone they had met before. It was as if they were starting out on a journey he had almost completed. They were making tapes in their bedroom; he had appeared on a record. Apart from Fisher, they were all at home with their parents; Stevie had his own place. They didn't have girlfriends; he had Julie, and she was the kind of girl they coveted: composed, confident, punky and sexy in capped sleeve T-shirts and Oxfam skirts.

Barrett and Carey hoped to one day burn with the same quiet, intense charisma as Stevie.

"When we're his age we'll be just as cool," reassured Carey.

Esther knew that he was fixated with the kinship he had felt with the original fans, the true believers — those who had seen the band on their first couple of tours, before they signed to a label. Barrett couldn't understand where they had gone and fretted that they had found something inherently phoney about him as if they shifted from one icon of integrity to another, mindful of *the sell-out*. He'd told her many times that every decision snagging him further into the machine — signing with a major label, employing a publicist, accepting a buy-on for tour support, the heavy selling of merchandise — had been made after a fraught imaginary dialogue with these devotees.

She didn't say, but she considered it an ideological debate conducted with ghosts. The kids like him who had stuck up their hair with sugared water and pinned button badges to their lapels had grown up, moved on. They weren't tripping from shop to shop any more in pursuit of articles of faith etched into records. They had kids of their own, bills to pay, more important things to worry about. In fact, when he talked like this it reminded her of their age difference. Few people of her generation expected rock stars to ponder socio-political issues or hold their integrity in such regard.

After they finished the meal, Esther shouted Holly in from outside where she was playing again.

"Aw, do we have to go, mum?"

"Afraid so."

Barrett ruffled her hair.

They paid and walked through to the small reception area at the front where they were ambushed by mirrors. Barrett saw his reflection four times over. He winced.

Group Hex's practice amps were the size of electric toasters and had to be banged on all sides to work. The sound, when it finally came through, was thin and tinny. On Barrett's seventeenth birthday a savings policy matured that his mum had taken out for him when he was born. He went to Digger, a music shop in town patrolled by the owner's notorious Alsatian dogs, ever eager to sniff around a customer's backside or gnaw at an arm. Barrett, dodging the dogs, bought a 100-watt amplifier and a speaker almost as big as a phone box. The amp had four inputs and Barrett told the others they could share it while they saved to buy their own. When they first plugged in a squeal of feedback was set loose and the overload made the sound woolly, but the joy of playing at volume for the first time sent them giddy.

"Rock *and* roll," screamed Fisher. "Group Hex? Group fuckin' sex more like."

★

Back at the villa, Barrett told Esther he planned to take the bus to Marbella the next morning and 'do his own thing' for a few hours. The website interview had put him in the mood, he said, making him want to seek out new music for his iPod. She guessed he was also hoping to find his new album on sale.

He woke at dawn and left the bed. Esther could hear his feet on the tiles, the fridge door opening at regular intervals and the fast crack of ring-pulls snapped from cans. He appeared to be moving around the kitchen constantly, the same number of steps each time. Wearied by the repetition, she fell back to sleep. Neither of the two electrical stores he visited had *Godspace* among their racks of CDs. They didn't have any of his back-catalogue either. He began cursing the Spanish. He could understand why they liked Flamenco music; it was in their blood. But not the big-hair rock and cod rap metal filling the slots on the plastic carousel. What value were lives lived out against a soundtrack so dire?

He swigged from a bottle of vodka in his pocket. Every ten minutes or so, trying to cut down a little. A poster advertising a forthcoming bullfight was on the wall in one shop.

"What's that about?"

The assistant smiled. He didn't understand.

"I thought this was a record shop," said Barrett.

"Records, yes."

"Well that's not music, is it?"

The man smiled again. Barrett walked out.

★

They rented a practice room above a working men's club. On their first visit, Barrett and Carey were led up narrow stairs to the dusty room they were to share with Thor, a heavy rock band made up of older lads from school. Thor were there, rehearsing at full blast, the smell of patchouli oil clogging the room. The singer nodded and motioned for them to sit down on a couple of chairs in front of the band; they were about to get a private performance.

While he waited for his cue, the singer began twitching his head and clicking his fingers. Gripping the microphone stand, he threw back his long hair and sang in a high-pitched voice. The music intensified and he lifted his voice higher still. The strain was too much. He made a weird, pained face as if a dog had jumped up and bitten his balls. The song slowed down. The singer slumped, exhausted. After a few seconds he approached the microphone gracefully, arms stretched open, fingers splayed. One of his eyeballs was missing. It appeared again. Then went. Came back. Went. Carey shouted down Barrett's ear:

"What's his eye doing?"

"I think it's sliding under his nose."

"Fucking hell. Did he burst something with all that screaming?"

"No, he's got a lazy eye or whatever they call it. He must have taken the plaster off his glasses when he was little."

As he watched and listened, Barrett grew contemptuous. It was all here before him, everything that was wrong, utterly wrong, with local bands. Thor were re-hashing blues riffs, not a drop of originality or invention about them. At every point Barrett knew what was coming next and it was hard to save himself from laughing out loud at the hopelessness and shame of it — stealing so brazenly, serving it up as if it had real worth, embarrassing themselves. Tell us something that matters, he thought: sing your life. And, while we're at it Mr Singer, stop trying to be Robert Plant when we all know you're an apprentice welder or something daft, dicking about with a few mates on a Friday night.

Carey thought they were abysmal too but had a secret admiration of their confidence, how sure they were of themselves.

*

On the bus back to the resort Barrett began thinking how wonderful it had been to have his records in shops throughout the world, bulletins from his life blown across land and sea, the familiar on foreign ground.

His bottom lip trembled. He fixed it still with the stumpy neck of the vodka bottle. He recognised there had been a countdown of sorts, starting when his records began to appear in charity stores. He stopped calling in; he couldn't bear to see them there. He told friends, pretending to dry his eyes, sniff-sniff, that they were like abandoned children, the sound of long ago youth and energy come to this, piled up and scuffed, the sleeves sun-bleached or warped through damp, unwanted. Their packaging also pushed him deep into the past. He'd not released an album on vinyl for years so these bulky artefacts, some with gatefold sleeves, had the effect of fossilising much of his career. The graphics were dated, particularly on the sleeve of *No Exit* where the letters were strung together as if on a neon-lit sign. When bands did this now, it was a pastiche of these old records. The slow soak of ageing was also evident in the subliminal elements: the ink on the sleeves; the washy colours; the thickness of the cardboard. And there was no bar code or mention of a website but, instead, a fan club address. In one shop, a series of stickers had formed a small mound on the sleeve as its price had fallen over months, possibly years. Barrett had almost felt it was his duty to drive up and down the country and buy them, bring them all home.

*

Carey took copies of the fanzine to Digger for them to sell. He passed the wall teeming with notes advertising instruments for sale and appeals for musicians to join bands. He couldn't understand why anyone would advertise for members, it devalued the artform. Groups, the ones that really mattered, were formed out of fellowship and shared values, not on how well they could play or whether they had a Marshall amp or Gibson guitar. It was a kind of love, best left to serendipity.

He counted the exclamation marks after phrases like, 'Must be able to play fast!!!' and 'Let's get it on!!!!' Led Zeppelin and Deep Purple-influenced bassists and guitarists were much sought after, and everywhere was the warning: no time wasters. A good name for a band, he thought: The Time Wasters. He had a notebook containing ideas for names; it was going in there. His favourite was The Pin Ups but he also liked Bread Roll Christ, Poppers, and Fountain Ear. If he left Group Hex he could see himself in The Pin Ups. They'd be wilfully enigmatic, a bit like Devo or Pere Ubu, each member in a cagoule with the hood pulled up tight by the drawstring, posing for photos on rocks out at sea, scary in the sea spray.

Three long-haired lads were perched on speakers, rolling cigarettes and nodding their heads to a song playing on the shop's hi-fi about a willow tree. Carey asked where the dogs were.

"What dogs?"

"The dogs that are always here."

"Dunno. Dead, maybe."

A tall bloke with wispy hair who seemed to be in charge took a handful of fanzines and placed them on the counter.

"Of course we'll try and sell these for you."

Carey was suspicious.

"There's nothing about heavy rock in them," he volunteered.

"Fair enough. You lot are the future now, aren't you? Punk, new wave and all that. We've had our day."

He seemed sincere.

Carey looked back as he left the shop. The owner-bloke was motioning with his head towards the door. He might have been letting one of the long-hairs know that a delivery had arrived or that the stand containing guitar strings needed restocking. Or, thought Carey, he might have been indicating that the kid just leaving, wearing an Italian combat jacket and hand-painted Doc Martens (blue) was a dick.

★

His reverie was broken:

"Sorry to bother you, are you John Barrett?"

He nodded, eyes half-closed.

"I'm a massive fan of your stuff."

"Cool."

Barrett looked into the face of a pale-skinned bloke he guessed to be in his late-twenties. He introduced himself as Andrew from Leicester, on holiday in Torremolinos.

"Would it be okay to sit next to you?"

"Sure."

"I can't believe it's really you."

"Well, there you go."

"How come you're here?"

He told him he was on holiday, chilling out after promoting his new album. He asked if he had bought *Godspace* yet.

"I've not actually."

It had been out over a month.

He was hoping Andrew wasn't in a band and wanted to send him a demo.

"I play in a band; could I send you a demo?"

"Sure."

"Will you take a listen and let me know what you think? What you really think?"

"Yeah."

(Barrett had a policy of not telling people what he *really* thought. He'd long ago learned that if you liked the stuff they were on to you again, asking if you'd 'get their music to the right people'. They'd ring record companies and magazines, passing off even faint interest as fervent, claiming he wanted to co-write their album with them, produce it, set up a world tour. Alternatively, if he said he didn't like it — even using bland phrases like it not being his cup of tea — they considered it unforgivably cruel. He had received several nasty letters and e-mails from bands he had inadvertently offended.)

He asked Andrew what his band were called and sounded like. He knew immediately that this was a mistake.

"We've had a few names actually. We started off as Beans and the Toasties but it was a bit long. Too comical as well, really. Then we were Local Heroes and at the moment we're Man Bites Dog which, I know, isn't great either. What do we sound like? Good question ... "

The cheek of it. Barrett had been making music for nearly 30 years while this shyster talking about himself with such self-importance was just out of the garage. He'd forgotten the dictum: don't encourage the punters, it was lethal.

"... I suppose we're a cross between pumped up funk and quite harsh rock. The one thing that stands out, that sets us apart, is Frenchy's voice. It's really fucking strong."

He looked across at Barrett as if hoping he'd be impressed that he'd used the word 'fucking', wanting him to know he was from the streets, born to rock. Barrett was staring out of the window, comfortably numb-drunk, wondering where all the donkeys had gone he used to see on postcards. Probably run over by the mad bastards on these roads, he thought, donkey juice on every car from here to Cadiz. Cue the saxophone solo.

★

Group Hex practised every Wednesday night. They had rough ideas for songs but were in love with sheer volume, playing the same chords over and over.

"It's like going to a twisted fucking Scout group, this," shouted Fisher.

Stevie D often turned up to tender one of his freestyle poems, set to random musical accompaniment; usually the pro-vegetarianism rant *Eat Shit You Fuckers*. Fisher would formally close proceedings by leaving his synthesiser and taking the microphone to sing *his* number—*Loveland*. On first listen it sounded like impromptu whimsical nonsense or 'winky wanky woo' as he called it:

> 'Let's go to Loveland,
> And float among the cosmos and the Milky Way,
> Flowers and trees and birds and bees.'

Loveland, he informed them, was actually a satirical comment on the state of the nation with its three million unemployed, a tyrant as Prime Minister and imminent mutually assured nuclear destruction. Towards the end of the number he'd implore the drummer or drummers (depending on who had turned up) to 'go punk'. As the beat picked up, he'd grab the microphone stand as if throttling it.

> "Margaret Thatcher,
> Give us a light,
> Margaret Thatcher
> Britain's alight!
> Margaret Thatcher,
> Fuck off you slag."

The drumming then slowed as Fisher dropped to a croon, indicating with a jolt of his forearm where he wanted stabs inserted:

"It's about time [boom-boom] that bitch [boom-boom] did the washing up, I said, [boom-diddy-boom] it's about time [twirl of the arm to indicate a drum roll] that bitch did the washing up."

★

"What advice would you give a band hoping to make it?" asked Andrew.

'I'd tell them to pack in, especially if the rest look as drab as you. I'm sorry mate but you've got the charisma of a crisp bag. I know now, clear as watery piss, that you are *not* going to make it. You're going to get a boring job like your dad did no doubt, marry a girl from the office and talk about your imaginary band that might have made it, could have made it, almost made it, for the rest of your life to give you some kind of standing among your dull-as-fuck mates. My advice is: forget it. And, next time you claim to be a massive fan, buy my record the day it comes out, okay? Understood?'

He thought this but didn't say it.

"Just do what you do, man, and do it well."

The lad sat back into his seat and smiled. Barrett contemplated getting off the bus and catching the next one. He had another idea.

"Mate, I'm not being funny but I'm totally whacked out. I could do with some sleep. I was up late working on new material last night."

"Hey, don't explain. I understand. Really. I'd be knackered too. Look, you get some shut-eye. Don't worry about me."

Barrett pretended to nod off, letting his head roll to his shoulder. The bus stopped and he felt movement at his side. When he sneaked a look he saw that the kid had got off. A postcard was on the empty seat.

'Hi John. Fantastic to meet you, Andrew Glassbrook. PS: Check out our tunes on good old MySpace. Just key in: 'Man Bites Dog'. Woof!'

He'd been decent enough, thought Barrett. Anyone else would have woken him and asked for an autograph or to have their photo taken together. He had also accepted him for what he was, the shape he was in; Barrett had sensed this immediately. Too often lately he'd felt the sting of disappointment from fans, read their minds: how dare he put on weight and look so much older.

*

After practices they usually called at the chippy across the road. They often took the tape recorder with them and left it on, taping conversations. One night, a man and woman, tipsy and leaning on the counter to stay upright, were talking to one another:

"Do you want chips, love?" he asked.

"I do *not* want greasy chips."

"How about rice, then?"

"No, thank you. Not normal rice anyway." She shook her head extravagantly. "I want that other stuff."

"What you on about?"

"That stuff I had last time."

He turned to face the others in the queue.

"What's she telling me, lads? Any ideas?"

Barrett asked if she meant noodles.

"No," she said. "You know, I want that posh stuff what they advertise on telly."

The Chinese lady looked up from wrapping chips:

"Fried rice?"

"That's 'em," shouted the woman victoriously, waving around her forefinger as if shooting a gun. "Fried rice. Not boiled rice. That's bloody boring, that is."

Carey smirked and checked that the 'record' button was pressed down. He said later that they should include it as an excerpt on their debut album.

"We won't find a better example of social realism."

★

The air conditioning on the coach was only working intermittently. A patch of sweat formed at the front of Barrett's T-shirt. His armpits were soon damp and runnels of water trickled down. He was sweating like a fat person, he thought: like in the jokes. This wasn't supposed to happen. He had been thin, wiry, until his mid-thirties when he began, as he called it, 'filling out'. He remembered it first being commented on when he called at the record company to run through a promo schedule. An assistant in the press office asked if he had been working out. He'd been aware of putting on weight over the previous year or so but hadn't undertaken a thorough inventory. Later that day he stared into a full-length mirror at home. He was shocked at what he found, how age had sneaked up on him. The flesh across his chest sagged. Wisps of hair formed a large butterfly, shoulder to shoulder. The strands were grey and where they had once been coarse, were now soft, fluffy. More bulk was at his torso and waist. He looked into his face. The skin was

32

blanched, the colour of over-boiled potatoes. He wondered what was it that made him look older. Something to do with colour and light, he decided. On the occasions he'd taken girls to his hotel room, he'd observed the on-the-road convention of draping a T-shirt over the bedside lamp. He felt like this, dimmed as if he soaked up light but didn't reflect it back. Leaning forward, he stared into his eyes. At least these were still in place, glossy brown and promising laughter and charm. He lifted a brow. He'd done the same years before in a publicity photograph that had formed the basis of a lengthy marketing campaign. The expression, held for a second or two, was projected on to posters and adverts, first across the UK, into the United States and, eventually, the Far East. He was still seeing it nearly two years later. One time, in Kyoto, this had made him anxious — the realisation that something as intimate and inconsequential as having his picture taken in a tiny studio in London could lead to this: feeling to be everywhere at once and yet, at that particular moment, lying on a hotel bed, missing home.

*

Scoffer's microphone broke so he left while he saved up to buy another. His replacement was a lad they'd seen around for years, Carl, who, unlike Scoffer, actually looked like a front man. He was tall with crimped and dyed blond hair, and wore a raincoat, even on hot days (especially on hot days, it added to the enigma). He was the sort of kid they routinely despised because of the attention he paid to his appearance but they knew him from before, when he'd dressed normal.

"Under all that crap, him wanting to be David Sylvian and all that, he's one of us," said Barrett.

As Carl joined, one of the 'floating' members, Ian, was cast

33

adrift. A month or so earlier he had undergone a personality transformation, from a typical seventeen-year-old who lived on the 'Bell estate, the son of a mum who worked at a clinic and a dad who drove mini-buses for social services, to an android. He now dyed his hair black, painted black eyeliner around the rims of his eyes (clumsily) and sucked in his cheeks as he walked the streets in a black jump suit with a red belt at his waist. He had spent a few weeks with the band stabbing at a synthesiser which he abutted to Fisher's so they could claim to be the *Kraftwerk Twins* — at one practice they began moving their arms and head like robots until Barrett told them to 'fuckin' give over'.

Ian announced, his voice solemn, that he and Carl had 'history'. They had met a week earlier at a nightclub where he had subjected Carl to a eulogy on cybernetics, the profundity of *Dr Who* and a painstaking, paints-peeling-off-a-my-wall dissection of Gary Numan's lyrics. Ian's leg had begun to feel warm and, reaching down, he discovered that Carl had pissed on him under the table.

"Well, you're boring me," Carl squawked before dissolving into the darkness.

Ian insisted that he couldn't work with someone who had humiliated him in public.

A band meeting was called, one of many. Carey said the issue came into direct confrontation with the band's libertarian stance.

"How do you mean?" asked Ian.

"We can't really have an open door policy if it's only open to certain people."

"He did piss on him, though," said Fisher.

"I know, and I believe Ian and everything, but aren't we making a value judgement on Carl? Shouldn't we take people as we find them, give them a chance at least. He might have changed."

34

"What? Since last week?"

"It only takes an instant to change, you know."

No one spoke for a few seconds.

"Does he do it a lot?" asked Barrett finally.

"What?"

"Piss on people."

"I think he's only ever done it to me."

Ian said he wasn't too bothered about leaving anyway because guitars were out-dated and he wanted to work with other synthesiser players.

"Another thing," he said. "I'll have more time to look after the video."

They asked what he meant.

He explained, but keep it quiet for God's sake, that his family had bought a video recorder. They weren't just the first on the 'Bell with one but probably the first in the *whole bloody town*. He and his dad were taking turns sleeping in the lounge to make sure no one broke in and nicked it.

"Obviously we've stuck a plaster over the 'on' light but when word gets round, they'll be after it."

*

Barrett had considered it a rock star's duty to look good (much as he hated the term *rock star*), so after the session with the mirror he undertook a strict gym regime. He talked evangelically in interviews about being fit, how it enriched his life. He was soon back in tight T-shirts and if he held his shoulders square and tensed the muscles across his stomach he believed he could pass for ten years younger.

Losing his hair did for him, wrecked the plan. He saw it was thinning when he was presented with a contact strip of photographs taken at a concert. It felt as if his youth, his livelihood and life itself were being plucked away by an invisible, callous hand.

'Why me? Why fucking me?'

He had always believed that good hair was essential. As a teenager he'd put records back in the racks when the haircut was wrong. Bald blokes worked for the council and cleaned their cars on Sunday mornings. They didn't make records or get up on stage; it was one of the irrefutable rules of rock 'n' roll.

He wished the bus would speed up, get him away from here, the memories. The bottle was almost empty, too.

*

A girl called Karen Pearson wrote to the fanzine and said she wanted to be involved 'with you guys who seem to know where it's at!' On the night of her visit the band and friends gathered around a table downstairs at the working men's club. They were wondering what a girl would look like who shared their passion for music, art and collectivism. She arrived in tight jeans and a frilly white top. She was slim, pretty.

"What's she come as?" whispered Fisher.

Barrett reminded him that fashion was divisive; it was the person inside the clothes that mattered.

They gave her the speech, so earnest it hurt. They were a community, explained Carey, of musicians, writers, artists, poets and activists. Over the next hour they mentioned Maoism, Dadaism, the Spanish Civil War, Mark Rothko, William Burroughs, the Bauhaus movement, situationism, the pursuit of freedom.

"A bit like hippies from the Sixties?" she asked.

No, nothing like hippies. This wasn't anything indolent or rhetorical but a total revolution, taking over the means of production, ending exploitation and making art from life itself. Music first, the rest to follow.

"I think I understand."

She said she wanted to be a graphic designer and Barrett suggested she could make a stage backdrop for the band. She told them a friend of hers was going to join them soon, a cool guy called Al. While she was speaking, a fair-haired kid in faded jeans and plimsolls entered the room. He looked shy and awkward, hands in his pockets. His cheeks were flushed candy floss pink.

"Here he is now."

He shook everyone's hands, smiling.

"Al?" said Fisher. "What's that short for?"

"Alastair but call me what you want, I'm not bothered."

A few minutes later Karen looked at her watch and announced that she was late for her bus.

"I'm going to dash. I'll be in touch, okay?" She turned to Al: "See you tomorrow."

They asked Al why his face was red. He said he'd travelled there on his bike. Barrett began telling him about the band. Al said he was working on a project too, collecting old bikes and rebuilding them with his elder brother, Rob. Any profit they made would go to Oxfam.

"Is Karen your girlfriend?" asked Barrett.

"No, I think she just feels sorry for me."

"How come?"

"I'm not bothered about meeting people and stuff. I probably wouldn't have come tonight if she hadn't insisted."

They talked for the rest of the evening, sipping half-pints of lager. The conversation was easy but, throughout, Carey had the impression that part of Al was elsewhere, already thinking about the journey home perhaps, whizzing through the streets on his bike.

★

Two days after returning from holiday, Barrett was summoned to his manager's office. Rupert Green had some good news and wanted to deliver it in person. Barrett travelled across London by tube. Green had previously ordered taxis to collect him from Victoria but explained that budgets weren't as generous as before and, besides, it wasn't cool being ferried around any more; that kind of extravagance was passé.

He arrived earlier than expected, panting. Chloe on reception asked if he'd like some water from the cooling machine.

"Please."

She meant him to fill up his own but he waited for her to leave the desk and operate the machine. He cupped the drink with both hands. Water spilled down his knuckles. He explained that he'd run up the stairs.

"That's why I'm a bit shaky."

"Right."

"Rupe's asked me in."

"I know. You're early."

"Am I?"

"Yeah. I've got you down for a one o'clock."

It was 11.30.

"One o'clock?"

"Yeah."

"I thought he said eleven, shit."

"I'm sure it'll be okay."

They taped practices, everything archived and listed, and began forming a set. Songs had working titles: *Funky Jam*, *Joy Division-ish #1*, *Fast One (With Slow Middle)*, *Bad Reggae*, *Loveland*, *Punky Veggie Party*. Walking home afterwards along the canal bank, they played the cassettes on Fisher's portable recorder. In the darkness, framed by trees and heading towards the twinkling lights and concrete sprawl of the 'Bell, they were often surprised at how good it sounded.

"It's the sort of stuff you'd hear on Peel."

This was the benchmark. Carey spent most weekday nights taping John Peel's show. The records he played were defiantly eccentric, some minimal, others crash-banged full of instruments. It was the sound of people finding an instrument (or sometimes fire extinguishers and beer trays, anything at hand) and doing what they wanted with them — playing them upside down, ripping strings off, setting them on fire, putting bass strings on a normal guitar, throwing a snare drum against a wall. Peel had made Carey and the others realise that anyone anywhere could be a small-town David Bowie — mysterious, vital. Except that Bowie and others from the mid-Seventies and before were now viewed as the Establishment, the old wave. The irreverence was crucial. Kick over the statues.

"Anything goes," said Fisher, swinging the recorder. "Fuck convention."

The lyrics and subject matter were eclectic too. Authors, poets and artists that Group Hex considered personal to them were being sung about or quoted widely as influences: George Orwell, David Hockney, Virginia Woolf, Edvard Munch,

Philip Larkin, Edward Hopper, Henry Miller. They felt dusted by intellectualism by merely being aware of these people.

Carey especially would fixate on particular tracks, or sometimes a band's name or a song title. These songs, he told Barrett, felt like they'd taken over his whole life, changing him in some way. He'd quote lyrics, snatches from singles that had sold a handful of copies, imagining them to be incredibly prescient or profound. For weeks his favourite track was about someone watching Concorde pass overhead while musing on 'fat ladies pulling shopping baskets'—all spoken in an eerie, bored voice.

"It's by the Native something-or-others. I didn't quite catch what Peelie said."

The track, with dozens more, went on to compilation tapes passed among the band and friends. These were given titles, usually culled from song lyrics—*Looking for the Joke (with a Microscope)*; *They're Calling my Name Over the Tannoy*; *The Last Mad Surge of Youth*—and housed in home-designed sleeves.

*

Chloe could smell Barrett, the sweat and the alcohol. She left her desk and opened the window.

"It's mighty hot out there," she said in a feigned southern American accent.

"Too right, man."

Fucking hell, he'd said *man* again; Esther had told him about that.

When Chloe sat down, Barrett looked across, eyes burning like struck matches.

"It does matter," he said.

"What's that?"

"Me, being early."

"No, it's no problem. Really."

His gaze unnerved her. She noticed he was mumbling to himself, closing and opening his fist.

★

While they were walking home one night after a practice, Barrett announced that he had a girlfriend. Kind of.

"Who is she?" asked Carey, trying to sound nonchalant.

"Tracey Morgan."

"Oh, right."

Carey felt let down. They had an agreement: the band above all else, every spare minute dedicated to it.

"I might pack her in though. Not sure yet. She said something that pissed me off a bit."

Tracey Morgan was in their class but, Barrett had assumed, in a different league. She walked around college carrying a hessian bag with a huge patch of a cannabis leaf sewn into it. Her hair was crimped and she wore long skirts that reached the floor. Barrett always imagined her lounging in a camper van at the weekends with her long-hair mates, smoking pot. They'd drive up to the hills or a beach and chase into the sea as the sun set, throwing each other in the air, splashing through the waves, laughing with their mouths open. Afterwards, blankets around their shoulders, they'd light a fire with driftwood and pass around bottles of beer. She spoke about people she knew — Pod, Sammy, Tetty, Mouse, and, of course, Jab, her 'lover', as if everyone knew them, like they were famous.

Barrett had made friends with her as they waited on the corridor before a tutorial. She unexpectedly congratulated him on being 'a very together person'. He asked her out. She said she was busy during the week but was babysitting at a neighbour's on Saturday night — did he want to come?

He rode there on his bike, shuffling it clumsily into the hall.

"I don't think they've got any beer in," she said. "Will wine do?"

He had a quick sip.

"Strong, isn't it?" he said.

"Get it down you."

She was trying to get him drunk, he thought. Clearly, she wanted sex. But she'd had all those hippy blokes who were years older than him and he'd not properly touched a girl yet. He was anxious. He was just a kid, bound to get it wrong.

"Shall we turn the telly off? It's just a distraction, isn't it?" she said.

Hell, she didn't just want a quickie, she wanted to concentrate, mull over it. He began sweating.

"It's a form of mind-control, television," she said. "They reckon that people watch on average four hours a day and it makes them anaesthetised to real life."

He took a sneaky look at her when she turned away. She had a cluster of freckles at the side of her nose. He wanted to lean across and lick them off, then move around to drink in her lips. She was wearing a white cheesecloth top with patch pockets. He longed to undo it and take hold of her. All he had to do was reach across and the whole world was his. What was he scared of? She was only a girl. Any minute now, he'd make his move.

"The music is going pretty well," he said.

"Oh yes, someone told me you'd got a bit of a band together with Dave Carey. I really like him, he's dead funny."

Barrett had a stab of jealousy. Did she tell people she *really liked* him too? He thought of what Carey was doing at that moment, writing probably or working on the set-list, while he was here with this girl, set for it. All he had to do was ask.

*

Rupert Green walked into the reception area and greeted Barrett warmly, offering his hand. Barrett ignored the gesture and hugged him instead, clinging.

"It's great to see you, Rupe. Amazing."

"You've obviously had a good holiday."

"Top."

Inside Green's office Barrett did his restless thing, pacing up and down in front of the desk, picking up bits of paper, staring out of the window. He spat on the palm of his hands, rubbing them together.

"You're a happy bunny," said Green.

"Top of the world, matey."

"You do know you're a bit early, don't you?"

*

"Shall we have a kiss?" asked Barrett.

Their lips met. She tasted salty. He reached in with his tongue. He started thinking about what she'd had for tea (pizza, he guessed). He manoeuvred her on to her back. She was compliant. She tossed the hair out of her eyes as her head settled on the arm of the settee. Her eyes locked into his. He undid her top and while he did, she reached behind her back to unfasten her bra. They fell out: two white scrumptious breasts. He froze. He'd gone too far. He'd only wanted to attend the exhibition, not make off with the displays.

"Is everything okay?" she asked.

"Yes, no, sort of. I was thinking — do you think the people might come back?"

"Not for ages."

"But what if they do?"

"They won't."

He didn't dare touch her breasts for fear of triggering a wanton response. He was sure she'd drag him in, eat him up and laugh him out of town. Sitting up, she made as if to fasten her top.

"If you don't feel comfortable, that's fine."

"I'm worried they might come back or the baby could wake up and we'd be in trouble."

Another idea:

"What about Jab? He won't like us doing this, will he?"

"We always said we'd have an open relationship."

They returned to watching television, holding hands. At 11pm he said he had to go. She kissed him on the cheek at the door.

"I'm really sorry for what happened," he said. "It wasn't me in there, not the real me. I used you, took advantage. I shouldn't have done it." He knew he should really be apologising for his ineptitude.

"I like you, that's why I let you do it," she said.

The ride home was downhill. As he freewheeled through the darkness he jerked out his arms and legs and felt like a shooting star. He decided it didn't matter that he hadn't gone through with the act. He'd asked someone out, had a date, been offered sex. That was more than enough. And how could he even consider a relationship with a girl who had referred to his all-consuming passion, his reason for living, as a 'bit of a band'?

As he made his way to the chair facing Green, Barrett stopped for a second and went into theatrical slow motion.

"So, I'm early. Fuck it. Let's get on with it. Hey ho, let's go."

"First of all, how was the holiday? Did the girls have a good time?"

"A good time was had by all, Rupe, believe me."

"What did you do?"

"This and that and, blimey Charlie, a bit of the other."

Barrett's vagueness and forced bonhomie irritated Green but he was determined not to let it show.

★

Although they were each starting out on their instruments, some had a distinct ear for music. Barrett and Fisher quickly learned to jam together, nodding their heads when changing chords or tempo. Carey, though, banged the guitar as if working at a lathe. He didn't know whether he was in tune or not and argued that this was irrelevant. It was about passion and drive and making unique, exciting sounds. To this end he was lent a distortion pedal, a Colorsound, by Barrett, which made his guitar sound like amplified white noise or the tinny, whining engine of a model plane.

While he believed he could beguile the group and their small circle of mates, Carey began to wonder whether the wider public would recognise him as a self-styled bastion of freeform, agit-prop guitar terrorism. Alternatively, they might view him as a chancer who spoiled an otherwise decent group. He quickly realised that you could pretend you couldn't play and say you were making it up as you went along, but no one did this for real. He listened to the rehearsal tapes and realised that an out-of-tune guitar, amplified and played out of time, was like opening and banging doors in your head: bloody annoying.

He accepted an offer of a guitar lesson from Fisher's dad, Trevor, who was in a rhythm and blues band that played in pubs and clubs around town. Trevor spoke in a pseudo-American drawl and had the rugged, detached demeanour of a high plains drifter. He called Carey 'boy'. He showed him how to strum a 'G' chord and Fisher joined in on keyboard. Trevor set off playing a lead riff, instructing Carey to hold down the 'G' in the background. Carey was soon stopping and starting, speeding up and slowing down. Fisher laughed. His dad frowned. Fisher stabbed the keys more enthusiastically to cover Carey's erratic timing. His dad listened intently and then stopped, slamming his hand across the strings to kill the sound.

"What was that?" he asked.

He wasn't sure whether it was Carey or Fisher playing hopelessly out of time. They set off again. On this occasion it was clear. He looked over to Carey, shaking his head:

"You've got your fingers up your arse, boy."

Friends began asking when Group Hex were going to play live. Carey hadn't given serious thought to doing gigs; it was a sop to tradition. He said this to Barrett, expecting him to agree. He didn't.

"It'd be fun. That's why we're doing all this practising, isn't it?"

They decided to enter a young bands' competition, to be held in the town square as part of an annual summer festival. Their

46

participation would be an arch political and cultural statement—they'd lose on purpose and make enough noise to spoil
everyone's day, thereby subverting the notion that any kind of
music could be considered more worthy than another. Take that!

★

"Come on then, what have you got?" demanded Barrett.

"A major television appearance, that's what."

"You don't say! An hour-long special dedicated to the new
album to be shown on BBC1 at Saturday teatime?"

"Not quite, but pretty good all the same."

"Go on, let's have it."

★

A few days before their debut concert the members of Group
Hex went to see Stevie D performing at a club in town called
the Hut. He took to the stage, which was no more than two feet
higher than the rest of the room, with his hair scruffed up and
his ripped jeans hanging from him. Half mad and wholly alive,
his eyes bulged as he screamed out his poems. Carey was
astounded at the rugged glamour coaxed from Stevie by a set of
lights, volume and serious intent. When he finished his set, he
tripped off stage and instantly returned to his peaceable self,
greeting Group Hex:

"Thanks for coming down. Good luck at the festival. It'll be
cool." Big smile.

Later, Carey asked how old he was.

"Seventeen."

★

"I've managed to get you a spot on *Lunch Brake*. They want you to do an acoustic version of an old number and a short interview."

"What's *Lunch Brake*?"

"I'm surprised you've not heard of it. It's supposed to be an antidote to the fluff that they normally put out on daytime terrestrial TV."

"When do they want me?"

"That's the catch — tomorrow."

"Tomorrow?"

"Yep. Someone's just pulled out on them."

★

Deck chairs were laid out in front of the stage like at a pier-end show. People meandered around fairground stalls, cardigans and jumpers over their arms and kids in tow. The sun was slipping away as nightfall closed in. Carey still hadn't given up hope of avoiding an appearance. Across the top of the stage was a banner for the contest's official sponsor, a building society. He nudged Barrett.

"Seen that?"

"Shit."

"Bad, isn't it?"

"Too right."

They demanded to see the organisers and were ushered into a caravan behind the stage.

"What's up lads?" asked a podgy bloke in a white shirt

stretched tight over his belly. "I've heard you've got a problem with our sponsor."

"I don't know if you've heard of Group Hex," began Barrett. "But we believe in taking a stand against things we consider corrupt or in league with rampant commercialism."

The bloke pulled a strange expression. Barrett continued:

"We feel it's inappropriate that we should play at an event sponsored by a building society."

"Why's that?"

"Because it's well documented that banks and such like invest their profits in dubious organisations."

"Don't you think you're taking it all a bit too seriously? You'll have a good time if you play. You might even win. They're a local building society too. It's good of them to support this kind of thing, there's nothing really in it for them."

Barrett said they would consult the rest of the group and report back in a few minutes. Everyone apart from Carey wanted to play, on the proviso that Carl made an on-stage announcement disassociating the group from all financial institutions.

An hour later they made their way to the stage. Carey felt bleached, rubbed out from the world. Before they were due to start, he wandered over to Barrett.

"John, where am I?"

"You're on stage."

"Am I?"

"'Course you fucking are."

"What do I do?"

"Play guitar."

"I can't remember the songs."

"What do you mean?"

"Everything's gone blank. John, fucking help me, will you?"

"What can I do?"

"What songs are we playing?"

He pointed to the set-list at his feet.

"I can't read it."

"The letters are big enough, aren't they?"

"Yes, but I can't read it."

Carey was on the verge of leaving, slipping by the speakers and down the steps, to the memorial gardens behind the town hall where he could start to look for himself again. Barrett grabbed him by the arms.

"Get it together."

"I can't John, I'm scared."

The MC was announcing them:

"Ladies and gentlemen, attention please, attention. We have for you now a local group making their concert debut [pronounced *de-boo*]. Please give a warm welcome to a smashing bunch of lads. Make some noise for Group Flex."

Carey looked down at his guitar. He saw enough strings to fill a harp. His fingers turned into fat sausages. Cement ran through his veins. Barrett acted swiftly and decisively. He slumped to his knees and turned the two buttons on the fuzz pedal to maximum volume and distortion. If it ordinarily sounded like a model plane, it was now a 747.

"It doesn't matter what the fuck you play. No one will hear the difference anyway."

On the first song Carey held a finger across a fret and strummed it over and over again. By the second, aware that he was effectively invisible within the wall of noise, he began moving his left hand up and down the neck as if contributing something valid. After they finished their fifth and final song Barrett led him from the stage.

Group Hex didn't win. First prize went to The Bug Club, a bunch of kids with bowl haircuts playing quirky rock'n'roll on trumpets and trombones. They could all play extremely well and had a dance routine — all in a line, shimmying to the right and left, crossing their legs and bending their knees.

"Look at those wankers," laughed Fisher.

Carl said he didn't think they looked old enough to wank.

*

Barrett shrugged and made as if to fasten a button on his jacket, getting set to leave. Green was used to artists behaving like this and understood it was part of the code of behaviour, the big yawn at life.

"They'll just want to talk about the old days, the shagging and stuff," said Barrett eventually.

"Well, if you will tell *Melody Maker* you're mad keen on free-love and an advocate of sex-for-all, what do you expect? Even if it was four hundred years ago."

"We've covered this before. It was supposed to be a bloody joke. I didn't know it would set me up as this great fornicator for the rest of my days."

"Look, I'll have a word with the *Lunch Brake* team and ask them to go easy."

"That'll just wind them up even more. You know what they're like."

"I know the people there. They're not going to want to fuck us over. Look, the show is a great opportunity to let people know you're back."

"How come they want me to play an old song? That's all they're bothered about, the past."

Green wished Barrett wasn't so shrewd. It was much easier managing shameless egocentrics or total fuck-ups than someone in between. He knew Barrett saw everything, even drunk. Only when his attention span waned did he stand a chance. Any minute now Barrett would ping an elastic band or realign the trays on the desk. Come on, bored. Green had learned to wait for the petition, 'Just do your magic' — a mandate to progress, for him to act as a buffer or resort to subterfuge.

"If you don't want to do *Lunch Brake* ..."

Green regretted saying this; it sounded as if he was hurt. Barrett had got his reaction.

"I'm not saying that. I'll do it if you really think I should. I'm just not sure, that's all."

*

Al had been at the festival. Carey was embarrassed to face him afterwards.

"We were shit, weren't we?"

"No. It was really good."

"Are you joking?"

"It had a real rawness to it, sort of edgy but still under control somehow."

They hadn't seen Karen since the night they had first met but Al had quickly become part of the gang. He came from a different background to them. His dad was a company director and his mum worked at a charity, organising its fundraising.

Barrett and Carey had quickly engineered it so they were invited to his house, a big old place on the edge of town. The only buildings like it they had been in before were museums or doctors' surgeries. The ceilings were high with ornate coving and the doors were made from thick, dark wood. The main staircase was as wide as a room, flushed with light from a magnificent arched window. Bookcases lined the walls and all around hung oil paintings: contorted faces, cleaved insects, crows by a roadside, telegraph poles scratched out against a rainy sky. They were surprised to find the odd concession to domesticity—a television, a conventional kitchen, half-read magazines—and realise people actually lived there, rattling around in all that space.

When they looked more closely on subsequent visits they noticed the dust, the cracks in the ceiling, the patches of damp, a broken window in the attic room and missing tiles in the downstairs bathroom. It was as if the people living there had other things on their minds or better things to do than fix the place up.

*

Barrett continued to pace Green's office, at one point affecting a strut. Green looked out of the window. He saw a pigeon fly on to the sill. String was caught tight around one of its legs. The foot had retracted and become a swollen purple stump. The bird hobbled along and sat down, plump and round. Green watched it while he thought of how much he disliked Barrett, how much he wanted him out of his life. He was the only client that made him like this, the one he broke his own rules for. And it was all done largely without the compensation of financial gain because the income from new material was negligible and he had no claim on past royalties.

*

Rock Focus was the local paper's weekly column 'bringing readers the best of the town's pop talent'. It was a total embarrassment, said Barrett. No one with any self-respect would go anywhere near it.

"Yeah, it's for small-town bores," agreed Fisher. "Sad bastards like The Bug Club who want to show off to their mams and dads."

Secretly, Barrett and Carey were campaigning to get the band in there. They wanted to take their message and music to as many people as possible. Souls had to be harvested and they realised that the mission would sometimes involve a liaison with the mainstream media.

Their manifesto had already been unveiled in *Word Hex* through a fabricated interview. Most of the piece was given over to their argument that the interview shouldn't actually be taking place (it hadn't) because musicians were no more important than, say, joiners or plumbers. Why bestow status upon someone because they could play a few tunes? The remainder was their standpoint relayed in neurotically bombastic terms: no roadies ("No man is subservient to another."); no cover versions ("How can you mean it when you're singing someone else's words and playing their music?"); no posed publicity shots ("Is there anything more fake?"); no elongated guitar solos ("They're the sound of pretension."); no encores ("It's a cliché, showbiz bullshit."); no cabaret ("Our hatred of people succumbing to nostalgic compliance is absolute.") and a rebuttal should they ever be asked to appear on *Top of the Pops* ("Never, as long as we have air in our lungs ... ").

Carey sent a letter to the paper under a pseudonym, extolling Group Hex's unique stance: 'They are the great hope in the black abyss of trite disposable pop'. A reporter phoned Barrett and a week later the article gushed how wonderful it was to find young people who were so passionate about music and didn't subscribe to the lethargy of most teenagers. They were a 'breath of fresh air in depressing times'. On the photo accompanying the feature they were smiling broadly, sitting together on a settee. They had made it absolutely clear to the photographer, a middle-aged man who smelled as if he bathed in aftershave, that they abhorred the standard rock 'n' roll protocol of staged poses, sunglasses, snarls, leather trousers and hanging around fire escapes. So please, don't ask. He hadn't.

*

Green's commitment to Barrett was based wholly on sentimentality. He had been a fan of Killing Stars as a kid. Barrett was the skinny warrior-poet of his generation, all cheekbones and fire eyes. Back at Green's flat, he had filed almost every press interview Barrett had done (not at the office because this was personal, a heart and soul thing). He still had the badges, the free satin patch and poster given away with initial copies of the second album. He knew it was unprofessional to have an emotional attachment to a client but Barrett was a reminder of why he had entered the music industry in the first place. When he was worn down by him he played the old material to re-invoke the energy, the explosion of ideas and the fuck-you stance.

*

The day after the article appeared in *Rock Focus*, Barrett and Fisher went into town. They were recognised in a bookshop and surrounded by a group of girls. The ringleader wore a short skirt and heavy make-up and said she was called Claire.

"Hey, you're quite fit, aren't you?" she said to Fisher. She flirted with him, patting his arm and throwing her head back when she laughed. "I'd love to be in your group. What do I have to do to join?"

Barrett asked if she could play an instrument.

"I used to do the recorder at junior school. Will that do?"

"Not really."

During the previous months Fisher had put forward ideas that had been dismissed by the rest of the band. He was interested in stagecraft but this was viewed as a dalliance with traditional show business. He had shown them designs for 'stage clothes'—hoods and shawls and cloth boots. The handmaidens pressing him close to the bookshelves revived another scheme.

"Can you dance?" he asked.

"No, but we can soon learn,' said Claire.

"I have something in mind that you might be perfect for."

He wanted them to dress as bridesmaids, but a bit, you know, sexy-like. He explained that at concerts, while the rest of the band played, he'd leave his keyboards and prowl around the girls with a whip, lashing at the ground. It would be like a bizarre ballet—beautiful, but, at the same time, *disturbing*.

On the bus home Barrett expressed doubts. He said he didn't think it was part of the post-punk new wave ideal. And wasn't it sexist?

"Oh give over, it'll be great fun."

"Their parents might object. They look about fourteen, fifteen at most."

"Will they fuck! They're from a council estate. They won't have seen their folks for years. They're ten-bob scruffs."

Barrett conceded that Claire was 'pretty fit'.

"I know," said Fisher. "I'm going to whip fuck out of that one."

Fisher held a few get-togethers but one of the girls' parents complained, asking why her daughter needed pretend blood and whether Fisher was registered as a dance instructor. He fumed:

"Fucking typical of this town, isn't it? I tell you, we're wasting our time here. It's beyond them. They're all in-breds."

★

For his part, Barrett was proud to be represented by a man from a class above, a man called Rupert. It was as if he had married outside his caste, done well for himself. When Green spoke, pronouncing the words ever so properly, he was listened to. He made sentences dance. The smile was easy. He was polite, decent, and if anyone missed the occasional clue — which Barrett didn't — they might not see that he was flesh wrapped around granite.

Experience had taught Green to view musicians as insecure, demanding and disrespectful children. Although they railed against anyone foolhardy enough to stereotype *them*, they were often the epitome of narrow-mindedness themselves. This meant that anyone in authority, taking responsibility or wearing a suit even was a *loser*. Meanwhile, the record company was a repressive, vengeful enemy and the wider, non-music-making public were dim-witted for having jobs, mortgages and conventional ambitions. Efficient pop managers, such as himself, were routinely viewed as glorified schoolteachers or, as one band mocked — irking Green immensely — *like someone's dad*. So, he had developed strict rules which he laid out upfront to all his acts. He wasn't their teacher or their father and he wasn't going to drive the van, procure the drugs or placate the bass player's usurped girlfriend.

"Have you got all that?" he asked Barrett at their first meeting.

"I have. Enough chips to open a decent-sized chippy, I'd say."

*

The band moved out of the working men's club and relocated to the attic at Al's house. He told them to help themselves to biscuits, tea, whatever was in the fridge. Yes, they could smoke and drink; his mum and dad wouldn't mind.

"They're liberals, anything goes!"

Al was obsessive about music. He had boxes full of compilation tapes and the band rarely found a group of which he hadn't heard. They trusted his judgement, bombarding him with questions:

"Is that guitar sound too Bauhaus? Should I chop it up a bit so it's slightly Gang of Four?"

At one practice Barrett took hold of Carey's guitar. He coiled his little finger around the volume control, teasing out sound. Abstractedly, he tweaked the tuning pegs with his other hand, tilting his head towards the speaker to listen better.

"The tuning is slipping, can you hear it?"

Carey lied that he could.

"And the action is rubbish. You almost need a clamp to hold down a chord."

Carey was uneasy whenever Barrett used musical terms like *the action*. It was the vocabulary of separatism, taking them away from the streets.

"If you get a decent guitar you'll feel a lot more confident about your playing," said Barrett.

The next Saturday they walked to Archibald's second-hand shop on the outskirts of town, amid the chip wrappers and discarded drinks cans, the taxi ranks and boarded up houses. Carey had first called there when he was about thirteen, pressed up to the wire grille at the window, staring at the shiny things framed by fairy lights. These were left up all year round as if Christmas never left this speck of the world. A fly's compound eye was needed to see everything jammed in there. And it was all designed to make lives louder, brighter, happier: drum kits, guitars, stylophones, bikes, lava lamps, football games, piles of magazines, model airplanes, flags, mouth organs, fishing rods, microphones, records, snooker cues, table tennis tables, amplifiers, postcards, record players.

At the entrance, hidden beneath oilcloth, was a device to pick up footsteps and trigger an alarm. The noise was so loud it made the floor vibrate. Customers would cover their ears and check for gunshot wounds. Old Archibald was out from the back immediately:

"Yes?"

He always looked at everyone dismissively as if he'd finally found the person responsible for posting dog dirt through his letterbox. His skin was yellow from spending too long under the fairy lights and his cheeks drawn and tense as if he'd eaten his lips in retaliation for a secret they'd revealed years before. The visitors to his shop were in his web now and he was going to eat them alive or toy with them a while, at least.

Carey and Barrett stood there, light-headed among the Calor gas and solder fumes.

"We're looking for an electric guitar. I bought one off you last year and I'd like to swap it for a better one," said Carey.

The alarm screamed. A woman entered with a lad aged about ten. She was carrying an electric guitar too. Archie asked what she wanted.

59

"This bloody thing doesn't work."

She said her husband had adapted a kettle lead and plugged it into a wall socket but they couldn't hear a thing, not a dicky bird. Archibald's teeth did a kind of jig.

"You stuck it into a plug socket and expected it to work? Without an amplifier?"

The woman said he hadn't told her nothing about no amplifier when he sold it to them; this wasn't on.

"Everyone knows you need an amp to hear anything. You could have blown yourselves to kingdom come."

He refused to give her money back. She said she'd return later. With her husband. To sort him out.

"Bring half the street with you if you like, love."

He turned back to the pair:

"Right, what was it you two buggerlugs wanted?"

Before they could begin negotiations, he warned:

"If it's a part-ex you're after, I'll be taking your picture."

He reached under the counter and waved a Polaroid Instamatic.

"Wonderful thing, this. I get you to smile like good 'uns and then I stick your mug shots on my wall in the back room — just in case you've nicked any of the stuff you're shoving on to me, even if you're claiming I sold you it."

He laughed a dry laugh that broke into a hacking cough.

They left with a Fender Stratocaster copy that Barrett said played well. The neck was narrow, making it easier to hold down chords. Carey was annoyed because the guitar they traded (which Archie had described as a 'beaut' when he sold it to him a year before) was now a 'plank with a few strings on'.

★

Green set out a glowing testimony to *Lunch Brake*. The show, he said, reached the perfect demographic audience for Barrett — ex-fans who wanted to know what he was up to, many of them women who still had a soft spot for him. They didn't read the *NME* any more or surf the internet but relied on the television and radio to tell them what was happening. He had been their heart-throb, a memory of 'lost youth they'd want to revisit'. Barrett sighed. Green smiled, apologised, and went on:

"They'll see you on telly and that same afternoon they'll be throwing your new album into the shopping trolley while they're scooting around Sainsbury's. Or, alternatively, getting their kids to download it from iTunes."

"That's a very patronising view of middle-aged women," said Barrett.

"Oh, fuck off. You know what I mean."

Green was fully aware that the album wasn't actually stocked by Sainsbury's or any other supermarket chain. Headfall, Barrett's record company, didn't have accounts with them because it couldn't offer sufficient discount. It was an independent affiliated to a major, specialising in acts that no longer justified large investment but had maintained a loyal and decent-sized core audience, basically the last stop-off point in the formal music industry.

"So you think it's a good idea?' asked Barrett.

"I do."

"Let's do it, then."

*

Al unexpectedly announced that he was packing in his A levels to start a job at an outdoor activity centre about thirty miles away.

"I can't stand being inside all day," he said. "And if I pass the exams it only qualifies me for an office job, which I don't want."

Within days he phoned Barrett and told him he'd fallen in love, with Lauren, an American college student staying with a party at the centre.

The band next saw him two weeks later as they filed into his parents' carrying their instruments. He was so happy his body appeared to be wrapped in lights, flashing on and off. He moved and spoke quickly and was rubbing his hands together, then wiping them on his jeans as though afraid of catching fire. Afterwards Carey said to Barrett:

"Have you noticed with Al that he's either really up or pretty down?"

Barrett said he had.

Group Hex entered another competition, to win a free session at a local recording studio. They sent in a cassette of tracks taped at a practice. A few days later they received a letter notifying them that as runner-ups they had won a day in The Crypt at half the usual rate.

"I didn't know just anyone could go in a studio. I thought you had to be famous or something first," said Fisher.

Carey was aware that in a studio the instruments were recorded individually and mixed together later. He suggested another approach:

"I think we should record the whole thing live and all play at once."

"But this is a chance to make it sound really good," said Barrett. "They can overdub, where they get about three guitars playing the same thing but on different tracks, so it's really powerful."

"It's false though, isn't it?" said Carey. "That's not how we normally play. How can it have feeling? I thought that's what we were about."

Fisher disagreed:

"What have we got to lose? We can practise loads so we get our parts spot-on."

Since when had this Barrett-Fisher alliance formed, wondered Carey. The bastards.

★

Godspace, Barrett's seventh solo album, had been heavily influenced by Mensch, a collective of left-field German musicians. A year or so earlier Green had lent him a set of their albums, worried that Barrett's approach had become too conventional. Mensch took what sounded like the sound of distant sawmills and hammers clanking on to concrete, taped it, slowed it down and fed it through masses of digital echo. Barely music, it was more the soundtrack to an almost forgotten dream.

Barrett had plagiarised their sound but where they used spoken samples—an American mumbling about burning fields ('The black smoke like a murder of crows, wings joined, sky all dark, no sound ...')—he sang lyrics of great portend. The opening song, the album's *motif* (as it said in the accompanying press release), was called *The Grave* and lasted eleven minutes:

'Walking from the womb, already I see my tomb.'

One reviewer had sneered:

> 'Barrett opens like Boris Karloff rising from his sepulchral majesty. You're meant to be afraid, very afraid, as he simpers on about what a drag it is to be alive but all we really hear in our mythical haunted castle is the sound of hysterical, derisive guffawing.'

*

Lauren was sixteen and, according to Al, the prettiest, cleverest girl in the world. Barrett and Carey met her at his house the next Friday evening. She was tall and boyish with fierce brown eyes, wearing a loosely stitched jumper pulled out of shape and almost reaching her knees. She didn't make eye contact or ask any questions, answering theirs with 'sure', 'cool' or 'no way!'

They trooped out to the nearest pub which was full of people washed and scrubbed for the weekend. Lauren had never been in a pub before. She was soon tipsy and began filtering through the various rooms. Al kept rising from his seat, concerned about her. Carey saw her talking to the locals — the bloke with a red face and a glass eye, the lads in the pool room. When she came back she was trailed by two or three of these and they backed up between the tables as if queuing for something but not sure what. She sat down beside Al and kissed him passionately for several seconds full on the lips. The men-in-waiting drifted away.

After Al and Lauren had disengaged, Barrett resumed their conversation. He wanted to know, as ever, what Al thought of new tracks, song titles and ideas. While Al spoke, Lauren turned to face him, staring at his mouth. She carried on until he became self-conscious and his words dried up. She forced her lips against his again.

★

Green had kept the review from Barrett but in his more antagonistic moods he was tempted to show it, if only to make a point: *this is what happens when you go off at a crazy tangent and pretend to be something you're not. I was hoping for a few weirder outros or the odd experimental middle eight, not a wholesale abandonment of your every musical and lyrical trademark.*

He had also been vague about the number of albums ordered by shops and downloaded.

"How's it shifting?" Barrett asked.

"Pretty briskly."

Barrett was astute enough not to ask for precise numbers. A gentle ambiguous truth sufficed.

The figures supplied to Green by Headfall showed that across the UK *Godspace* had sold approximately eight hundred copies into shops and a similar number had been legally downloaded. Green had been hoping for healthy upfront sales to save revealing to Barrett the extent to which his career had contracted. How could he tell a man who, famously, was once said to have had a copy of one of his albums in every ten homes in the UK, now had such paltry sales?

Green could see that future releases would probably become mail order or download-only and Barrett was set to join the ranks of ex-pop stars selling a few hundred copies of each album — though claiming it was a few thousand — to a resolute set of ageing fans via the internet, with whom they were practically on first name terms.

At closing time they walked back to the house. Al's brother, Rob, was home from university, sitting in the kitchen reading a book. He was fascinated by his brother's new girlfriend and bombarded her with questions: did she like England? What was it like in New Jersey? What music was she into? How long was she staying? She answered at first but then reverted to body language: a nod, a shrug, an upside-down smile.

"What do you think of our pubs?"

She pulled an 'I dunno' face. He had an idea.

"We've got some peanut butter. You Americans love that, don't you?"

"Where is it?"

"In the cupboard."

Walking past him, she opened the cupboard door and took the jar from the shelf. Screwing off the lid, she dipped in her fingers, scooping out a handful.

"Well, mind my manners!" said Rob.

She froze, glaring at him. Her nostrils were flared, her top lip raised.

"It was a joke," he said.

She didn't move.

"…a joke, I didn't mean it."

"FUCK YOU!" she screamed, slamming down the jar as she left the kitchen.

Al ran after her and returned a few minutes later. He tried to explain:

"You shouldn't have said that. Americans have a different sense of humour than us. How was she supposed to know it was a joke?"

★

When Barrett left the office, Green sat back in his chair. He started thinking about the pigeon. He'd seen birds like that as a kid. His mother had told him that if you caught them and undid the string they were okay; the trouble was catching them. Barrett was like that fucking pigeon. He needed unfastening, from himself.

Taking off his glasses, Green rubbed his eyes. This time he hadn't issued the regular gentle, ambiguous truth but a complete falsehood. An appearance on *Lunch Brake* for an artist like Barrett was almost worthless and, most likely, another stage in the shutdown of his career. Green could visualise everything: Tommy Hulme, the presenter, prattling on about Barrett's supposed lascivious past (sardonically, with a few rehearsed puns) while Barrett smiled self-deprecatingly, interjecting a few lines of his own to prove he could 'laugh at himself', a necessary property of ageing rock stars. Barrett, in return for playing Hulme's stooge, would be granted two minutes (maximum) to run through one of his old hits. In a bid to relay his artistic worth, he would change the words or elongate the middle section, anything to reinforce his self-image as an individualist, someone constantly changing, experimenting, eternally relevant, man.

Green was also apprehensive of him appearing on a show that viewed piss-taking as high art. It would look as if Barrett didn't have the capacity to discern or, worse, accepted any offer of television, however vulgar. He would be further branding himself as a curio, a frothy lightweight, a quick hit nostalgia fix. Green had agreed to the booking only because he was eager for national exposure. The radio and press pluggers had garnered little and a sign of life was a necessity. Barrett, like all artists, had to have a drip-drip level of attention, especially around a record release and Green felt obliged to drop in this sweetener, giving the impression of behind-the-scenes busyness and showing that the record hadn't been released into a void. He felt he owed it to Headfall, too.

Only now, alone in his office, did he face what he'd known all along but ignored like something large and cumbersome left in a room but covered by a dust sheet. Barrett wasn't going to sell additional copies of *Godspace* by appearing on *Lunch Brake*. If he sold any extra albums it would be from his back catalogue, from which neither he, Headfall or Barrett earned anything because he was still in debt to previous labels.

*

Carl left the band before the half-price studio session. No hard feelings, he said, but he wanted to form an ensemble with a lad who'd put an advert in the paper for 'synth-slaves'. Guitar bands were on the way out, he proclaimed. The future was in bleak soundscapes scaring people half to death, reflecting back to them the desolation of their lives and environment. They should check out Cabaret Voltaire and Throbbing Gristle for more enlightenment. They already had.

"Everything is fucked up," he said, cheerfully. "They're flattening everything and rebuilding in concrete, all these underpasses and walkways, the precinct in town. The world's going to be completely different a decade from now, if they've not bombed it to fuck."

He had been reading up on Dada and Futurism. His new band (which wasn't, he insisted, a 'band' in the conventional sense) would embrace the philosophy of Filippo Marinetti, the founding father of Futurism. They would mesh performance, literature and visual art, and encourage their audience to interact, to 'create' with them.

At his final practice with Group Hex he passed around the set-list he had already contrived for his new project, song titles awaiting songs. Among them were *The Rats Shall Eat The Survivors*, *Hamburger Face* and *They Stuffed Our Shoes With Paper*.

Afterwards Barrett said he was glad he'd gone.

"He's been getting on my nerves with that dance he does, the thing with his knees going to one side."

Carey knew exactly what he meant. Fisher had another complaint:

"I can't stand the way he lets his mouth sort of hang open when he stops singing. He looks a right spaz."

The three of them agreed that this petty and peevish attention to detail made for great bands.

★

Back on the telly. At last, thought Barrett, as he walked through Soho. A drink was in order, to celebrate. A social drink. While the rest of the world worked and slogged and drifted to nighttime, he'd get there first. Let the suits rush around and the bus drivers wrestle for space with the taxi drivers and van wollahs. Let the builders fill the skips, fasten up the scaffolding. Double vodka, then two or three more. For good luck. Which pub? Which pub to fall into from these twenty thousand streets under the sky? Did it matter? Any. The Porcupine, just off Charing Cross Road. Fine. He skipped through the door, as good as.

69

"Vodka please, a double."

"With ice?"

"Please."

Ice was a treat, it made for a different drink than the one in his jacket pocket.

The barman didn't smile. The other drinkers didn't trade one either. Most were clinging to the bar as if it was driftwood. One read the paper, the racing page. Another stared at the optics and the packets of peanuts hanging down on a board, as if looking for a note he'd pinned up long ago. A fruit machine whirred, playing the same three or four notes constantly. Barrett thanked the barman and lingered a few seconds, hoping for conversation. Nothing doing. He sat down and opened a discarded newspaper left on a chair. He read the same stories repeatedly, only realising when he'd got a few paragraphs down. He looked about him and was suddenly downcast: full of old men, bloody awful, feels like 1952 in here.

He drank the vodka and slipped back out to the street. The day had turned overcast. Drops of rain dabbed his face. He pulled shut the lapels of his coat and kept hold as if hugging himself. The rain grew stronger. People hurried by, others gathered in shop doorways or under bus shelters. He passed the massage parlours and strip clubs, the fluorescent glow at their doorways laying out a carpet of lemony light across the wet pavement. One of the women sitting inside smiled at him. It seemed friendlier, less professional than usual. Maybe, he thought, it wasn't the routine step-this-way enticement but genuine pity for a poor wretch getting wet out there.

Before, he'd loved days like these when the sky turned black and rain flushed away protocol, making everyone the same — little creatures searching for shelter and each of them with a tale: the taxi driver, the bookshop girl, the lovers in the cafe, the faces at the windows in the pubs. What were their lives? What was their story? How did they get there? What would they do when the rain stopped? Barrett didn't need a notebook; images and ideas fell into his mind like footprints in fresh cement, stored for later when he was back home, guitar in his arms.

The rain trickled past his collar, down his neck and into the hollow between his shoulder blades. This wasn't a poet's rain, he cursed, but merely drip-dripping water. Only when he'd been famous, when people were listening to his words, buying his records, had it counted for more.

★

The band were rehearsing one evening unaware that Al had arrived home from London where he'd accompanied Lauren to the airport. His mother entered the attic and motioned to Barrett. The band stopped playing.

"John, could I have a word?"

She said she'd heard noise coming from Al's room but he'd not responded to her shouting. Barrett ran down from the attic. It was quiet now. He knocked on the door, pushed it open and switched on the light. The room was a mess. Drawers were levered from their runners and tossed aside, bedding everywhere. A magazine was torn up lying next to bits of coloured cardboard. Barrett looked closer and saw that they were plane tickets and a passport. Al had attacked his tape collection too, unspooling lengths that had fallen like the guts of a dead animal around the room. Amid the chaos, Barrett saw Al lying face down on the bed.

"Al," he said.

He wasn't sure if he heard a murmur or not. He reached over, patting his shoulder. The denim of Al's shirt was soft, the flesh beneath sinewy. Al was in the room, flesh and bones in clothes and still breathing, but Barrett felt that most of him, the substantial part, was missing.

★

Barrett travelled home from London by tube, covering the last twenty miles or so by overground train. He struggled to stay awake under the soft sway of the carriage's rhythm. Esther had offered to pick him up from the station but he said he wanted to 'do some civvy'—his own term for undertaking something routine, something *ordinary* people did.

He ambled through the station car park, down a narrow alleyway and past a couple of fields. He came to a new estate of large detached houses built in sandstone. He looked through windows as he walked, into these boxes of illuminated life. They formed a cartoon strip without a narrative—people watching television, working at computers, reading newspapers, moving from one room to another. He began to pity them, these stuck, going-nowhere people. They had no relationship with hope. They tapped at a computer, talked on the phone or to each other in person but that was it, everything. It didn't lead anywhere. Even now, he thought, late in his creative life, he still had hope (as much as ever, actually). There was always the chance of something happening, breaking through: the next song, the next record. He couldn't imagine a life without hope, when you weren't pushing for something that people could share and enjoy, a song or a book or a film, something you'd made up yourself. This was why you were given a life in the first place; you were duty bound to make it special.

Now that Carl had left and Scoffer showed no signs of return-ing, Barrett said it was probably time for an overhaul. He suggested a name change. Group Hex sounded a bit too, kind of, you know, sort of … comical.

"When I say it to people I feel funny inside. I cringe."

"I know what you mean," said Fisher.

Barrett volunteered 'Killing Stars' as an alternative. He wasn't sure where it came from, a film possibly, but it had been in his head for months. He said it also made sense that he took over vocals.

"I've been writing most of the lyrics."

Over the previous few months he'd been turning up to prac-tices with songs mapped out, the parts written, and a clear idea of how he wanted each instrument to sound. He'd tamper with knobs on the amplifiers, fussing over the precise tone or the depth of reverb. The floating zoo strategy had been jettisoned too with kids no longer showing up randomly at practices.

"No staying power," said Fisher. "Paper tigers."

Shaun, a kid Barrett and Carey had met at college, became the sole drummer. He had long hair and wore denim; Barrett liked this because it was contrary to new wave etiquette. He was self-taught and had an economical style of playing built around the snare and hi hat, which meant the rhythm was lean and not the regular bang-bang-bang and mad dash for the cymbals.

Darren Shackleton, a friend of Shaun's, became the bass player: they came as a pair. He announced that he wanted to be known as Shack and listed as such on subsequent tapes and records, thank you very much. He liked different bands than the others, including a few that Barrett dubbed 'twiddly bastards'.

"I don't want you tossing off," Barrett told him at his first practice. "The bass has to be solid, underpinning the guitar and that's it. Nothing fancy required. Leather strap, play with a plectrum and no finger picking. And always, always, make sure it's a long-scale bass, not one of those puny short-scale things."

"That's a lot of rules."

"I know: obey them."

"Aye-aye, captain."

★

The rain had stopped and the private lane leading to Barrett's converted millwright's house on the edge of the village, was becoming dusty again.

He entered through the back door. Esther was playing at the kitchen table with Holly. They had emptied dried pulses and beans into small plastic pots and were sticking them down with glue.

"This is us, daddy."

Holly had drawn a picture of the three of them. Esther was a long, thin worm. Holly, a small one. And he was a roundworm. They had hair. He didn't.

"Is daddy really so chubby?"

"Easily. Easily peasily pudding and pie."

He left the room to hang up his coat. He tried to hook it on a peg under the stairs but it kept slipping off. He threw it to the floor. He didn't return to the kitchen but slipped upstairs and into bed. The curtains were open. Streetlights had come on and made distant rooftops shine silver. A crow shuffled along a wall top. He put his hands together and jammed them between his thighs. The air outside was smoky. It was the time of year when bonfires burned in fields and back gardens, as if it wasn't enough that summer had ended, it had to smell like it too.

The bed was soon warm, the sheets newly washed. He felt like a child, sick in the afternoon. He had often been ill as a kid, with asthma. He used to think it strange that life went on without him, classmates at their desks, cars moving along the street outside. His mum would come up to him, soup on a tray, flannel for his forehead.

"Dad won't be back for ages yet," she'd say.

Neither of them wanted him to return and the house blown cold again. He always brought something of the outdoors with him — the smell, the weather, the messiness — and scattered it to all corners, grumbling.

"What's he doing in bed?" he'd ask.

"He's ill."

"You sure he's not pulling your leg?"

"He's been coughing all day."

"Take him to the doctor's, then."

"I have."

"Good for you."

"What does that mean?"

"What do you think it means?"

His parents often spoke as if they were having a sword fight, jabs and thrusts until someone was run through:

"Oh, piss off."

⋆

The band decided to record *Manifesto* which was the first page of *The Communist Manifesto* set to a three chord progression. Carey had read portions of Marx's text and relayed its sentiments so the others could share his enlightenment. He decreed that if you were northern and working-class and had witnessed the Conservative government ravage the textile, coal and steel industries, it was your categorical duty to align yourself with the ultra-Left.

"Well said! I'd rather have a kiddie fiddler in the band than a fucking Tory," said Fisher.

The Crypt was based beneath a terraced house and owned by Bob, a bloke in his thirties who had spent years in cabaret groups. He had knocked together two cellar rooms, put carpet against the walls and wired up an eight-track sound-desk. Scattered on various chipboard ledges covered in foam (which served as seats) were technical leaflets about recording equipment, and porn magazines.

"Which way shall you swing," he asked when they entered. "Technology or pornography?"

Carey watched the others take their turn to play. They were proficient, getting it right on the first or second take, asking to do it again if they felt they could do better. Barrett had written extra parts which he laid over the basic tracks. They were strong, adding another dimension or counter-melody.

"These new bits are like raisins in a bowl of corn flakes," gushed Fisher.

Carey went last. He was handed a pair of headphones. He could see outlines of band members through the thick glass separating him from the control room. Barrett was sitting close to Bob.

"Are you ready, Dave?" asked Barrett. "Are the cans working okay?"

The *cans*? What was all that about?

"Sure."

They set the tape rolling. The red light lit up. Carey came in late.

"I'll run it again."

He came in too early. Bob reeled it back. After five or six attempts, Carey timed it right. He was so elated, he lost the rhythm. He was taken back to the beginning. Again, he came in late. Bob held up his fingers to help him, counting down from four to one, to no avail. Carey saw Fisher move towards the microphone on the desk linked to the recording booth.

"Are you okay in there?"

He wanted to tell him to fuck off.

"Fine."

His voice was parched.

Bob, small and bald and wearing a scruffy T-shirt, said a tea break was in order. He darted around like a wren, plugging out leads, talking fast, asking if anyone wanted a brew, two sugars or one. Come on lads, make your minds up.

"I'll tell you what, Dave," he said. "When we start again, you just play along to the track. I won't tape it. Try and get yourself warmed up while we talk among ourselves."

"Okay."

It was an old trick. Bob *was* taping but had taken the pressure off Carey by making him believe it was a run-through. He was more relaxed without the red light and was doing fine until he stopped after the first chorus.

"Shit," muttered Bob. "We nearly cracked it then."

The red light went back on. Carey was worse than before. He could see the band were getting bored, toy fighting with one another.

"I think it's slipping now," said Bob. "It might be best if we look at dropping you in."

"What's that?"

"We can do it bit by bit, jabbing you in wherever it goes a bit wonky until we've got through the whole song."

They did as Bob suggested, recording the track in short stages over the course of an hour. At one point Bob and Barrett thought the control room microphone was switched off. Carey overheard their conversation:

"Are you happy with that guitar sound?" asked Bob.

"I think so. Why?"

"I've never heard anything like it before. It sounds like a grinding machine."

"We'll have it low in the mix."

"Very low, I'd say. Maybe at that pitch where only dogs can hear it. Dead dogs!"

Barrett chuckled. Carey wished him dead.

Later, at the mixing stage, Carey rediscovered his composure, suggesting subtle but important changes, coaxing Barrett to vary his vocals in a few places. On the occasions Carey's guitar was isolated it sounded awful — a grainy, gushing sound. Merged with the rest though, it added a rough energy.

"It's like a load of cement covering the cracks," said Shack.

Carey nodded his appreciation:

"Every classic band needs that element of cement."

"We should call the album that — *Element of Cement*. I can see it in the racks now," said Shack.

About an hour before they finished, Carey saw a pile of letters under the mixing desk. He reached down. It was the same one he had received but addressed to someone else. He looked at the others. They formed a roll call of every band within a thirty-mile radius. Each had been roundly congratulated and designated 'lucky' runners-up with the offer of a full day's recording at half the usual price. Bob noticed.

"Hey, you're not supposed to see them."

"A bit late now."

"I had to get the studio up and running," said Bob.

Barrett and Fisher laughed and agreed it was a great scam. Carey thought it was sneaky.

★

Barrett woke a few minutes later, hearing Holly shouting.

"Daddy, are you up there?"

"Here, in here."

His mouth was dry. While he waited for Holly to follow the trail of his voice, he fished into the bedside drawer and felt for the smoothness of a bottle. He unscrewed the top and swigged down the contents.

"Hello kiddo," he said to her silhouette.

"We wondered where you were."

"Just having a nap. Daddy's tired."

"Are you getting up soon?"

"In a few minutes."

"Come on, I want to show you my picture. It's good, I tell you: *really* good."

"I'll soon be with you."

He pulled on a shirt and went down. Holly was drawing in the living room, her belly flat to the floor.

"Don't look, I'm just changing it a bit," she said.

Barrett went through to the kitchen.

★

Back home, Barrett played the studio tape continually. His parents were out so he had turned up the stereo full blast. He barely heard the telephone when it first rang.

"Hello."

"It's Rob here, Al's brother."

Barrett knew immediately that it was bad news. He had to remind himself to breathe, drawing it in as one gulp.

"I'm afraid Al tried to kill himself today…"

Barrett couldn't speak.

"… he's okay though."

"What did he do?"

"He slashed his wrists."

★

Esther had started the tea, chopping vegetables and dropping them into pans. Barrett wanted her to add the garlic and spices so the house would smell different to the one he'd grown up in; his mum, dad, and the past was on his mind now.

He sat at the table. Esther saw the bulge in his top pocket. She crouched to put a tureen into the oven. While she placed it on the wire ledge, she took another surreptitious glance. He'd craftily levered off the top and was swallowing the vodka down hungrily.

"John," she shouted.

It startled him.

"What?"

"Can't you give it a rest?"

"Actually, no. I can't give it a rest."

"Why not?"

"You know why."

"I don't, tell me."

"Because if I do, I feel shit. I've told you before, I'm weaning myself off. A little bit less every day."

"Well is that it for today? Have you had your lot?"

"Depends."

"What on?"

"This and that."

Barrett wanted to say, but couldn't summon the words, that it depended on whether he started to feel nervous, hollow inside. And whether his hands shook. And whether he was scared of the phone ringing or the television being on loud because it was like something poking at his skin, going all the way through. Or his stomach aching as if he wanted to go to the toilet or throw up. Or whether his mouth became dry and he could taste something that reminded him of a leaking battery. And, and.

"Anyway, you've not told me," she snapped.

"Told you what?"

"What Rupert wanted you for."

"I'm doing a telly tomorrow."

"Tomorrow?"

"That's right. The Barrett is back."

★

A few days later Al returned home from the hospital. Barrett called round. Al's mother answered the door and led him to his room. It was early summer and he noticed how different the house looked in sunlight. The place was lifted up, suspended in the air.

Al was wearing a white T-shirt and washed out jeans, the healthiest nearly-died person Barrett had ever seen. Al said he was going to be fine. The counselling sessions were booked and the wounds across the inside of his arms had started to heal. Barrett asked to see them. They were like notches on a prison wall counting out days.

"Why did you do it?"

"I don't know. I get down sometimes."

Barrett looked around and noticed how bare the room was: no pictures, a few coins on the windowsill, a small neat pile of clothes folded on top of a wooden bedding box.

*

After their meal, which Barrett picked at, he sat by the stereo working through a pile of vinyl records. Esther was relieved to see him drinking from a can. She thought there was something routine, domesticated even, about a man taking swigs from a can in the evening. Every ten minutes or so, he shouted for her to come through from the other room where she was getting Holly ready for bed.

"Listen to this bit coming up, how it drops down and they pick it up again."

She turned an ear to him and nodded approvingly. He lifted his thumb; the music was too loud to hear themselves speak anyway. She shouted all the same:

"You look like that kid you always get at a teenagers' party, sitting by the record player all night choosing the music."

He smiled. He liked the image.

*

Carey sent the demo of *Manifesto* to the *NME*. He didn't think he'd hear back because everyone said it didn't matter how good the music was, it was all down to connections. The industry was a closed shop. And journalists didn't play tapes anyway; it had to be a record.

Two weeks later Carey was in his bedroom working on a novella (he hadn't stopped to think how pretentious this sounded when he told people). His mother shouted that someone from the 'Elemy' was on the phone.

"Hello," said Carey.

"All right, how's it going? Sean McArdle, *NME*. I'm trying to track down someone from the band Killing Stars."

The man had a Scottish accent. He sounded as if he'd been drinking.

"I'm Dave Carey. I play guitar in the band."

"Ace. Got to tell you man, I've just played your demo tape for about the twentieth time. It's fucking brilliant."

"Really? You like it?"

"No, I don't *like* it," said McArdle. "As I just said: I think it's fucking brilliant. I've not heard anything so raw and exciting in fucking ages. Have you been in bands before?"

"Not really."

"I can't believe that. The production is fucking superb. When are you next playing live? I've got to see you."

He told him they had no concerts planned.

"Look, I've got a mate who puts on shows here in London. I'll have a word with him and get you on somewhere. Would that be cool with you?"

Carey said it would be fantastic and thanks very much.

"Listen, don't thank me. If it weren't for the fact you're making great music I wouldn't be calling you right now. It's the fucking music."

Esther took Holly up and went to bed herself soon afterwards. Barrett began drinking from a bottle of red wine. It refreshed him; his thoughts glistened. He pulled a single from its picture sleeve—yellow vinyl. He slid it back in so he could take it out again. He had the urge to lick it, closing his eyes and imagining it tasting of banana. He remembered having the same thought when he was about fourteen, wanting to devour music.

★

McArdle organised for them to play in London, first on of three bands in a room above a pub. They hired a van and filled it with instruments and amplifiers, cushions and pillows. It felt like a school trip.

On the way down, Carey sensed the differing factions. He and Barrett were the 'teachers' (or rock's first social workers, as Barrett joked); Shaun and Shack were the cocky kids and Fisher was the maverick—Barrett had once referred to him as a 'godsend'.

"He's the most way-out kid in town and he's in our band."

When they reached the outskirts of the capital, Shack was at the back window giving marks out of ten for the girls they passed.

"God, the birds here! They're so much better-looking than what we get back home. Even the ones that are about thirty look fit."

Carey reminded him of the band's clearly stated non-sexist policy.

"Let loose, Mr C, and be free," said Shack.

Fisher and Shack organised a game of 'paps, pups or pips' where girls were graded on the size of their breasts.

"Look at them! Paps, definitely."

"No, they're pups, they are."

"I bet they're all filthy bitches, this lot," cried Fisher.

He carried on, becoming increasingly crude.

"Take it easy," said Shack. "I'm as dirty as the next man, unless the next man is you and happens to be a twisted fucker."

"I know—good isn't it?"

★

Surrounded by his old records, a lad Barrett knew from school came to mind—Craig Smith. When he visited other mates, the records formed background music while they talked about girls, teachers, football or what they had seen on television the night before. Smithy though, really did listen and would stare intensely as Genesis' *Foxtrot* or Judas Priest's *Rocka Rolla* revolved, nodding his head slowly. The few words he spoke were whispered not in sentences but as lonely fragments.

Barrett recalled a shopping trip they had once made together, an eight-mile bus journey to an outlying town solely to buy a couple of button badges. Snow came down and the buses were taken off the roads. They walked back, the snow turning to slush. After being with Smithy for a few hours, during which time he barely spoke, Barrett felt he was becoming him. They fell into the same walking pattern, side by side in their ox-blood Doc Marten boots and three-quarter length beige duffel coats. Smithy didn't seem to notice the symmetry but Barrett had to break it, stopping regularly and pretending to retie a lace. It took more than three hours to get home.

Fisher sat back down among the cushions, empty cans and chocolate wrappers.

"Just thought — what are we wearing tonight? What's the stage gear, man?"

"What we're wearing now, normal clothes," said Barrett.

"And what about my grand idea?"

A few days earlier he'd told them that he intended to wear his sister's knickers *over* his trousers and a see-through flexi-disc taped across his face.

"Not really us, is it?" said Barrett.

"But it's our duty as artists to blow minds for a living."

"Well, let's get established first in case we blow our chances."

Unbidden, Shack announced a fondness of Abba.

"Abba?" said Fisher. "You're joking, aren't you?"

"No, I think they've got really good tunes, how they're put together and that."

Fisher shook his head, disgusted. Shack turned to Barrett for support.

"Tell them John, *Arrival*'s a good album isn't it? You know, cleverly done."

"Fuck off."

"You're just scared to admit it."

"I can't bear to even look at that album, their self-satisfied faces in that poxy helicopter. It makes me want to puke."

"Okay then, you might not like the music but which one would you shag?"

"The monkey one with the beard."

Shaun asked how they were going to recognise McArdle.

"I've seen his picture in the paper a few times. He's got curly hair, I think."

As they drew close to the venue Shack spoke to Carey about *Word Hex*. He said it was okay in places but a bit too ... he couldn't think of the word.

"You know, when something's too much. What is it? It sounds like hysterical and it means more or less that."

"Histrionic?"

"That's it. It's got some good stuff but you go over the top. People switch off when you start ranting and raving."

"But how can you not get passionate about subjects like the bomb and what Margaret Thatcher is doing to this country?"

"I don't know, you've just got to stay cool I suppose."

*

Woody, another of Barrett's schoolmates, would happily use up Smithy's share of the talking. Barrett remembered visiting him one Saturday afternoon to listen to a Black Sabbath album. Woody asked if he had ever headbanged. He said it was great, it made you feel drunk.

They had to break off from the head-shaking when Woody's mum knocked on the bedroom door with plates of roast beef sandwiches. After she'd gone they resumed with a gentle swing of their fringes. As the beat picked up, Woody slipped off his glasses. The guitars and drums came in and they began shaking their heads furiously. The music stopped. They heard a scraping sound. Woody sat upright, eyes spinning.

"What the fuck?"

They stared about them, brains at sea. The grating sound was traced to the record player. The top half of a roast beef sandwich had jammed against the arm, causing it to lift and fall intermittently. The other half was in Woody's hand. He cracked up laughing:

"I thought we'd summoned the devil."

Barrett smiled at the memory, pleased that this small world, *his* world, peopled by the likes of Smithy and Woody, seemed to count for something because he'd made it through, sung their lives.

*

They found McArdle in a pub down the road from the venue. His head was hung low over the table as if he was about to fall asleep. They couldn't see his face at first; it was covered by thick hair.

"Hello, we're Killing Stars," said Barrett. "Are you Sean McArdle?"

McArdle jerked back in his chair.

"Huh, yes. Good to see yer."

The band tried to engage him but he stared down at the floor. When he did speak he made forthright, bitter statements. They were telling him about their day in the studio when he cut them short.

"See him there? He's a total arsehole."

He pointed to a bloke dressed in black sitting alone at another table. He was jotting in a notebook.

"Who's he?" asked Carey.

"Steve Herbert. He writes for the *NME* as well, except he can't fucking write to save his life. He's a fucking joke."

"Right."

"Don't go fucking near him, that's my advice. And don't let him know I like you because he'll fucking rip you to pieces on principle."

"How come you're like this with one another?" asked Fisher.

"Because he's a cunt."

"My boss is a cunt too."

"Yeah?"

"Too fucking right."

Fisher had picked up McArdle's swearing habit.

"How come?"

"Where do I start? He's sneaky, he's selfish, he's greedy."

"What do you do?"

"I work in a scrap yard. I'm supposed to be taking out engines. At least that's what he told me in the interview. Most days I'm throwing washers in skips, shit like that. One, two, three, four, five, six, counting them out. Nuts and bolts as well. Do you know what I'd do if I got half a chance, if I could corner that bastard out of work one day? I'd cut his fucking face with scissors."

McArdle recoiled.

Carey whispered to Barrett:

"I think Jase is freaking out McArdle."

"I know, funny isn't it?"

★

Barrett pulled out more singles: Wah! Heat, The Pop Group, Wire, The Au Pairs, The Passage, Echo and the Bunnymen, The Birthday Party, The Normal. He put Magazine's *Shot by Both Sides* on the deck, listening to it on headphones. One time his dad had knocked on the bedroom door while Magazine were on, the bit about drugging you and fucking you on the permafrost.

"What's that headcase on about?" he asked.

"I'm not sure exactly."

His dad couldn't understand why his son liked music so much and wanted to be in a band. Playing the guitar was 'plinky-plonky rubbish' to him, messing about. And he didn't like the friends he plink-plonked with either. They were all a bit weird. Why didn't he have any *normal* lads as mates?

Barrett began thinking about his mum and dad again: the rows, the shouting and swearing, plates flying across the room, her threatening to leave. He remembered the time his mum jabbed a hot iron into his dad's chest, sending him falling to his knees, screaming. She poured water over the burn from a plastic jug she kept at the end of the ironing board. The iron had scorched his shirt and left a small 'V' on his skin. Afterwards it became known as his 'Starship Enterprise' because it looked like the badges they wore on *Star Trek*.

Barrett and his brother knew to watch out in case they were caught in the crossfire. A sauce bottle once struck Barrett on the back of the head. He was knocked over and lay face down on the carpet for a few seconds. His mum fussed over him, worried she had killed her six-year-old son.

"Oh God, are you all right?"

He pretended to be lifeless. She cradled his head. He imagined them both somewhere peaceful and quiet. He willed the moment to last forever. He wanted the room to be hazy when he opened his eyes, the colours and shapes fused. It was as clear as before.

"You're okay, you're okay," she blurted, holding him to her.

She smelled of chip fat and washing powder.

★

Killing Stars played to about fifteen people — fanzine editors and Japanese tourists chiefly. After each song the applause was light and broken and they could hear the bar staff talking to one another.

Carey was burning up with nerves again, focused desperately on the two or three chord sequences of each song, simplified for him by Barrett. He strummed a wrong chord at one point and Barrett glared. They were about to play *Manifesto* when Barrett spoke to the audience:

"If you listen closely you might recognise the words to this one. It's about the redistribution of wealth from rich fuckers to the people who really need it. Remember [he put up his finger]: honour good men, be courteous to all men, bow down to none. Or else … "

He began the introduction quietly, holding the strings only part-way to the fretboard so they sounded brittle (he explained later to Carey that it was called 'dampening'.); this wasn't rehearsed.

"Class struggle, it's the history of class struggle," he sang above the rhythm.

He turned his back to the audience and counted in Shaun with nods of his head, lips puckered. Fisher came in at the same point, his face twisted in concentration.

★

Every few months or so Barrett's mum said she was leaving, promising to come back for her 'lovely sons' in a couple of days when she'd found somewhere for them to live. She disclosed these half-baked arrangements to Barrett and he became her confidante. David, three years younger, was expected to tag along.

Once, she actually made it through the front door. Barrett was bundled into the car by his dad to help look for her. About a mile from the house they spotted her walking down the road. Her hair was messy as if she had bolted from the hairdresser's half way through a cut.

"There's mum," cried Barrett.

He saw his dad smile. Got her.

She recognised the car and left the pavement, squeezing through privet bushes that bordered a grassy area in front of a block of flats.

"What's she playing at?" said his dad.

She had crouched to hide herself but the arc of her back was visible.

"Wind the window down," he ordered.

Barrett struggled with the handle.

"Bloody hell, give it here."

His dad pulled at it. Before it was even half way down, he was shouting:

"We can see you, you know. You look bloody stupid. Come on, come back home with us."

"I'm not going anywhere," said the voice in the bushes. "Just bugger off and leave me."

They could see the white of her face through the leaves. Passers-by were stopping to look. After a few seconds she stood up and began walking close to the hedge. He drove alongside, leaning across:

"Come on, get in."

She came to the end of the fence and tried to climb over a low wall. She caught her knee and winced. Rubbing it, she sat down and dangled her skinny legs over.

"What you doing now?" he asked.

"Sitting here. I can if I want. It's a free country, isn't it?"

"Everyone's looking at you."

"I don't care. Let them look. Doesn't bother me. Let them all see what you're like."

"Come on, you've made your point. You're showing yourself up in front of your kid."

"I'm not."

"You are."

"Am I showing you up, John?"

He didn't know what to say. His dad turned to face him.

"She is, isn't she? You don't want to see your mum behaving like this do you, son?"

When he said 'son' his voice softened and this made Barrett feel funny inside, as if bits of him were melting.

"I'd like us all to go home, mum."

She slipped off the wall.

"Open the bloody door then, will you?"

They drove in silence for a few minutes before she spoke again.

"I want you to know Ray that I'm not doing this for you. I'm doing it for him, understand?" She motioned with her head to Barrett. "And for David."

"Message understood. Loud and bleeding clear."

★

After finishing *Manifesto* they headed to the tiny room at the back of the stage that passed as a dressing room. Chairs were stacked around a battered upright piano. McArdle followed, carrying a coat over his arm. He was so drunk he bumped into people and furniture, barely able to apologise, making sounds rather than words. He cornered Barrett, speaking to him from about three inches from his face, his eyes wide and red-rimmed.

"I got to tell you, gotta tell you man, that was fucking totally, I mean totally fucking amazing. I'm shaking man, buzzing. I want to do the interview here and fucking now. Let's do it, me and you."

McArdle had a small tape recorder and spent a few minutes trying to get it to work, cussing and slamming down the lid. Carey hovered nearby. Barrett was chewing gum and laughing louder than usual. He used the word 'altruism' in reply to one rambling question; Carey had no recollection of this being part of his usual vocabulary. McArdle was holding on to Barrett, tugging at the bottom of his jacket, probably to keep himself upright but also as if he was literally touching the cloth.

The article on Killing Stars didn't run in the next issue of the *NME* or the one afterwards. They wondered if it had been shelved or even whether 'McArdle' was an impostor. Meanwhile, they gave him the nickname McGargle in tribute to his prodigious drinking.

*

A few copies of *Godspace* were stacked next to the CD player. Barrett placed one in the tray and pressed the headphones against his ears, closing his eyes. He was at the stage where enough time had elapsed since he'd recorded it, so he was hearing it (almost) like everyone else did.

*

Carey, Barrett and Fisher went to as many concerts as possible, usually with Al who seemed less prone to moods than before; they assumed the counselling was working. They were fanatical about seeing and hearing all they could, drinking it in. The apprenticeship had to be thorough; this was going to be the rest of their lives. Carey had been reading D.H. Lawrence and dubbed these excursions a 'savage pilgrimage'—everything had to be classified and have a greater purpose. Most nights they got in free, claiming they were a reviewing team from *Word Hex*. The next issue was at the planning stage.

A few college friends formed a band called Area 51 and the four of them volunteered to help out at their show at the Hut, humping the gear. The gig was pay-to-play and members of Area 51 had to sell tickets, with most of the proceeds going to the venue.

The concert was on a Monday night. It rained heavily all day. After parking the van, Barrett entered the club with Kersh, Area 51's guitarist. They stamped down hard to shake the rain off their clothes. As they did, their feet stuck to the threadbare carpet where oceans of beer had been spilled over the years and turned to glue. They laughed. Sue, the girl who organised the concerts, was passing in black leggings and black Doc Martens, holding a tower of metal ashtrays.

"Where shall we put these guitars, Sue?" asked Kersh.

"On the stage—where do you fucking think?"

Kersh had hired special lights from Digger and hand-painted images for a slide show to accompany the music. They struggled for nearly an hour putting up the screen he had borrowed from college. All the time, Sue was marching across the floor giving a countdown until the doors *had* to be opened.

"I don't think there'll be a rush," joked Kersh.

"Well that's your fault not mine, matey."

Fisher offered to man the door. No one rolled up during the first hour the venue was open. Finally, about fifteen minutes before they were due on, a group of five or six girls made their way down the stairs to the 'reception'—a piece of wood balanced across two columns of beer crates. They had been drinking and were laughing and joking, their arms around one another.

"We're on the guest list," said the one at the front proudly.

"I'll just check. What's your names?"

"Debbie Earnshaw, Carol Holmes and Dawn Sutcliffe."

As Fisher scanned the list of names she piped up:

"We're groupies, you know."

"Are you?"

"Too right. Are you in a band?"

"I am actually."

"What they called?"

"Killing Stars."

"Killing Stars? I know all about Killing Stars, I do."

"What do you know, then?"

"I know you played a gig in London and you're going to be in the *NME*, so there. My boyfriend told me."

Fisher realised they were the girlfriends and sisters of Area 51.

"How many are in there?" asked another.

"You're the first to show up."

"You're joking."

"I wish I was."

The girls fell quiet and moved through to the main room.

Area 51 took to the stage and played to their girlfriends and sisters; Carey, Barrett and Al; three bar staff (who talked throughout); the sound engineer; and Sue, who left after a few minutes and entered the office at the back of the bar area, slamming the door behind her.

Occasionally the girls left the main room to visit the toilets at the entrance. They were despondent. One stopped to talk to Fisher who was dodging between the reception area and the concert hall.

"They've put weeks of practice into this," she said.

"I know."

"Why do you think no one's come?"

"I know full well why they haven't. It's simple: this town is full of twats. They're at home watching *Coronation Street*, putrefying in their living rooms. They'll turn up later for the disco though, you watch. They're only into music that they already know. They're too scared to venture outside their little boxes and give new stuff a chance." He waited a few seconds before adding: "As I said — twats."

Afterwards, in the early hours, the three members of Killing Stars convened at Fisher's house. Al was there too. It was still raining.

"I hope *we* don't do gigs like that," said Carey.

"We won't," said Barrett.

"How do you know?"

"I just do. We're a good band."

"So are Area 51."

"I know, but there's a difference."

★

97

The number '1' appeared in the small screen on the CD player, lit white against luminous green. The drone of the cello intro to *Paradiso Paradox* rang out followed by several bass notes heavy with reverb. As the song picked up Barrett felt as if his heart had stopped beating. Then he was nauseous.

★

Five weeks after the interview had taken place, the article appeared in the *NME*. Killing Stars were listed on the cover, next to established groups. The piece stretched to quarter of a page and the praise was unremitting. Barrett wrote 'edgy, true-to-life vignettes, hard but with a soft centre'. The instruments were 'inter-woven and interlocked, tuned in and turned on like a 200 horsepower shagmobile with a velvet-lined interior'. Their music had 'pop sensibility' melded with 'rain-lashed, über-strop'.

Within a week they were contacted by six record labels; three concert agencies; five fanzines; two managers (London-based); two radio stations; three publicists; a producer; someone calling himself a 'plugger'; and a bloke offering to make badges with their name on.

Barrett informed the band that they didn't need a manager; they already had one. He'd promised the job 'more or less, sort of' to someone who had approached him at the town festival. Barrett said he wanted someone who, unlike the rest, hadn't waited for the endorsement of the music press before recognising their potential, but had trusted his own eyes and ears.

He passed around a name-card: 'Gary Aspinall: Artiste Management'. Dotted around the letters was a series of dancing musical notes. Barrett told them Aspinall was in his late-twenties with a carefully sculpted quiff, rings in both ears and Buddy Holly glasses. He was, said Barrett, the first openly gay person he'd ever met.

"What did he say to you?" asked Shack.

"He was all excited like a kid, clapping his hands and saying how much he loved what we did."

"But do we really need a manager?"

"We've got to have him," said Barrett. "He's queer!"

They didn't understand.

"Just think of the guts it takes to be bent in this town. Fucking hell, he's a hero. And dressing like he does. You've got to respect anyone with that kind of courage. That's punk — proper punk. Being what you are and not caring what people think."

They saw his point.

Carey said they didn't know if he was any good or not.

"We'll find out, won't we? And if not, we'll just fire him," said Barrett. "Look, those two that called after reading about us in the *NME* will be bandwagon jumpers. Gary's local, more accessible. He has to be worth a go. He's got his own office."

"Where is it?"

"In a side-street in town. I think he said it's above a butcher's."

*

Godspace wasn't just shit, Barrett decided: it was pretentious shit. Well-intentioned, earnest or enthusiastic shit might have been forgivable but this was music that was ponderous and middle-aged. Why had no one stopped him? Why hadn't Green given him an indication? They both knew the code. He was supposed to say it needed 'working up,' 'tightening here and there,' or even 'a bit of a re-think.' Green had let him release this hopeless sprawling mess and encouraged him to dress it up as high art.

★

Aspinall was keen, turning up to his first band meeting carrying a ring binder and calling everyone by their first name. He booked them immediately on to an eight-date support tour with a band that had just recorded their second John Peel session; McArdle had put a word in for them. They didn't need hotels or to miss work or college because the dates were on the northern leg.

At the first show they sat around for almost three hours while the main band sound-checked. They worked painstakingly on the drum kit, spending more than an hour on the snare drum alone: bang, bang, bang. Then the microphones: one-*two*, testing, one-*two*, one-*two*. When they were happy with the sound, they ran, laughing, through a series of cover versions, speeding them up and slowing them down. They ignored the members of Killing Stars sitting around the empty hall, shuffling their feet nervously, tapping on tables, strumming unplugged electric guitars. By the time they finally left the stage, refusing to acknowledge Killing Stars, the audience had started to file in. They gathered at the front, unsure whether the concert had started or not. Killing Stars were barely able to try out one song before the sound engineer interrupted and said, 'Done.' Earlier he had turned the on-stage speakers up full and giggled when they instinctively covered their ears to shut out the feedback.

"The name of this band is Killing Stars," announced Barrett an hour later when the gig properly began.

Carey was aware immediately of Barrett's presence, how he held the stage. During the third song Barrett put down the guitar and was almost on his knees, pleading, acting out the lyrics. It was the kind of melodrama they normally sneered at but it fitted; he kept his cool. He began to ad lib again. He motioned for the band to fall quiet and set off walking around the stage, pacing like a tethered animal. He unfastened the microphone from the stand, tapping it on his forehead and then cupping it in his hands. He went to sing but shook his head as if he had forgotten the words or considered them unworthy of expressing the intensity of his emotion. He was now almost at the edge of the stage. He bent over, looking directly into the faces of the people pressed up close.

"We're living in strange times."

The sound engineer responded by extending the echo so the words 'strange times' reverberated around the hall.

"I said we're living in ... strange times."

Fisher was jabbing at the keyboard, grimacing when he played the odd wrong note, sitting back and flicking Vs at his instrument. Shack was locked into the rhythm, jogging on the spot like a boxer, eyes set to the back of the hall. His collar was turned up and he exuded self-assurance. Shaun didn't drop a beat.

Seeing Barrett like this, Carey suddenly felt emotional. He had known him almost all his life and imagined he was capable of it but hadn't been completely sure. Here it was now: full-blown. He looked at the faces in the crowd. They were entranced. He'd never thought this before, not properly, but at that moment he saw how handsome Barrett was, the black hair, liquid eyes, fine bone structure. Carey switched his thoughts back to his playing, not wanting to forget where he was in the song. He was counting in his head: one, two, three, four, change chord, one, two, three, four, back again. He didn't hear the music or feel it, it was a maths exam.

Barrett let the microphone fall limp in his hands, feigning indifference. He was nodding his head and moving his foot up and down, uttering intriguing phrases at random.

"My baby's on valium ... you're becoming part of the machinery ... we have to make these evenings last, they're always flashing past ... a billion stars are a moving sight."

They finished with a new song, *Believe in the Sign*, and the audience cheered loudly.

Al told them afterwards it was the best gig he'd been to, ever.

"I'm telling you: that was amazing."

He had been down at the front when they played. He was drenched in sweat, his T-shirt pulled out of shape.

★

The next morning Esther found Barrett slumped in the same chair. At his feet were empty wine and vodka bottles and the scattered records. She left him dozing and went into the kitchen to make coffee. When she returned he had stirred and was rubbing his hands slowly across his head. He had a thoughtful look as if concentrating.

"What is it?" she asked.

"Blimey, I'm on the telly today."

"Are you going to be okay to do it?"

"Up for the cup, me."

"Did you drink all that booze?"

"Me? No. It was those elves. I swear. I was just sitting here stitching some shoes when these two little fellas came in and started supping my stash, dancing around like madmen."

His eyes were shining. She smiled.

"What song are you doing on *Lunch Brake*?"

"Not sure, yet."

"Why are you so happy? Is it because you're on telly?"

"Can't a man be happy these days?"

"I suppose so. It's just a bit odd, that's all. What's it all about?"

"I saw the light last night."

"What light?"

"You know, *the* light: the truth, the way."

"You're confusing me."

"My new album, what do you think?"

"It's good."

"No, what do you really think?"

"It's good."

"It's not, is it?"

"It's different."

"Different? You're just trying to be nice. Admit it. I know the truth. I can take it; I was born standing up. It's toss, isn't it? Utter toss. And do you know what? I'm glad I know it for what it is because now there's no more kidding anyone."

"Well, don't start talking like that on the show. You're supposed to be plugging the thing."

"Hey! Ever the professional, me. I'll tell them it's a milestone in the history of rock. The usual baloney."

He was disappointed that she hadn't argued that the album had some worth, the odd track maybe, perhaps one of the shorter ones.

★

After the concert, members of the main band were slumped in the dressing room which was little more than a corridor with pegs along the wall. Breathing hard like athletes after a race, they were enjoying the attention of various people with backstage passes fastened ostentatiously to their clothes. They, like Killing Stars, had been well received. The sound had become clearer, louder and more powerful when they plugged in. From the first note the crowd had bobbed up and down en masse, singing along and shouting for particular tracks.

Barrett positioned himself by the dressing room door so everyone could see him.

"Good gig, lads," he shouted.

They nodded, not sure who he was.

"But you were out of order before, the way you treated us. Three hours for a soundcheck while we get less than five minutes isn't on. And you [he turned to face the sound engineer], what's so funny about whacking up the feedback and laughing when it almost deafens us? I want you to treat this band with respect. You're the main band, I know that, and I appreciate there's a pecking order but tomorrow we'd appreciate a reasonable soundcheck."

A bloke in his mid-thirties or thereabouts interjected:

"And who are you exactly?"

"John Barrett, of the Killing Stars. Who are you?"

"David Silverman, I happen to manage this group."

"Good for you."

Barrett left the room, closing the door gently behind him. Carey had to stop himself from cheering; it was one of the most impressive things he'd ever seen. Barrett had stuck up for himself, stepped outside the role of being a shoulder-shrugging kid, said it like it was. And he wasn't yet eighteen.

★

Barrett walked past the entrance to the television studio. He thought it absurd: he could go into any other building along the street, sit at a desk or chat with someone and the interaction would be insignificant, witnessed by only a few people. Or he could go through another door, have cameras pointed at him and be seen by millions.

He strolled into the reception area. A large monitor was on the wall behind the main desk. *Lunch Brake* had just come on air. After a few seconds of clapping and cheering it cut to Tommy Hulme running on the spot. He was wearing a sharp blue suit with narrow lapels, his hair cut short. He moved his eyebrows up and down frantically.

"Come here," he beckoned. Eyebrow up: "Remember this?" Eyebrow down, a theatrical point to the right. It cut to a piece of film from years before, of Barrett appearing on *Top of the Pops*. It broke down, stuttering as if the tape had snapped.

"Cor," said Hulme, pulling his lips together. He waited for a reaction from the studio audience. It wasn't enthusiastic enough.

"I said, ladies and gentlemen: 'Cor'."

This time he extended 'Cor' for about two seconds.

He returned to the autocue, moving his head across and smiling so everyone knew he was reading from it. He continued:

"Twenty years ago, that. Yes, twenty years. John Barrett, the chiselled and feisty hit maker extraordinaire, will be along shortly. So lock up your daughters or, better still, your grandmothers, because he's back and on the prowl."

*

When the tour finished Killing Stars were invited on to another, playing mainly college venues with a band that had recently had a top twenty hit. Already the organisation was slick, with everyone having specific roles—hiring the van, planning the route, booking the bed and breakfasts, overseeing the guest list and rider (two perks of which they were initially unaware).

Barrett and Carey were resolute about challenging the stereotype of rock musicians. They were ruthlessly polite. They were punctual. Hotel rooms were left tidy. The van was returned in spotless condition. The whole system of running the band, to every last detail, defined Killing Stars. It was something they'd schemed for years in Carey's bedroom, their particular take on the dignity of labour, a loyalty to fellow workers.

At first Shaun, but more especially Shack, balked at the ideology.

"We're supposed to hang loose, aren't we? Isn't that what rock 'n' roll is about?"

"Who do you think tidies up the mess that bands leave?" asked Barrett. "Not the owner of the hotel, that's for sure. It's some woman from down the road getting paid next to nothing, struggling to feed her kids. That could be *my* mum or gran. Or yours. If we want to make a difference we've got to live it. Do you know what this is about? I mean: *really* all about?"

"I think so."

"I'll tell you. It's about being fundamentally a decent person, not an arsehole. Having feelings for other people, trying to understand their point of view, showing humanity."

"I just want to play bass and have a good time."

Shack seemed to realise how trite the remark sounded. He

smiled. This small gift of conciliation had no impact on Barrett.

"Well, you might be better off in another band if that's what you want," he snapped.

"Come on John, you don't mean that," said Fisher.

"I think I do."

"See —*think*."

"Hey, come on," said Carey. "We've a war to fight with the system and its minions. We can't do that if we're battling with one another."

"He started it," said Shack.

"And I'm always prepared to finish it," said Barrett.

"Okay, okay, I'll put on a pinny and vacuum reception if it keeps everyone happy," said Shack.

*

Barrett noticed a toilet across from the sea of leather sofas and smoked glass coffee tables in reception. He locked himself in a cubicle, sat on the toilet lid and started to drink vodka. He was anxious, on edge. He'd not done any major television for a couple of years, since the third repackaging of his greatest hits.

When he left the toilet the receptionist was back at her desk. She glared at him. Barrett guessed she thought he'd come to service the drinks machine or deliver a parcel and had used the toilet without permission.

"Can I help you?" she asked.

"I'm on the telly soon. Just checking in."

"On what show?"

"His," he said, pointing to the screen.

"Tommy Hulme?"

"That's the chappie."

"I'll ring through to Dustin's office and let him know you're here."

She tapped her pen while she waited for the call to be answered.

"He doesn't appear to be at his desk. I'll e-mail him and let him know you're here. Sorry, what was your name?"

"Honest John Barrett."

★

Killing Stars began to notice the same group of fans at their gigs. They waited to speak after shows, nervously asking for autographs, thinking of questions to extend their time with them. They wanted to know what guitars they used. Was the track *Where Have all the Yoppers Gone?* about anyone in particular? Did they have badges for sale? And what's been the best night on the tour, so far?

"See you tomorrow."

"Tomorrow? But we're playing in Wolverhampton. How you going to get there?"

"We'll make it, don't worry."

And they did, the same thirty or forty people, sometimes fifty. One of them saw Barrett outside a venue and said he had something to show him. The lad rolled up his sleeve. At the top of his arm was a tattoo: 'Killing Stars: Believe in the Sign.' Barrett felt the breath leave his body. He had to get away. He pretended he had to collect something from inside the hall. Walking away, he swallowed hard to save himself from crying.

As the tour progressed they became friends with the headline band.

"You're weird, you lot," said their singer.

"Why?"

"Because you're not weird, if you know what I mean. Are you vicars' sons or something, all these rules you have?"

Barrett revealed their solid working-class credentials.

"Good on you, then. But don't forget to enjoy yourselves, man."

"We won't. We acknowledge the need for levity amid the struggle to revolutionise."

"See! Well fuckin' weird."

★

Barrett watched the monitor while he waited. They had cut from Hulme to a piece about an awards ceremony. A midget had been sent along as the programme's roving reporter. Everything was filmed at his height to see which film stars and celebrities patronised him or, alternatively, ignored his size. Not funny, thought Barrett: just crude. In a few minutes he had to mix with these people, go along with the joke, entertain them. He needed another drink, a long one. He headed back to the toilet.

★

Al missed a few dates towards the end of the tour. They found out later what had happened.

Lauren had written from America telling him she'd fallen in love with someone from her home town. Included in the envelope was a collection of her new boyfriend's poems; she sent them believing it would help Al understand why she had to be with him.

Before hanging himself Al destroyed everything that he

hadn't got round to before: photographs, books, letters, records — as if it wasn't enough to die, he also had to remove from the world all evidence that he had existed.

The band gathered at Fisher's.

"I just can't understand why he did it," said Shack, breaking the long silence.

"Because life must have been so shit for him," said Barrett.

"But what about his mum and dad?"

"I imagine when you're that low you don't think about anything apart from getting away from the pain."

Barrett kept saying they had to do something.

"What like?"

"Anything that keeps his name alive, somehow. I can't stand the idea of him slipping away. I want to feel like I do about him today for the rest of my life. I don't want to ever fucking get over it."

"We could put his picture on our first record sleeve," suggested Carey.

"I don't think he'd have liked that. He was really shy."

"What then?"

"I don't know, but I tell you: all this has made me want it even more. We owe it to Al — you know how much he loved this band."

"To be honest John, I don't think he saw it like that. He was just happy listening to the songs."

"No, you're not getting me. I'm saying it's doubly important that we get our songs through and that people get to know what's happened in our lives, so we can keep his memory alive."

A week after the funeral, Barrett and Carey were still talking constantly about Al.

"He was effortlessly cool, wasn't he?" said Barrett. "Not competitive or ambitious. He didn't give a toss about possessions. All he owned apart from his books and records was a pair of jeans, a few T-shirts and those tatty plimsolls. Because he liked me it made me feel good about myself, that I wasn't shallow. Now I'm sort of cut loose."

Carey said he felt the same.

★

A tall man with floppy hair walked towards him, smiling so his teeth were on show, top and bottom.

"John, John Barrett? Nice to meet you, mate. I'm Dustin Cowley, producer of *Lunch Brake*."

He smelled of expensive aftershave and was wearing sensible shoes and designer jeans. *Woodwork teacher wanker*, thought Barrett; this had been the stock insult for the straights Killing Stars encountered.

"How's it going?" asked Cowley.

"Great."

Barrett sensed Cowley had been forewarned that he had a drunken guest. It made him determined to act sober and confound the bastards. In the lift Cowley asked again:

"How's it going?"

"Great."

"Where are you off to next? Got more promo?"

Barrett was used to media people asking this. They wanted to know who they were competing with and confirm that they were among others clamouring for an artist's time; the celebrity thing only worked with the tacit agreement that they all chased the same prize.

"I'm going to bed actually," said Barrett. "I'm absolutely knackered."

"Been busy then?"

"Yeah."

"You've got a new album out, haven't you?"

"Yeah."

"I haven't heard it myself but I've been told it's really cool."

"Well then."

Cowley looked perplexed by this response.

★

Short news pieces began appearing in the music press speculating to which label Killing Stars would sign. *Zigzag* ran a longer article: 'Who's Looking to the Stars?' Aspinall declined to do any direct bidding.

"They'll come to us," he said.

Barrett grew apprehensive as other groups were offered deals. Aspinall said stalling gave them 'more edge'. Eventually, he began negotiations. He offered them first to a label that had courted them for a few months, though none of its staff had been in contact for a week or two. The head of A and R had recently changed and the new incumbent wasn't convinced. Aspinall asked why not.

"They're lacking that certain something. Too low-key, somehow."

"Low-key?"

"I'm not sure the lyrics have a broad enough appeal. It's obvious they mean it but songs about factories and bombs — I can't see it."

"I did my best," Aspinall told the band afterwards. "God, I must have been with him for two hours. I couldn't persuade him."

That same day they received a letter from another label. They were thanked for submitting their demo tape (which the label had actually requested) but, at this moment in time, were not what they were looking for. They were wished all the best in their desire to break into the music industry, yours sincerely.

★

"Do you want some make-up?" asked Cowley.

Barrett usually declined make-up but decided he didn't want to look whited-out any more; he'd glow with the rest of them.

"Oh yes, please. Lots of puffy."

He was introduced to Cheryl, a girl in her early twenties in jeans and a white T-shirt. Her hair was tied back and she looked radiant as though she'd just jumped from a horse after galloping around a field. She dusted his cheeks with foundation. The gentle patting made him sleepy. His chin slipped to his chest for a second.

"Had a late night?"

"I did, actually."

"You're on Tommy's show, aren't you?"

"Yeah. What do you reckon to him?"

"He's great. He's just like you see him on screen, dead funny."

"Does he flirt with you?"

"Nah. He's married."

"He looks too young."

"I think he's older than people think."

She asked why he was on the show.

"I've got a new album to plug."

He was a great admirer of people like Cheryl, he determined, shop-floor people who were easygoing and didn't condescend or self-promote. Honesty was under-rated.

"My mum was really into your stuff when she was younger," she said.

So was discretion.

Cowley returned, beckoning Barrett.

"Come on John, we're ready for you."

He led him down a corridor, talking all the time:

"Tommy's going to open by asking you a few general questions about what you've been up to lately, some stuff about the new record, that kind of thing. He's obviously going to talk a little bit about your reputation: which stories are true and which aren't. We were hoping to close with a short spot of you playing but we're running ridiculously late so we'll probably have to leave it this time around. Next time you're on, hey? With a full band, possibly."

"Fine."

Except it wasn't. They had broken a promise, although, as he'd just realised, he'd forgotten his guitar anyway.

★

The band met that evening and went to the pub. After a few minutes and barely a few sips of his pint, Barrett said they might as well go home.

"I knew this would happen. It's all bullshit. All that fuss after the *NME* piece and then nothing, absolutely nothing. They just like fucking people about."

"There are a few others I've not got back to yet," said Aspinall. "I think you might be over-reacting a little bit."

"It'll be the same with them, blagging tapes and not playing them. It's a stitch up."

"We could always try and make the music less low-key, I sup-pose."

"No, we don't go down that road," said Barrett. "We are what we are and if they don't like it, tough luck."

Barrett headed home alone, desolate. Al dead. No deal. Life shit. He pulled up his hood. As he opened the knackered, permanently-squeaking garden gate, the house wavered through tears as if it was on fire. He pushed past his mother and collapsed on the settee.

"What's wrong, love? What is it?"

"They've turned us down."

"Who has?"

"That record company."

"Which one? That lot who've been phoning all the time?"

"Yeah."

"Are they allowed to do that?"

"They can do what they like."

"That's not on. Can't you report them?"

"Don't be stupid."

"Hey, don't take it out on me. I'm only trying to help. They shouldn't make promises, building you up and letting you down. You're only kids. What's Gary said about it?"

"He's useless."

"You're always saying how professional he is."

"He is for round here but not for London. It's different there."

"What are you going to do now?"

"Pack in."

"You can't do that, not after all the practising. Another com-pany might like your songs. There's a lot of them, isn't there? Why did they say they didn't like you anyway?"

"We're too low-key."

"What does that mean?"

"Nothing. They just say these things. It's the first thing that comes into their heads."

★

Suddenly, Barrett felt fantastic. His head was clear and his heart full of blood and happiness. He sensed acute physical strength and sharpness of mind but it was simultaneously blurry, as if he was in the moment but it was behind him too. He guessed it was the pile-up of drink, nerves and adrenaline. As he marched behind Cowley he made up his mind. The tipsy guest was a television cliché. Everyone knew the form. But he wasn't going to be the playful puppy let loose. He wasn't even going to be drunk (he *was* drunk but there was a difference in being drunk and acting drunk). Instead, he'd be the truth-king, on a mission to blow up television's falsified reality. It was the world, your life, the lot of it, boiled down to an anecdote or a wisecrack: question, answer, laugh-laugh, cue the music. No one acted like that in real life; no one fizzed like Tommy Hulme, apart from cocaine addicts.

"Ladies and gentlemen, a big hand for John Barrett."

As he made his way to the chair at the side of Hulme's desk, the house band played a few jazz-tinged bars from one of his old songs.

"So, John Barrett," announced Hulme.

The camera panned to Barrett. The protocol was to react by smiling or nodding, preferably both. He stared at Hulme, graveyard eyes.

"Right, I know this might appear an odd question and laugh

if you want, but, tell me, what's it really like being John Barrett?"

"What do you mean?"

"My friend! The women, the adulation."

"I adore women," began Barrett.

Hulme smirked. Bring on the banter.

"We all adore women, John, we really do, but what is it especially with you and them?"

"I'm not happy unless I'm fucking them, at least according to you."

★

Barrett went to his bedroom. His acoustic guitar was propped up against the wall beneath a poster of Bob Marley. Why other bands and not his, he asked himself. His music had so much more worth and potential. Already he had mastered dynamics, loud and quiet. He could switch rhythms so the guitars chopped and chewed or gelled together as one. He knew how to form lead parts, thickening the sound with keyboards and then leaving it sparse, pinned delicately to a picked chord or the click-clicking of a solitary hi-hat rhythm. All this came natural, as easy as breathing. Born to it, born to go.

What happened now? Without an outlet for his music, it became a vanity. If he carried on he would be viewed as someone who hadn't accepted the truth — that he wasn't good enough. But if he packed in, he knew the bitterness would ferment. He could see himself walking his home town twenty or thirty years on, telling everyone what should have been. He couldn't bear not being special.

The streetlights came on outside, orbs of purple light flickering to an orange glow. He blamed Aspinall. Should never have trusted him. What was he thinking? What was he doing hanging around town if he was any good as a manager? Those boots. The quiff. Those fucking name-cards.

★

"Whoa whoa, fella," yelled Hulme, holding up his hands as if protecting his face.

"You asked."

"True, but I didn't ask you to relay it in such crude terms."

Hulme did an upside down smile to camera:

"Moving on, and I think we should good people, you've got a new record out John, tell us about it."

"Truthfully?"

The presenter leaned back in his chair.

"I wouldn't expect anything less."

"It's toss or as I said to my wife this morning: utter toss."

It was classic panic TV: cameras moving from side to side, the audience laughing nervously, then silence sprawling wide as night.

"So, I take it that you're not too keen on it?"

"That's the same question as before, asked in a different way. You're buying time while you think of something to say."

"Oh, I'm sorry," said Hulme.

"Good. Do you know what else you should be sorry about?"

"I think I'm going to find out."

"What you said before, your speech at the start of the show. I've got a four-year-old daughter who means the world to me. She doesn't want to hear that stuff."

"What stuff is that?"

118

"Notches on the bedpost, all that nudge-nudge shit you came out with."

"I think if you take a look at the biography supplied by your record company it makes quite a point of trumpeting your libido. If you live by the sword, you die by it too, so to speak."

Hulme pressed down on his earpiece so everyone knew he was receiving messages.

"I think we've one or two very anxious producers backstage."

The audience laughed. Barrett turned his chair to face them.

*

Barrett heard the front door open and guessed it was his dad, home from work. Soon afterwards he could smell potato hash; they always had hash on Wednesdays.

He thought fancifully of death, of taking his own life, running a razor blade across his wrists. His would be the poet's suicide, an ethereal wasting away, blood trickling down the sheets, droplets forming elegant splashes on a neatly written note. His music would live on. A posthumous album could be assembled from the songs recorded at concerts and rehearsals. He visualised the cover of the *NME*: black with a tiny box in the centre given over to a photograph of him singing. Underneath, in tiny letters: 'JOHN BARRETT, R.I.P.' He scolded himself for being so stupid. That night with Al in his ripped up room had shown him starkly the difference between disappointment and depression. And there was still hope: more labels to hear from, more concerts booked. He picked up his guitar and began strumming. A few minutes later he had written a track he later titled, *The End of Music*.

"Why are you laughing? He's not funny," said Barrett. "He's just sarcastic. Can't you see he hasn't got a soul? None of this lot have. It's fake. They're scared of real life. Terrified. Don't encourage them by laughing."

Ironically, a few giggled.

"Look, so I've had a drink. At least I'm alive. This lot here, they're already dead. They all want to be something they're not."

Hulme had recovered his poise.

"If you don't mind, John."

"I do actually. Shut the fuck up."

★

Aspinall received a phone call from Rob Murray, a name he'd heard before.

"I'm not sure who he manages but I think he's pretty big-time," he told Barrett. "It's only fair to tell you he's been in touch."

"I'll ring him and see what he has to say."

Aspinall was taken aback.

"Where does that leave me?"

"We can sort things out later."

"Come on, that's no good."

"I'm sorry you feel that way."

"I'm bound to, all the work I've put in."

"What work?"

"What work! How long have you got? It's been non-stop

since that *NME* write-up. Sending tapes, writing biogs, sorting out pictures, chasing promoters. Bloody non-stop. These things don't just happen, you know. It's all graft."

"Well maybe that's the problem."

"What is?"

"That you're so busy rushing around, you haven't had time to stand back and take an overview, to work on the big things — like getting us a deal."

"I'm not having that, John, I'm really not having it. It's exactly the kind of bullshit that bands come out with when they're about to fuck someone over."

Barrett hadn't realised Aspinall was so robust.

"I'm not going to fuck you over."

"You are, I know it. That's what people like you do."

"*People like me*, what does that mean?"

"You're cunning. I could tell from the moment we met that you had an agenda."

"I thought that was a good thing, knowing what you wanted."

"Not always."

"I've got to talk to Murray at least."

Aspinall stared at the floor. Barrett scrutinised the office: the plastic figurine of Elvis on the window sill; the tray of index cards on the table (one for each of his acts, including one re-listed 'TBC' because Barrett said seeing the words 'The Bug Club' made him feel ill); the CND badge clipped to a Legalise Cannabis poster; the peeling wallpaper; the files on the floor in cardboard boxes; the tatty carpet; the calendar daubed in black marker. Barrett liked the homespun, hopeful air of it all but felt he now had to force his belief in it. If he were to return in four or five years he was sure it would all be gone, the room rented out to someone else or given over to storage, maybe left unoccupied, gathering dust. Aspinall would be working in a clothes shop in town, talking bitterly about his days as a pop impresario, how he had been let down, ripped off.

As much as he wanted to take it with him (the office, Aspinall, his home town) and shape it into something that could fend for itself in the music business, it had to go; it was holding him back.

★

Barrett was now standing, not sure whether to speak directly into a camera or address the studio audience. He looked from one to the other. Hulme was trying to attract his attention, still pretending it was droll and vaguely under control.

"Yoohoo, Mr Barrett. We're over here."

"You're over there, I'm not."

"Indeed, you're more out-there, aren't you?"

"What an arsehole. The thing is, he's a bright kid. He's chosen to do this rather than something worthwhile with his life. What's he being paid? Tell us, how much are you on? How much am I bid for this soul?"

"A good deal more than the royalties you received from your last album."

"See, he doesn't give up, does he? What a peevish man. He is your God, folks, people at home, people in here. Your new God. Oh so much cleverer and smarter than you. So worship him, worship all this shit."

He reached the front row of the audience. The faces were pale. He'd run out of words. He felt light-headed, dizzy. He held out his arms and fell to the ground as if he'd been shot. Hulme's voice stretched out like a wire across a divide.

"Well, don't let anyone tell you we don't do things a bit differently here at *Lunch Brake*. Time, surely, for a short break."

*

Rob Murray invited Barrett to what he referred to as his 'HQ', in west London. He went by train; it was the first time he'd been to London on his own and he was pleased that he found his way through the rat-run of tube stations.

The office was above a boutique that had barely any stock in the window, just a pair of shoes and three or four folded sweaters. Barrett was incredulous; it looked like a remnant sale after a fire. The floorboards in Murray's office were exposed, sanded down and varnished. Across the walls were photos of famous bands blown up to almost life-size. One featured a member Barrett didn't recognise. He presumed it was an early line-up. He didn't know some of the other groups either — legends-to-be, he guessed. He was struck by how similar they all were: mouths slightly open, heroic eyes, uniform in their sullenness. Laid out side by side like petulant dolls, they had a humorous quality too.

While he waited, Barrett began to feel out of place, intimidated by the surroundings. Then he was angry with himself. He could cope; it came with the territory. He'd get used to it.

"John," said Murray, holding out his hand to shake.

"Nice office," said Barrett.

"Do you think so?"

Barrett wasn't sure whether this was false modesty.

"Yeah, it's great. Really trendy."

As they passed the photographs, Barrett asked about the mysterious member.

"Oh, he left years ago. I think he's a postman in High Wycombe or somewhere. We don't talk about him any more!"

They sat opposite one another in his office, divided by a large desk. Framed magazine covers were on the walls, alongside gold and silver discs. Barrett squirmed, imagining himself watched by the other band members and their friends. He thought of the pronouncements he'd made after rehearsals, the blood on the forehead speeches. Now here he was, the bright light of showbiz shining on him, everything that was conventional and mainstream distilled into the room: the slick manager; the self-congratulatory trophies; the expensive trinkets (gold lighter, executive toys); the cigar butt in the ashtray; the view from the window (a walled garden with 'Private' slapped all over it). What did it have to do with walking home along the canal after a practice or the mills shutting down, making everyone's mam and dad unemployed? Or songs about the lifts on the 'Bell stinking of piss?

Give it a break, he thought. So he was supping with the devil, staring him in the eyes. But he was also learning the enemy's song and afterwards he'd be better armed, full up on knowledge. It was all experience.

Rob Murray puffed out air as if he was getting ready to say a great deal.

★

Hulme stood over Barrett:

"I knew he was on something. You could tell a mile off. He's probably OD'ed."

Cowley called Rupert Green on his mobile.

"Did you see that?" he yelled.

Green was on his way to the office in his car. He'd asked Chloe to record *Lunch Brake* for him.

"I'm in town, Dustin. What's happened?"

"Your man has shit on your chips, Rupert. Nothing you're involved with will get on here again. Do you hear me?"

Routinely you pissed on your chips; this was evidently much worse.

"What's he done?"

"Just watch the tape, watch the fucking tape. And it wasn't even original, for fuck's sake. Someone's just told me David Essex did more or less the same thing in *Stardust* and we've all seen the Pistols with Bill Grundy. I tell you, we're over Rupert, over. The man's a fucking idiot."

★

"I'll call it as I see it, no messing," said Murray. "I love the band and want to manage you. I think we can go on to big things, simple as that."

Barrett said they sort of had this mate who was kind of looking after them at the moment, a good bloke, but it probably wasn't working out as they'd imagined and despite his best ...

"Look John, there isn't a band that has walked through that door without this same story. It's as old as the hills and I tell them all the same thing. Really, it's nothing to do with me — it's your choice. As I see it you can do one of three things. Number one, you can sack him, plain and simple. Secondly, you can pay him off. Or thirdly, you can keep him on in some capacity. Have him humping the gear, picking up the birds, getting the beers in, anything you want. He won't like it and he'll be sick of it in a few weeks if he's got anything about him, but it's a gentle let-down, at least."

"We all like Gary but lately I've been wondering whether he's up to it."

"You're saying it yourself, then. Trust your instinct. Every time. Tell me, how many deals with major labels has this Gary done?"

"He's only just making contacts now, building them up."

"I'm sorry but I'm telling you now, hand on heart, he is *not* going to find Killing Stars a major record deal. He will nibble around the edges, get a few people to like him or view him as some kind of oddity but they're not going to trust him enough to sign his band. Do you know what they call unsolicited demos sent to record companies by people like him? Idiot tapes. How cruel is that? They don't play them. They shove them in plastic bags and get the cleaner to chuck the lot out once a week."

★

Barrett kept his eyes closed. The sounds around him merged and became like the distant rumble of an aeroplane high in the sky. He could hear odd spikes of chatter cutting through:

"Do you think we should lift him?"

"Has he broken something?"

Eventually he felt himself being carried. He moaned, feigning pain.

"Careful with him."

He was taken to a medical room and laid down on a narrow bed. The place smelled of TCP. A thin blanket was put over him. After a few seconds he realised there was only one other person in the room. He sneaked a look. She was a middle-aged woman with fleshy arms and wide hips.

"Hello," he whispered.

"Oh, come round have you?"

"I seem to have."

He made as if to sit up. She hurried over.

"Take it easy. You've had a bit of a turn."

"What happened?"

"I'm not the person to ask. I work in the offices upstairs. They've got me down because I'm the designated First Aider."

"Will I be able to go soon?"

"Not likely. There's an ambulance on its way, I'm led to believe. Now you lie down and take it easy."

She said she was looking for a form to put down his details.

"No, they're not here. I'll have to nip out and see where they're kept."

When he heard the door close Barrett climbed from the bed. He left the room and followed the 'Fire Exit' signs along the corridor to a glass door at the back of the building. He pushed it open, it wasn't alarmed. The air outside was cool against his face. He walked down a side street. He kept on, across roads, down alleyways, past schools and warehouses. No one recognised him. He had anticipated people staring, asking whether he was the bloke they had just seen on television. How could something so momentous occur, he thought, and yet he pass through the streets undetected, unchanged?

★

"I thought punk had changed everything, blown it wide open," said Barrett.

"Come on, who's released all these albums by new bands in the past few years — the majors. They've bought up the rebellion, sold it back to the kids. Don't get me wrong, I'm not saying punk was a complete waste of time. A lot of the early singles put out from back-bedrooms kicked a few complacent A and R men up the arse but they're on top of it now. I know this is ridiculous for you to grasp right now but once you sign with us you *will* be on daytime Radio One, you *will* be on *Top of the Pops* and more than likely you'll go top ten. See, I can put a team together that all but guarantees these things. The system only fails if you fuck up badly. You might want, I don't know, to get Bolivian pan-pipers on your first single or release a track called *Fuck Wank Piss*. Well then, in that situation we're not going to get all those things, obviously. If, however, you supply a decent string of well-recorded tuneful songs, it really is like pressing a button. And I'll tell you now, one track we should definitely go with as a single, maybe after a more up-tempo number first — that one about the lad dying, the ballady one. It's totally brilliant."

"It's about a mate of ours called Al."

Barrett wanted Murray to ask about Al but he didn't.

"It doesn't seem fair," said Barrett after a few seconds. "All those bands struggling for recognition, really believing in themselves. When it comes to this, one person having so much power."

"But if they're any good, people like me always come along when the timing is right. It's about surfing the right wave. A band making your sort of music five years ago, for example, wouldn't have had a sniff."

"But what if people like you don't come along?"

"They get proper jobs, get married — that's life."

"Seems harsh to me."

"Life *is* harsh. It's the way of the world, I'm afraid. You get lucky or you don't: simple as."

*

Barrett reached some railway arches that had been converted into workspaces, most of them occupied by firms in the motor trade. A group of lads were sitting with their backs against a skip outside a body-repairer's. They were wearing paint-flecked boiler suits, protective masks hanging around their necks on elastic. Further down, at the corner of the street and a few yards from a shopping arcade, a young woman beckoned Barrett to her. She looked foreign. He assumed she was lost and wanted directions.

"Business?" she asked.

"No thanks."

He began to walk away but she moved alongside him. She was wearing a short skirt, tight to her thighs. Her legs were mottled.

"Don't you want a good time?"

"Not really."

"Everybody wants good time."

She sounded East European.

"And where would we have this good time?"

"Over there," she said, pointing to wasteland flanking the railway line.

"Someone might see us."

"We could go some place else if you like. My flat maybe?"

"How far away is it?"

"Three, four hundred metres. Quite close. You wanna come?"

He nodded. He asked her name.

"Natasha."

She saw him smile.

"Why are you smiling?"

"Russian girls are always called Natasha, aren't they?"

"How do you know I am Russian?"

"Aren't you?"

"I am, sure. But not all girls who are from Russia have the same name."

She wrinkled her nose.

Kids were playing at the entrance to the flats, pushing one another and toy-fighting. They looked foreign, too. Barrett stopped briefly.

"Natasha, I'm not going to get beaten up, am I? And robbed? I've seen this happen in films."

"No no, I promise."

He believed her.

★

Murray noticed that Barrett looked deflated.

"It's not so bad really. Look at me, I've been in the business more than twenty years and believe it or not I still enjoy it. The main thing is to listen very closely because everyone is told what they want to hear or what will cause the least damage or kid them along the longest. No one ever tells the truth: that version of the truth where there's nothing intended apart from passing on information. It's always a loaded truth."

"What version of the truth are you telling me now?"

"Good question. I can see I'm going to have to watch you! I'm telling you the version where I want you to believe that I'm sort of inside the pack but outside it too. That I'm basically an honest, straightforward guy who sees the madness in it all. I want you to trust me and believe I can get you the best deals possible and put you in touch with the right people."

Murray clicked the silver balls together on an executive toy before continuing:

"I've hit you with a lot of stuff today, most of which you'll struggle to take in. I've not touched too much on how much I like the band because I don't want to do what everyone else does — flatter you and then sucker you into a deal. I hoped that as soon as you stepped into this place, saw the bands we worked with, had a good look and listen to me, that you'd take it for granted that I'd only have you in here if I was absolutely and totally knocked out by your music. As it happens, I didn't send an office junior to check you out, I went myself. I liked it so much I went to the very next gig on the tour. And, no, I didn't ask to go on the guest list or come creeping up after the show. I paid, stood at the back, listened to the music, watched how the kids reacted, and knew, *just knew*, that I could do something with your band."

*

Barrett decided he liked this kind of thing. It reminded him of life on the road, meeting people, seeing places, 'going freestyle' as they called it in the band. He'd not done enough of it lately. He'd become fastened down like everyone else, too many days the same, drifting.

Natasha climbed a flight of stairs. She was wearing black slip-on plimsolls, the type Barrett wore in PE as a kid. Her calves were firm and the way she bounded up made him think she was probably in her mid-twenties, not her thirties as he'd originally thought. He took a swig from the bottle in his jacket pocket. They came to a landing containing four doors, each painted pillar box red with an oblong piece of frosted, wire-reinforced glass in the centre.

In the flat, a light was on in one of the rooms. Natasha walked towards it and spoke to someone inside. Barrett peered over her shoulder. An old woman was cradling a baby. Her face was leathery and lined, her body wrapped in dark clothes. She looked as if she had blown in from the Steppes. For a second he felt as if he'd walked into a cartoon. If he opened another door he might find an Arab in flowing robes, a cowboy or a mountie behind another. The baby had crow-black hair, small darting brown eyes and was swaddled in the same frayed hessian cloth worn by the woman. She was stroking its lips with long thin fingers. Barrett noticed that there was hardly any furniture in the room. The few pieces in there were made of chipboard, the edges worn away, plastic handles missing or hanging off. The settee had a stained cloth thrown over it. Natasha shut the door gently.

"Is that your mother?" he asked.

"No, no. My grandmother."

She led the way to a bedroom where she drew the curtains and switched on a lamp that had a pink shade with tassels hanging down. A cot was beneath the window. Barrett sat on the edge of the bed. The place smelled damp.

"What would you like me to do to you?" she asked.

"Nothing."

"You watch me?"

"No thanks."

She looked puzzled. A tub of Sudocrem was on the window sill and, poking out from under the bed, a changing mat decorated with cartoons of bears holding balloons. She set her face into an austere expression. Barrett felt he had to explain:

"I can't have sex with you. Not here, like this. You've got your kid in there and your grandma and I'm married anyway."

"You must pay."

"I'll pay. How much is it?"

"Depends what you want. Whether it the wank off, blow job or total sex."

He counted out notes from his trouser pocket.

"Total sex?" she asked.

"No, that's for you, for your time."

"Is this joke?"

"No, really, it's not a joke."

He asked whether other men had sex with her, knowing who was also in the flat.

"Yes, it is never any trouble."

★

Barrett remembered something:

"Out of interest, how much do you think the advance would be from a record company?"

"Quite a few thousand pounds, quite a few..."

"We always said we wouldn't do anything just for the money."

Murray grinned:

"That's easy to say when there is none."

★

"Shall we talk for a bit?" he asked.

"Okay."

He noticed how relaxed Natasha became, knowing she didn't have to go through with the act. She had been in England nearly a year, she said. Her husband was in Russia, hoping to follow on. At first she had worked in a restaurant but lost her job after being late a few times. She had been 'sleeping with gentlemen' for four months. Her friend had told her it was a good way to cover the rent.

"What are the men like who come to you?"

They were mostly okay, she said. Some worked under the railway arches and visited at lunchtime because they no longer had sex with their wives. Others drove over in cars, sometimes big cars. Barrett asked whether anyone looked after her. Not really, she said, but there was Alex, another Russian, who lived in a nearby block and was a friend of her brother's.

"He look after me in a way," she said. "He's very big."

She puffed out her narrow chest and tensed the muscles in her arms and shoulders to replicate his size.

"Were you scared of me at first?" he asked.

"No."

"Why not?"

"I could tell you were a good man."

"Really?"

"Sure. You can tell. It is easy. I see it in how you are walking, looking around, your clothes."

This touched him.

She finally asked him a question:

"What job do you do?"

"I'm a singer."

"Singing in pubs, yeah?"

"Not really."

He expected her to ask where he did sing then, but she didn't. He pondered: perhaps in Russia people sang on street corners or outside cafes. Or maybe at weddings, funerals, potato festivals. She said three times that England was a nice country but her cold tone made it sound disingenuous. He encouraged her, saying she should move from London and go north where her family would be the only Russians in town. People would want to meet them, help them out. She would soon find work. Everything would be great. She had stopped listening.

As he spoke he realised he was being idealistic — projecting his fervour on to someone else, issuing false hope; Esther often chided him about it. Many times he'd told people who could hardly work a camera that they could be photographers or he'd encouraged weekend painters to push for exhibitions. He did this because he'd done it — lived a life devoted to creativity — and was uneasy with his elevated station, wanting others to sample it too. He was aware that he'd been like this since a kid. He cringed over one memory, which rasped across his thoughts as he spoke to Natasha. He'd been at a holiday camp with his parents. Most of the week had been spent in the games room with his brother, playing table tennis or feeding coins into slot machines. In the corner, sitting behind a trestle table, was an oldish man. He had wooden trays in front of him containing rows of coins from which he gave out change. The other kids barely noticed but Barrett watched him until, on the final day of his holiday, he approached the table. He wanted to know the man's name, be his friend, and, most of all, to express how sorry he was for him. He waited until the room was almost empty.

"Hello."

The man reacted as if was the first time he'd spoken in years. "Yes?"

"I just thought I'd talk to you."

"What about?"

"Your job. Do you like it?"

"Why are you asking?"

"I was just wondering."

"A job's a job."

"You seem a bit lonely, that's all. Have you ever tried to do anything else?"

"No. Now bugger off, will you?"

"Sorry."

"You should be."

★

Back home, Barrett briefed the rest of the band about his meeting with Rob Murray. Shaun and Shack were adamant: they wanted to sign with him and then a major record label. It wasn't for them, being one single, three-minute heroes on John Peel and—as they put it—a lifetime to follow as grease monkeys, factory hands or office fodder. Fisher said he was desperate to get away from the scrap yard, what ever it took. Any day now, make no bones about it, he was going to 'banjo' his boss.

"He'll be spitting his teeth out of his arse, he will."

Anyway, he added, what's the fuss? They could change the system from within, spreading out the cash and the love to good causes: CND, Rock Against Racism, the Green Party. Barrett picked up the theme, saying that once they were established, they could set up their own record label and help other bands. They could insist on choosing their own support acts (Carl's new projekt—the 'k' was crucial—Giraffe in Flames, had already nominated themselves). Carey didn't join the debate. He didn't think it fair when he was considering leaving.

★

As Barrett stood up to leave he asked Natasha if he could kiss her. She leaned towards him. Her hair was short but uneven at the side as if a well-meaning friend had cut it or she'd had a go herself. He pecked at her cheek and instinctively pulled her towards him. She was tense. Suddenly he was desperate to see his wife and daughter.

They left the flat and Natasha accompanied him back down the stairs. As they descended the second flight he heard voices and footsteps. He was walking into a trap. Why else were they there? They had seen him enter, guessing he'd been drinking and was unfamiliar with the neighbourhood. He was sure he was about to face a gang in hooded tops, baggy jeans and train-ers. They were going to bump into him, ask him who he thought he was, splash blood over their trainers. He'd strayed too far from home ground, had it coming. Before, there had been protection — the band, security, roadies, fans, someone from the record company — and late night jaunts in unfamiliar cities were easy. This was him the same as everyone else now, but shorn of the instinct that made him cross the street to avoid danger or listen for footsteps behind him. He was going to get taught a lesson.

★

Barrett refused to accept Carey's neutral stance.

"Can we have your votes please, the Swiss jury? You got this thing off the ground with me in the first place. You've got to contribute."

"Well it's obvious, isn't it? Everything's hunky dory with managers and major labels as long as you're making them money. They'll indulge you while the records are selling. It's when they stop that you've got problems."

"But we won't run out of songs like other bands do," said Shack. "We'll keep it going. I can never understand it when bands go shit. We'll just have to make sure we don't."

Fisher started up his savant routine, shifting his gaze from each of them quickly, rambling on.

"There are many ways to look at this. It's like water making its way to the sea. Me? I say trust what's in here [he patted his chest]. That's what makes us different from the weasels and arseholes in this town. We *do*. And they don't. Get me?"

Shack moved his head from side to side slowly. Fisher, exasperated, continued:

"Look, it's simple. We can be all wishy-washy, sitting on the fence, not knowing this from that, and where will it get us? Nowhere. That's the life a person deserves who is like that, a non-life. Instinct, that's what I'm on about. Following it. Being brave enough to."

"What are you telling us?" asked Barrett.

"I'm telling you that you met this Rob bloke, you know what he's about: what do *you* think we should do? What is your instinct telling you, because what ever it is, that's the right way. And it's right because we're a gang. That's what this fucking band is and if one of us feels it, we all feel it."

"Rob's okay I suppose but he's very music biz."

"What do you mean by that exactly?"

"Well, I didn't like him at first, straight off. He's so sure about everything, like it's definite that what he says is right. But I think the music should come before everything and if we want to record it well and have it heard by as many people as possible we've got to work with people like Rob Murray. I know it goes against a lot of stuff we've said in the past but everything in life is a compromise. If we do it with a good heart it will work out okay. People know when you've got integrity."

★

The first flash made him step backwards. Barrett slumped on the stair behind, curled in on himself. More bursts of light exploded. He screwed up his eyes, holding up his hand to deflect them. He heard voices:

"John, John, can you tell us what happened today?"

They were all speaking at once. He realised, with relief, that they were film crews and journalists. He wasn't going to die or end up in a coma, then.

He had momentarily forgotten about Natasha. She was clinging to his arm, covering her face with her free hand. His name was shouted repeatedly. They wanted to know who he was with, how he felt, why he had done it, where he was going next. It *had* happened — he had purged himself on national television. He looked beyond the scrum and saw vans parked outside and people with walkie-talkies flitting across the car park.

"Who are you, madam?"

"This is Natasha, Natasha Gagarin, my eastern European publicist," said Barrett.

"Who else do you represent, Natasha?"

She shrugged.

Barrett had been drinking continuously in the flat. As each camera flashed he imagined these puffs of light to be soft bullets. He smiled. He was being gently shot to death in the lobby of a tall building, the same as John Lennon.

"Where is my wife?" he asked.

These were Lennon's last words.

"At home," someone yelled facetiously.

"There's blood on my shirt," he whispered.

There was no blood on his shirt. The throng fell quiet. The fierce lights appeared to dim.

"Don't know what happened but somebody lost their mind tonight ... " he sang quietly.

"Is that something from one of your songs, John?"

"... the smell of sulphur and I weep as I embrace the sky."

There was a gap of a few seconds before the rabble started up again. Barrett shouted for Natasha to go back upstairs and lock herself in. When she left his side he began making his way through the hoard. They were reluctant to move and he had to push using both hands to clear a path. After one of these surges a small bald man in a tight tracksuit top moved into the space. Barrett noticed that his head was ringed in shaving cuts. He had a small mouth and narrow razor teeth. He spoke:

"Mr Barrett, surely you've gone too far this time."

He went to fend him off but the man held his ground.

"Take your hands off me," snapped the reporter.

"Look, I'm too tired to be bothered right now," said Barrett.

"I'm not. Come on, let's have it."

*

Killing Stars signed to RM Management. Aspinall was offered a position as 'co-manager' but declined.

"You're joking, aren't you? I'll be doing the shitty stuff, getting all the blame and none of the glory. I don't want to be a rubbing rag, thank you very much."

"I'm really surprised you're taking such a negative attitude. I've had to fight your corner with Rob," said Barrett.

"God, listen to you. Talking the talk, already. *Negative attitude* — that's what people say when they hear something they don't agree with. And for your information, I don't need you to fight my battles."

"I'm sorry you feel this way."

"Don't patronise me, John. Look, I can live my life perfectly well without Killing Stars in it. I always knew that you viewed me purely as a way to increase your weirdo quota or something sad like that, using people. I've already made contingency plans."

"What are they?"

"I'm very close to signing a deal for the Bug boys, if you must know."

"Gary, they're a novelty act."

"And what are you lot? Everything's a novelty act when you get down to it. You're this week's politicos with a pop bent. There'll be another along any minute, believe me."

*

This wasn't right, a stand-up row on the news.

"Are you being paid for this stunt?" asked Barrett.

"I resent that remark."

The reporter unfastened the zip of his tracksuit top as if getting ready to fight. Barrett looked at the bloke's microphone. The logo on it revealed that he worked for a cable television company.

"Look mate, I'm in enough bother. Couldn't you pick a scrap with someone else?" asked Barrett.

"But you're the person who has offended me."

"What, by asking you to move?"

"But you didn't ask, did you? You pushed."

"Right, I'm sorry for pushing you but can you now get out of the way, please?"

The rest had stopped to watch. This story couldn't get any better.

"I'm not prepared to move until you answer my question, a question I have every legitimate right to ask."

"Go on, what is it?"

The reporter immediately dropped the pitch of his voice, making it appear as if they had fulfilled an outstanding arrangement to meet at a tasteful location and discuss the state of Barrett's career in acutely solemn terms.

"John Barrett," he began slowly. "Foul language on daytime television viewed by millions; lewd, drunken behaviour; caught in the company of a woman thought to be a prostitute just hours later. Tell me, where do you go from here?"

"To hell."

"Please. Be serious."

"I am, believe me. I know my place. Hell it is."

"Answer the question."

He kept the microphone to Barrett's mouth. Scratchy radios and the bleeping of mobile phones could be heard. Barrett knew the throng would soon start up again.

"John, John," they chorused.

He looked across as the bald head stabbed with flecks of red bobbled away. The reporter was still battling, heaving people aside, his face glowing like a Halloween lamp.

★

A few days after they had signed with Rob Murray, Carey told them he wanted to leave.

"I can't play very well, I don't enjoy the gigs and the record-ing—what's the point?"

Carey thought Barrett might say there was nothing wrong with his guitar playing. He had done this before, persuading him it gave the band 'edge' or was 'original'. By saying nothing he was confirming that it was abysmal.

"I don't want to stand in the band's way," said Carey.

"You won't. You've done so much to make the group what it is. You're the one with all the ideas."

"You're past that now, ideas. It's gone up another level. A few levels, actually. Rob's already told you it would take at least three months to record an album when he gets the label deal. I don't want three months of being a nervous wreck, worrying about my playing. You lot can play so well. You're lucky that you all came together when you did. The odds on that are really slim. Meeting Rob too, that's incredible luck. Most bands slog around for years without anyone noticing them. That gig Area 51 did, that's what it's like for most groups night after night."

"Dave, if you think you're doing the right thing then go ahead and do it. Just as long as you're sure."

"I was sure until you said that."

"Well then, think about it some more."

*

Barrett made it to the road. A few reporters were still around him but most had stopped and were dictating pieces to camera. He wandered into the traffic and flagged down a taxi.

When he arrived home journalists were lingering by the gate. They were surprised to see him and took a few seconds to remember their roles.

"John, John, can you tell us what happened today?"

"Whole world's gone mad, hasn't it?"

"Do you have a comment to make?"

"Tea or coffee? And how many sugars?"

Esther came to the door.

"Make them a cup of tea, will you?" he said. "These lads are parched, standing out here all day waiting for a miracle."

She was overtaken by rage.

"You make them a cup of tea."

"What's up with you?"

"Come in, I'll show you what's up. The news is about to start. You can see for yourself."

★

After the band meeting Carey went home to work on his novella. He broke off from spells at the typewriter to think about whether to leave the band or not. The easy luck of Killing Stars had beguiled him, despite what he had said to Barrett. It had been relatively simple: bring some people together, write a few songs and, a year or so later, an offer of big-name management with a record deal to follow.

He believed it would be the same with his writing. He'd send it to a publisher and the rest of his life was set: the beautiful solitude of writing and reverie, quiet in his own space but also well known, fêted. He'd still do the music too, his own material. He'd buy a portastudio — was it a Fostex that Barrett had mentioned? — and return to the weird sounds they had started out with, the yelling and the whispering over 'manicured' noise. He was aware that if Killing Stars made it, there would be kudos in him being an ex-member. He liked the idea of becom-

144

ing a cult figure signed to a label such as Some Bizarre, Rough Trade or Mute.

Novels, with music as a side-career; a life couldn't be any richer.

★

Barrett sat down in front of the television. His eyes were almost closed when his image flashed on the screen.

"Executives held urgent talks this afternoon after a flood of complaints about the television programme, *Lunch Brake*. In an edition broadcast live, the former pop star, John Barrett, let fly a volley of expletives. Staff at the television company have received a record number of complaints."

They moved to an interview with Dustin Cowley. His skin was light green.

"We had no idea that Barrett had planned this publicity stunt. Unfortunately this kind of thing is always a possible, if unlikely, occurrence on a show that goes out live. We're obviously deeply upset if anyone was offended and will examine our policy on live interviews in the future."

Back to the presenter:

"A few hours after the incident Barrett was seen in the company of a woman he claimed to be his publicist but who is, in fact, a prostitute."

Natasha appeared on screen, head down. A tall man was by her side, his arm around her shoulder. She whispered into the microphone:

"I did not know who he was. That he was a famous man."

The last part of the item saw Barrett making his way through the scrum of reporters, past the aggressive bloke in the zip-up top.

"Well then?" demanded Esther.

"Two things. I'm not a *former* anything, me. I'm of the here and now, I am. That I am. And it was most definitely, definitely, not a publicity stunt. I meant it." He waited a second and added, "Man."

"I can't believe you."

"What, you think it was a stunt?"

"No, I can't believe your cheek. Coming in here and not apologising, trying to be funny about all that's gone on. Did you sleep with that woman?"

"I wouldn't have had sex with that woman if she had paid *me*. Sex did not and would not happen, me and her. No, no way, never. Kaput."

"Oh, come on."

★

Carey finished for the night by writing a scene where his protagonist looked out over a polluted river:

> 'It was swamp-still with strips of wood, tyres, plastic bottles, shopping trolleys and traffic cones breaking the surface. In the gloomy half-light, a few sparrows or starlings were the only signs of life. They picked at crumbs that had broken off from discarded polystyrene tiles, mistaking them for bread. Further down, vandals had thrown in a section of road works. Traffic lights were switching from red to amber to green beneath the water in ghostly blobs of colour.'

He read it back, pleased with himself. Writing, it had to be. If it wasn't novels straight off, it would be journalism college and on to a job at a local paper, learning his craft, immersing himself in words and language. He was going to leave the band.

★

"It wasn't like that," he protested. "There was this weird Russian woman in the flat, her grandmother I think, or mother, I can't remember now. An old lady anyway. And a baby. I did give her some money, yes. Out of charity, more than anything. I swear I didn't touch her. I don't know how I ended up there in the first place. It all sort of happened."

Esther set her face hard and angry. She was only twenty-eight but for the first time and through eyes cloudy with drink, Barrett saw her projected to her mid-thirties: resentful, disappointed. He dare not say, but secretly believed that most people, especially women, faded away at thirty-five or thereabouts. They yearned for something magical to have happened by then and when it inevitably didn't they were left to sleepwalk the earth, dreams rusted into the ground.

"What made you act like you did on *Lunch Brake?*"

"It was getting to me, Est, really bad. They were taking the piss, giving it that I was an old bloke, going on about past glories. I don't know whether you're really mad about it or what Rupert thinks but I swear I don't regret it. I think it's kind of funny if anything. It had to be done."

He noticed that his daughter wasn't around.

"Where's Holly?"

"I've taken her to my mum's."

"Has Super Rupe called?"

"Yeah, he's suicidal."

Barrett laughed.

"No, I mean it. You've got to ring him. He wants to put together some kind of news release. The papers have been on his back all day."

★

Rob Murray, as promised, 'pressed the button' and within three months of signing with him, Killing Stars landed a major record deal. They moved to London into flats provided by the record company and began 'pre-production'.

Carey completed his A Levels and started a one-year journalism course at a college based a couple of hours' train journey from home, living in digs with a middle-aged couple through the week. He and Barrett regularly sent each other postcards. London place names — Maida Vale, Soho, Ladbroke Grove, High Street Ken, Shepherd's Bush — quickly became commonplace in Barrett's notes. Carey downplayed his life (he wasn't sure why), grumbling about the shorthand and the boring public administration classes:

'I'm not sure when we're actually going to do some writing,' he wrote on one postcard. 'I told the lecturer I planned to write novels and he said it was his duty to remind me (m'Lud) that I was undertaking a *journalism* course and there was, despite what I may have thought, a distinct difference between the two disciplines. Ouch!'

The original plan was for Barrett to play all the guitar parts on the album but after a few weeks he wrote to Carey and told him his replacement had been appointed, someone recommended by Murray.

'He's called Alfie and he's a good bloke. Not at all full of himself. From Nottingham originally, so sort of northern. He plays the rhythm parts on just two or three strings and he's made it sound more echoey and spooky.'

He also had news on the label's intentions:

'They love what we're getting down on tape. There's all sorts of talk about how much of a push they're going to give us. Be warned, much warned!'

Alfie, what sort of a name was that, thought Carey. His gran's dog had been called Alfie. And Nottingham wasn't in the north.

★

Rupert Green had dealt with several crises in his career but none played out in public like this before. As he drove to the office he thought back to the negotiations when he'd taken over Barrett's management. He'd gone to see him perform and was convinced before he'd even sung a note. Barrett had walked on to the stage, seeping dynamism like petrol. The lights hewed his features, making him appear broad and strong. The audience was hushed. Barrett looked into the darkness beyond the lights trained on him, half snarl, half smile, and introduced *Me Me Me*.

"This song is dedicated to someone I love dearly, someone who means the world to me, more than words can ever express — me."

Green was angry that he'd not administered his original plan. He had seen other artists, usually drawn from once big selling groups, re-establish themselves by downsizing while making it appear a creative decision. Instead of under-selling large concert halls, they played at intimate clubs or offbeat venues such as churches. Overheads were kept down by having minimal equipment, road crew and backing musicians, and it was passed off as the muse stripped bare and laid before a discerning audience. Writers from broadsheet newspapers (which had long-ago adopted rock as a staple of their arts coverage) were invited and invariably seduced by the engaging mixture of simplicity and humility. As he explained to Barrett, profits from these tours were significant and went principally to the artist, allowing them to maintain their country houses, padding around in slip-on shoes, releasing a CD on their own label every year or so (available at the gigs, of course) and it all had a communal, quasi-spiritual vibe. Green told him that the goatee, ponytail, baggy trousers and conversion to Buddhism were optional.

"See, cash and credibility: what could be better? And, imagine, all those pinko writers from way back that used to call on us to join the revolution and who so reviled the establishment — they're all now working for *The Times* or *The Guardian* or popping up on Radio Four having tea and biscuits, talking pompously about the new wave epoch. They'll absolutely love you, darling."

"Bollocks," scoffed Barrett.

"Pray, why so?"

They often spoke to one another in this affected way during the early days.

"You make it sound like you're selling me a mortgage. I don't want to play to the same 200 people every October in Cleethorpes or Weston-super-Mare. It's preaching to the converted, running on the treadmill. Anyway, isn't it usually those blues dullards who go in for all that?"

Green hated the blues too; it was a common bond between them. They saw it as the duty of everyone inspired by punk to find nothing but disgust in the brain dead clunk-clunk-clunk of R and B.

"Come on, perhaps we've been a bit harsh on the blues in the past," goaded Green.

"Get away. I'd put flame-throwers on the lot of them. I nick stuff but at least you don't know where I'm going with the chords or what's coming next. They just plod on and on with that self-satisfied look on their faces like they know something really clever that we don't. Let's have it right, how can a few honkies from Slough or wherever play the blues? What do they know about rattlesnakes and sloshing about in a Mississippi swamp looking for rats to eat? Another thing: mouth organs. I fucking hate them. If you ever hear a mouth organ on one of my tracks you have my full permission to stick it up my arse, sideways."

*

Moving away to college reduced the impact of leaving the band for Carey. He made new friends, walked different streets. He soon had another diversion. One weekend while back home visiting his parents, he met Lucy. It wasn't her real name but because she was 'juicy' he said he had no choice.

"Sorry, it just fits," he said.

"I don't mind, I quite like it."

They were in The Galleon, the only pub in town with a decent jukebox. She said she liked Joy Division and The Jam.

"What's your favourite Jam track?" he asked.

"When You're Young."

It was his too.

"How come?"

"It makes me feel happy and I love the video. It's them singing away under a bandstand somewhere. There's this cute kid in it, sticking his tongue out."

"It's actually a very dark song."

"I know — 'The world is your oyster but your future's a clam'."

"Well spotted."

★

Five years on, Green wasn't laughing any more. He'd heard all Barrett's jokes, seen the knowing smiles, the winks, the click of the fingers, the long pauses, the sarcasm, the pretend lightness of being of a man weighed down by himself. It was old charm crumbling at the edges. Green now considered the too-cute humour and boyish demeanour unbecoming for a middle-aged man, like squeezing into someone else's clothes. It was also fake. Barrett had seen himself on television and in photographs too many times and knew the impact of every gesture, every expression, so he went through life impersonating himself.

On a sporadic basis Green resented all his clients but none so much as Barrett. Who did he think he was? When did an artist over forty last have a hit that wasn't a novelty record or re-release, usually set to a hip hop beat? He could forgive the kids their selfishness and stupidity, but not Barrett. Why had he allowed himself to be suckered? He could have marvelled at his live performance and left the venue the same as everyone else, a fan. No, he had fallen for Barrett's claim that, between them, they could make the world sing his songs again and how the new material was the best he'd written and he'd improved with experience, infusing his music with more depth, more subtlety. More bullshit.

★

Lucy was doing A Levels at school but on Saturdays worked at a café in town. She finished at 7pm and Carey would meet her on the canal tow-path as she made her way home. Sitting astride the lock gates, he felt heroic in the half-light. He had a clear feeling of change, of not being a kid any more. Most of his life had been played out by the canal, he realised, the seasons coming and going — buddleia along the edge sheathed in colour and butterflies in June, becoming grey and dry in November, arched like burnt out sparklers; the murky water freezing up in winter; smashed stars on ice from bricks thrown by kids.

Now, in that same place: a girlfriend, someone who cared. He'd watch her approaching, a black dot growing bigger, dark outline becoming colour. Smiling, as ever. Pleased to see him. And him her. In love. Group Hex and Killing Stars soon seemed a long ago yesterday.

*

Green broke protocol and issued an immediate news release by e-mail. He would usually have waited for approval from Barrett but the need was too pressing. He didn't run it by Guy Williams either, the independent PR consultant who had worked with Barrett when he was signed to a major label. Green knew Williams would want to put out a holding release, something bland while the heat diffused. But this was no time to circumvent the issue. When you had fucked up so catastrophically, you had to apologise long and hard, beg for mercy.

'Pop singer, John Barrett, today apologised for his behaviour on the television programme *Lunch Brake*.

He accepts that his conduct was inappropriate and offensive to both the production team and, more importantly, the viewing public. By way of explanation, Mr Barrett has a drink problem. He plans to seek treatment and fight his way back to good health.

The outburst was not an attempt to draw attention to his current record release. He would like to assure fans and the public in general that his conduct was an aberration.'

After it had been sent, Green wondered whether it formed a melodramatic letter of resignation to Barrett. While writing it, he had been fully aware of its incendiary nature and the impact it might have. He didn't care. If he had to shock or shame Barrett to his senses, tough.

★

"Hiya," Lucy would say as she reached Carey.

He'd look at the floor. At his scuffed shoes and frayed trousers. The shyness at the beginning was always beautiful. He knew where it was heading: kissing and cuddling and some more. And then the talking, lots of talking.

She was attractive but humble, suggesting her good looks had taken her by surprise. He'd seen pictures of her as a kid. She was a skinny thing with a morose face, stomping about in wellies and an anorak. Her eyes were small, just a couple of dots. Aunties probably told her she was cute, thought Barrett, and she was, but it was more that her face was unusual, almost pixie-featured.

"I'm not sure I'm a big fan of non-juicy Lucy," he teased. "Far too bony."

In other photographs, taken at different stages of her life —

aged ten, thirteen, sixteen — he could see the edges and angles rounded, the colour flushed into her, the wet sticks of a half-lit fire bursting into life. By the time he met her, she was radiant.

*

Esther went to bed first, still angry, leaving Barrett flicking through the music channels on television. He came across one of his old videos. He rued that nothing was allowed to slip into the past any more, the clock stuck fast. He could see his absolute younger version: the full head of hair and its soft texture, the liveliness, the clear skin. He remembered the belief he had at the time, how he would always remain cool, one step ahead, his status increasing and enduring. He was going to be one of the select few — The Rolling Stones, U2, Bob Dylan, REM, David Bowie, Bruce Springsteen — artists who remained credible but still had commercial success and who's every album felt inter-woven with life itself, a cultural landmark.

He'd believed that, like them, he had the third eye, watching for the footfalls, the errors of judgement that brought the lot crashing down: writing the wrong songs, signing with the wrong label, wearing the wrong clothes, saying the wrong things, working with the wrong producer, everything wrong.

Watching his own video and thinking of the years in between, he saw clearly again that he hadn't dodged the bullet. The decisions he'd made had been calculated and astute enough but the scene, the world, moved to its own rhythm; something he'd not taken into account. Where once he'd enjoyed critical repute, he'd slipped up, slipped back, fallen out of favour and not been strong or established enough to 'ride the storm' (as the label called the backlash). For a long time he'd done what most drowning-not-waving artists did — prevaricated or grabbed at things, worn the desperation too thinly, revealed himself as a hustler. They were all hustlers, every last one, but the test was to remain enigmatic, to keep hidden all that grotesque pushiness and self-love.

Slouched in his chair, it was as if he was watching a son or grandson. He smiled at the earnestness of the boy, his enthusiasm. He's got a lot to learn, he thought; a long way to go.

★

Lucy's bedroom was strewn with albums. They were piled up, tipped over, in and out of sleeves. Carey's collection was filed alphabetically, stacked on shelves. He envied her robust approach: her records lived and had the scars to prove it. She could recite lyrics, understand what it all meant — its importance, how music (new wave, especially) trapped life in a bell jar. Occasionally they'd talk about Killing Stars and he wondered whether she secretly wished he was still a member. They agreed that the band had probably lost momentum by spending almost a year recording their debut album. Carey told her that he'd heard before of bands signed amid great hubbub only to be launched with little support from the label or dropped before actually releasing anything.

He was unaffected by their initial notices: a short, non-committal review of their debut single in *Record Mirror*, a solitary play on John Peel. Carey presumed they'd be isolated occurrences, noticed only by the few who were looking closely enough, ex-members particularly. Unusually, the *NME* had no mention of the single on the week of its release. Carey had not seen McArdle's by-line for a while. He guessed he'd moved on and that the band had been a crusade of one.

★

The next morning Barrett asked Esther to buy the papers. The story had made them all, as a lead on either page three or five. *The Sun* flagged it on the front, down a side column: 'Oh f**k! Four-letter Shame of Pop Legend.' The broadsheets each carried a photograph of Barrett taken outside the block of flats, microphones and mini tape recorders pressed to his face.

He began reading. Esther saw him grimace.

"What is it? What?"

"They're saying I'm a pisshead."

She grabbed the paper and scanned the article. It claimed he was a 'self-confessed alcoholic' and was about to have treatment. No one had written this about him before.

"I can fucking sue them," he said. "They've made it up. What right have they got? They'll all know now. It's pointless."

Esther was confused. He tried to explain:

"It's all about image, isn't it? To myself as much as anyone else. I know I don't sell many records these days but the thing that gets me through is that I've managed to stay alive creatively. I've been seen to be in control, on top of everything. Think of the others who were around when I started. They're all re-forming their old bands now, turning into cabaret idiots or they're in the paper put over as saddoes — serving hot dogs from a greasy van somewhere. Now I'm just like them: another boozed up loser. Do you know those e-mails and letters I get from fans? They mean the world to me, the fucking world. They'll stop now. They'll give up on me."

After finishing the journalism course Carey moved with Lucy into a rented terraced house. She was eighteen and he was nearly twenty; it felt as if they were playing at being grown-ups.

The rattle of the letterbox woke him one morning. The central heating wasn't working properly and it was cold, breath turning to steam about his face as he descended the stairs. They had been stripping the walls in the kitchen ready for re-decorating and the exposed plaster soaked up the light, making everything grey.

★

He told Esther that no one was supposed to know about the drinking. It was, as he saw it, a betrayal; proof that he wasn't a man at peace with himself. The serenity and strength he claimed to embody would mean nothing when fans learned that for many years he'd been unable to get through without a bottle at hand. The short sentence relating his 'long-standing drink problem' was like raindrops falling on a watercolour painting, washing him away.

"The fans won't desert you," said Esther. "They'll want to offer their support. You're only human."

"I don't want your sympathy."

"That's the last thing I'm offering."

"What do you mean?"

"I couldn't feel sorry for you, John. You're not the type of person people feel sorry for. They know you'd resent them for it."

He liked this idea.

"Do you really believe that you're some kind of superman, and people buy into that?" she asked.

"I think so."

She shook her head. She'd had enough.

"What's wrong?" he asked.

"How long have you got?"

"Don't be like that."

Esther turned to face him.

"It's you, basically."

"Me? Do you mean the drinking?"

"No, not that. Well that's part of it but not the main thing. It goes deeper than that. I'm more bothered by what you stand for or what you think you stand for — precisely what you've been talking about."

"What I stand for?"

"How you think your life is more precious and important than anyone else's. The thing is, surprise surprise, you don't *feel* any more than anyone else and you don't *hurt* more than anyone else. In fact, you're exactly the same as everyone else. It's all in your head. If you think it or suffer it or even hear about it, you see it as profound, something only you've thought of."

Barrett didn't understand. Her remarks didn't relate to what they had been talking about. It was as if she'd waited for an opportunity to make this speech, so here it came. And he hated people emphasising words at random for extra *impact*. She continued:

"In a nutshell, you're in love with yourself and everything — the mess you're in now, for example — is down to that. The world has to revolve around you. It's the only way you can make sense of anything — if you're looking out from bang in the middle. This wouldn't be so bad if you acknowledged this but, no, you have to make out that you're some kind of Christ figure, bearing everyone else's suffering. Take your records. Let's start with *Burning Blue* ... [*Burning Blue*, his first solo album, had sold more than a million copies in the UK. It was acutely confessional, chronicling the breakdown of his marriage to Judy, his first wife. The subject was covered on every track. In fact, he appeared to have plundered every circumstance and incident from their relationship and turned it into a rhyming couplet: days at the seaside, walks through woods, nights of lovemaking, wholesale passages of dialogue between them, promises they'd made, friends they shared, everything.] Christ, did anyone ever hear the last of that? How long were you doing interviews for? How long did you wallow in your victimhood? Two years? Three? Has it ever stopped? Now, I've no doubt you were well and truly pissed off when she left, but talk about a song and dance. Ha, that's funny: song and dance. I know: you're an artist, you're creative, you're supposed to lose yourself to melodrama now and again, it's your job, but, come on, how far from the truth are we allowing you to go here? If you were honest, how long would you say you grieved over Judy? I'll give you the benefit of the doubt and guess it was six months, top. More like three in reality and I'm sure you were happily accepting offers of solace from other girls in the meantime: an option most of us non-pop stars don't have, by the way. People who get dumped always feel like you did, it's normal. They get sick. They crack up. It does feel like a little bit of them dies. They take years and years to get over it. It's a horrible messy experience. Just because you come up with these lyrics about kissing their eyelids in the morning and keeping their clothes as mementoes, doesn't mean your suffering is any greater than theirs. The only difference is that you can express it better than most and have the platform to do it. I hate that you see yourself as special. It's just monumental self-indulgence and, do you know what, it's boring. Boring to be around, boring to live with, boring to know."

★

The *NME* was on the kitchen floor. Carey put it on the 'work surface', a laminated cupboard door placed on top of the washing machine (the vegetables had to be chopped before the spin cycle kicked in). He saw a familiar face on the cover. It was Barrett, smiling, the Golden Gate Bridge behind him. Rain sloshed against the kitchen window, not evenly but in intermittent bursts as if hurled from a gigantic bucket.

Carey headed back to the bedroom but stopped and sat down on the stairs, hurting like a child punished for something he hadn't done. Killing Stars, their first single: on the cover. Getting the McArdle quarter-page feature before they had signed was incredible good fortune; this was almost unprecedented. The paper would have to remain loyal now because their credibility was intertwined. Success was as good as guaranteed.

★

Esther's anger didn't compromise the clarity of her words. It was bitterness formed from acts of kindness she'd secretly regretted, suffering she'd needlessly endured, and problems caused by Barrett but left for her to resolve.

He feared she was planning to go through his albums one by one, track by track. He put up a paltry defence.

161

"You could say this about any writer, anyone who's creative. It's not fair to pin it all on me."

She took a few seconds to respond.

"But I don't live with *any* writer. I live with you and it's you who is the problem."

"Okay, I can understand what you're saying but I don't see why it should piss you off so much."

She interrupted:

"Can't you see it? I thought you had some wonder-vision that allowed you to see so much more than the rest of us, all the way into souls. But now you're telling me you can't see this — something so patently obvious, something in front of your face."

Her voice became softer.

"Look, it's not the indulgence I mind so much. I can see it's part of what you are and what you do. It's just that there's nothing beyond it. I never believe you're truly with me, with anyone. It's all internalised and ritualised. Sure, you can write a bloody song about it but actually living it is a different thing. It's like with Holly…"

"Don't go there, please…"

"No, I will go there. I'm going there because it's the only way to make you understand. Yes, it's lovely that you should put one of her drawings on the cover of an album and it's fantastic that half of the album is about how great she makes you feel, lighting up your life, making you complete and all that, but it doesn't make you a great father. Being a great father is about being there for her, spending time with her, holding her, listening to her, being driven mad by her, answering all her questions, day after day, hour after hour. You've never done that — you've left it all to me. Does it never cross your mind when you're writing these songs that you might be being just a tiny bit hypocritical?"

★

That morning Carey was due to attend an interview for a job as a trainee reporter. He dressed quickly while Lucy was asleep. His suit felt as if it was someone else's. It was too baggy, the trouser legs gathering at his feet like broken concertinas. He stared at his reflection in the bedroom mirror while knotting his tie. He looked pretend posh, nothing quite right. He gelled his hair at the front and stuck it down at the sides — anyone could see he was cool and would recognise the deliberate irony of the suit and tie, surely.

As he left he checked that the *NME* was still in his briefcase. While it was open he made a quick inventory: one tangerine (now a little hard because it had been there since his last interview); a few pieces of copy paper (thin, powdery sheets on which reporters typed stories — in case he was set a practice story to complete); one pen; a button badge with the name of a new wave band on it; 17p in change; a spiral-bound notebook; and a letter sent to him while he was at college from the National Union of Journalists about a strike at a weekly newspaper in Kent.

★

Barrett was about to ask how he was expected to be at home with Holly, being all these things, when he had to tour, record and promote his music — bringing money into the house (as his dad used to say). Weren't all rock stars errant fathers or mothers anyway? He didn't get a chance to speak.

"...You don't actually live your life like everyone else, where you're answerable for your failings or the things you do. Everything is done by proxy in your songs. Like when you took Judy away from her husband. You didn't have the guts to see him and explain. No, you pleaded for forgiveness on your records. Those tracks were just a sop to your conscience and that doesn't count. Like it doesn't count when you criticise yourself in a song and get all that praise for honesty and frankness when in real life writing that song and being that frank was all it ever was. It's too easy, your life. You move through it as if you're a ghost."

"Why have you never said this before?"

"I have, in different ways."

"I never noticed."

"That's another problem; you only see what you want to see."

Barrett hurt deep down but while she'd been speaking he thought how beautiful she looked, how quickly her mind worked, how in love with her he was. He had always known she was intelligent but, until now, it had remained blunted by diplomacy. Here, it was spread wide like a butterfly opening its wings and he was overwhelmed. She had said what he already knew (or suspected) but hearing it spoken aloud had the effect of freeing him, making him feel new again. Okay, maybe she had gone a little too far. No one went round to see their new partner's ex-husband, did they? And she had been unnecessarily sarcastic. Otherwise, it was more or less everything.

*

On the bus to the job interview Carey decided: best get it over with. He opened the *NME* and read the article on Killing Stars:

'The sun shines into the eyes of John Barrett. They narrow to filter the light. A smile forms at his lips. He is handsome and scruffy-dangerous like the kid at the fairground spinning the Waltzers, born hip and burning red-hot. The T-shirt he wears has been pulled at the neck and falls twisted on his shoulders. He doesn't care. I ask whether he can believe it: the US of A, the world — all his.

"Yeah, I believe it."

He looks me straight in the eye and makes me feel unsettled.

"You're not kidding, are you?" I ask.

"Nope."

Carey read the rest of the article carefully, fearful of every sentence. Within the first few paragraphs Brecht and Kafka were mentioned. He had studied the music press since he was ten years old, believing wholeheartedly in its prose but, until now, oblivious to how it embellished a personality, making it richer and darker. He glanced across to the photographs, reminding himself that the piece was about John Barrett, someone he knew so well.

When he finished he stared once more at the large picture of Barrett, arms thrown back, eyes drilling the camera. The other band members were in the background, milling around. Carey searched for his own face among them; the group looked lopsided without him. He'd been on the other photos, of course, taken by friends giving up a Saturday afternoon, posing at the quarries or against pebble-dashed walls on the 'Bell — fuzzy, out-of-focus, grey photos.

He should have stuck it out, he thought, got over the stage fright. Performing was only a small part of the deal. He could do the rest, easily: travelling the world; choosing sleeve designs; the interviews; the photo-sessions; the Golden Gate Bridge. He put the paper away. As he slipped it into his briefcase he wished it was a coffin and that he could shut Barrett away for ever, take him out of his life.

As an afterthought he looked who had written the piece: Steve Herbert, McArdle's detested colleague.

★

Esther was unsure how Barrett would react, whether he would come out fighting; it had served him well in his career.

"I'm sorry," he said lightly. "Everything you've said is true, just about. You've said all that I am and I'm glad."

"Why?"

"I want to be with someone who really sees, who knows me. I've never had that before. Or maybe I have but the people I've been with have chosen not to tell me, which is no good. You're so much more of a better person than I am and I'm glad I'm with you, that despite all those things you've said, you see something in me of value. It's going to change now anyway, isn't it?"

"How come?"

"Well, I can't really see a way back, can you? I'm not going to be able to dream up this counterfeit personality on records. Who's listening anyway? All that matters now is you, me and Holly."

She saw that he was about to become sentimental. She hadn't finished.

"John, why do you drink?"

The question seemed to fall from above like a solitary shard of ice.

"I don't know."

"You know you've got a serious problem, don't you?"

166

He shrugged.

"You've got to face it."

Suddenly he imagined his old self looking down — the fresh-faced kid, the fastest runner in school, the cheekiness and the charm — and he was embarrassed by what he'd become, this folded-in drunk, tired, a failing career piled on top of him. He'd find that kid again, he told himself, and run through fields, love Holly and Esther with all his heart. Never drink again. Not a drop. If Esther didn't believe him he'd show her the hiding places for his bottles and empty every last one down the sink.

*

The newspaper office was on the main street in town. Carey pressed the bell on the counter.

"Hello, I've come for a job interview with the editor."

He was led into Jack Sutcliffe's office, a small box at the back of the building separated from the news room by a sliding door.

"Hello son. All bright-tailed and bushy-eyed are we?"

The editor stared at Carey, making sure he'd got the joke.

"Yes."

"Right then, let's get cracking. Do you know what my ambition is?"

Carey was confused. Had he got their roles mixed up? Sutcliffe was at least forty, maybe fifty. Wasn't he a bit old for unfulfilled ambitions?

"Well," began Sutcliffe. "What would make me happy, wondrously happy, would be a nice quiet job as a car park attendant in Ilfracombe, somewhere like that. We went on holiday there last year, me and the wife. Have you ever been? The car park is on the cliffs with a little flight of steps to the beach so holiday-makers can trip-trap down with their picnic baskets. Beautiful little spot, it is."

He stood up and began miming winding tickets from a roll, putting money in an imaginary bag tied to his waist.

"Remember, I'd have a proper coat on, like they wear. 'Here you are, Sir. Here's your change. There's some room by the bottom end, just past the Volvo. Hope the weather stays fine for you.' Have you ever heard any Rachmaninov or Rimsky-Korsakov? [Talking to Carey now and not pretend holiday-makers.] Piano concerto No. 4. It takes you away from yourself, to somewhere else."

He was sitting down again, fingers fluttering in the air as if using invisible chopsticks, hearing this wonderful music in his head.

"Enough of silly old Jack. Tell me, why do you want to be a reporter when you could be a car park attendant soaking up the sun all day?"

★

"There must be a reason why you drink," she said.

"Habit."

"But what made you form the habit in the first place? There has to be something."

"Filling in time, I suppose."

"Come on John, talk to me."

She had said his name again. He loved it when she did this, especially so tenderly. He wanted to kiss her.

"I've thought about all this, I really have. But I don't have an answer. It's nothing clichéd like drinking to forget or anything like that. I just like being drunk. I feel wrapped up with it, safe from everything. I know it's fucking my body up but my brain wants it and has to have it."

"Do you think it's down to something that's happened in the past?"

"It might be the disappointment."

★

Carey got the job and joined the team of six reporters at the paper, most of them at least twice his age. Telephone directories and old copies of the paper were piled up through the office. Thumping typewriters caused the tables and floor to shake. His time was mostly spent covering the local court and inquests, calling on the police, fire and ambulance.

"Anything for us?"

Most days there was 'nothing doing' but on others there was a lot of living, and dying. Carey covered all manner of stories: joy-riders smashing a car into a reservoir wall ('Three Dead in Horror Smash'); a 53-year-old 'mother of four' finding her husband suspended from the loft by a rope ('Hanging Tragedy'); the secretary of the local chrysanthemum society predicting a good turnout at the autumn show ('Hoping for a Blooming Success'); the Najib Hamed Appeal raising cash to send six-year-old Najib, stricken by a rare cancer, to Disneyworld ('America Here I Come!'); and the head teacher at St. Joseph's School revealing that intruders had caused serious damage when they broke in and left the taps running in the toilets ('Vandals Wreak Havoc').

As the sole trainee Carey was often sent to reception when a member of the public called in. He would face old ladies complaining that the verges on their estate hadn't been cut all summer and the grass was now past their (bandaged) knees, or a councillor asking for a photographer to take a picture of him next to a pothole in the road. At least once a week a teenage girl in tracksuit bottoms, chewing gum and carrying a baby, would turn up demanding that something was done about the damp in her flat.

"It's making us all ill. Put *that* in the paper."

★

"The disappointment?"

"I've always felt it. I was disappointed when I wasn't famous, then I was disappointed when we made it because I didn't like a lot of what it involved. And now I'm disappointed because it's gone. It's that thing of nothing being normal. It's hard to explain. I remember one time, I was with the band recording the first album and mum rang the studio. She was telling me what she'd done that day: the shopping, paying the bills at the Post Office, seeing Mrs so-and-so from down the road. I didn't listen, didn't give a toss."

"Everyone feels like that sometimes about their parents."

"I know but this was different. I was thinking, 'Do you think someone like me should be bothered with this drivel?' She knew I was angry with her, too. And people changed once we started having hits. You saw it in their eyes, how pleased they were to meet you. They'd do anything to keep you talking, flattered because you even looked at them. I played this gig once, a showcase thing, and the record company got a load of people down. They were literally lined up waiting to meet me and I had to work through them one by one. There was this girl who worked in promotions. She'd broken her leg and was in plaster.

It felt like they were waiting to be healed, one touch from me and they'd be okay again, throwing crutches in the air. And what's it all about, what is it I've got? Nothing really, less than most people in fact, except that I can get on stage and be something for an hour or two. It doesn't seem much for all that adulation and fuss, does it? After a while, you come to expect that people will be amazed to meet you and when it doesn't happen you feel let down. I'd do photo sessions and get upset if the photographer was speaking to someone from the label, not bothering with me. I'd sulk — actually fucking sulk, just because they weren't speaking to me or talking about something I was interested in. How wrong is that? It's what you've wanted all your life, to be special, but at the heart of it you're lonely because nothing is what it seems. All the stuff with the girls stems from this. You're looking for something real, even for a few hours. But apart from the act itself, sex with strangers isn't real. You feel worse afterwards, more lonely than before."

He stopped for a second:

"We've gone through this before though, haven't we?"

"No, not like this. Am I missing something? Where does the drinking come in?"

"I suppose it gets you through. Look at it this way: if fame and wealth doesn't make you happy, where do you go then?"

"Other people cope. They don't become alcoholics."

"My problem is that I'm cursed. Not as in devils and stuff but in that I don't know what I want. Never happy, I suppose. Like I said before, *disappointed*. I want it and then I don't. In interviews years ago I used to call it restlessness but it's deeper than that. At least when I've had a drink I feel like it's suppressed."

★

Carey was aware that Jack Sutcliffe sounded amusing — a 'character' — when he described him to anyone but he was hard work really, sucking a pen and mewling, constantly fretting and pacing the office. He was fearful of the paper being sued or the directors berating him for mishaps. He'd worry excessively about getting people's ages wrong or making a Geoff a Jeff. He also hated it when anyone used words outside standard journalese. Carey once put 'plethora' in a report.

"That's just showing off," Sutcliffe scolded. "Do they say plethora around here while they're having their breakfast: 'Mum, can I have a plethora of Shreddies this morning?' Do they buggery!"

He spoke of the directors as if they were sombre Dickensian characters with distended bellies and mutton chop sideburns, kicking orphans down the street. On the few times they visited from head office, Carey was surprised that they were fairly young, calling everyone by their first name, interested in what they were doing.

It was better in the old days, said Sutcliffe constantly. When journalism was a proper profession and you had time to check things thoroughly, telling a good tale to what ever length you wanted. It was all bloody wallpapering now, sticking in free puffs from PR companies in London, getting your ear bent by toffee-nosed girls with names like Pandora and Ursula. Recipe pages and gardening columns wasn't journalism. Claptrap like that belonged in magazines. No, he said, people around here bought the local paper to read about their next-door neighbour growing giant sunflowers or getting caught in a public toilet with the manageress from the Co-op, trousers round his ankles.

★

At lunchtime Barrett called Guy Williams. He was put on hold. While he waited, he looked through the window. The trees were almost bare of leaves. Williams answered:

"Who's been a naughty boy, then?"

"I know, I know."

"I've had to field a few calls today."

"Yeah?"

"Apparently You Tube has had a record number of hits for your three-minute slot yesterday and a couple of people in the office have uploaded a screen saver of your rather hissy slump to the floor."

"Oh dear."

"Anyways, all that aside, what can I do for you, John?"

"Have you seen today's papers?"

"I have. We get them all here, every last one."

"What do you think?"

"Well, there's some choice stuff. I get the distinct impression that Rupert has been dabbling. Has anything bothered you particularly?"

"Just the bit about the drinking."

*

When Killing Stars began to appear regularly on the radio and television, Carey's colleagues asked him about Barrett. He told them he was pleased for his old friend. He deserved it. He'd worked hard. Music was in his blood.

"Do you really think that?" asked Chris, the sports editor and next-youngest member of staff.

"No, I fucking hate him!"

"I would too. He looks a right tosser if you ask me."

"Nah, he's okay actually."

"Are you going to do a piece on him for the paper, then?"

"That might be difficult."

"Why?"

"Let me see: because it hurts, basically. Him having such a fantastically glamorous life and me stuck here with you miserable lot, plus, of course, our friendly neighbourhood neurotic boss."

"But is he happy, hey? You know, deep in his soul."

"Knowing him, he probably is."

"Told you — wanker!"

★

"Did we know that before or is it a revelation?"

"No, it was a kind of secret. I like a drink, you know that, but that doesn't make it a problem."

"I wonder why Rupert's announced it then, which he must have done. They wouldn't make something up like that without any corroboration. They ain't as stupid as people think."

"It's libellous, isn't it?"

"Truth is an absolute defence, remember, and if Rupert has been indiscreet enough to issue a press release telling everyone you're a raging dipsomaniac it's well within their rights to run with it."

"Do you think that's what he's done?"

"It looks that way. I don't think he needed to either. There's more than enough to chew on already."

"Did he contact you?"

"No. There were no messages from him. I thought there might have been but he must have decided he could handle it."

"Well he's not handled it very well, has he?"

"I'm not sure in the long run it's going to do that much harm. It's all rock'n'roll isn't it? It'll be old news next week. They ain't going to keep hammering you. They'll get bored after a bit."

Barrett said he planned to put out his own news release refuting the allegations. Williams said he didn't think it would make much difference but there was nothing to lose.

★

The cycle of the year quickly became routine for Carey at the paper: Christmas fairy (a kid from a local school decked out in clip-on wings and lifted up in a small crane) switching on the town centre lights; Pace Egg play on the market car park at Easter; droughts or downpours in summer (and at least one kid drowning in an abandoned mill pond); fêtes; Halloween parties; the civic bonfire; Remembrance Sunday; anti drink-driving campaigns.

The weekly deadline fell on Wednesday, so Thursday was an unofficial rest day unless a big story broke overnight, which seldom did. Carey and the others spent most of the day drinking tea and chatting while Sutcliffe 'put the paper to bed' at the printers. The only proviso was that the tray had to be cleared — a wooden box containing notices of weddings, deaths and reports from old folks' organisations.

One Thursday, a week before Carey's third Christmas at the paper, he was told 'Mr Barrett' was on the phone.

"Dave, it's me — John. You made it then?"

"Made it?"

(Wasn't he supposed to say that to him?)

"To the papers, like you said."

"Oh yes, I made it."

Barrett said he had a couple of nights off and was at his mum and dad's.

"They haven't divorced yet, then?"

"No, still thinking about it. Look, do you fancy going out tonight?"

"Tonight? Won't you get mithered if we go local?"

"I'll keep my head down."

Carey remembered; he had a night job for the paper.

"Damn, I can't make it. I've got to review a play."

"What is it?"

"Well, it's a musical actually. They're doing *Viva Mexico* at the Memorial Hall."

"Really? Sounds brilliant. Can I come with you?"

"They're just local amateurs — are you serious?"

"Too right."

★

Esther and Barrett worked until the late afternoon preparing the press release. She wondered if she had been too aggressive the day before, even whether she had really meant it. She was thinking back to when they had first met: it was all there then, everything he was. They were at a house party thrown by one of her girl friends. Barrett knew the girl's boyfriend; he'd done some artwork on his record. Esther was on the edge of a conversation he was having with three or four people in the kitchen when he asked her opinion.

"Sorry, I wasn't listening," she said.

"Come on, we know you were. You were having a damn good nosy, weren't you?"

"Okay then, I was. So?"

"See, I thought so."

She was positioned almost behind him so he had to turn from the others to speak to her. They were soon locked in their own conversation. She had never been asked so many questions before. She found it simultaneously exhilarating and taxing. A half hour went quickly by and he was so relentless she wondered if it was some kind of technique; it felt hypnotic. He asked what her dad was like, what job he did, whether he liked it, what was the happiest and saddest moment they'd spent together, did she carry a photo of him around with her? He was the same about her mother, and younger sister. He looked deep into her eyes and it was as if a tiny invisible monorail ran between his eyes and hers and he was travelling into her. She didn't find it uncomfortable or strange but considered it talking in a way she had always wanted to talk, saying what she really felt, knowing that someone was genuinely interested. She began asking *him* questions. He answered with the same detail he'd demanded from her, staying close to the subject, never slipping into anything hackneyed or becoming evasive. She started with his dad.

"I love my dad but he's hard work," he said. "Very northern, traditional, believing in certain things. He loves me loads but you have to look closely to find it, if that makes sense."

She knew he was many years older than her but this wasn't alluded to and he didn't talk down to her. Within a few minutes she'd forgotten how she had first seen him — one or two stones overweight, tired looking. The longer they spoke, the more handsome he became. She noticed his mouth, its shape and the slight curl of the lips at the corner. When he smiled, these hooked up and reached his eyes to form a U shape. It had the effect of radiating warmth.

★

They met outside the hall. It had been almost four years since they had last seen one another. Carey planned to shake Barrett's hand but they were soon hugging. Barrett was so pleased, he began jumping up and down, holding him. Carey was ashamed of the resentment he'd tended.

"Doing any music?" asked Barrett when they separated.

"I've done a few bits but nothing serious. I'm working on some ideas."

People were filing past. They followed them into the hall; they were the only ones under sixty. As soon as the show started they had to suppress giggles. The dialogue made reference to young, handsome banditos but these roles were played by four old blokes whose make-up looked to have been applied with a blunderbuss. They coughed and wheezed through the dance routines which amounted to turning around slowly, holding a sombrero over their heads and shouting Olé. After a particularly rousing song one of them winked at the audience, twisting his mouth to one side as he did so and almost causing his false teeth to slip out.

In the interval Carey won a raffle prize kindly donated by *one of the loyal and committed patrons of the Players* — a length of fuse wire wrapped around an H-shaped piece of cardboard. The old folk in the audience clapped and woo-wooed as if he'd won free drinks for life.

Out on the street afterwards Carey was surprised how interested Barrett was in him, wanting to know all that had happened since they last met.

"You've read my letters."

"I know, but I want more information."

"What kind of information? You're making it sound like an episode of *The Prisoner*."

"Tell me about the people you work with, for a start."

He reeled off a couple of Jack Sutcliffe anecdotes. Barrett smiled.

"You're so lucky knowing people like him."

"Lucky?"

"He's real and sounds like he's actually got a personality."

"I thought everyone had a personality."

"You'd be surprised. We don't seem to meet many people who are authentic. There's always a kind of trade-off going on where either you want something from them or they want something from you."

"You've always had a good antenna."

"True, but there's such a lot of static around it gets hard sometimes."

★

Barrett put on his glasses to read the computer monitor. Esther stroked his shoulders.

"I shouldn't have said those things."

He felt for her hand.

"No, you were right: everything you said."

"You can't help what you are," she said. "I knew when I first met you how it all worked."

She was referring to how pleased she'd been to have his attention that night, as if he had painted her gold. Maybe she'd even engineered the meeting, the way she moved closer to his circle. The smiling, the looking into his eyes, the slightly cooked up wackiness — it hadn't been left to chance.

They moved on, to the Lord Howard pub a few hundred yards from the hall. Lucy was already there. Carey introduced her to Barrett. He asked how long she'd known Carey (four years, thereabouts); what bands she was into ('tons' but mainly The Smiths, Echo and the Bunnymen, Jane's Addiction, Husker Dü, The Go Betweens and the Violent Femmes); how she'd met Carey ("His mate chatted me up in the pub but I fancied Dave more"). He asked if she liked Killing Stars.

"They're all right but the singer's a bit full of himself."

Barrett laughed.

"You know your music, don't you?" he said.

"I do."

"I always think there's something a bit different about girls who really like music, the same as girls who really like sport."

"Why's that?"

"I think it shows they understand men, what they're about. I've always wanted to meet a girl who's into music but who's also girly, if you know what I mean — not a parody of a bloke."

"You must meet lots being in the band."

"Not really. There are basically two types: girly girls who say they like music but are not really into it all that much when it comes down to it and then girls who are usually not so pretty but who like it in a way that blokes do, collecting rare limited edition singles imported from Venezuela, stuff like that. Is that sexist? Am I making any sense?"

He was testing her out, hoping she wouldn't censure him or affect puzzlement.

"I think you are, making sense that is."

Carey returned with the drinks. He asked Barrett about the band, how they were getting along with one another.

"We're doing pretty well to be honest. It's not so much a social thing as before but it works. Things get done."

Barrett apologised again for being out of touch for so long.

"I've meant to call you loads of times but something's always come up. I feel that with you and me it's not that important anyway because we go so far back."

Towards the end of the evening Carey had an unusual feeling. He sensed he'd been too eager and noticed that his voice had become expressive, going up and down in range almost as if he was performing. He did it, he felt, under Barrett's encouragement, turning himself into a kind of eccentric turn. He began to ponder: why did Barrett still want to be his friend? What did they now have in common? In fact, what had Barrett ever liked about him? He had always been the quiet one, the monochrome next to the colour, the brakes on the speeding car, the minister in charge of photocopying and form-filling in the parliament of Killing Stars.

As they were parting, Barrett asked Carey if he planned to stay at the paper. No way. A local weekly paper was a precursor to a daily paper, radio, television — anything you wanted; that's if you planned to stay in mainstream journalism. And Carey didn't. Had Barrett forgotten already the long conversations about how he was going to write novels and screenplays?

Carey realised he'd not asked him about America or touring Europe; or who had designed the sleeves; or why they were doing videos after vowing they never would; or why songs he'd co-written like *Brixton Riots* and *El Salvador* hadn't yet appeared on any records. They hadn't talked about Al either, how much they still missed him. Next time.

★

Barrett was disheartened that it had come to this — tapping at a computer trying to think of the right words to save his good name, his career. He used to have people do this for him, people he could ask to 'sort it' and they did, no fuss.

Esther put on the main light in the living room. Plates from lunch were on the floor. The television was on with the sound turned down. Barrett couldn't stand the domesticity, the ordinariness. He sipped some vodka; he'd told her again that he needed to come down slowly.

★

The rain fell softly as Carey and Lucy walked home afterwards, both tipsy. Carey tilted his head to catch drops in his mouth, trying to suck flavour from them. He turned to Lucy:

"What did you think of him, then?"

"He's nice, not at all as I imagined him to be."

"How did you imagine him to be?"

"He always comes across as a bit cocky on the telly. I suppose I thought he'd be arrogant but he isn't at all. I can see why you and him would be good friends. Did you tell him we're getting married?"

"Nah."

"How come?"

"We'd have got a lecture. We always said we didn't believe in marriage because it was what *straights* did."

"He might change his mind when he meets the right person. Most people do."

★

They finished the press release too late to make the next day's papers but sent it anyway by e-mail to the addresses supplied by Guy Williams:

'John Barrett's speech on the television programme *Lunch Brake* yesterday was a calculated and bold attempt to highlight the hypocrisy and phoney nature of television. He does not seek to apologise for his behaviour, nor the strong and necessary language he used to convey his heartfelt message.

"I did what anyone with a modicum of intelligence should do when faced with television creeps. I meant every word," he said.

Barrett counters claims that he has a drink problem. He is taking advice from his solicitors and plans to sue newspapers that have made these allegations. He also denied sleeping with a prostitute. "I met her while out walking and visited her flat. It was as simple as that. Nothing went on between us."'

No one acknowledged receipt of the release and, over the next few days, there were no follow-up news stories.

At the weekend a friend of Green's contacted him to say one of the broadsheets had run a lengthy feature about the *Lunch Brake* incident. Green phoned Barrett; they had just started speaking to one another again.

"I don't know what it says exactly but it's supposed to be very positive," he said. "And the writer says he knows you. See if Esther will nip out and get you a copy."

She drove to a petrol station and bought the paper, parking in a lay-by to read it. As she entered the house she beamed a smile.

"Is it that good?"

"Better," she said.

The headline was 'Dear John':

'So, he's a friend, an old friend, but that's irrelevant: John Barrett, I salute you. It's peculiar seeing a mate become famous, then not so famous. It's as if they go off to war and you're never quite sure if they'll come back and whether they'll be the same people if they do. When I saw Barrett on *Lunch Brake* it was like seeing one of those Pathé film reels, someone caught on celluloid in the heat of battle in a far away place.

His behaviour has been seen as either unadulterated boorishness or a piece of exhibitionism designed to sell copies of his new album. The condemnation has been loud and sustained. Swearing and shouting might not be particularly edifying but to view Barrett's outburst as some kind of infantile tantrum is to miss the point. It made sense. Perhaps you need to know Barrett to understand.

I was a close friend of his and a member of his first bands. I liked him immensely. Everyone did. He was never still or quiet. When I think back, I see him fidgeting, shadowboxing and running on the spot, desperate to be somewhere else: the next lesson, the next street, on the swings instead of the roundabout. We knew he'd be famous. It was a matter of time.

I remember seeing him the day after our band (perhaps *his* band would be more accurate) had been turned down by a record label that had long given us the impression it would sign us. We were all disappointed but he was devastated. It didn't help that one of our best friends had died a week before. I saw then how much he cared, how much passion he had for the music. We tried to comfort him but he was inconsolable. And furious.

By the time the band got its first deal (I left just before) we were heavily politicised, not to mention ridiculously self-aware. We saw punk as a cultural and social revolution. We were defiant and pious and dissected our lives and the lives of people around us. We were looking for hypocrisy and duplicity. At one point we planned to call our debut album *The Fakefinder General* because that's what we were: ever vigilant for phonies, agents of the state and patrons of the bland.

I have not seen Barrett for nearly twenty years but I know instinctively that he will not have changed greatly. I imagine his life hasn't been easy. Fame and privilege will have rested awkwardly on his shoulders. His sexual promiscuity is much vaunted but I view this as evidence of someone with a zest for life. He wanted to hear more music than everyone else, read more books, go to more places, learn more things: always more.

On *Lunch Brake* I could still see him as a kid, the same street-fighting dancer, revolution romancer. He used to write poems, some of which became incorporated into his lyrics. One of them was about how the system (we were obsessed with this unwieldy, transcendental monolith) treated its dissidents. He wrote that it, 'Turned what it didn't understand into a joke.' Barrett, as I write, has become this joke.

The public and the media like its fools and are unconcerned with circumstance or antecedence. That Barrett has, in the main, spoken good sense and remained principled all these years doesn't seem to count. His one act of folly seems set to form a permanent shadow over his CV. He will not be viewed as the insurrectionist, the truth speaker or even a situationist but a plonker, dipstick or liability—three terms used in the press this week.

To know Barrett is to understand his fury. He is not

a pretentious man and will not have expected undue obeisance from the *Lunch Brake* people but it was clear that the sole purpose of his appearance was to be mocked and reduced to stereotype. I'm glad he refused to play this allotted role. He could have been more subtle perhaps but revolutions are seldom quiet. Everyone loves a scene, TV people especially. It is ironic that Barrett has been releasing sincere and thoughtful albums for the past decade to scant attention but a three minute outburst on terrestrial television has put him near the top of the national news agenda.

The impact it will have on his career is difficult to assess. It reveals the extent of Britain's cultural shift that twenty-five years ago he would have been viewed as an anti-hero and maverick but now he is merely the fool facing a life on the margins, away from harm's way. He deserves better.'

The by-line read: David Carey.

"Good old Dave," said Barrett to Esther.

"You've never mentioned him before."

"I have, lots of times. Come on: Dave, David Carey. You've not forgotten, have you?"

"Forgotten?"

He smiled.

"Oh *that* David."

"Him, Fisher and Al were my best mates, the gang within the gang. Me and Dave grew up together, formed the band and everything. The trouble was his phobia about playing gigs. He baled out just before we started to get anywhere."

"Why don't you ring him and thank him for the article?"

"I should really. A lot of water's passed under the bridge. It's good to see his name in print. I thought I'd hear about him being a famous novelist one day because that's all he ever wanted to be."

Green was hopeful that the article might provoke a re-evaluation of Barrett's outburst. He'd seen other artists recover from similar incidents and been viewed later as enigmatic or prophetic, their careers revitalised.

An unexpected proposition came his way. He phoned Barrett:

"John, it looks as if some good has come of your exultant return. I've just been made an offer by Nesta Publishing. I've checked them out on the internet and they're quite big — tall building and head offices in New York big. Anyway, they've asked if you'd like to commit to an autobiography."

"How do I do that?"

"They want to hook you up with a ghost-writer. You'll work through your life story with him and he'll knock it into shape and present it to them, their English office at any rate."

"Sounds easy enough. What's the payola?"

"They've mentioned a few figures that seem pretty good to me."

"What's pretty good?"

"Enough to buy a house on that estate down your lane, say."

Barrett often professed an indifference to money but his experience of the music industry had taught him that advance payments were a sign of commitment to a project. The more offered up front, the harder they worked to recoup it.

"Aren't they a bit tacky, rock books?"

"Not necessarily. We can do it on our own terms to a degree. I asked if they wanted to marry you off with a particular writer but they say they're happy to go with whoever we want, as long as he can deliver. I've only had one phone conversation with the MD over there but it seems they're a lot more gentlemanly than we're used to in the music business."

The deal was done over two weeks with the advance to be paid in three stages: on signing the contract, delivering the manu-script and publication. Green asked why the majority was due on delivery.

"Just in case Barrett goes nuts on us again," said Jake Norden, the editorial director at Nesta's UK office.

Barrett asked Green to contact David Carey and invite him to ghost-write the book.

"Is that a wise move?"

"I think it's a bold and enigmatic move."

"Don't you think he might know rather too much about you and have too much insight?"

"Possibly, which is why it's bold and enigmatic, my friend. Remember, it's an autobiography, so although he'll write it, it's still my voice and I'll have final say. And the runes, they say we come together again."

He put his hands together in mock prayer.

"Why don't *you* get in touch with him? He's your pal, not mine."

"He is but could you do it Rupe, please? It'll be too weird talking to him straight off after all this time."

Green was used to rock stars refusing to undertake tedious chores, often because it affronted their ego. Barrett was differ-ent. He was genuinely afraid of social contact. Tour managers had reported back many times that he'd been unable to queue at a service station café or buy a drink at a hotel bar. He'd try occasionally but hurry away, flustered. Green had asked him about it once.

"I can't stand how corny it is. Waiting your turn, being regimented like that. I get nervous. I think I'm going to blurt out something stupid. I can feel myself sweating, my face going red. Then my mouth goes dry and I start sucking on my tongue. I know it's fucking stupid but it's the way I am."

"But you've done gigs in front of thousands of people."

"That's different."

Carey was invited to a meeting with Green to discuss the book. He took the day off work and travelled to London by train. Inside Green's office he noted the small designer fridge containing bottles of beer, mineral water and coke; the piles of CDs; the sound system blasting out music; the settees; the posters on the walls: it wasn't like this at the paper.

While he checked his computer for e-mails, Green continually picked up one of the two phones on his desk or the mobile in his pocket. A T-shirt supplier called. The ones they'd sent weren't black but a kind of grey, said Green, sigh. The same thing had happened last time. It wasn't good enough. Shaking his head, he put down the handset. He looked at Carey:

"Thanks for coming, Dave. I'm sorry about all this ..." He pointed to the phones and paperwork scattered across his desk. "Right, shall we get started? Is it right that you grew up with John?"

Carey told him they had lived on the same street and gone to the same school. They were in their first band together.

"That's it, I remember now. It was in your article."

Green explained that it might have been expected they would choose a more established writer, but Barrett had every faith in

Carey. He realised immediately that this sounded patronising and apologised. Carey said he understood:

"I suppose you're sticking your neck out using someone like me who has only ever really worked in local papers and done the odd bit of freelancing."

While Carey was talking, Green buzzed Chloe.

"Any sign of our fella?"

"Not yet."

"Give him a call, will you?"

Chloe had to ring the house because Barrett refused to carry a mobile. Esther answered and said she was surprised he wasn't there. He'd left hours ago.

"You'd better tell Rupert though: he's not too good."

"Not too good?"

"He's been drinking heavily."

"Oh dear," said Chloe.

She broke the news to Green.

"Fucking hell," he said, getting up from his chair.

Carey felt he ought to say something.

"It's fine, I can see him another time."

"It gets me down, this."

"Is he drinking a lot?"

"He's an alcoholic. Absolutely 100 per cent."

"He was really strong as a kid, someone we all looked up to."

"He's been through a lot since, good *and* bad. I suppose you're going to have a fair old job making sense of it for the book."

Green fell quiet for a second before snapping back:

"Look David, John's not going to turn up now. He's probably waylaid in some pub. I think you understand the gig with all its idiosyncratic challenges. If you want it, it's yours. I've already had the contract from Nesta. They've moved surprisingly fast on this one, probably to cash in on John's current notoriety. All you have to do is sign it and we're away. It's fine by me, of course, if you want to get it checked out by a lawyer."

"No, I'll sign."

Carey saw it as a portent that Barrett was returning to his life. The time between had been long, a lot of rusted up years. His mind raced. This book first, then on to more deals, recognition, air breathed into novels and screenplays jammed in drawers. He had the gig now, after all — the association, the required gravitas, trusted to tell a story rich in cultural significance and brimming with all that made for a life well lived. Any shilly-shallying and someone else would be in there, someone less deserving. He wasn't going to let this slip through his fingers.

The walls of his flat were lined with books. He had more than 2,000 but had read, cover to cover, no more than a tenth of them. He was ruthless about the time he'd dedicate to each. An author had five pages, ten at most, to convince him, otherwise the book was slotted into one of the shelves — he couldn't bring himself to actually discard any. He liked the feel of books. He'd some-times rub the paper between his fingers to examine its texture, noting whether it was white and flat and dry, or rough as if it might leave yellow powder on his fingertips. He scrutinised the typesetting, the fonts, how it sat on the page and the density of the ink. He preferred discreet covers, pencil shading and soft colours; a book had to beckon him quietly. And he was steadfast to particular authors, hunting down everything they had writ-ten, buying books two or three times if they had different covers.

Among his collection were about fifty rock biographies. He considered the standard poor. Most were written by quasi fans or hack journalists. He could do better. The autobiography of John Barrett would be rich, engaging, informed, lively — adjectives he hoped would feature in reviews .

The supposed trip into London to see Carey and Green provided cover for Barrett. He had decided he needed a break, time alone. He headed to Brighton. Years before, the band's first publicity shots had been taken on its beach. He recalled it being mid-summer, the sky as blue as the ones Holly now crayoned. They larked about, filling their socks with pebbles and seeing who could throw them furthest out to sea. Later, sockless, they walked along the Lanes, peering into the antique shops and realising that for the first time in their lives they could buy almost anything on sale, courtesy of their record company advance.

The pictures they used from the session were close-ups, their faces salt-stung and bright. They later travelled down the coast and the photographer took shots from a distance so the band became silhouettes against the sea and sky, everything shimmering. A few days afterwards Barrett wrote *At the Edge of the Sea*, in which, as he told the *NME* at the time, he tried to 'trap that beautiful day forever, like a ship in a bottle.'

He arrived at Victoria Station and found a seat on the train. The carriage soon filled up. A man sitting opposite tried to make conversation, mentioning a building they passed. Barrett had been drinking since the early hours and when he tried to answer his tongue was dry like the corpse of a small lizard. He nodded instead before making his way to the toilet to down more vodka. He saw himself in the mirror. The harsh light lit up creases on his forehead. His eyes were half shut.

Back in his seat, he looked through the window to the sky.

Rain was set to fall. He liked the places trains took you to: the unsweetened side with its austere buildings and sharp-edged metal, the silos and the loading bays, cranes, gravel pits, mounds of soil and stone. Then to the countryside: reservoirs, hedges, a solitary tree in a ploughed field. And, close up: gorse, silver birches, elms, poplars and sycamores — when he was young his mum made him list them when they went on journeys.

He was suddenly nostalgic for home, his proper home in the north, and for the rainy days he remembered when clouds colluded at the tops of telegraph poles until they finally burst, flooding the roads, making lakes on the school field.

The day after meeting Green, Carey decided to take a walk through town. He wasn't heading anywhere particular but roving, much like he'd done as a kid. He felt different. He was an author-to-be now, gathering material, resuscitating the past. He reflected on how the place had changed and the best way describe it in the book. Home towns were always considered a big deal. They shaped the artist and filtered into the music.

He'd always imagined he'd be about sixty before he could walk the streets and think how there used to be a school here or there, a shop on the corner, a row of houses. He could do it already. The mills and factories were mostly gone, replaced by houses, industrial estates or random patches of grass surrounded by small wooden posts guarding the sites where buildings had stood. In odd places factory walls were left standing without a roof. When they were kids, Carey, Barrett and the gang used to walk through these sites, shouting so their voices echoed and throwing stones at pigeons sitting in openings where windows had been. They were a liberating army, the first in after the bombs had dropped.

Carey's mum had worked as a sewing machinist in one of the mills, making blankets, sleeping bags and kids' coats. Barrett's mum was in the offices, filing. In the mid-1970s cheap imports led to short time until round-the-clock working became a four-day week, then three, two, one, gone. Carey recalled the listlessness back then, the town shuffling its feet and waiting to move on. People ambled along the canal bank or smoked by the brook, watching sludge gather around carrier bags and discarded tyres. Blokes would talk for ages because they had nothing better to do, asking kids what they were getting for Christmas and where they'd been on their holidays. Carey remembered one bloke telling him to be a good lad for his mam and dad and work hard at school so he didn't end up like him, *on the scrap heap*.

"How old do you think I am?" the man asked.

Carey had no idea.

"About fifty?"

"I'm thirty-four, you cheeky bugger."

He couldn't understand why he was offended; it was close enough.

We are old now, thought Carey: him and Barrett and anyone else who had been little then.

Barrett got off the train and walked down the main street away from the station. He saw the sea at the end of the road. The sun was setting and gave the water a reddish hue. He thought of how much he liked wandering, bumping into life. He took a swig from his bottle and kissed the air.

After strolling around for an hour or so he came across a small guest house advertising vacancies. This will do, he thought: rough and ready—much better than some faux-posh hotel. A woman aged about forty, in jeans and a tight white blouse, answered the door. She had a pretty nose and honest blue eyes and wore a silver clip to keep the dyed yellow-blonde hair from her face.

"Can I help you?" she asked.

Carey went back to where they had grown up, among a rat-run of redbrick terraces. His old house was empty with a 'For Sale' sign attached to the wall. He looked through the front window. Bin liners were on the floor with bedding and coat hangers spilling out. He tried to recall how the room had been furnished: the settee under the window, a clumpy coffee table in the middle of the room.

He didn't need to knock on doors to know people had died or moved on. Everywhere there were kids' bikes propped up where old people used to live, different dogs barking the other side of gates, different washing on lines. He remembered the tiny lady with frizzy hair from the greengrocer's. She used to ask him fiercely personal questions like was it true that John Barrett's mum and dad were splitting up (it was, in a way, but Carey said he didn't know and she sighed as if his vagueness had caused her physical pain). She'd gone, cancer. And her husband too, heart attack. He'd seen their death notices in the paper.

The canal was a few rows behind and, beyond that, new council houses built where the Bluebell estate had stood until a few years before. The 'Bell had comprised blocks of flats that were like something turned inside out with its guts on show: corrugated edges, twisted metal and stones set in concrete. The disaffected were scooped up like cockroaches from all corners of town and let loose there — the unemployed, the sick, the single mothers, the passing-through, the druggies, the dossers, the boozers, the thieves, the depressives, the down on their luck. *No Escape Estate* on Killing Stars' first album had been about it.

They weren't supposed to play on the 'Bell but would run along the decks, holding competitions to see who could jump down the most stairs (carrying the injured winner home later). When it was hot, tenants dragged chairs on to the landings and supped bottles of cider and cans of beer. These get-togethers lasted until the early evening when there was often shouting and police vans speeding past. Carey, Barrett and the rest followed on bikes and skateboards, their little legs moving as fast as they could go. They'd hear the swearing and raging, see the men with their shirts off, arguing on the balcony, knocking over chairs, telling the police they were interfering bastards. After a few minutes, quietness descended and scratchy voices were heard on police walkie-talkies. Bored now, the kids set off home again. Carey often took one last look over his shoulder, seeing the blokes and their wives making up, shaking hands with the police. Show over.

Barrett was in a playful mood, freed up in a new town. 'Can I help you?' Was that the question? Yes, he thought, you can help me: get upstairs now you sexy little thing and await my arrival. I like it gentle and I like it rough. I like it solemn and I like it silly. I want you naked and I want you in something see-through, diaphanous, you know: suggestive. Chiffony, is that a word? And I want you experienced and efficient so I can lie back and think of nothing but the pleasure. But I'd also like you shy and reticent so I can teach you, show you. I'll want to kiss you, eat you all up and touch you all over. The fun we'll have will be wholesome and frivolous. Come on, why are we waiting?

Carey made his way through the new estate on the 'Bell's former site. The houses were built from light-coloured bricks and had walkways and stretches of green—convenient for dumping old settees, and kids. A gang was lazing around a roughly made fire, bonfire night approaching. He passed a smashed up bus shelter and several kicked down fences. He said hello to one kid and was asked if he was a *bummer*. When he came to a house that was cared for—hanging baskets over the front door, a tended lawn, everything neat and tidy—it upset him. He felt like a deserter, someone who had slipped away from a warzone and left the good souls to a slow death.

At least Barrett had made it through and found poetry in it all. But, thought Carey, the working-class heroes in his songs were different than this plague of weasely would-be Americano gangsters in tracksuits and baseball caps. These kids hit the streets agitated because England was grey and wet and half-asleep, the very things Barrett and Carey had found perversely inspiring. Maybe, he pondered, he was out of touch and it was the same as ever but dressed up differently. Kids might be in their bedrooms strumming a guitar or loading a tune into a computer, writing a few words about a girl at school or feeling as if they didn't belong, already shaping themselves as outsiders. And how fortunate to be able to do everything from home on their computer—writing and recording music, designing sleeves, doing the photographs, having websites, e-mailing songs around the world.

Where the houses ran out, the town became a rash of retail parks and leisure centres, franchised restaurants and multi-plexes. A few years earlier councillors had rejected a plan to uncover the river passing through the town centre (headline, one of Carey's: *The Venice of England?*). Warnings were issued that it would become a civic litterbin with down-and-outs and depressives throwing themselves in and bored teenagers hurling in shopping trolleys. The paper carried letters saying the smell would be horrendous and rats as big as dogs would drag toddlers into the sewers.

Barrett smiled. She opened the door wider, trusting. He told her he was looking for a room. She put her hands to her hair and readjusted it. He breathed down his nose so she wouldn't smell the drink on his breath. Her figure was compact, the breasts and thighs at the corners of a parcel of flesh. While she was talking he thought that it was women like her who had formed his sexual apprenticeship. He'd grown up fantasizing about actress-es in *Hammer Horror* and *Carry On* films: voluptuous, pouty, husky voiced and milky skinned women who made sex playful, something you fell into. He hated calibrated sex.

"The room's up there," she motioned. "Up two flights and on your left."

When he reached the town centre Carey called at the San Marco, a coffee bar on the main street.

"How are you today, my friend?" said Luca, the owner.

Carey was impressed that Luca's Italian accent was still

strong despite living in the town for more than thirty years. He liked it too that he happily served up pie and chips, egg on toast — anything you wanted, apart from Italian.

The San Marco was practically the only place in town unchanged from their childhood. Carey and Barrett used to sit there drinking cappuccino, plotting. One time they spent an afternoon writing down entries for a competition in the local paper. Readers had been invited to suggest names for a night-club that was about to open, a suit-and-tie place dedicated to 'chart music'; they crossed themselves every time they said this, begging forgiveness for uttering such heinous words. *Bastards*, *Twatz*, *Shafters*, *Disco Pants* and *Knobbers* were on their list. They didn't win.

Carey sat at a table with his coffee and pulled out a notebook. He began listing the things that hadn't been around when they were young: computers, the internet, video recorders, remote controls, credit cards, satellite television, microwave ovens, DVD players, mobile phones, CDs, iPods, camcorders. He recalled the first digital watch appearing at school. Someone's uncle had brought it back from a foreign holiday. Kids took turns pressing the button to make the face light up red. Life had gone truly space age. At about this time, Carey had received the Aiwa tape recorder with its large buttons and flip-up lid. During the first week he secretly recorded conversations, usually between his gran and mum. His gran was in awe of the technology, refusing to believe it was her voice.

"Do I sound like that?"

She jabbed Carey on the arm:

"You've done something to make me sound like that, haven't you? Come on, admit it, you little bugger."

The idea to form a band came from the Aiwa. Everything started there.

The attic room in the guest house contained two beds separated by a small wooden table covered in circle stains. Barrett pulled back the bedclothes: clean enough. He went back down and told the woman he'd take it for the night.

He lay down on one of the beds and reached into his trousers but he'd lost the impulse somewhere between the woman answering the door and booking the room. He pulled the cover over his head and made a cave. If only he could stay there forever, he thought, under the covers, in a locked room, at the top of the house, at the end of a corridor. Left to drift in and out of sleep, warm. Nothing sticking through: telephone calls, people to speak to, obligations. He kissed the blanket, rubbing its texture over his lips, trying to realise its taste. He imagined he'd heard his dad, in the next room possibly, across the landing, at the bottom of the stairs. That voice, with its coarse timbre, searching for his son, wanting to know what he was up to.

'What you doing in here?'

'Having a kip.'

A kip, that's all. Not even a proper sleep. Just a little word for a little thing to be doing. No harm to anyone.

'You ill or something?'

'No, dad."

By saying 'dad' he was already appealing for leniency, palling up.

'Well, what do you want to be in bed for? It's not bloody night time.'

'I'm tired.'

'Tired? You've done nowt.'

He reminded himself it wasn't real.

Carey looked across to the entrance of the shopping precinct. In the mid-1970s the area had been turned into a labyrinth of ramps and corridors for months while it was installed. Workmen were visible through the grilles in makeshift walls, scouring deep into the earth. Everyone said it was going to be like America.

The town's only independent record shop, the Black Sedan, was a victim of the development. Carey remembered grumbling about the closure at the time, how it was scandalous and *typical*, but the necessary trip to another town or city to buy punk and new wave records added to their lustre. It didn't seem right that thrilling music should be on open sale in their dead-end hometown; tracking it down had to involve some kind of trial, a test of commitment.

Parker's, their favourite clothes shop, had also closed with the influx of chain stores. A first visit there without a parent in tow was a coming of age. Before this, local kids bought their clothes from places that were like hardware stores, with everything kept inside wooden drawers. Parker's was open-plan, a semi-lit cavern teeming with bomber jackets, fly-collar jumpers, Budgie shirts, patch-pocket flared trousers, smiley badges, Trax boots, bootlace ties with silver fasteners in the shape of marijuana leaves, sweaters with stars on them. Racks of clothes were wheeled on to the pavement and suspended from rope over doors and windows. Staff allowed customers to make their own way across the uneven floor to spin revolving racks or wander through wooden slatted doors to the changing rooms and stare at jeans posters for Levi, Brutus, Lois and Wrangler, usually showing peachy skinned girls stroking horses.

Carey often wondered if the Killing Stars single *All Gone* was about Parker's:

'How much would I give to be in that place,
Looking at you, into your face
All the pretty things racked up, hanging high
Me and you laughing, reaching for the sky.'

He meant well, always had. Barrett knew that of his dad. It was just that he believed kids had to be pushed, especially boys. It couldn't be left to chance. And wasn't he like everyone else's dad? Knock on any door on their street and they were all the same. They shouted and bawled, had a drink after work and a drink in the evening and a drink before bed. They weren't alcoholics though. It was a hobby, neatly chiselled into their day, chamfered to fit their down-time. The rest of the time they were grafting hard, paying the rent or covering the mortgage, putting bread on the table.

Lying there listening to the intermittent hiss of the radiator and the seagulls' shrill on the fire escape, Barrett wondered whether he was lying down now because it had been forbidden then. But there was still no peace, not the real thing (perhaps he hadn't drunk enough yet). He was being told to get up, do something. It wasn't his dad anymore but the ghost of his dad or maybe his conscience or just a voice in his head; he didn't know. It was saying how dare you and who are you to wallow, to indulge like this? Don't think yourself so special, kid. We've all had it rough, every one of us. Get up and get on with it. You shouldn't be crawling into bed, the covers over your bloody head. And haven't you got a wife back home, a kid to feed?

Once they were kitted out at Parker's, Carey remembered that older kids headed to Tramtracks, Blazes, the Candy Peel or the Candlelight—out-of-town cabaret clubs offering three course meals (prawn cocktail, steak and chips, Black Forest gateau) and two course entertainment (a comedian and a covers band). He recalled talking to some girls while they sunbathed on the school field at lunch time. They boasted that they had been to the Candy and met an older lad with his own car. They laughed:

"You'll never get in there, with your baby face and newspaper round money. There's no room on the car park for your Chopper either!"

"I'm not bothered."

"How come?"

"I'm into proper music."

"What's that then?"

"Punk."

"That's crap, that is."

"It's not."

"It's all spitting and noise."

"It means something."

"If you say so."

Barrett was unsure whether to ring Esther or not and save her worrying. But he didn't want to hear her voice; not what she would say particularly but the sound of it. She was too young for that harsh tone of admonishment and he didn't like that he drew it from her. For a while, several years even, he'd enjoyed the mischievousness of drinking, daring to be different and outside the conventions of everyday life. He used to chuckle at her chastisements and consider them a barometer of affection, that she cared enough to try and put him right.

At first Esther had tolerated his smirk, ostensibly enjoying the playfulness of his drunkenness, but there was no fun to be had any more in teasing her that he needed one more drink, my love, or exaggerating his state, sending himself up. She was through with all that.

Carey excused himself the research of going back to their old school. He had been there with the paper on various stories, feeling the same dread each time. He and Barrett had been in a CSE stream, corralled into non-academic subjects such as metalwork, craft, technical drawing and woodwork, and kept away from anything conceptual or artistic. They had discussed this many times when they were in the band together, how it was almost as if they were viewed as pre-ordered staff for local firms needing engineers, mechanics, draftsmen and joiners, or, in the mills, sweeper-uppers and luggers.

He recalled some of their classmates. Andy Sutton was a bony, freckly kid with his hands perpetually dipped in the front pocket of his anorak, where he kept his space dust. Everyone else had grown bored after a packet or two but Sutty was addicted. He'd hold his mouth open while it popped and cracked in his teeth and along his tongue.

"Fucking hell, Space Canaveral or what?"

Teachers tried to include him in lessons but soon accepted that his life was as combustible and random as freshly damp-ened space dust. He often went missing for weeks, explaining it in staccato sighs.

"It's me mum's new boyfriend, see. Well, we were all meant to be going up there. Newcastle. And he came late. It was supposed to be the whole weekend as well. But we got there later than expected. The car broke down, see. And my older brother reckoned he could fix it. He couldn't, really. So we called the AA."

After he'd meandered on for a few minutes, teachers waved their arms as if rubbing him out. Very good, now turn to page seventeen in your blue-backed books.

Barrett closed his eyes and fell asleep. When he awoke a few minutes later he lay on his stomach and then turned, stretching. Outside the window, light was leaving the sky. He drank some more and shut his eyes again. As he slipped in and out of sleep he made a note of where everything was in the room, his personal compass points: wardrobe, sink, window, door. He hated waking up and not knowing where he was, how to get out.

Other classmates came to mind. Debbie Tench had an ever-open mouth and greasy hair; Wayne Lomax spent lessons drawing fantastically detailed penises and scrotums; Andrew O'Hara was continually showing off his collection of porn so invasive it almost qualified as biology. Craig Lucas was one of several headcases. He and his gang once went on a cat-killing spree. They spoke about it as if they were taking part in a comedy sketch.

"How many did you get last night?"

"Just the one but by fuck it copped it."

"And in what way did it cop it?"

"With an iron bar, no less."

Lucas mimed the action of striking out with a bar. Much laughter.

"Did it die straight away?"

"No. It did this funny walk as if it was pissed. Then its back legs collapsed and it keeled over."

Carey and Barrett did little schoolwork because it was viewed as effete or toadying to the teachers. It had to be handed in surreptitiously, out of sight. They sublimated their real personalities, both growing fringes to shut out the world close up. While the rest fished out *Motor Cycle News* from their carrier bags (never holdalls or satchels), they pored over the *NME*, happy—flattered even—to be referred to as *weirdoes* and largely left alone. They developed an encyclopaedic knowledge of music, forming a network with older and younger weirdoes in the school, borrowing albums from each other, making tapes of their favourite tracks.

Barrett got up from the bed. He stood by the window and fished randomly in the back pocket of his jeans. He pulled out a picture of Esther and Holly that had been taken in a seaside photo booth. He recalled their laughter as they wrestled with the soft toys that Holly insisted went on too: Sylvester, Pink Panther and the scraggy dog she took everywhere. Suddenly, he was missing his 'girls'. He sat down, clutching his face. The feeling of emptiness reminded him of one of his 'little deaths'. These came on him when he was young, a sadness that descended arbitrarily before slipping away to leave a sensation of incorporeality, being there but not being there. It often happened a day or so before an outbreak of asthma. Barrett had spent weeks of his childhood with chest infections—the song *Indoor Boy* was a reflection on the subject. The illness would begin with a tickly cough and he'd have syrup to soak the itchiness but then the wheezing started and the cough-coughing through the night. When the breaths became brittle his mum or dad took him downstairs and made him stand on the doorstep, drawing in fresh air.

Notionally the school uniform had been 'smart clothes in brown, blue or grey', but some kids wore tight nylon tracksuit bottoms that doubled as pyjamas, occasionally with milk stains down the front and studded with dried nuggets of cereal. Most days Barrett wore a jumper with a roll neck collar and a Black Sabbath patch on the front shaped as an upturned cross.

Carey remembered telling Barrett that his mum had always dreamed of him wearing a blazer to school. She saw it as incontrovertible evidence that he was going to make something of his life. He refused. He had no choice. He knew kids would point at him, asking who he thought he was and after a few days of this, they'd be tripping him in the corridor and shouting after him that he was queer. The blazer would end up in a tree or kicked around the floor until it became creased and dusty, the poshness literally rubbed away.

If they went from school to a friend's house at dinnertime the kid's mum was often still in bed, the breakfast plates on the settee, a milk bottle on the table. The fire they had forgotten to turn off would be blazing out heat on three bars with a small mongrel dog curled up next to it, drowsy with the heat. Happy to see a sign of life, the dog would wake up and set about them, jumping up and barking. On the hunt for something to eat, the kid would open the kitchen cupboard to reveal packets of custard, small bottles of food colouring, cream crackers and bottles of sauce — nothing you could actually eat without feeling sick afterwards. If they went back later, after school, the place was full of kids drawing at the kitchen table or riding bikes down the alley, the dog trailing after them, nipping ankles.

Barrett made regular visits to hospital for tests, having to blow in tubes, give blood and undergo X-rays. They checked for allergic reactions, injecting his arm with traces of dust mite, bird feathers, cat and dog. Back home his mum put a plastic sheet across his bed and vacuumed the room every day to keep down the dust. He was given an inhaler and had it with him at all times.

The illness became part of his self-identity. He liked, as he described it in one television interview, 'the cadence of wistful infirmity' (he told his press officer afterwards that he had affected this ridiculous level of pretension but the interviewer hadn't realised). His asthma had been mentioned once in a press release issued by the record company, naming other famous coughers: Keats and Orwell.

"You make it sound like I had TB or rickets. I wasn't Tim fucking Cratchett," Barrett complained.

For years afterwards he found himself in discussions about other people's childhood illnesses and afflictions: kids in callipers, kids with a hole in the heart, kids with tumours. Everyone, it seemed, had spent their childhood on a sick bed, sipping tomato soup and being propped up with pillows so they could look out over the garden. He also stopped mentioning his there-but-not-there sensation in interviews — others had experienced it too; it was pretty commonplace.

Most kids in their neighbourhood didn't live with their real dads. They called their mums' boyfriends by their first name and were indignant if you mistook them for their actual dad. He was somewhere else, Glasgow or Liverpool or on the other side of town with a new woman.

Carey remembered Alan Ainsworth's step-dad. He had white hair and was continually chewing, although they never saw him put anything into his mouth; he might have been gnawing his tongue. Barrett, Carey and Alan were watching television one night while Alan's mum ironed in the kitchen. Alan's dad came in from his shift just as *Monty Python* had started, the bit with the naked man playing a piano in a field. The three of them giggled nervously. It was as if he'd caught them fiddling with each other under the bedclothes. He put down his flask and tool bag.

"Do you think that's funny?" he barked.

He pointed at the telly. They didn't know what to say.

"Well, do you?"

They did, but stayed quiet.

"It's about as funny as a dog having a shit, that is."

It fell dark outside. Barrett resented the routine of nightfall, how it seeped from the sky, crept through the streets and sent everyone scurrying away, a good day gone dead. Why was everyone obedient to its call? He wanted to stay up, talking, playing music, drinking, shouting, kicking against its divinity.

Every night he was fearful that the morning wouldn't come. Where ever he was, before he settled down to sleep, he looked for trees or tall buildings, locking earth to sky, bolting everything down so it couldn't float away in the darkness. He slept with the curtains open, anxious to see the first drift of light against the window. In summer, windows were left open too so he could hear the birds or traffic building up on nearby roads, evidence that the day was coming.

Woody was one of the few who lived with his real dad. Barrett had christened him 'Luigi' after calling round one day and finding him wearing the coolest sunglasses he'd ever seen. The rest of his apparel was strictly dads' stuff of corduroy trousers, patterned cardigan and Hush Puppies. The glasses, though, were straight out of *The Godfather*.

Carey recalled that Luigi had driven them to their first proper concert—Hawkwind at a large concert hall. On the way there Luigi spoke gravely as though they were preparing for war: don't talk to anyone; keep a good grip on your tickets; go two at a time to the toilets; leave a few minutes before the end to avoid the rush; if anyone steals your seats, tell the usherettes. Woody told him they didn't have usherettes at gigs, unless that was the name of the support band.

"Well, you know what I mean, whoever's in charge."

Woody said no one was in charge. His dad told him to stop being a clever arse.

Soon after they entered the hall, a skinny bloke ambled on to the stage carrying an acoustic guitar. He began singing caustic songs about pregnant teenagers and getting beaten up on council estates. The crowd was in uproar. People left their seats and moved down the aisles to get closer:

"Fuck off."

"Twat."

"Get off."

Barrett, Carey and Woody went to the toilet. While they were standing at the urinal they saw a dishevelled longhaired lad turned slightly to the side, fiddling with himself. Woody wasn't shy:

"What you doing?"

He turned around.

"I'm trying to piss in this bag."

He had a crisp bag, half full of piss. He was drunk and struggling to hold it, splashing the floor and his shoes.

"What you going to do with that?"

"Wuzz it at that bastard on stage. He's lucky it's just piss."

He turned back to the job in hand before looking over again.

"How old are you lot?"

"Fourteen," they chorused.

"You look about nine."

Carey and Barrett noted the name of the bloke with the acoustic guitar billed as a 'punk-poet' on the posters: Patrik Fitzgerald. They were going to buy his record, the one about having a safety pin stuck in my heart, for you, for *you*.

In the mornings the sun lit bright Barrett's folly. Looking out, whether across streets, fields or buildings, the dread of the night before seemed absurd. Why had he needed the drink—and so much of it—to ease him through? Some days, on waking, he managed to steer clear of a drink for two or three hours but the countdown to nightfall always left him dangling.

On only one occasion could Carey remember their class becoming united. It was the Friday morning after Blondie had appeared on *Top of the Pops*. They had each fallen in love with the band's singer (no one knew her name). She was angelic and sexy; red lips, golden hair; smiling and snarling; opening her mouth and gritting her teeth. The metalwork lesson had hardly started when they began talking about her.

"Did you see her?"

"She's beautiful."

"I think she's called Debbie something."

Their feelings were so intense that talking about her felt like a bloodletting; the pressure had to be released. The room had tall windows and was bathed in splashy light.

'Den-oo, be-doo, I'm in love with you.'

The drinking had eventually become a physical need. His body demanded the tang on the tongue, the sweet-sharp burn down his throat, the trickling into his chest and stomach, then the afterglow. The bottle itself was a source of fetishistic pleasure, similar to when he handled his asthma inhaler as a kid. He liked to roll the top between his fingers while attached to the grooves in the bottle's neck. He adored the sound of metal scratching against glass as it whirred round. He'd run the top's sharp edge against the pad of his thumb, pressing it down hard to make an imprint in the flesh.

The first drink of the morning formed a mouthwash. He'd swill it on both sides of his teeth before swallowing. It tasted bitter ("similar to vinegar or aftershave," he told Esther) but it travelled to the extremities of his body—feet, hands, head—

acting like wind blowing life into embers. Once he had re-lit the fire, every swig became easier, more pleasurable. Being drunk was wonderful.

They had heard something of punk on television and were intrigued by Patrik Fitzgerald, but saw it close up when Paul Kennedy marched into the school yard in leopard skin trousers and a capped T-shirt covered in zips. His hair was spiked high and a small white feather dangled from a stud in his ear. Until that morning most self-aware kids had opted for a look of sullen pseudo-spirituality, forged largely in the image of David Carradine from the television series, *Kung Fu*. The standard look was duffel coats or denim jackets with sew-on patches, head down, hands in pockets, lank hair and a permanent slouch.

A mob gathered around Kennedy, asking questions as if it was a press conference.

"What you dressed like that for?"

"I'm a punk."

"What's that?"

"The fight-back, that's what."

"How do you mean?"

"Stuffing it up them."

"Who?"

"The teachers, your mam and dad, anyone who tells you how to live your life."

He parted the crowd by putting the back of his hands together and moving his arms in a large arc as if doing the breast-stroke. Later that day he was sent home and told to change back into his uniform. He moderated the look over the next few weeks, adopting a kind of militaristic chic with sharply pressed trousers and black-framed glasses without lenses.

Barrett and Carey were hugely impressed. Whatever Kennedy had drawn from punk to give him such self-assurance would stand for them too. Others felt the same. Within a week it had blow-torched the school, turning into relics anyone still smelling of patchouli oil and padding around in desert boots.

Barrett had vague plans to jot down some lyrics in Brighton but had no inspiration, or a pen. Perhaps a drink would help, he decided. A social drink, a drink like his father used to have, among men. They could stare at the walls, the floor, their pints, and say something or other about nothing or other on the weather, the football, how it's all changed around here. Then he could think about going home tomorrow, making up with Esther, taking Holly to the park or the museum to see the stuffed birds. Last time, she'd asked if they could be brought back to life so she could ride on one. She wanted to know how high you could go before bumping into heaven.

Kennedy had a small box of seven-inch singles that he took everywhere with him. He passed them around, explaining how rare some of them were, that the see-through vinyl with hand printed sleeve was limited to the first thousand copies. Most of the artwork was basic, done at home in a few minutes with paint, scissors and glue.

"That's the whole point," he told Barrett.

He was always breathless, just back from somewhere: catching a coach to Newcastle or London; sleeping in a park; meeting up with a brilliant new band at a service station; *snogging a bird* on a fire escape. He told them of his plan to liven up the school disco. Next week, or the week afterwards, not sure yet, he was going to wear rubber gloves and flick milk at everyone and pretend it was spunk. Everyone knew he wouldn't do it but was impressed by such deviant thinking.

While Barrett admired Kennedy's whole-heartedness, he viewed his abrupt change of persona as cartoon-like. He resolved to make his own conversion to punk more subtle. He unstitched the Black Sabbath patch on his jumper and fixed button badges to his coat.

★ ★ ★

Carey began making notes for the book, concentrating first on their childhood days. No one but me knows this, he thought: I was there.

Neighbours had several ways of describing Barrett when he was a kid. He was enthusiastic, a bit of a handful. He had ants in his pants or was a bloody fidget. Carey thought that these days he might be taken to the doctor's, put on tablets. He could even have a *mentor* shadowing him at school, helping him calm down: some of the other kids don't like it when you jump about so much, talking all the time.

The Barretts lived two doors down from the Careys. The houses were divided by thin wooden fences strung across small front gardens. Carey's first memory of him, first memory of anything, was a sunny day when they were both about four years old. Barrett was shouting, cocking his leg at the fence ready to climb over. While he was yelling and waving he didn't notice his mum had moved behind him, crouched down scrubbing the doorstep. Barrett moved back and stepped into the bucket, knocking it over. Water rushed across the path soaking his mum's shoes. She was quickly upright.

"You silly little boy. How many times have I asked you to be careful? Get in the house, get in this minute."

Most kids, thought Carey, would have hung their heads low or cried but Barrett lifted his chin and made an 'O' shape with his mouth, showing off. As his mum soft-slapped the back of his legs, he laughed as if he was being tickled.

The furniture at the Barrett's looked as if it had been gathered up on an afternoon scoot around a few second-hand stores. Nothing matched. The coffee table was teak and expensive-looking while the threadbare settee with its cigarette burns and stains might have come from a youth club. The seascape prints in the front room had turned seasick green from years of sun staining.

The house reeked because everyone in the family smoked, Barrett and his brother from when they were young teenagers. They were incessantly borrowing *ciggies* from each other and bickering over who owned which packet and where the lighter was or whose turn it was to go out and buy a box of matches.

The talking never stopped, so there seemed to be more than four of them. They interrupted one another, shouted, spoke at the same time. The telly was left on but unwatched, save for when a particular programme might snag their attention for a few seconds .

Carey was amazed at how quickly they fell out, the ferocity of these arguments, and that they made friends again so quickly. They all swore too: bugger, shit, piss, bloody and bleeding. His dad, Ray, sometimes cried out 'fuck' when he was angry. If Barrett's mum swore, she'd turn to Carey:

"Excuse my French!"

This made him feel awkward.

"You're all right, mum. Dave doesn't mind a bit of swearing, do you?" said Barrett.

"No."

"He does, you can tell. Look at his face."

"Really, I'm not bothered."

"Come on," she'd say, teasing. "You've been brought up proper. I bet your mum and dad aren't effing and blinding all day like this lot."

"They swear sometimes."

"What? When your dad bangs his hand knocking in a nail or something? That doesn't count."

Ray Barrett was exceptionally tall. Unlike most dads on the street, he worked in an office, for an insurance company. He wore expensive suits. The trouser legs were narrow and the material seemed to change colours; it was black from afar but shone purple and gold like oil on water when you got close up.

He smoked with great dexterity. When he took a cigarette from the packet, he closed the lid and bounced its tip against the cardboard, drawing in his cheeks and looking about him. He sucked hard when it finally made his lips, grunting and coughing extravagantly. He'd flick the ash away by twitching his thumb against the filter.

On light nights when the street was full of kids chasing up

and down booting footballs, Ray joined in. He'd pick the teams, encouraging everyone to *pass and move*, *control the ball*, *find a man*.

Barrett's mum would sometimes sit on the doorstep, knees pulled up to her chin.

"Are you going to join in, love?" Ray would shout.

"No thanks."

"Come on, Kath, show us how it's done."

"Not likely."

Carey knew there was something different about Barrett's mum. He could remember being in their kitchen when he was seven or eight years old and sensing that time spent near her was special. Her skin was the colour of butterscotch and she had large brown eyes and thick black hair. She wore tops with low necks and he sneaked glimpses of her cleavage. His mum said once that she was a good-looking woman and that 'all the fellas at work are after her'.

Once when he visited their house, Carey was told by Ray that he'd installed a pub in the kitchen.

"Come and see this."

He had a huge tin of beer on the table. He pierced the lid with a stumpy metal device.

"Watch this."

He pulled a small lever down and a thin stream of beer funnelled through a nozzle.

"See, I can pull my own pint whenever I want now. They call it a Party Seven but it's more fun if you're having it on your own!"

John was standing in the doorway between the kitchen and the front room. His dad called him over.

"Come on. Don't stand there like Piffy. Let's show him our party piece."

Ray crouched down and shuffled on to his back, the diamond patterned lino beneath him as he positioned his head under the spout.

"Fire away."

John pressed the handle and a jet of beer looped out. The first splash landed on Ray's forehead and he gasped, shaking his head. It was in his hair and down the front of his shirt. Eyes closed, he searched for the flow with his mouth and began gulping it down. When he'd had enough he leaned forward spluttering.

"Turn the bloody thing off, turn it off."

On the street and at school Barrett was the tallest for his age. He was athletic and agile and usually won the races around the block and back. Everything he did was in twitchy bursts as if he wanted to get to somewhere else as quickly as possible.

One summer, on a hot day that set the tarmac bubbling, the pair headed to the swimming baths. Carey, for once, was undressed and ready first. He saw kids standing by the pool. They were staring into the water and for a moment he thought someone had drowned. As he drew closer he saw a man dressed in white pushing a large net on a stick into the shallow end. Kids were giggling and there were cries of encouragement as the net was forced down. At last Carey could see. Lying on the bottom were two turds framed by pastel blue tiles. The shimmering water made them look alive. Kids were making faces.

"Yuk."

"Shut up, will you? It's not funny," yelled the man.

The changing room doors flew open. They were slatted and

wooden and on a spring like in cowboy films. It was Barrett. He didn't sense anything untoward and raced forwards, puffing out his chest as he charged across the tiles. He jumped into the water with a loud splash, landing close to the net. The kids saw it as bravado and cheered loudly. The attendant was remonstrating with Barrett before he had even had risen to the surface.

"You bloody fool, what the hell are you up to? Can't you see what I'm trying to do?"

Barrett's dark hair broke the water and he squeezed his nose with his thumb and forefinger. He looked around frantically. Kids were laughing and pointing. As he pulled himself up the stairs and out of the water he saw the turds for the first time.

"I bet you know something about how this got in here, don't you?" shouted the man.

"No, it wasn't me. It was Winnie."

"Winnie who?"

"Winnie the poo, you must have heard of him."

Everyone burst out laughing. Carey thought how brilliant it was to think of something so quickly and not mind all those people staring.

Mr and Mrs Bentley owned the local corner shop and were widely considered to be the oldest people in the world. Their skin was almost transparent and Carey couldn't bear to look at the back of their hands because it looked as if it was about to tear. They both spoke in the stuttering dry voices that children affected when pretending to be old people.

Carey went in one day with Barrett. Most kids nodded as they entered or muttered a quick hello, but Barrett was more profuse.

"Morning Mr Bentley. How are you today? Feeling well?"

"Not too bad, John, for a fella my age. And how are you and your mam and dad?"

"All very well, Mr Bentley, very well indeed."

Mr Bentley looked across to Carey and winked, letting him know that he thought his best friend was a cheeky so-and-so.

"What can I do you for today?" he asked.

"Today, I think I fancy some pear drops," said Barrett.

Mr Bentley turned from the counter to face the shelves behind him stocked with jars of boiled sweets. While he scanned the rows, moving his finger across, Barrett picked up a *Mars Bar* and a *Milky Way*.

"Can you see where they are, lads?"

"Just up there, near the top," answered Barrett.

Barrett stuffed more chocolate into his pockets.

Outside, Carey asked him whether he felt tight stealing from an old man.

"A bit, I suppose. I don't do it all the time, just when I'm hungry. He's probably loaded anyway—he's had that shop for years."

Soon afterwards a paper round came vacant and Barrett was taken on. One morning Carey decided to go with him. They met at the shop.

"Keep an eye on him, David," said Mr Bentley.

"How come?"

"Ask him."

"Why have I to keep my eye on you?"

"He doesn't believe I deliver all the papers."

Mr Bentley leaned on the counter.

"Listen, I've had lads doing that exact same round as you for over thirty years and no one's ever done it as quick, no one. I know you run about like your arse's on fire but you're back here before you leave."

Carey had never heard Mr Bentley swear before. He didn't think people that old could. He giggled.

"And what are you laughing about? Do you know more than you're letting on?"

"No, honest."

"What is it then?"

"You, swearing."

"I know a lot more swear words too and you'll hear them all if I find out your pal's shoving these papers in someone's bin."

"I don't do that, Mr Bentley, honest. I'm just dead quick," said Barrett.

About half way through the round they came to a small private estate with neat lawns.

"Watch this," said Barrett at one door.

He pressed the newspaper roughly into the letter box and rattled the flap before giving the bottom of the door a few prods with his foot. The curtains were closed at every window.

"You'll wake them up," whispered Carey.

"That's the idea."

After a few seconds, they heard coughing from inside and the slow scrape of slippers across tiles.

"Hang on, hang on," rasped a voice.

An old man answered, still pulling up his trousers. His hair was askew, his eyes tiny blue dots. He fished in his pocket and handed Barrett a coin.

"Thank you, Mr McVay. I thank you most sincerely."

"Aye, so you do."

He had a strong Irish accent.

"And who's your mate, here?"

"This is David."

"Hello, David," he said. "Now, if you're thinking of coming here next week and I've won the lottery, don't, because I won't be here, will I, John?"

"No way."

"I'll be over the sea and far away with a beautiful woman in my arms, won't I, John?"

"Definitely."

"See, he knows, you know," he said, pointing to Barrett.

"I've got to go now," said Barrett sharply. "Old Bents beats me with a big stick if I'm late back."

"Now don't you go telling lies like that. He's a lovely old chap and wouldn't hurt a fly."

"He does. He whacks me hard when no one's looking. He looks a bit weedy but he can't half give you a crack when he's mad."

"Give over. You're having me on."

Barrett grinned. Mr McVay turned to Carey:

"Every morning he does this to me, every morning. He's a funny little chappie, for sure."

When he reached the gate, Barrett turned and waved cheerily, this time using Mr McVay's first name.

"Take care, Eugene. Oh, and don't forget."

"Forget what?"

"Up the IRA!"

Mr McVay cracked up laughing. Carey noticed how much younger he looked than when he'd first opened the door.

Ray took them to their first football match.

"There'll be thirty thousand fans there, pushing and shoving," he said.

They went on the bus. Carey didn't understand how they got

from their street to the ground. It was houses and fields, cars and buses, streets and streetlights, and then they were there. When they got off, Ray said:

"I'm just going to have a swift half."

They were left outside a pub entrance. It began to rain. They leaned against the wall with their hoods up. Carey didn't know how long it took to drink a half but it seemed ages. They counted how many people passed. Barrett got mixed up at about one hundred and thirty-four. They had a competition to see who was best at being cross-eyed. Barrett won, his eyes almost disappearing under his nose. They practised spitting. Barrett could do it furthest but Carey was most accurate. Seven times out of ten he hit the grid. There were suddenly fewer people around and they could hear roars from the ground.

"Does that mean someone's scored?" asked Carey.

Barrett looked at his watch.

"Nah, they haven't started yet. It's five to three."

The people passing by were now hurrying. A bloke jogged down the pavement holding a kid's hand. They both had scarves tied to their wrists.

"We're going to miss the kick-off," said Carey.

"I know. Shall we go and get him?"

His dad was sitting at a table in the corner. A pall of cigarette smoke hung over him and his mates.

"It's your lad, isn't it Ray?"

"Aye, he's been a bugger all week so I've brought him to see this lot as punishment."

"I think I'd prefer a slapped arse myself!"

"Are you ready, dad? We're going to be late."

Carey noticed Ray had changed colour, to a funny shade of red.

"Do you want to get yourselves a bag of crisps?" asked Ray.

"I'm only going to be a few minutes."

"Dad," said Barrett. "We're going to be late. Come on, please."

Ray downed his pint, picked up the cigarette packet from the table and buttoned up his coat.

"I'll see you next time, lads, or in the ground if you can drag yourselves away from here."

Outside the pub Ray stopped and bent down to talk to Barrett. Carey walked around him (it seemed to take a few seconds) so he could see what was happening. Barrett still had his hood up.

"Don't you ever do that again."

"What?"

"Show me up in front of my mates. Do you hear?"

"I won't, dad. Honest."

"Make sure you don't, otherwise there'll be no treats like this for a very long time. I don't want any mither. I get that from your mam all week."

Carey was awe-struck when they got inside the ground. (Afterwards, he couldn't recollect any detail from the match itself, only the noise, the overcoats, the rich green of the pitch, the people gathered together singing and cheering.) At half-time Carey asked Ray if he could go to the toilet. When they made their way back to the terraces, they lost their original place and had to stand behind a pillar. Ray sighed.

"Couldn't you have gone to the lav before the kick-off?"

"I didn't want one then."

"Well you should have thought-on."

They couldn't see the game properly now and it was all Carey's fault, said Ray. The afternoon was ruined. He should be able to control his bladder at his age; he wasn't a little kid any more. Ray caught Carey covering his ears during the chanting.

"Get your hands down. It's supposed to be noisy, it's a bloody football match."

Carey felt like crying. Grown-ups weren't supposed to talk to children like that. He wished he was with his own dad. He hated Barrett's dad.

The bus home was packed. Carey and Barrett shared a seat and his dad sat in front, next to an older boy. Carey heard him ask the lad if he'd enjoyed the game.

"It was okay, I suppose. Shame we didn't win. I knew we wouldn't though, just knew it."

"Why were you so sure?"

"They weren't tackling or anything."

The lad's clothes were damp, his cheeks rain-stung and rosy. He had thick hair on top but the sides and back had been cut very short. Carey looked closely and could see where someone had run up and down with an electric razor, making uneven furrows. Ray asked the lad why he was so wet. Hadn't he been able to get under the stand with everyone else?

"I was queuing up for some Bovril at half-time and it was pouring down. The queue went on forever."

He rested his head on the window. The rain formed swirling patterns on the pane.

"Mister," he said. "Will you wake me up if I fall asleep? I live near Churnet Street."

Ray said he would. After a few minutes the lad nodded off. Barrett asked his dad whether he was going to wake him.

"I don't think so. Look at him, he's fagged out."

"But he'll miss his stop."

Ray said the lad needed his sleep more and, anyway, the bus driver would feel sorry for him and double back to drop him off at home. The three of them got off, leaving the boy slouched in his seat.

"That lad will have to walk all the way home from the bus station now," said Carey to Barrett.

"I know."

Friday night was 'disco night' at the Barrett's. The chairs and settee were pushed to the edges of the room and the record player turned up full. The records were housed in a wire device that resembled a toast rack. Ray grabbed at them, plonking them roughly on the player.

"We like the sound of the scratches, don't we? It gives it more rhythm."

Ray conducted proceedings, imploring everyone to 'get up and get with it'. The brothers, and Carey if he was around, were encouraged to sing along, jump about (on and off the furniture even) and bang on the coffee table with broken pens until the mood dropped for the finale when Ray played the same three songs each week: *Vincent* and *American Pie* by Don McLean and Elvis Presley's *Mama Liked The Roses*.

"Get your collars up," he ordered.

They stood in line, the family and any visiting kids, emoting like crazy, acting out scenes from the songs, crying tears for imaginary cameras.

Carey's mum didn't approve of him playing with Barrett. She said he was a different lad afterwards, as if he left a mark on his skin.

"You've been with John, haven't you?"

"No."

"Come on, tell the truth."

"Okay then, I have. Not for long though. How do you know?"

"I just do."

"How?"

"It's the way you walk in here full of yourself and start answering back. Just like him."

"But John's not bad or anything."

"No, just cheeky."

"That's okay, isn't it?"

"Depends."

"On what?"

"What side of cheeky he falls on."

"He just sticks up for himself, that's all."

"Right then."

At lunchtime one day they were sitting on a wall at school. Some girls walked over. Sharon Ellis had a new haircut. It was now blonde instead of mousy brown and curled out from her face. She was chewing gum.

"What do you think of my new hairstyle, then?"

"Good, really modern" said Carey.

"What about you, John?" she asked.

"Don't like it."

The gum nearly fell from her mouth.

"Why not?"

"It looks false, the way it all curls out at the sides. Hair never grows like that naturally."

"What do you know anyway?"

She padded the floor with the sole of her foot as if stamping out a fire.

"You asked my opinion."

"I didn't."

"You did."

She was close to tears. Her friend pulled at her arm.

"Come on, he doesn't know how to talk to girls, he doesn't."

"You're so full of yourself, you are," cried Sharon.

As they walked away, a lad shouted over to Barrett that he was a tight bastard.

"She deserves it," he said.

"How come?"

"She's thick and she thinks she's something."

They had just finished a football match during a PE lesson and were making their way to the changing rooms. Kids pulled down their shirt cuffs to warm their hands, blowing out long trails of freezing air that hung about them like small, lost clouds. Simon Lloyd was carrying one of the painted staves they'd used as a goalpost. He had dark skin because one of his grandparents was black. Keith Hanson snatched the stick, held it over his shoulder and began shaking it like a spear.

"Hey Lloydy, what's this?"

He didn't answer.

"Come on, what's this? You know, don't you?" He made monkey noises, banging his chest with his free hand. "It's a fucking Zulu spear. I bet your mam and dad had these when they were in the jungle."

Some of the kids smiled nervously. Barrett turned round:

"Pack it in, Keith."

"Why?"

"Because it's not funny."

"Are you his bum chum or something?"

"You're only picking on him because he's smaller than you."

"I'll pick on you in a minute."

Barrett kept on walking.

"Piss off," shouted Hanson.

Barrett shook his head.

One morning Carey and Barrett were in the playground waiting for school to begin when they saw two figures beckoning them to the fence.

"I think it's your mum and dad," said Carey.

They ran over.

"Have they taken the register yet?"

"No."

"Come on then."

"Where we going?"

"You'll find out. Come on, get a move on. You can come too if you want, Dave."

The boys raced round to the gate. Barrett's parents were giddy as if they were on the run from the police.

"I'll do you a note tomorrow saying you've had a sore throat and I'll have a word with your mum, Dave," said Mrs Barrett.

They all climbed into Ray's car.

"We're going to the seaside," he said.

"Brilliant."

They stopped at two or three pubs on the way and arrived in the early afternoon. They were hungry. Most of the cafés were shut but at the end of a street running parallel to the sea front, they came to The Singing Kettle. The name was written in ornate letters, some of them tilted, on a board suspended by a chain across the main window. An elderly man was leaving as they entered, shadowed to the door by a lady in a pinafore. She was about to spin the sign to 'Closed'.

"Sorry love, are you shutting up?" asked Ray.

"I was, but come in."

"Are you sure?"

"I'm sure."

As they walked through, she put up the closed sign and fastened the bolt. They had the café to themselves.

It was a long room with a counter running down most of one side. A pall of steam rose over the metal urns and pipes from where she drew hot water. The high autumn sun leaked shafts of light that quivered where they met the heat. The menu was on a pin board. At the far end Barrett saw a jukebox. Ray flipped him a coin. He had never known his mum and dad so relaxed and for them to seem so happy together. He put in the money, stabbed at the buttons and Don McLean started up:

> 'A long, long time ago
> I can still remember
> How that music used to make me smile …"

*   *   *

Carey had imagined the day, the joy of it, for years. He strolled into the building with a studied nonchalance, smiling at Rita on reception, passing through to the editor's office. He told him about the book offer. Sutcliffe sat back and unhooked his glasses so they dangled at chest height on a piece of string.

"I suppose I ought to congratulate you."

"It's a big opportunity, Jack."

"Aye, I imagine it is. Remind me, what does this fella sing?"

"He's had lots of hits. You'd know them if you heard them."

(Carey, the same as all Sutcliffe's staff, felt like a teenage nephew in his company.)

"You know me, strictly classical."

Carey hoped he wasn't going to rhapsodise on classical music or his other passions — opera and wine, and anything else he could be snooty about to sanction a slow shake of the head and his favourite lament:

"Didn't you know that?"

Waiting a second before adding:

"Did you actually go to school?"

Instead, Sutcliffe asked:

"Do you think you're up to it, writing this book?"

"I like to think so."

"I know we've had plenty of stories about this Barrett fella in the paper but not for a while, if I remember rightly. If he's still as famous as you say he is, you're in with the big boys, aren't you?"

"I'll manage."

"I hope you do."

The first pub Barrett came to was hosting an Irish Night. Shamrocks and frothy Guinnesses were chalked on a blackboard at the entrance. He scoffed. He couldn't think of anything worse than plastic Micks whooping it up, fiddles and bloody whistles. He'd met scores of Irish in the music industry and on the road and while they were coming at you with the blarney, the brogue and the twinkling eyes, they were counting the money ('One for you, two for me.') or planning the subtle seduction of your girlfriend. And they hated the English, always. Still fighting the old battles, a blighted potato in their pocket to grip should the bitterness wane.

Was he up to it? In with the big boys. Thirty-odd years on a runty provincial paper, what did Jack Sutcliffe know about anything? Still, and much to his own irritation, Carey began to fret. How exactly did you ghost-write an autobiography? Was it like a long newspaper story? How did you discern between exhaustive and laboured, brisk and superficial, discursive and indulgent? What had he got himself into?

A few hours later he became bullish. A book was a book, it didn't have to sing and dance. Mustn't let people (or himself) stand in his way, put him off. He thought sourly of the rejections for his novels and the knock-backs from national newspapers he'd approached with feature ideas; his piece on Barrett had been one of only a handful accepted. He recalled an incident from years before. He was fifteen, getting the band together with Barrett. On the walk home from school he bumped into Jonesy, a sneery kid who lived a few streets away. Carey told him about their plan.

"You? In a group?"

"Well, yeah."

"You can't be in a band."

"Why not?"

"You just can't."

Jonesy shook his head, smiling to himself.

"You don't look like somebody in a band, for a start."

"Don't I?"

"No way. I can't believe you think you do."

"How are you supposed to look?"

"I don't know but I tell you this, the idea of you being in a band is fucking hilarious."

Carey could recall the exact privet hedge they were passing, the makes of cars parked along the road. And that Jonesy's face was not his usual salmon colour but slightly redder from climbing the stone steps leading to Matlock Crescent.

He vowed: not this time. Mustn't let anyone (or himself) stand in his way, put him off.

Two couples passed Barrett on their way to the pub. They recognised him and fell into a conference. He knew what was coming.

"It's John Barrett, isn't it?"

He shook his head.

"You are, I know you are," said a bloke who looked to be in his mid-thirties. His head was shaved and he wore a black T-shirt with a celtic tattoo on his upper arm.

"I'm a massive fan of yours. I saw you on telly last week where you kicked off. Priceless, totally priceless."

Barrett started to move away. The four of them matched his stride.

"Come and have a drink with us," said the other man who, with his short hair and lean body, looked like a squaddie. "Just the one, hey, if you're going somewhere?"

"I don't drink Guinness," said Barrett meekly. "And I'm on my way to a recording session."

"Come on, one pint. It'll do you good."

"Okay, Oi'll have the one then," he said in an Irish accent (which they didn't notice).

"Good lad," said squaddie.

Barrett felt his skin tighten.

Carey was granted a three-month unpaid sabbatical to write the book, the first in the paper's history. He floated through the flat for the first few days, taking baths, turning the computer on and off, staring out of the window. He'd never had time to reflect like this before and was thinking about his own life as much as Barrett's, adding up.

An early plan to write for the music papers had been thwarted by the responses to his introductory phone calls. They were off-hand with him, pretend breezy, a sardonic tone in their replies, almost as if they were bored by the sound of his voice before listening to what he actually had to say. He wasn't sure if he was suitable anyway, whether he was cynical and dogmatic enough for the role.

Despite telling friends when he started at the paper that he was passing through, he'd been there more than twenty years. He had his reasons. The salary was reasonable; there had been regular promotions (largely cosmetic but still tokens of appreciation); and it was a job he could do easily, leaving him the energy for creative writing in the evenings and weekends. Also, he planned to harvest experiences from work to colour his novels, the little tragedies or joys he came across most days, the quirks of life: characters like Russian Joe who believed he had to keep six radios switched on permanently and tuned to different stations to ensure his brainwaves were 'static' or Mad Alwyn whose house was crammed with pieces of metal and wood he'd found all over town.

He still saw friends from college and many were continually swapping jobs, almost — as Carey saw it — for its own sake, taking on more stress, going through second or third divorces, never satisfied. He told them it was quite pleasant 'having your arms around a job'.

"I've got good karma," he said. "Happy in my own space."

Whether this was true or not, he wasn't sure.

His marriage had lasted nearly six years before Lucy packed up and went, her belongings jammed into bin bags, saying that while she loved him, she wasn't *in love* any more. She'd married twice since and he wasn't sure where she was now living; the Christmas cards had stopped. Four girlfriends had come and gone after her, each lasting between three months and two years. He'd liked them at the time, loved them possibly, but none were *the one* (or a replacement for the one he'd lost).

He mused on the minor detail, the shading of his life: pub quiz on Tuesdays; a collection of *Private Eye* and *Mad* magazines (in binders, stored away from direct light or heat); copies of every letter he'd sent or received from childhood kept in plastic clasp-lid boxes; a set of mugs from seaside towns he'd visited; a vast collection of CDs and vinyl listed alphabetically on a computer file.

The plan had been to form a self-image of quirkiness and individuality but he wondered if he'd become the sum of these parts—a typical, single, forty-something man, immersed in hobbies and living by a set pattern. How was anyone to know that his heart still belonged to punk and new wave, to 'anarchy, love and peace?'—his parting shot in each issue of *Word Hex*.

The book would save him, he determined, re-build him. The sabbatical would become the rest of his life.

Walking through the pub, Barrett found himself between the two men with their partners behind. He thought of stalling, promising to follow them in and slipping away. Too late, they had already covered his escape route. The pub was packed, the smell of alcohol so strong that Barrett imagined it was possible to get drunk from merely breathing in the fumes.

The throng at the bar was three or four people deep. They passed pints over their shoulders. Some wore T-shirts with slogans across the chest: 'Made in Cork' and 'All the way from Tuam' were two he noticed. A huge tricolour hung from the ceiling. Barrett could hear music, a flacketty-flacketty sound, but wasn't sure whether it came from a jukebox or band.

"I'm Mick, by the way," said the bald man, turning to Barrett.

Mick! Barrett laughed.

"Why are you laughing?"

"An Irishman called Mick, fancy that."

"What?"

The music had got louder.

"An Irishman called Mick, fancy that," shouted Barrett.

"I'm not Irish, not strictly…"

Barrett pretended he had been jostled so he could turn away and miss most of what Mick was about to say. He still heard. Mick's great-great-grandfather had left Waterford in 1910 and travelled to London to find work. Barrett nodded, bored. The story, as much as Barrett could hear, involved food parcels sent home, hardship, building sites, freedom fighting and families large enough to populate entire villages. Mick's mate finally reached the bar.

"What do you want to drink, John?" asked Mick.

"A shot of vodka please, on its own."

He heard him yell to his mate:

"Ian, he wants vodka but get him a pint as well."

The pair winked at one another. Barrett felt sick.

They found a table. Barrett wasn't sure but it looked as if they had persuaded the previous occupiers that it was their duty to make space for a rock star. Mick sat close to him. Barrett could smell his breath.

"I can't believe I'm here with you. It's incredible," said Mick.

He had already said this three times. Barrett smiled and reassured him that it was all really happening.

"I saw you at one of the bigger venues in London. Bloody hell, where was it?"

He asked his partner. She shook her head. She couldn't remember either.

"Anyway, you were brilliant, giving it all this ..." He tensed his face and pretended to play a guitar earnestly.

Barrett noticed they had each placed a mobile phone on the table. He asked whether he could borrow one to 'phone the missus'. Mick pushed his close to Barrett's face, insisting he use his.

"I can't work the bloody things. Can you tap in this number for me?"

Mick did so and passed the phone to Barrett.

Carey quit roaming the house and set down to work, reading through his collection of press cuttings on Barrett. The same few words were repeated in most of the reviews and interviews with Killing Stars: melancholic, bleak, gloomy. He found a review of an early single in *Melody Maker* that made him smile:

> 'Bloody hell lads, cheer up. You're not scraping around an African refugee camp sucking on a grain of rice a day or working your dreary balls off in a Siberian gulag wearing zilch but a tatty government-issue vest, so loosen up. Unfasten your raincoats and sing like you're glad to be alive.'

Melancholic; bleak; gloomy. Carey didn't recall Barrett this way. As a young kid he'd been filled up with happiness. Maybe Al's death had been the catalyst; everything seemed to change afterwards. Or perhaps it stemmed from his mum and dad, the fights, the falling out. But many of Barrett's songs were specifically about loss and death. Carey re-read the lyrics to *Obituary* printed on the album's inner sleeve:

> 'I know death comes in the end
> Comes as nobody's friend
> But you were different somehow
> You had immortality
> You were always there for me
> Why is it different now?'

Barrett had always been reluctant to explain his lyrics in interviews. He told *Sounds*: 'I hate lyrics that have a defined beginning, middle and end, and tell a literal straightforward story. They should be like jigsaw pieces you can fit together as you want.'

Carey found a fanzine containing one of Barrett's first interviews. The band had just signed their record deal and he was uncharacteristically candid.

```
Q: A lot of your songs deal with serious subject
   matters, often death, is there a reason for
   this?
A: I can't get my head around why people die.
   How you can have this mind knowing lots of
   things, having done lots of stuff, and then
   they're gone. At that second, none of what
   went before means anything. A fly passing by
   has more knowledge than a dead person. It
```

```
knows how to move, where the light is, where
danger is, whether it's hungry or not. The
other thing is that some kids from my school
died and it really haunted me. I even visited
their graves. I couldn't take it in, why they
had died and I was alive. What had they done
for it to happen?

Q: How come these kids died? Was it a road acci-
   dent or something?
A: No, they were separate incidents. Three died
   within the space of about a year.
```

Further into the article Barrett talked about making music:

```
"When you get a group of people playing
together at full blast and everything's
sounding great and you're lost to these songs
you've made up yourselves, it's the best
fucking feeling in the world."
```

The joy, Carey wasn't going to neglect that.

The phone lit up to show the call had been answered but Barrett couldn't hear anything. He gave it back. Mick put it to his own ear.

"No, she's there," he said. "It's a woman saying hello."

He returned it to Barrett. He still couldn't hear. The music fell quiet for a second and Barrett could make out Esther's voice.

"Where are you?"

"In Brighton, taking it easy."

The fiddles and the drums and the banjos started again, drowning her out.

Esther phoned Rupert Green immediately and asked if he would accompany her to Brighton.

"Do you know where he is exactly?" he asked.

"No, but I've got the number logged of the person whose phone he's just borrowed. He's obviously with him at the moment and if we're lucky he'll be with him a while yet."

She looked at her watch. It was 10pm.

"Rupert, we'd better go straight away. He's not been right since *Lunch Brake* and I'm worried about him. I'll drop Holly off at my mum's. If John has made a drinking buddy they'll go their separate ways when the pubs shut."

Green said he'd drive and book a couple of hotel rooms en route.

Esther dialled the number back. The call wasn't answered. She left a message:

"Hello, it's Esther here, John Barrett's wife. I see that he's just used your phone to call me. I'd be very grateful if you or John could ring me back as soon as possible, thank you."

Carey knew the kids Barrett had spoken about in the fanzine. Alan McCready had been in the school year above theirs. They noticed him because he always wore the same tartan jacket with imitation sheepskin around the collar and cuffs, and was usually on his own.

The newspaper report of his death said he'd left home one morning, telling his mum and dad he was fed up because some kids had been picking on him at school, jabbing a compass in his leg, flicking chalk at him. He walked a mile or so and climbed over a barbed wire fence where the canal ran alongside the railway track, an area known well to Barrett, Carey and the gang because it was where they often put pennies on the line. McCready lay down in front of an oncoming train.

Carey recalled what happened a few days after his death, when they were sitting on discarded car seats on wasteland.

"We helped kill that kid," said Barrett.

"What?"

"All he wanted was a friend."

"But we hardly knew him."

"Don't you remember, that day we saw him? He was standing over there."

He pointed over the railway fence to a steep embankment matted in and bracken and hawthorn. Carey had forgotten they had ever seen McCready out of school.

"Didn't he say he was looking for a football?"

"He never played football. Kids say things like that when they want to be your friend, anything to get talking."

"We didn't know."

"I did but I just ignored him."

"But we didn't know he was going to die."

"I knew he was lonely. We all did."

"The paper said he was a bit backward."

"So?"

"Well, you know."

"You could tell McCready was all right. All we had to do was talk to him."

Barrett began walking away.

"Where you going?"

"Home."

Barrett realised he had been brought into the pub as a kind of exhibit. Mick shouted people over and they squeezed through the crowd to reach the table. Barrett was continually shaking hands and signing beer mats.

He looked around and saw that the music was emanating from a band at the back of the pub, on a raised section. They were playing pro-republican songs; one was about the devil coming to earth in the form of a British soldier. Several people joined in the chorus or were tapping their feet, banging on tables.

Mick had skirted the subject for a few minutes but finally came to his point.

"Is it true about you and all those birds?"

Barrett's eyes were almost shut.

"Aye, it's all true, me hearties."

The vodka and the Guinness, the noise and the bodies; it had the effect of sealing off Barrett. He dared himself to submit to star-roving, his term for the state between sleep and being awake but inebriated, when time, with a little coercion, could be blown away like dust. He sat back in his chair. Mick had put it in his mind now: *all those birds*. When he'd been in the band, it had all been about hanging loose, sharing the passion, strumming a guitar, talking, laughing, holding and kissing. Then upstairs to bed. Living fully and resplendently in the moment, a tap turned on from heaven above.

"I've met and been with all manner of female form," he mused in one radio interview.

Paul Ashover was another of the kids who'd died. Carey remembered walking with Barrett in the school grounds and seeing him sitting among the saplings that skirted the football pitches. He had a crisp bag pressed to his face.

"What's Ashy doing?"

"It looks like he's sniffing crisps."

They had heard on the news about kids sniffing glue and thought Ashy had misunderstood and was trying to get high on prawn cocktail crisps. He was still there when the bell rang, gorging on whatever was in the bag, holding it over his nose and mouth.

The bag *was* full of glue. A few weeks later his face was encrusted with sores and he staggered as if drunk, one leg haphazardly thrown in front of the other. He disappeared from school soon afterwards; he was only fourteen. They occasionally saw him walking the streets, stopping and shouting as if disciplining a small child, obviously hallucinating.

He died within a year, discovered on the landing of a block of flats on the 'Bell, a pool of blood around his head. Another gluesniffer had stamped on him after having a vision that he was on fire.

The third kid was Craig Hoyle. During the summer holidays he'd gone with friends on a bike ride to some quarries. They waded into one of the pools to cool down. Craig swam out and shouted that he was struggling. His mates thought he was joking until he disappeared under the water. Firemen pumped through the night and his dad waited at the water's edge. As daylight broke, the body was found.

All manner of female form. He'd had sex with one girl who demanded it urgently and vigorously and then cried before taking a bath in her clothes and shouting down from the hotel balcony. Another covered her body in strange messages written in lipstick and mascara: *Them That Die'll Be The Lucky Ones; The Gutter Of The Heavens Hangs Over Me*. Several times he had to rummage through their bags to find phone numbers of friends or parents and have them picked up from the hotel.

Sometimes, after sex, he'd stare into their faces. He'd wonder what made them glow even in the half-light. Was it the shape of their face; how it was framed by the hair; the arch of an eyebrow or the angle of the bone across the cheeks? He eschewed girls who dyed their hair and built their faces around heavy make-up. He preferred those that others might pass off as plain until you hooked into the fullness of their lips, their bright eyes. Or maybe a thin neck, a forearm covered in downy hair, a small flower-patterned clip holding the fringe from her eyes: he'd fall in love with the detail. Then he'd wish himself away from the hotel and the entourage, imagining them together on a beach or sitting on grass in a park, places where ordinary people went.

Once or twice, fans had offered up their girlfriends sacrificially, proud of an association with Barrett. He declined but considered the moral dilemma to be disengaged if the girl stayed at the venue while her boyfriend went home. The girls usually excused their behaviour by saying the relationship was drawing to an end anyway. They'd grown apart. They were more like brothers and sisters now.

"But I'll be gone tomorrow," Barrett told them.

He loved saying this; it sounded like a lyric.

"That's okay."

"How will you get it back on with your long-termer?" he'd ask, realising the phrasing implied a kind of sentence.

"I'll deal with that in the morning. Like I said, we're getting round to splitting up."

He'd look in their eyes earnestly (not sure if he meant it or not) and thank God he'd fallen on the side of mystery and romance.

Leafing through the fanzines, Carey was reminded of the desolation of the late 1970s and early 1980s. It was like recalling a serious illness from which he hadn't expected to recover. Margaret Thatcher was on many covers with her condescending smile and spray-on hair. Various editors had given her eye-patches, inserted Frankenstein stitches on her cheeks, fastened horns to her head, put an axe in her hand. 'Evil Cow' was daubed across her forehead on one. She was depicted beside Ronald Reagan (Ronald Raygun, more usually) on a few, with the insinuation of a sexual relationship between them. Over time, Carey had felt his attitude softening on many issues but his hatred of Thatcher was undimmed. He didn't feel remotely sorry to see her image desecrated.

The main themes on the inside pages were the threat of nuclear war and the fight against racism — most were adorned with the CND symbol and Anti-Nazi League arrows. Alongside interviews with bands, most of them pictured scowling and flicking Vs, editorials raged against the government, bureaucrats, unemployment, the US, bland pop music, the police, the nuclear family, capitalism, meat-eating, censorship, vivisection, supermarkets, the tabloid press, Radio One DJs, religion, the anti-cannabis lobby and *Top of the Pops*. There was a lot to be angry about.

Carey recalled the fanzine writers they had met when the band started out. They were usually skinny and humourless ghost-faced kids, pathologically shy, refusing to make eye contact. As they mumbled prepared questions, their voices were barely audible:

"In your view have the ethics of punk been compromised by the willingness of too many bands to take corporate inducement?"

These protracted interviews would soon begin to feel like a dull ache. Absolute concentration had to be maintained at all times because one deviation from the punk/fanzine dogma and the lot could come crashing down. They learned quickly that these kids might have been under-fed and over-earnest but they could run people through with their pens. Give them a few loose words and six months to staple their fanzine together and they were screaming in 30pt bold caps: '**HYPOCRITE**'.

Often, to avoid this kind of retribution, Killing Stars 'set Fisher on them', knowing he'd tender some of his winky wanky woo, leaving them bewildered. Carey still had a tape of one of these interviews:

"Jason, how would you describe the band's politics?"

He replied slowly, sculpting the words as if from wet clay:

"Well, as one would say. No, as *I* would say because I hate the word 'one' because it reminds me of my boss and he's a cunt. Where was I? Politics? Well, in this country, so to speak, as we are now and have been before, as a matter of opinion, to my opinion shall I say—if you don't mind—and I sense that you don't, because you have asked the question to me, that this country is, well, how can I say, strung up on a hamstring kind of thing."

Barrett's star-roving was interrupted by a face pressed close to his. He was circling down, back to the pub, the Guinness spittle and the racket.

"It's me, Mick," said Mick, noticing the glassy look in Barrett's eyes.

Barrett wanted to say, 'Are you taking the Mick, Mick, with all these Micks?' but wasn't sure he'd be able to form the sentence properly.

They were asking him something. And they were different people from before, faces he didn't recognise. What were they saying? What did they want? One of them had straggly hair and a large piece of wood in his hand. He was wearing braces over a stripy shirt. Barrett realised he was holding a guitar and appeared to be offering it to him. Did he want him to sign it? Tune it up?

"John, he wants to know whether you'll play a song."

Carey found a piece he'd written for *Word Hex* on Russia's invasion of Afghanistan. He also fished out the lyrics to *El Salvador* about America's activities there:

> 'Trapped in the middle
> The eagle and the bear
> Talons in El Salvador, claws in Afghanistan
> Political puppets for a power regime
> Heads fall limp at the cut of a string
> Mutilated bodies left to decay
> This is the dawn of the tyrant's day.'

The threat of nuclear war had felt omnipresent. Coming to your town: melted faces, mushroom clouds, Hiroshima, death,

Nagasaki, disease. Carey used to wake up anxious, imagining that a car door slamming on the street was the aftershock of a fallen missile. Protect and survive. Stock up on tins of food. Stay indoors. Hide under the table. He used to worry that they'd soon be stockpiling rings drawn from the fingers of the dead and comforting wide-eyed women, like in scenes from *The War Game*. Everywhere, there were reminders of this doom-to-come: marches, documentaries, badges, posters. The war hadn't started but they already felt they were suffering from radiation sickness. And it was relentless, suffusing them with despondency, their lives placed in a polythene bag.

Barrett told them repeatedly that he was in no state to sing.

"Just a couple of songs," they begged.

"I can't remember how to walk, never mind sing."

"Go on, a couple of your old hits."

"I don't know the words. It's a long time ago."

The man with the guitar was joined by others who Barrett presumed were the rest of the band. Outside this circle, another group of people were urging him 'not to be soft' and to 'get on with it'.

"Come on then," he said.

Most nights on television, workers were interviewed who had been made redundant, heads slumped into their donkey jackets, seething about Thatcher, grumbling that the unions had sold them down the river. At school, if anyone was brave enough to aspire to anything half-decent it was seen as arrogance or that they were kidding themselves, living on dreams. When Carey told his careers teacher he wanted to be a writer he was handed a leaflet about trainee manager schemes at Marks and Spencer.

"There'll be some writing involved."

Carey remembered conversations with his dad, being told he'd be bloody lucky to get a job at a newspaper, any newspaper, never mind working as a *writer*. He'd better take anything available when there were three million unemployed.

Barrett took the guitar and made his way through the pub with people patting his back, shaking his hand. Mick followed close behind with his hands on his shoulders like a trainer leading a boxer to the ring. They arrived at the 'stage'—a piece of speckled linoleum laid across the floorboards. People were holding up mobile phones; they had called friends and were about to relay John Barrett live from their local pub. Why couldn't they enjoy the moment for what it was, thought Barrett. The idea was to let go, give yourself over to the music, the band, the people you were with.

A couple of blokes jumped on the lino, wrapping their arms around Barrett and smiling madly while their friends took photos. The flashes of light temporarily blinded him and made faces taper like the flame from a candle. Behind him, the band were taking up their positions. The drummer tightened the snare drum with its key and wiped his sticks with a cloth. The bassist had his hand stretched across the neck, holding down the strings to stop them buzzing. At first Barrett didn't see the ensemble to his right. Fucking hell: a fiddle player, a couple of blokes with penny whistles, another with a hand-held drum—proper Mick stuff.

Barrett felt for the borrowed guitar at his midriff and ran his hand across the wood. He stared into the faces in front of him before lifting his gaze to the tricolour above them, noticing once more the shamrocks and harps on various flags. Only one song was apt here, a song that everyone in the room would recognise and which meant something to them all. He spread out his arms as a signal to the band that it began quietly and put his forefinger to his lips, imploring the audience to fall silent.

Carey played Killing Stars' first two albums consecutively. The sound had changed markedly from when he'd been a member. It was layered, the guitars powerful and flickering into edgy, fleeting rhythms. Fisher's keyboards provided dashes of melody, hooks to stand as counterpoints to Barrett's vocals.

When the debut album had been released originally, Carey had said to friends that it was too polished, implying that Barrett had made compromises, toning down the political content, smoothing out the sound. He realised now that songs like *Brixton Riots* or *El Salvador* would have been incongruous. Neither album contained any quirky, offbeat numbers or concessions to half-hearted ideas. Instead, the tracks were crafted and blended as a lyrical and musical whole.

On the second album Barrett had included a track obviously about Al called *Adventure Lit His Star*. Until hearing this, Carey had consoled himself that Barrett's success was good fortune or through force of will.

'I had a friend, born inside a teardrop ...'

Carey hurt when he first heard the song and many times afterwards; it was so honest. Unlike most rock stars, Barrett hadn't glued together a few meaningless or arcane phrases and passed it off as profound. This was the real thing.

Listening again, Carey recognised that it was all there, the times bottled: the fear, the streets, the boot-boys, the damp, the bomb, the hanging around, the onslaught on hope. And despite the reviewers' fixation with the gloominess, Barrett had still found room for optimism — the mentions here and there of a girl's smile or small acts of kindness, as if he hadn't given up on finding a way to some kind of happiness.

"And did those feet in ancient times walk upon England's mountains green ..."

A few giggled, not sure if it was a joke. The drummer tried to lock into the tempo but the other musicians were motionless. Barrett continued, looking defiantly into the faces a few feet away. His voice was sweet and tuneful. The drummer gave up. Barrett took over the slow rhythm, tapping the body of the guitar. From the back of the room, a slow handclap broke out, and booing.

"Ireland for the Irish!" shouted a man to Barrett's left. People laughed.

The booing grew louder and the shouts more hostile. Although he was on almost the same level, they respected the performance space, though several moved forward a few inches. He sang every verse, remembering the words from school. He had to increase the volume slightly as it went on, to make himself heard. At the end a few clapped, probably in admiration of his audacity, but most booed. They were largely pantomime boos, good-natured aside from the odd person making hand gestures. One man with a thick moustache and red cheeks was motioning that Barrett was a wanker.

Barrett called the fiddle player to his side. He was wearing scuffed Dr Marten boots and tight black trousers with holes at the knees.

"Play us some of that fucketty-fucketty stuff, will you?"

The fiddler didn't understand.

"One of those daft jigs."

Barrett had a plan. He was going to further antagonise an audience already roused to a pitch of near-violence. This would be everything at once: High Theatre, performance art, rock-'n'roll; the most wonderful piece of agit-prop situationism ever ever. He could imagine Carl and Fisher out there, all those kids from years back—the new wave apostles, loving it, pleading for more. Give it them, give it them good. Do it for punk. Do it for Art. Let go. Burn down the house.

He waited until the fiddling and whistling had built to a decent level and moved to the microphone.

> "You're a shit-shovelling load of dirty Micks
> As thick as the day you were born
> And fancy that, the Pope's a twat
> And the Virgin Mary's a tart."

Out of respect to his hosts he sang it in an approximation of an Irish accent. He made it through the first verse successfully but as he moved on, making it up as he went along, he was showered in beer. A middle-aged woman threw the first pint, hitting him clean in the face. He gasped. The man at her side jumped forward and punched Barrett in the shoulder causing him to stagger back from the microphone stand. Barrett leaned forward again, determined to continue. Nothing could hurt him, he thought. This was a dream, wasn't it? Star-roving. No one got hurt in a dream. The stand was slammed to the ground.

The microphone went with it, the feedback causing it to squeal like a dying alien. They were all about him now, three or four ready to fight and more behind. Mick was holding out his arms, fending them off.

"He's pissed, he doesn't know what he's doing."

His mate Ian was also on the lino, pushing them back. He turned to Barrett and motioned with his head to the fire door behind.

"Fucking get through there, before they kill you."

Barrett pushed the bar but it didn't budge.

"Give it a boot."

Barrett was so drunk he couldn't lift his leg more than a few inches from the floor. Ian shoved him aside and crashed his heel against the metal bar. The door flung open. It was completely dark outside. Barrett ran and began falling down stone steps. He fell hard on his back, his head thudding against each step as he made his way to the bottom. He tried to get up but the pain was excruciating. Scrambling to his knees, he crawled into the stairwell. He couldn't see anything but felt beer crates and barrels around him. He heard footsteps and voices above.

"Where is he?"

A taxi passed the side-street next to the pub's yard.

"The bastard's probably in that cab now, laughing at us."

The door slammed shut and the music started again. Barrett brought his knees to his chin and wrapped his arms around them. Blood trickled down from the wound on his head. He dabbed it with his finger and transferred it to his tongue. It tasted metallic. He reached inside his coat and pulled out the vodka.

Mick and Ian stayed in the pub, promising to follow their girl-friends home later. They had to keep talking about what had happened to convince themselves it was real. The pub emptied after a while and the bar staff put towels over the taps and brushed glass and crisps from the floor. Mick took the phone from his pocket. It flashed that he had seven messages. They were all from Esther.

"Christ, I've got a shit-load of messages. I bet they're from Barrett's wife. Do you think I should call her back?"

"Why not?"

"He might not want her to know where he is."

"Get her rung. Wherever he is now, I reckon he could do with some help. He's going to have a steaming hangover in the morning at the very least."

Mick phoned her. She asked him to stay at the pub until they got there. She was in a car, she said, about twenty minutes from Brighton.

"But he's not here," said Mick.

"Where is he?"

"I don't know, he ran off."

"Ran off?"

"Yeah. He got into a bit of a scuffle. He's okay though, I think.'

Mick promised he'd wait.

The pair left the pub and sat on a low wall outside.

"What do you think she'll look like?"

"Smallish, blonde haired, fit as fuck. Aren't all pop stars' wives like that?" said Mick.

"Suppose so."

After a few seconds Mick shook his head:

"John Barrett, in this pub! It's untrue."

They sang a few lines from a couple of Killing Stars songs, using their thighs as drums.

Green's Jag drew up. Esther got out quickly and walked over. Ian whispered to Mick:

"Pretty close, except for the hair."

They told her what had happened, how he'd goaded the audience.

"But his grandparents were Irish," said Esther. "He's got figurines of Mary and Bernadette all round the house that used to belong to them. He's always doing this. He's got this stupid idea that getting everyone pissed off is some kind of artistic statement."

She asked where they had last seen him. They led her to the back of the pub and pointed at the door.

"How could he out-run a gang of people if he was so drunk?" she asked.

They hadn't thought of this. As she spoke, they heard a moan. Esther followed the sound. Blood had run down Barrett's forehead and congealed. When he turned to her, the headlights from a passing car picked out his streaked face.

"John, are you okay?"

He said his back hurt and he had a tingling sensation in his legs. She asked about his head.

"I just need a plaster on it. It's my back that's killing me."

Barrett wanted to get into the car and go home but Green insisted they call an ambulance.

At the hospital a nurse stitched the head wound. She said the consultant would examine his back in the morning; he could move his toes, so nothing was broken. He was put in a side ward where he quickly fell asleep. Esther took the almost-empty vodka bottle from his coat.

Once more, Barrett made the papers. Someone from the pub had taken his picture and sold it to *The Sun*. He was photographed 'star-roving', eyes shut, mouth open. The story didn't match the picture. It said he'd barged in shouting obscenities about the Irish and insisted he was handed the microphone. They hadn't picked up on his admittance to hospital but Green knew it was a matter of time. The town's evening paper, the *Argus*, carried this later as an exclusive, reporting that he had suffered a back injury in a fracas outside the Golden Lion.

Green was less perturbed by this new controversy but it crossed his mind that such regular unsavoury appearances in newspapers often formed a countdown to tragedy. He couldn't understand how Barrett wanted to be king of the world and simultaneously not care if he lived or died.

On the drive back to London he thought of the times he had tried to help, from heartfelt advice to booking him into a clinic (which Barrett didn't attend). He remembered the conversations:

"You're drinking too much, John."

"Leave me be, for I know what I'm doing."

"But how did you get to this point?"

"I'm just like all the rest, the golden children that end up drowning themselves."

"You're sounding like William Blake now."

"Rock 'n' roll does it to you. Come on Rupe, you know how it works. There's booze everywhere. You do an interview and you're given some. You get to the venue and there are crates in the dressing room. You drink before the show, after it. You're on the ceiling after a gig. Then there's always someone wanting you to stay up back at the hotel: have a drink, pal. In the morning the whisky bottles are all over the room. So you take a sip before breakfast. You're pissed from the night before and you realise you feel good, that you're kind of passing through everything. And you get to like the glide. So you have another drink after breakfast. Before you know it, you're supping all day."

Green knew all this but there was a difference between heavy drinking and alcoholism. He had seen that as Barrett's career had wound down he'd used the freed-up time to nurse himself through and accommodate the cycle of drinking — sleeping in late, not bothering to wash or dress, not returning phone messages. Barrett had boasted that the hangover, which had formed at least an intermittent restraint while he was busy, was largely avoided because he had mastered the skilful courtship of sleep and intake. The secret was to keep the ball rolling, the vodka flowing, so there was no drop-dead stop. Only if he slept more than four hours continually, which he hadn't for years, did it set in deep. He told Green he had learned to wake every hour or so, take a sip and kiss himself good night all over again. He didn't mind the rigmarole. It was worth it.

"I'm an inveterate soak."

"That's what cock-eyed romantics call being a pisshead."

"Oh Rupert, must you be so brutal with me?"

Barrett had tried occasionally to stop drinking but Green wasn't sure which was worse: scrubbed up and pious sobriety or the habitual alcoholism to which they had both adapted. When he stopped, Barrett was aware that he lost his sharpness and

258

became like everyone else. As a kid in Killing Stars he'd been emphatic about everything. If anyone asked or even if they didn't, he'd tell them and refuse to qualify or temper his opinion. People liked this, it made him someone to follow. Off the drink, he saw all sides, took his time, stopped and thought. He also kept infuriating lists, counting down the hours and days since his last drink, dragging everyone into the crusade.

"Two days now, Rupe. Two days since I touched a drop."

"Great."

"Is that all you've got to say?"

"Double great."

"That's more like it."

A few days later, the lists were torn up or lost.

Green parked in the courtyard below his office. He'd decided to sleep on the sofa bed adjacent to his desk, ready for an early start in the morning. As he pressed the security code into the doorpad and made his way up the stairs he realised he'd all but given up on Barrett. The pep talks were a waste of time. Barrett and his ilk (addictive personalities, though he wasn't sure of the definitive term) were beyond his understanding. Sure, he could talk with them on roughly the same level, share the same jokes and taste in music, but no matter how rational they appeared, how convincing, there was always a door open in their head that they couldn't shut. And through this door came both the need to drink and the self-deception that made it permissible to them, whatever the consequences.

★

The phone went.

"Hello," said Carey.

He'd been making notes for the book and it was the first time he'd spoken all day, so his voice was chalky.

"I suppose you've heard the news."

It was Chris from the paper.

"What?"

"Barrett's in bother again. Apparently he's in hospital in Brighton."

"What's happened?"

"They think some Irish guys beat him up."

"Shit."

Carey put the phone down and began to panic. Not now. Don't screw up. Keep it together, John, for my sake. You owe me this. He rang Green immediately, on the pretext of concern about Barrett.

"Hello Rupert, it's David Carey here, the fella who's doing the book on John."

He asked about Barrett.

"The doctors haven't had a proper look at him yet but it's obvious he's damaged his back. As soon as he's on his feet again, I'll make sure you can collect the material you need."

"That's fantastic, but the main thing is that John gets better and sorts himself out."

He had really wanted to ask if it was okay to visit him in hospital and begin the interviews: time was pressing. He phoned again an hour later.

"I've been thinking, Rupert. As you know, I've only got three months to complete the bulk of the work and if I'm late meeting up with John I'm going to get behind."

"I could ask Nesta to put back the delivery date if you're running late."

No, no, no—it had to be now. Otherwise the book might get postponed indefinitely or cancelled altogether. Carey didn't want to return to the paper with its have-a-go heroes; ex-footballers pushing over piles of pennies in pubs and Jack Sutcliffe talking about all-our-yesterdays journalism. He had started to resent the books on his shelves too. They mocked him by having someone else's name on their spine. It had to be now.

"If I see him in hospital I'll be gentle with him, Rupert. Nothing too demanding, I promise. It's not like I've any need to be confrontational or anything. It might even form part of his recuperation."

He brushed himself on the shoulder, checking for slime.

Barrett drifted in and out of sleep. He came round properly by lunchtime the next day. His mouth was dry. He said his head was throbbing. Esther gave him water.

"Do you know what's happened to you?"

"Not really."

"You fell down some stairs outside a pub."

He pulled a face to show he didn't remember. She stayed by his side all afternoon. In the early evening she went back to the hotel but within an hour a nurse phoned and asked her to return immediately; Barrett was acting strange.

When she arrived he was sitting on the floor by a radiator in the corridor, his body tense.

"They want me to do it but I can't. I've told them I can't but they won't believe me."

"Do what?"

"Walk across this ledge. It's too high. I'm going to fall."

"There's no ledge, John"

"What's that then?" he said, sarcastically.

"It's some tiles on the floor, that's all."

He blinked and kept his eyes shut, shaking his head as if he thought she was stupid.

"Who's asking you to do this, John?"

"Him there."

He pointed down the empty corridor.

"He's all smiles now that you're here but when you've gone he'll be out again making me do it when I've told him I can't. I've not been trained."

He started up again:

"They have these things to watch over us, making sure we do it. They're in the walls, little things."

"Cameras?"

"No, not cameras. These little creatures. They can burrow through plaster. You'll see one in a minute. They're always breaking through."

She asked him if he knew where he was.

"I'm waiting for Al. He's in a class."

Esther assumed he thought he was at college.

"You're in a hospital, love, not college. And Al's dead. He died quite a while ago, remember." She had never called him 'love' before but it felt right now.

"Give over, he's not dead. Don't say that. It's bad luck. He was here before. He's done the training for all this. He knows the ins and outs. There's only him who'll believe me. He won't — that bastard there."

He pointed down the corridor again. He was moving his elbows and knees in an eccentric circular motion. She looked behind to the two nurses and spoke quietly to them:

"Has he had strong medication?"

"Only painkillers."

"Is it the bang on the head?"

"It could be, but it's unlikely."

Esther tried to coax Barrett back to bed.

"Leave me alone Est, don't move me. It's too far down."

She was relieved he knew who she was.

It took nearly fifteen minutes to persuade him to get into bed. Barrett skittered across the floor nervously as if walking along a rope bridge. Lying on his back, he stared intensely at the ceiling. Esther was beckoned to the nurses' station.

"Is John on any kind of non-prescription drugs?" she was asked.

"Not that I'm aware."

She suddenly remembered the vodka, that he was an alcoholic.

"He has a drink problem."

"How much of a problem?"

"Quite serious."

"That's probably it, then. He's suffering withdrawal symptoms. We'll have to give him something to help, otherwise he'll be climbing the walls."

Carey set off for Brighton in the early afternoon. The journey began in bright sunshine but the sun dipped behind clouds and the sky turned sludge grey. Flies crashed into the windscreen, dotting it with red and black specks. He switched on the radio. The songs were about heartbreak and loss.

He called at a service station. Children were everywhere, playing on the machines, running around. He was reflecting again: no kids of his own. What would be left behind when he'd gone? Wasn't this everything with him and Barrett, the need to leave a mark? And why was he alone? Why had his wife left him, all that 'in love but not *in* love' routine? It was nothing personal, she said. These things happened, and it was as upsetting for her as it was him. But what did the next man have that he didn't? And why did her affair (he hated the word 'affair'—so flimsy for something so catastrophic) have to begin when they were still together, still married? Come to think of it, and why with someone they both knew?

Years before, at one of the paper's Christmas parties, someone had told Carey that he was the species of man known commonly as 'goodus blokeus'.' He knew what this meant. On the surface it was a compliment but it picked him out as someone light on charisma. He was the *nice* guy.

He collected a plastic tray from the pile and ordered lasagne. He sat down and chewed on the food. It smelled of blocked drains and was clinging to his teeth. While he ate, he became aware of a lad standing nearby in a red and white uniform. He was waiting to clean the tables and stared across the room blankly. He looked like something that had been re-heated in one of their microwave ovens and his sad, defeated expression was making Carey feel worse. He headed back to the car.

The hallucinations stopped. Esther told him it was as if a demon had taken over his body and then left again.

"Did my head go all the way round?"

"Not far off."

The skin on the back of his hand where the drip had been inserted was black like an inkblot but with a yellow border. Esther stared at it. Barrett did too. They chatted for a few minutes and she sensed his mood change. He turned his head away.

"What's wrong?" she asked.

He gathered his breath in short sucks.

"Stuff, being here."

"You'll be out soon."

"I knew this would happen."

She asked him to explain. He told her about the time his dad had taken him to the asthma clinic at hospital when he was a kid.

"He loved me, you know, my dad."

"I know he did."

"He didn't like me being ill. He had this strange attitude, like he believed if we all ignored it, it would go away. But once he realised I was really ill, he'd do anything for me. He used to stand with me at the back doorstep in the middle of the night, helping me get my breath. He spoke to me then like we were pals. You think about things in here ... something happened that day at the hospital."

"What?"

"Dad got talking to this old bloke in the waiting room. He was about seventy and wheezing away. He was chatting and then stopped, looking right at me. He said he could remember when he was as young as me and how time had flashed past. He clicked his fingers to show how quickly it had gone. It's never left me that image. And here I am now. It's my turn."

She shook her head.

"It wasn't being in hospital that meant it was nearly the end of his life. It was because he was old — probably twice the age you are now."

After a few seconds she asked if he was missing the drink.

"No."

He said it so blithely, it made her suspicious. She glanced across to the men in the other beds. Had he already set up a supply route?

"Not at all?"

"I could knock a slug back if you passed me a bottle but, no, I'm fine."

"Is that because you've gone through a kind of cold turkey and don't want it to be in vain?"

"It's more to do with the fact that I'm stapled to this bed and even moving an inch kills me."

Esther had arranged to meet Rupert in a restaurant after the hospital visit. He was already there when she arrived. He stood up and pulled out a chair. She looked down, folding the napkin on the table. Rupert noticed she was crying.

"He's going to be okay," he said.

"It's not that."

"What is it then?"

She shook her head. Rupert ordered drinks.

"I'm not sure I can go on," she said.

"If it's upsetting you, I'll take over the regular visits. Dave Carey is seeing him tomorrow."

"No, I don't mean that. I mean I don't know whether I can go on with John. He's going to die, isn't he?"

"He's strong. He's a fighter as much as he's anything."

"The drink will get him in the end, though. He's not come anywhere near stopping in all the years you and I have known him, has he? We're just faces at the window."

"It can feel like that at times."

"You've been here before, Rupert, you know musicians inside out — what happens next?"

"Some pull through, it's not unheard of."

"I don't want this."

"I know. I'm aware of how much you care about John."

"That's it — I'm not sure any more whether I do. Not enough as I should, anyway. I think I'm through, Rupe. I don't want to spend my time running after him and I don't want people to feel sorry for me any more. Why does my life have to be forever tangled up with his mess?"

"You're down because you're in the middle of a crisis. I got like that when he freaked out on *Lunch Brake*."

"I feel like I've run out of love. There's a limit. I don't want to be one of those people at someone's beck and call, having no life of their own."

"I'd no idea you felt this way, no idea."

"That's because I'm good at covering things up. I've had to be. It's a role, isn't it? I play it because I believe I should but when you're bombarded with all this, you're not sure whether you mean it or not any more, whether it's just a habit. I love him but it's not the proper love between a man and a woman. I feel like his mother sometimes or his daughter. And he's never been a proper father to Holly. It's like he's a hologram of a father. You can see him but there's no flesh and blood."

"He thinks the world of her, you know."

"He says he does but that's because he's sentimental. He hasn't put the hours in, he never will. To me, this alcoholism thing is a legitimised form of self-love. It gets you out of everything."

"They say it's a disease, don't they?"

"Only because it suits some people to see it that way. If John was living penniless on the street, I'd understand it. People like that turn to booze and drugs so they can escape and go off somewhere else in their heads. John's surrounded by luxury, everything he could possibly need. His alcoholism is an indulgence. I know that might sound harsh but I don't care any more."

"Where do you go from here? Are you seriously saying you're thinking of leaving him?"

"I don't know."

Walking across the hospital grounds, Carey became apprehensive; it had been a long time. At the entrance he passed an old man in pyjamas and a dressing gown, holding a metal frame from which a drip was suspended. Carey felt guilty for being youngish, light on his feet and healthy.

He arrived at the ward and moved along the central corridor, peering into the ante rooms. He heard Barrett before he saw him, his laughter. He was sitting up, joking with another patient.

"Dave. Bloody hell!"

"You look surprisingly well," said Carey.

"It does you the world of good surfing down stone steps using your head as a brake. You don't look too bad either: a bit grey at the gills but otherwise, as was."

"Are they looking after you?"

"Can't complain."

"I thought you might have gone private."

"Come on, Brother Carey, and how would I square that with the branch?"

"What have they told you about your back?"

"They think it's going to heal okay but I'm going to be laid low for weeks."

"I'm here about the book."

"Right, pull the curtains round so these reprobates can't hear us."

Carey sat down. He thanked Barrett for the commission and began explaining how he wanted the book to be an original and incisive piece of work. And how sorry he was he'd have to ask so many questions but everything had to be just right, accurate, true to life.

"I trust you," said Barrett. "Do what you think best."

Barrett grimaced.

"What is it?" asked Carey.

"If you'd have stuck with the band you wouldn't have to go through all this. Before we start, remind me: why did you leave exactly?"

"I couldn't play."

"You could. You had your own sound, that thing with the fuzz box."

"I never felt I belonged on stage."

"No one *belonged*, you had to tell yourself you did. It's a shame because in the beginning it was always me and you and Jason, with Al sort of around the edges. That was the real gang, wasn't it? A good group isn't about everyone being able to play well. You need people to shape it, give it heart. With you, I always saw you doing sleeve notes, sorting out the artwork, all that stuff where you have to know what's cool. The best bands, the ones that matter, are a group of people singing about their lives, their mams and dads, the streets they came from, the crap jobs they've had, everything. And serving it all up pure to the public, saying, 'This is what we are — do you recognise any of it?' All the better if you were dragged up because punters see a kind of glamour in squalor. Ideally they'd like you to have been brought up by wolves, living half wild on the streets. That's what rock 'n' roll is, why bands from these shitty estates get to be massive. And do you know why people like all this? It's because they're envious but rooting for you at the same time. Their own gang — the kids they grew up with — didn't stick together. They see you as someone who made it through and they want to be part of it. That's why they buy the records. It reminds them of what could have been."

"You're still making speeches, I see."

"Too right. It's my job; someone's got to do it."

"How's it felt being back in the news since *Lunch Brake*?"

Barrett grinned.

"Well, it's taken me right back to the old theme of me as the grand fornicator. Any age, any size: bring them on, lie them down."

"I was going to ask you about all that."

"Right then, let's get it nailed straight away, so to speak. Basically I got it tangled up in the rock'n'roll myth. It went with the travelling, life coming at you at faster miles an hour. I know the *Melody Maker* piece was a mistake but lots of girls viewed our liaisons the same as I did—a fantastic way to pass the time. It was so easy to get them, if I'm being honest. All I'd do was glance over and they'd be hooked. One time, I was with a group of people in this hotel. I was jetlagged so bad I couldn't keep my eyes open. There was this gorgeous black girl. These other blokes, all of them at least as good-looking as me, were chatting with her, sort of competing for her attention. At the end of the night I put my key on the table for a second so she could see the room number. I went up and within five minutes she was at the door, not just wanting sex but telling me how I exuded this magnetism. I kidded myself that the charm would have been with me whether I was famous or not but it was the fame and only that which made the difference. It meant I could short-circuit everything. All I had to do was be enigmatic and that meant doing nothing apart from being there."

"Did you fall in love with any of them?"

"The corny answer is to say all of them because I did, in a way. When you're like me and fancy yourself as a creative person it's well within your capabilities, believe me, to be both carnal and romantic at the same time. But, if I'm being truthful, I'd say that until Judy came along I'd never loved anyone, not truly, madly, full-up-to-the brim overflowing with it, anyway."

Barrett and Judy had known each another for years. She booked bands into The Hut, replacing surly Sue. She also managed a few local groups and had stayed in touch when Barrett left town, sending him tapes, asking for advice and the odd phone number.

They had arranged to meet one afternoon in Hyde Park. He hadn't seen her for almost a year and was surprised how much she'd changed. She was wearing an Echo and the Bunnymen T-shirt, the one with the band silhouetted against a night sky.

"You look different," he said.

"In what way?"

"Not sure. Cooler, I suppose. No, slacker."

"Cool or slack in a good way?"

"In a good way. Yeah, definitely a good way."

They were sitting beneath a tall beech tree, its leaves forming a huge green umbrella. She smiled.

"What are you smiling about?"

"How nice it is here."

Carey changed the subject.

"We never did the clichéd teenage things, did we? All that stupid tantrums stuff."

"No. We rebelled for real. Punk and new wave was a kickback to our parents' generation. If you go back and play those early records there is a real hatred of what they represented. So many of the songs were about how dumb and horrible it was to get married and have kids and a mortgage. Look at the sleeves. Loads of them were pretty sick pastiches of this idea, like it was inherently evil to aspire to it. "

"Why do you think this was?"

"We saw it as the place where all the boring stiffs from school were heading, kids who never questioned anything. They were going to settle down, make babies and turn into their parents. The other thing was that our parents' generation was a nightmare. Most of them were in their twenties in the 1960s but they didn't *swing*. They were putting on their best gear for Whit Week, eating ham sandwiches at the in-laws on a Sunday night, waiting for buses in the pissing rain. They lived their lives in black and white. Naturally, this meant they wanted to repress us as much as they'd been repressed themselves. We never got any encouragement to have ideas about anything artistic. The whole thrust of punk was that we were lifting the lid off the whole thing. It was all retaliatory. Learn to play an instrument? Why bother when you can make your own noise? Go to art college if you want to paint pictures? Bollocks, we'll cut this stuff up and stick it down and call it art if we want. Kids were writing novels without any punctuation in, doing plays where it was just shouting and swearing. That was the last time this country had a genuine grass roots cultural movement."

"What years are we talking?"

"1976 to late 1982, possibly 1983. You'd have to ask a sociologist, I suppose."

Carey thought: was Barrett so solemn—pompous even—back then? Didn't he used to laugh at himself, doubt himself? Or had they always sermonised like this and it was he who had changed, softened, over the years? No, he decided, it was more simple than that—he'd grown up, and Barrett hadn't. It was what happened when you stopped reading, stopped learning, in late 1982, possibly 1983, and surrounded yourself with sycophants. Say what you want, anything, and it was assumed profound because it came from the lips of someone considered charismatic, worthy. You stayed a forever kid. He was glad the tape recorder was running because he wasn't listening, not properly. It was a drone, the same thing re-hashed—punk, new wave, righteous anger, the routine paean to the outsider. He wanted to challenge Barrett, rip into his half-baked theories, but reminded himself that it was his job to reflect his subject's viewpoint, not provide a critical analysis. If Barrett wanted to sound like a stuck record with pretensions to intellectualism, it was *his* lookout. Carey would write is as he found it, ha-ha.

Judy said she loved parks. Barrett said he did, too. She asked if he'd seen the couple sitting on the grass at the entrance, their arms around one another.

"No."

"I'm surprised."

"Me too, because looking is my trademark. You've read my lyrics."

"I'm sure."

"What does that mean?"

"I think you only look at things you choose to and then go into great detail, acting like you're the first person to see things in that certain, special way."

"Very astute," he said, stroking his chin. "Very astute indeed, Miss Moneypenny."

The talking was effortless. He realised how easy it would have been to put his arm around her, hold her hand.

"Did you actually like your mum and dad?" asked Carey.

"I'm not talking about my folks specifically. They were like they were because of the way they'd been wired. It was that post-war austerity thing, powdered eggs and ration books. They were happy just to be alive, breathing in fresh air, walking around without bombs raining down on them. This was a step up from *their* parents and then we came along and wanted to take it a bit further. Another thing is that we had Margaret Thatcher. She focused the rebellion by being such a bitch, talking in that yucky fake posh voice and openly declaring war on the working-classes. It wasn't like now where you can't see your enemy and the repression is so subtle."

"We were proper working-class warriors, weren't we?"

"What do you mean, *were*? I still am, more so. I've been talked down to so many times by arseholes who think they know more than me because of their toff accent or because they went to public school. I resent the way we were written off at school. Most people haven't got a clue what it was like in that kind of environment where you had to pretend to be thick so you didn't get picked on."

"How have you reconciled earning lots of money with your left-wing views?"

"Don't ask that."

"Why not?"

"It's naughty."

"It's a valid question."

"Okay then, I sends a lot to charities and to the poor and sick in all corners of the world, I does."

"You're evading the issue."

"No I'm not, I'm issuing the evasion."

Carey had to unclench his teeth.

A few weeks later Judy was in town again. They met at a Giraffe in Flames' show in Soho. Carl had abandoned synthesisers and recruited Johno, an old pal from school, as 'lead prankster'. The pair staged impromptu 'happenings' while a tape of what sounded like mating whales played in the background. They had saved their most extravagant show for the capital, Carl throwing offal from the stage while Johno, in full radiation fall-out suit, used a gas primer to set alight an effigy of Margaret Thatcher. The fire alarm sounded and the audience decamped outside.

Afterwards Barrett and Judy were alone at her friend's house where she stayed when she was in London. Barrett was sitting on the floor, his back against the settee. Judy was lying across it, slouched so her head rested against the cushions near its arm. They had been drinking at the concert, giggling on the car park, and had gone through a bottle of wine at the house. She asked him about his new album, what bands he was listening to, how often he thought of home, was he happy. She stopped talking. He closed his eyes. He didn't have the usual sensation of drink coshing him to sleep but was alert in his tiredness. He momentarily forgot she was there, while also being aware that sharing the same space felt good. He felt her hand on the top of his head. She stroked his hair. He opened his eyes.

"It's not fair," she said.

"What isn't?"

"Me and you."

"I know," he said.

"Why did I have to get married?"

He turned to face her, smiling.

"You had to. You needed the chains of tradition and compliance to bind you tight."

"Don't joke."

She was crying.

"I'm falling in love with you," she whispered.

He'd heard this said a million times, in films, in songs, but it had never sounded so sincere.

"But maybe that's what's given us both edge, especially you with the music, having to fight for things and not getting them on a plate."

"Possibly, but I could have done without it, thank you very much. We were a long time in that fucking school. As it happens, we were okay, we made it through, but what about the ones who didn't? That kid who killed himself on the railway line, others that had the shit kicked out of them every day. Do you remember that psychopath Robert Smithson who used to hang kids off the bridge over the motorway? While we were suffering all that, other kids elsewhere, rich kids, were being told they were great, kept away from the nutters, and, lo, they're now running the country. Most of the top blokes at record companies went to public schools. Fancy that, they're even running rock'n'roll, the branch of the corporate family business that's supposed to champion the underdog and provide a dissenting voice."

"Do you ever get accused of having a chip on your shoulder?"

"Of course I do. That's how they disempower you. They're clever. They have ways of discrediting arguments that get too close to the truth. Do you know what is our greatest weakness, the working-class? We want to be liked. They don't have that problem, the middle-class. They like themselves enough as it is. We're always seeking approval, doffing the cap. We're too easily hurt and put off doing anything."

This was all good material. Carey was surprised at Barrett's lucidity; Esther had warned him he might be tired and confused.

"You seem really with-it."

"I know, it's weird. I feel like my mind's racing. Have you ever been in hospital?"

"No, not to stay."

"I don't know whether it's because it's all white and bland and everything is done for you but, this last day or so, I've had this feeling of seeing things more clearly. All the peripheral stuff is washed away."

It was getting late. They could hear voices outside, nurses shouting to one another across the car park, the day-shift meeting the night-shift.

Barrett and Judy were discreet, not leaving anything to chance. They sometimes wondered themselves if it was really happening. Judy largely managed the affair. He was happy to follow and impressed that she could organise things without being prim or bossy. She told her husband she had to attend weekly A and R meetings to clinch a deal for one of the bands she was managing; it meant she could spend regular nights away.

If they went to a pub it was always a good few miles out of London and he wore a hat and glasses as disguise. After hours, they sometimes went to the band's rehearsal room in King's Cross, using a side entrance. They'd turn off the lights and build a nest from the lengths of foam Shaun kept in his bass drum to deaden the sound. She made herself at home among the broken amps and old set-lists, never complaining. The softness beneath them and on all sides (the walls were carpeted too) made it feel as if they were in a place specially made for lovers.

After they made love they became aware of tiny specks of light, so small and grainy that they had to look away to see them clearly, like distant stars in the sky. This light came from windows covered in wood and carpet. A contraction in the wood or a patch of stretched fibre let the streetlight trickle in.

"Let's head for that star," he'd say.

She would hug him, nuzzled to his chest.

Carey asked him about the dressing room speech — the night he'd confronted the headline band, and also when he'd stuck up for the black kid at school.

"It was almost as if you'd been trained to do that."

"How do you mean?" asked Barrett.

"You never stopped talking at home did you, your family? You learned to express yourself really well from being about five years old. No one could argue like you. And you're the type of person who people like to please because your approval makes them feel good about themselves. You're not easily afraid and you don't mind getting hit if it's something you believe in."

"Carry on, I've never had this kind of psychological profiling before. The *NME* did me dozens of times but never asked about my family. They were more interested in whether I preferred Camus or Beckett."

"I think a lot of what you are is down to your dad. It helped that he was hard work. You never had paternal love on tap like some of us did. He made it difficult for you to earn, so you tried more than most."

"Are you saying my ambition was a way of justifying myself to him and to make him love me?"

"I think I am, yes. He might have been bad for you as a dad but good as an inspiration. I know this sounds simplistic but there is a definite pattern of rock stars either hardly knowing their dads or having a turbulent relationship with them."

"Who like?"

"Bob Marley, John Lennon, Marvin Gaye, Morrissey, the Gallaghers, Kurt Cobain ... I think because they didn't get lots of what you might call 'little' love when they were growing up, they went looking for big love from an audience when they were older."

"You're not planning a career switch to psychiatry, are you?"

"No."

"Very wise."

Barrett rented a flat in Chelsea especially for their meetings (she called them trysts but he hated this word so she said it even more). He was afraid of them being photographed at his house in Barnes, which was known to the press. They'd later talk fondly of the nights they'd spent at the rehearsal room, early in their relationship.

"I was testing you out," he said.

"What do you mean?"

"Seeing if you were prepared to rough it. I had to be very careful. A lot of girls are just after the money and the glamour but you passed the test, well done."

"So now I get the posh Chelsea pad, do I?"

"And me, thrown in."

They had made love in the flat one winter afternoon, the bedroom window flushed orange from the streetlight. Outside, everything was covered in new snow and when the wind picked up, flakes danced like a swarm of wasps. They could hear muffled crunching underfoot as people passed by. She asked how much he loved her.

"Too much."

"How much is that?"

"I wouldn't like to say."

"Stop teasing."

"How can you measure love?"

"I don't know."

He thought of a way that transmuted love to heroism.

"Look outside," he said.

"Aw, I don't want to move."

"Come on."

She tutted and manoeuvred across the bed, holding the covers tight to her chin. He watched as she stared at the street below. He had looked outside earlier and, covered in snow, it seemed like the laws of nature had been temporarily suspended and the whole city might drift up to heaven. She had a beautiful back.

"What do you see?" he asked.

"Cars, houses."

"No, not that. What's around the cars and houses?"

"Snow, ice."

"Well, if you told me I had to go out there and walk until I dropped, I would. I'd freeze for you."

She grinned.

"Don't laugh," he said.

"I can't help it."

The nurses took increasingly conspicuous glances until one came to the bedside:

"Are you comfortable John, with all this talking you're doing?"

"I'm fine. This is Dave, by the way."

She nodded as she straightened the blankets.

"What's it all about?"

"He's writing my life story."

"Well, put me down for a free copy, won't you?"

She moved off a yard or two and stopped:

"They'll be round with dinner in a few minutes. It might be an idea if you broke off soon. Is your wife visiting tonight?"

"She better be!"

"Shall we finish for today?" asked Carey.

"If you want."

Barrett looked about him as if he was checking. He spoke quietly:

"When you come tomorrow, do think you could bring a bottle?"

Carey didn't understand.

"You know: a bottle."

"John, I can't."

"Please."

"You're supposed to be giving up, getting yourself right."

"I'll have it for security, so I know it's here."

Carey shook his head.

"Go on Dave, one bottle."

The first few times he asked her to leave her husband, she refused.

"I can't," she said. "He's a good man."

"I'm a good man."

"You're both good men, that's the problem."

He was affronted, unable to believe he was competing for her affection; he was used to winning without a fight.

"Right, that's it. I'm going back to my harem and I'm going to shag every last one, good and proper."

"That's up to you."

"God, you're annoying,"

She asked for time to think. Over several weeks and months she changed her mind constantly, sometimes positive she should join him and then that she shouldn't. They got drunk together to help make a decision, and to forget that a decision had to be made. They got drunk alone. It was the first thing they thought of in the morning, the last thing at night. She was afraid of shifting the course of her husband's life to accommodate their selfishness but at other times they felt it was nothing to do with them, this thing that had happened. They had no choice.

She left her husband but said she wasn't ready to commit herself wholly to Barrett straight away. She needed space between. He complained, thinking of schemes to bring them closer. He invited her to work as tour manager or to oversee the merchandise. She declined.

"I don't want to lose my identity. I'm a feminist, remember, unwilling to subsume my personality for anyone. Especially you."

"Why especially me?"

"You eat people, you do."

"Come on, it won't be like that."

"Thanks but no thanks. Something else puts me off, too."

"What's that?"

"If I do the merchandise I'll have to put up with people saying 'merch' all the time and I bloody hate it."

"That's a much better reason."

"I can't believe this," said Carey. "You've gone nearly a week in here, presumably not touching a drop. You don't want to go back to the beginning, do you?"

"It's not like that. I just want some in case. They'd give me a drink if this was a drying-out place. They're not geared up here to help someone like me. They're just treating the medical condition. It's not right to stop my drinking dead like they've done. I need to come down slowly."

"I'll ask the sister."

"Don't get them involved. I know what's right for me."

"John, you're putting me on the spot here."

"Why—because I've asked for one measly bottle of vodka? Can't you do that for an old friend?"

"But there's more to it than that."

"No there's not. It's pretty straightforward: will you get me a bottle or won't you?"

"I don't know."

"Well I might not know a few things, as well."

"What do you mean by that?"

"It works two ways."

"What does?"

"Everything."

"You're talking in riddles."

"That's because you choose to see it that way. I'm talking pretty straight. Basically, I think I might need a drink and I'm asking you as an old mate and someone who needs something right now to get me one, to do me a little favour."

"What's the *something I need* right now?"

"You know."

"I don't, that's why I'm asking."

"Well you want something I have: information, this book."

"Are you saying you'll only co-operate if I bring you a drink?"

"No."

"What are you saying, then?"

"That things work two ways: give and take."

"John, I'm not being stubborn for the sake of it. I want to help you stop. This is weird enough as it is, meeting you twenty-odd years on, after all that's happened."

"All I'm saying is that the best way to help is to get me a bottle. I'll have it here in case of emergency. I know how these things work. I need something, otherwise it's like taking away the floor when someone's learning to walk. I promise — that's precisely what they do at those clinics. They wean you off. Just get it and put it under the bed."

"What if I don't?"

"I've been a bit weak this last hour or two. I might get worse overnight and feel like I don't want to see anyone tomorrow."

Carey turned and left.

About an hour later, Esther arrived on the ward. Barrett challenged her immediately.

"What's wrong?"

"What do you mean?"

"Something about how you've just walked in here. You've got your head down."

"Nothing's wrong."

"It is. Is Holly all right?"

"She's fine."

"Good, you had me worried then."

Esther couldn't resist:

"I thought that was *my* job."

"I knew something was wrong. Come on, let's have it."

"How are you? Did you get on okay with Dave?"

"Don't change the subject."

"Not now, John. Let's save it until you're out of here."

"You can't do this to a man, get him intrigued and then say leave it."

"It's nothing new. No, actually it *is* something new."

"If it's about the boozing, Mr Barrett has a strategy in hand."

"It's not just the drinking."

"Is it *Godspace*? Has its awfulness got to you, finally? I promise I'll burn every copy when I get out of here and, believe me, my next album will see a return to arcane concepts like verses and choruses."

"We've got to talk John, properly. About me and you and where we're going."

"That *is* heavy. Perhaps we *should* wait until I'm out of here."

They spent an hour or so talking of nothing much, both understanding the entente. After she'd gone Barrett thought how easily women changed, the seesaw of emotions. On the night he'd been hallucinating, through a tiny pin-prick of reality he'd seen how much she cared for him. Now she was different, set hard.

Back at his seafront hotel, Carey tried in vain to absorb himself in one of the novels he'd brought with him. The dilemma swung on a creaking hinge in his head. One bottle, just one. How easy was that? No, he couldn't. He went to bed early, flicking randomly through the television channels with the remote. One bottle. Surely he couldn't be held responsible if Barrett turned to drink again afterwards. The book. Did he have enough material from the cuttings and his short time with Barrett to go ahead without his further co-operation? Would Nesta want to publish an unauthorised account, a biography instead of an autobiography? Jack Sutcliffe, life at the paper. Christmas fairies, death crashes, amateur dramatics in that dusty church hall. He couldn't go back. The book, by whatever means.

He turned off the light and television but couldn't sleep. This new mood of Barrett's, as they parted at the hospital — the conviction, the ruthlessness. Carey wondered how someone could change so abruptly, a brick wall appearing across an empty road. It reminded him of the beginning of the end of his marriage. She was the same that night, uncannily so. She arrived home in the early hours, much later than she said she would. He found himself in the kitchen, lifted from his bed and taken downstairs as if by a force outside his control. She took a few seconds with the key and looked surprised to find him there. She smiled tensely.

"I didn't think you'd still be up."

Her eyes were glassy; it might have been walking into the well-lit kitchen after being out in the dark. For a second he thought of pretending it was an ordinary night. He could make her a cup of tea; tell her he'd been unable to sleep. He might have said he'd been worried and needed to know she was safe before turning in properly. She'd thank him for caring, linking his arm on the settee and leaning into his shoulder. He didn't recall thinking what he was going to say next. He just said it.

"Where have you been?"

It was as if he was listening to someone else speak. His voice was loud.

"What do you mean?"

"Come on, where have you been?"

'Come on?' He'd never said that before.

A cold draught had blown in when she opened the door. He shivered.

"I've been out with friends. What do you think I've been doing?"

Secretly he believed (or wanted to) that there was nothing to tell but he was drawn by something innate, a need for confirmation. When it was over, all this suspicion and tension, and she'd cried that her heart was all his, it could subside again and rest for months, possibly years. He imagined that she'd forget about it in a few days but if it skittered across her mind the memory might be paradoxically reassuring; she was loved enough to induce this urgent need for evidence of devotion. But this didn't happen.

"Let's go through to the other room," she said.

He knew immediately. It was in the tone of voice, soft and conciliatory. The fighting was over and it had only lasted seconds. She slipped off her shoes before sitting down. He stayed standing. She told him straight. She wanted to leave. Her eyes, focusing miles beyond him, had struck midnight. She was already wherever she wanted to be: down the street, across the town, away. He watched her mouth as she talked. It was as if she was speaking in a foreign language. He pressed for more information. It had all disappeared, she said: the magic, the oomph, the sparkle. He wondered whether he should have stayed in bed all along, pretending to be asleep. If he hadn't been in the kitchen, the tiles icy beneath his feet and his hand clasping shut the pyjama fly-hole, this might not have happened. Why did he have to push at everything, test it out?

When they finally went to bed, she fell asleep quickly, breaking into a steady rhythm of breathing. In the dark — thinking, thinking — he became convinced she'd found someone else. She hadn't been herself lately. The day before, he'd asked if she had a cold coming on. This sheen of assurance had been daubed on her, it wasn't the girl he knew.

★

Seagulls circled the hospital car park. Carey watched them floating and diving in the clear morning air. One broke free and landed on the wall near the entrance. A toddler passing with his mother stamped hard to scare it away.

Barrett didn't seem as genial as the day before. His skin was the colour of old snow and Carey thought the talking and going over the past might have slowed his recovery, set him back a few days. Barrett didn't ask for the bottle. Carey hoped he'd forgotten — maybe this was the confusion Esther had talked about.

This time, Carey was determined to stick to the band's historical narrative and not go off at tangents. When the tape recorder was switched on, Barrett's mood picked up noticeably.

★

She moved out. In the haste, some of her clothes were left scattered around the bedroom — a night-dress; the leggings she wore for exercise workouts; shoes tipped on their side. Carey couldn't bring himself to pick them up and kicked them to the edge of the room. Her hairs were everywhere. He had to fish them from the bath plughole where they had set as a clump of black stringy syrup.

They spoke on the phone the day after she left. He sensed she was fixed to a course of action, methodical and efficient in a way he had never known her to be before. She said she didn't want to condescend to him; if she didn't love him wholly it wasn't fair that they were together. Give it a try, he pleaded. Just a few weeks. She said it wouldn't work. You shouldn't have to *try* with love.

"Please Dave, accept it. It's hurting me so much knowing what I've done but it would have been much worse pretending everything was okay. I care for you too much for that."

★

"On a day-to-day basis, what is a rock star's life really like?"

(Carey almost chuckled; he sounded like one of those dreary fanzine writers from years before.)

"You know this stuff already."

"Most people think they do but it's probably nothing like they imagine."

"Well, you're travelling an awful lot. Photos one day, promo the next. We'd get flown to places like Belgium and asked these deep and meaningful questions that were ridiculous, really. Stuff like, 'Vot vould you say voz the most cherishable aspect of the stance of the Killing Stars in today's modern oeuvre?' You end up treating them with contempt, taking the piss; not that they notice. I enjoyed the meet-and-greet things where you'd visit some country and the label boss gives a little speech about how great you are and how many records you're going to sell in their *territory*. The best ever was this tiny American bloke wearing horrendous crimpolene flares. He had a daft wig, a shiny black one. He stood up and said, with a serious face, that when he first heard Killing Stars he'd had an 'eargasm'. He described me as a 'robo-hunk'. The band was in stitches. Other than that, life is as you'd imagine it: a lot of hanging about, filming videos, sound-checking, knocking about a studio for months on end."

★

Her leaving coincided with the hottest summer for years. Lawns turned sappy yellow. The paper ran drought stories every week. All this sunshine, thought Carey, perfect for the seaside and long country walks, but all he had was misery warmed up. He thought about her constantly but struggled to recollect her face as if he was assembling fragments of a ripped up photograph. The circumstances of the break-up ricocheted around his head. He was driven, looking for clues to solve a crime that felt like murder. Every detail was analysed and a searchlight taken to her gestures and moods, both recent and long ago. He believed comments (or just a facial expression, a thought inadvertently revealed) that had once seemed insignificant might now resonate with a new profundity. After picking through the relationship itself, he moved on to his past, her past, their families, their childhoods. He was convinced that among all this was the flawed gene that had caused him to be chucked up from life with all this time — miles and miles of it, days and days — stretching out before him.

He felt ill, sickly and tired. At night he thrashed around the itchy, empty double bed. When sleep finally came it was broken every few minutes as if it coexisted with an electrical charge that caused his body to convulse.

In letters and phone calls he asked her to reconsider, to come back. He called on friends and made them stay up late: talking, talking. He lost weight. He drank so much beer he thought he could smell it about him permanently. He was a wreck.

★

"What did you think of record company people?"

"They were all over us in the beginning, sorting everything out, almost to the point where they'd cut up food for us before we ate it. It was embarrassing, really. You feel like a god, like you can literally murder someone and people will deal with it. I was driving home once after three or four days of being waited on, pushed past queues at the airport and in restaurants, everyone telling me I was great, and I had this horrible loneliness as I was driving. You get addicted to the attention. Another time I was bombing down the middle of the road in my car, cutting people up at the lights. I realised I was pumped up with that adrenaline of thinking it was my right, that I was better than all these little people. The downside of the whole thing, of course, is that it makes it harder to be alone."

"Do you think the experience has changed you?"

"Totally and utterly. I promised myself I'd revert to plain old me when it stopped but it's impossible, it cuts too deep. Wasn't it John Updike who said celebrity is a mask that eventually eats into your face?"

"I didn't know you read Updike."

"I don't. I just remember good lines and pretend to have read all these cool authors."

★

Carey felt marginally better if he kept on the move, dodging the
sadness. He worked his way around college friends who had
dispersed to various points, working for local newspapers. He
decided to spend a weekend in Wales with Tim and Heather.

It had barely registered when Tim said on the phone that
Heather was pregnant with their first child. As soon as Tim
opened the door, Carey knew he had made a mistake. Heather
was behind him, further down the hall, and they were both
wearing meek smiles; he could see it was taxing them to fashion
this condolence. They led him in and offered a seat at the table.
The front room was like a museum exhibit, a facsimile of an
Edwardian house with an open fire and rugged dark furniture.
On the table was a wooden chopping board, a butter dish and a
dainty teapot. They didn't waste any time:

"We're sorry to hear about your break-up. We were really
surprised," she said.

"I was, too."

They looked astonished by his response. He sensed the hopelessness of his role. If he was flippant it was seen as camouflage
for acute sadness but if he sang his grief, he'd *taken it bad*. He
knew that no matter what he said, it would have no affect
because they had set aside the weekend as a memorial to his
failed marriage.

Heather made a slightly better job of the compassion. Her
face was long and thin and she continually stared down at the
floor and flashed her brown eyes as if about to cry. Carey was
sceptical of their empathy; he felt they saw the downfall of his
marriage as a warning and his decline somehow burnished their
success, especially with a kid on the way.

They were both teetotal but had bought Carey a bottle of wine. Tim, eyes beaming, wanted to know what had happened, why she'd gone. He was fiddling with the string on his elderberry tea-bag (why couldn't they drink normal fucking tea like everyone else?).

"Was everything all right in your love life?" he asked after an hour or so of talking.

The cheek of it. Straight out, like that. Carey didn't answer. He rocked his head from side to side, trying to relay that he wasn't going to budge.

"Our love life was fine, thanks."

"But was it fine for her?"

"Do you want any supper?" Heather interrupted.

When she came back, carrying a tray of cheese sandwiches (thick crusty bread and brinjal pickle), Carey noticed how pretty she looked. Her eyes were soft and kind and she looked girlish now she had relaxed. She drew up her legs beneath her on the settee and the skin above her knees was soft and creamy with an outline of muscle where the flesh creased. After they had picked at the food, Tim asked Carey again if everything was okay and was there anything he could do for him. He said no, but was tempted to add:

'But I wouldn't mind shagging your wife.'

Then he remembered she was pregnant, and cringed.

The next day they insisted on taking him out. He woke early and while he waited for them to get up, he leafed through the books on their shelves. They smelled damp and some of the pages had stuck together. Wherever Tim had lived over the years he had never heated the houses properly. Visitors had to leave their coats on rather than expect him to turn up the gas fire a few notches; it was their problem if their body thermostat was fucked — they didn't eat enough vegetables and garlic or hadn't taken enough exercise (unlike him).

They had a new car. Carey guessed Heather had persuaded him they needed something reliable now the baby was due. He climbed into the back seat. Tim wound down the window and the air rushed into Carey's face. On other mornings he had woken fresh, cheerful almost, and it had taken an hour or two for the sorrow to properly arrive. Not today. He was six feet below the water lilies. He stared at the back of their heads, love framed nicely in the windscreen. At the traffic lights Tim rubbed her thigh playfully and she gave a wrinkled expression of reproach. Carey hated their happiness. He wanted to pound his fists against the interior of the car, throw himself around. Instead, he sat quite still and took part in polite chit-chat.

*

The bottle of vodka still hadn't been mentioned. He's forgotten, thought Carey. He kept the questions coming.

"What were the relationships like in the band when you were together?"

"We were like the rest — so close at the beginning that we almost had our own language but afterwards we wouldn't stay in the same hotels. I'm always surprised that any bands stay together. It's almost like an experiment in human behaviour, to see how you can most fuck people up. You're given money, you have your egos flattered, you're expected to be creative and make lots of decisions with the music, the artwork, the photos, which PR you're going to use, which promoter. Then there's the label or the management trying to box people off, working out little strategies so they can make sure they land on which-ever side is left with the most power, the most earning potential, installing the odd persecution complex along the way. In every group someone invariably gets a drugs or drink habit, so into the mix goes paranoia. Pile all this on to whatever neuroses were already there from childhood, and I'm surprised bands even stay together for one album, never mind institutions like The Rolling Stones or U2."

★

A month after leaving, she phoned Carey unexpectedly and asked to see him the next afternoon. He spent more than an hour preparing to drive over to the house where she was lodging with three other girls. It felt like an audition. He fretted over what clothes to wear, trying to recall the ones she'd liked. He polished his shoes and checked in every mirror that he was young and handsome, or near enough.

On the journey there the sun was warm through the windscreen and side windows of the car. He hadn't driven far before sweat began trickling down from his armpits. He thought he heard a fly buzz over his shoulder and jerked to swat it: nothing there. Dotted along the main roads were car showrooms with signs fixed on top of gleaming vehicles: 'Test Drive Today', 'Low Mileage', 'Car of the Week'. A newsagent's shop had a swivel board on the pavement and it revolved to read either 'FAGS' or 'CIGS' in bright pink and orange. Along one stretch, factories were pressed tight against the road, the walls blackened by exhaust fumes. He passed a council football pitch where a group of seagulls were holding a meeting in the centre circle. One broke free and set off in flight, the rest following on.

He pulled on to the estate where she was now living. Privet

hedges had been flattened and litter was strewn around. He parked about thirty metres from the house because he didn't want to be watched as he got out of the car. The garden of her new home was a parched lawn containing a few tufts of grass, a decaying fossil of dog shit, cigarette packets and an empty milk crate. The front of the bricks around the door had fallen off and earwigs danced among the debris. How desperate had she been to escape? He pressed the bell. No sound. He jabbed it again. Not working. He pounded the side of his hand against the door, his heart beating ahead of the rhythm. After a few minutes a girl with brown hair and a round face opened it.

"Can I help you?"

He told her who he had come to see and asked if she was in.

"I think so, I'll just go and look. Who shall I say wants her?"

"Dave."

She came to the door. She had an abstract, whimsical expression on her face. She led him down the hall and into the kitchen. The sink was crammed with dozens of pots. Clothes were drying on a radiator. Milk cartons and tea bags were scattered on the worktop. Carey was strangely calm. He felt like a new boyfriend, fresh and full of promise. Maybe she wanted a new start.

*

He had to ask, even at the risk of reminding Barrett about the bottle.

"When did you start the drinking?"

"It was a gradual build-up. I remember my dad saying how he'd get thirsty at about nine o'clock at night and before he knew it he'd drank three or four bottles of beer or he'd slipped out to the pub. Everyone has their own version of nine o'clock, I suppose: that point when you realise nothing else is going to happen with the day except roll on to another. With me, the problem was that it wasn't nine o'clock. It started off in the late afternoon, then lunchtime, and then it was almost as soon as I woke up. I craved it, had to have it. It wasn't so much the getting pissed, I had to do it to set myself up, get on an even keel."

★

Carey drove to a town centre pub. He realised they hadn't done any afternoon drinking in all the years they'd been together; it was something you probably did either at the start of a relationship or now, at the end. He bought the drinks.

"I think we should sort out the divorce paperwork. We need to get things properly agreed," she said.

It wasn't reconciliation then, but more of her new-found efficiency.

"What's the rush?"

"The sooner we do it, the better. So we can move on."

He ordered more drinks. He asked again why she wanted to split up and whether she'd met someone else.

"I'm leaving you for *me*. I want to know what I'm about, who I am. We met very young."

She started to drink brandy and lemonade but her mood didn't alter. It grew dark outside and drizzle patted the pub windows. He drove her back to the house and she kissed him goodbye; a quick, flashing kiss. He watched her put her new key into the door of her new home and disappear inside.

On the drive home, he didn't care any more. It was over and, for a few minutes at least, accepting this felt a merciful release.

He started singing to the dashboard, banging on the steering wheel. The dialogue they'd had was irrelevant. The truth was in her manner and actions: the occasional looking away when he spoke, her fierce staring when *she* said anything. He was sure she didn't mean to hurt him but was clearly determined to remain faithful to her decision, aware that showing any kindness or warmth might galvanise his hopes. She had done the job well, he thought: the set of her face, the body language. The message was clear — any attempt to form a bridge between them would hack away more of his dignity. It was over, done with.

*

Barrett pressed his hands down on the grey blanket as if to concentrate his thoughts.

"If you've got a drink, you've always got company. I need to be around people but when I've had a drink it takes away this need."

"Don't you like being alone?"

"Me being on my own isn't like anyone else being on their own. Imagine it: from the age of eighteen I've had people with me all the time, telling me I'm great, making me the centre of attention. When that goes you really miss it, anyone would."

"What's the answer, how do you deal with it?"

"It all depends when you ask the question. Right now, I'm thinking I'm going to be okay."

*

Carey wanted to recreate the life he'd lost as quickly as possible. He started going out, specifically to find a replacement woman. He was back in places he'd last been in years before with Barrett and Fisher when they'd gone there primarily to mock: American-themed pubs, overbearing music, perma-tans, high heels, short skirts, pleading eyes. He tried to imagine what everyone was talking about, why they laughed so much. What were they shouting down each other's ears so vital that it justified such effort? They all seemed so comfortable in the bright lights and clamour, their gestures exaggerated, their cool in place in the heat. Perhaps, he thought, they were laughing to stop themselves from crying, these Friday night people, most of them divorced or separated, let down, abandoned.

And he was one of them now, watching the pub doors, eager for someone to walk in and make him happy and wholesome again. Maybe, it crossed his mind, these people were really, truly laughing but he didn't get the joke because he was humourless and cynical and scornful. Unlike when he was there as a teenager, he now felt they saw him for what he was, if they could be bothered looking: a saucer-eyed, fake-shy ex-college boy, oozing sensitivity and aloneness, believing with all his little heart that he was different than the rest, more thoughtful, more everything.

"Are you all right?" asked a friend he was with. He hated being asked if he was all right. Was his affliction so obvious?

"Yeah, fine."

"You seem a bit quiet."

He hated this, too.

"Sorry."

Now it sounded as if he pitied himself.

"Just give us a shout and we'll move on if you want."

"Okay."

They went to a night-club. He was hoping beyond hope to see either *Bastards*, *Twatz*, *Shafters*, *Disco Pants* or *Knobbers* lit up over the entrance.

★

"It all sounds a bit pathetic, doesn't it?" said Barrett. "Like I'm a kid or something, needing people to hold my hand all the time."

"Not really."

"Maybe I'm not as bad as I'm making out. I have good days and bad days. I remember before the band even formed that I'd have times when I felt sort of fragile, nervous of speaking to people. I used to love it just being in my bedroom, playing guitar. I resented it if even my mum came in."

"How did you do the gigs, then?"

"I really don't know. It just came easy. I thought everyone could do what I did: just getting up there and feeling comfortable. I cracked a few jokes at the first gigs we did and had people laughing. Honestly, it was effortless. It was the one thing I could do really well and it brought me everything. It must be weird if you're good at something and it's of no use in life or it goes unrewarded. I couldn't imagine that."

Carey could.

★

Bojangles. They'd called it Bo-fucking-jangles. Don't take me in there, thought Carey. Don't kill me.

He went in. He drank more beer, room spinning. He was persuaded to dance. He shuffled around dutifully, looking at the women around him. There were two distinct age groups: pale-skinned, bony things just out of their teens, eager-faced, moving quick and sleek. And women of his age, getting close to thirty, their skin darker somehow, bodies sturdier. They moved less frenetically, with trust in the rhythm. Some of the younger ones smiled at him and it felt to be the kindly greeting of the fifth former to a teacher passing on the corridor.

What would Barrett say, he thought, seeing him here, dancing pathetically to this shit, shit music? Still in his home town, in the same job, in exactly the same space but now doing it for real: blending in, looking for women. He could hear Fisher in his head: 'It's like punk never happened. Where's the individuality, the expression? Where's the poetry? They all look the fucking same. Baaa'

Please don't play Killing Stars, thought Carey (as if they would). Don't flush out the old new wavers from the shadows and have them strutting around self-importantly when it didn't mean a thing because they were each stuck: wife (or ex-wife), kids (or no kids), job (same old), jacket and tie (a condition of entry) — a disgrace to the legacy they claimed to celebrate.

*

"I feel like that," said Carey.

"Like what?"

"Unrewarded, I suppose."

"I thought you were happy at the paper, staying in your home town and all that. In fact, I've often envied that kind of serenity you have."

"Serenity?"

"Don't you see it that way?"

"I think I'm just good at feigning it. I don't feel like that underneath."

"How *do* you feel?"

"I'm supposed to be interviewing you, aren't I?"

"I thought we were just talking."

"Right then ..." Carey paused like someone about to climb several flights of stairs. "This is hard to describe but I've been pretty much on edge for years, frustrated. I've seen what's happened to you and I've been pleased for you. But you moving about, doing things — interesting, creative things — has made me even more aware that I've been standing still. Imagine how you'd feel if you'd done all that music and just put the tapes in boxes all over the house. Imagine having all these things you wanted to say and share, and no one ever hearing it."

"Quite a lot of writers don't break through until they're older."

"That's not much comfort. I want it now. I've wanted it to be *now* since I left the band all those years ago."

"I do know how you feel," said Barrett. "I'm not in a dissimilar position really, these days."

How dare he, thought Carey. How dare he claim empathy. Barrett had made all those records, travelled, met thousands of people, done hundreds of interviews, lived a full and productive life. So, he was selling far fewer records these days, but that was because he'd said all he had to say, exhausted himself. His recent albums had been doodling, a man *looking* for something to say, pumped up fat on a privilege afforded him because of what had preceded it. Carey wanted to blurt, 'But I've not even been born yet'.

He smiled instead, serenely.

★

It was his lucky night. She was dancing close by. He wasn't sure how they would come together. The woman with her bumped into him and made extravagant gestures of apology. She said something he'd not heard since he was at school.

"My mate fancies you."

He looked across and moved closer. They began dancing together. After a few songs he asked if she wanted a drink. She said she already had one. He explained that this was convention, a precursor to them engaging in conversation. He was testing her out: she would either appreciate his oddball humour. Or think he was a dick.

"Well, why didn't you ask for a conversation in the first place?" she said, and reached for his hand to lead him from the dance floor.

She was called Jenny, she said, and worked in an office as a sales administrator. He asked what this meant but she said she didn't want to talk about work because it was boring. She asked if he was married.

★

"Me and you are so similar," said Barrett. "We have this weird relationship with hope. It's like a lizard's tail we're trying to grasp."

Didn't he use that in one of his songs, pondered Carey: is that what he does, recycle metaphors?

"It doesn't matter how many records I've made or how many books you write, we'll never get what we're after."

"What do we do then? How do we cope?"

"We can give up on hope, I suppose, or bring it more up close so we've a greater likelihood of achieving what we really want. But, having said that, how can we fundamentally change when the pursuit of what we're after actually defines us?'

Carey smiled: *actually* and *fundamentally* in the same sentence. It was the sixth-form debating society relocated to a hospital setting with U2 providing the soundtrack. We still haven't found what we're looking for. Punch the air, thump the chest.

★

"Nope, definitely not married."

He asked her the same question.

"No, thank you."

Carey realised that because he wasn't sure who he was any more, he could be anyone he chose. He became breezy and witty, showing off, drinking himself familiar. While he spoke to Jenny, his friends were looking across; one gave him the thumbs up.

After talking for about an hour, they left the club together. He had intended to take a taxi home and pick up his car in the morning. He found himself walking towards it.

"Do you want a lift?"

"That would be very nice of you."

She was attractive, with a narrow face and deep set blue-green eyes. She had black hair and a long fringe that fell across her face which she brushed away without affectation. Inside the car, the windscreen was misty with condensation. He was impressed that she wiped it clear using the sleeve of her coat.

He was well over the legal drink limit. It didn't matter.

Nothing mattered. As he drove, he thought what he would do if he was stopped by the police. How could he explain that this wasn't his scene and he was ghosting through a kind of parallel life until he rebuilt himself again? He looked around for a police car pulling out from a side street or zooming up behind, lights flashing. He knew exactly how he'd react: he'd sit on the edge of the pavement and cry, all that pressure and stress squeezing up on all sides until he burst. As if in a dream, a police car *did* appear behind them. Jenny spotted his anxiety.

"Is that a copper?"

"Yes."

"How much have you had to drink?"

"Too much."

★

"Perhaps we shouldn't change but celebrate what we are," said Barrett.

"How do we do that?"

"By accepting it's what makes us different, this relationship with hope. Think of all the little lives out there, how inconsequential it all is. We've got charisma because of how we're wired, something about us. "

"I like little lives, I want to write about them."

"You won't have a bestseller, then."

"I'm not bothered about having a bestseller."

"Everyone wants to reach as many people as possible."

"I just want to get started and have something out there, anything."

"Do you want it as much as you've ever wanted it?"

"More so. I feel the soil coming in on me, I really do. It's at the stage where it's physiological. I need it to happen to remove the pain."

"That bad, hey?"

"I'm scared now."

"What of?"

"The look in your eyes, just then. It's reflecting back to me what I see in my own sometimes. I don't want to want it so much. I want to live like everyone else."

"See, it's like I said — life is bigger, it's bigger than you."

"That's REM, isn't it?"

"Well spotted."

★

Jenny reached for his arm.

"Stay calm and concentrate on your driving."

Her counsel moved him. The police car turned off the main road. He'd escaped.

"Shall I drive to the tops?" he asked.

He thought how formal it sounded compared to what was sure to follow.

"That'd be nice."

He parked in a lay-by on a moorland road and they climbed on to the back seat. She was eager. As they kissed hungrily, the car was lit up intermittently by vehicles passing by, headlights on full beam. He imagined the conversations. Everyone liked to spot the shaggers, to see otherwise decent people from good homes taking their turn at quick-fix sex in the darkness above town.

Carey couldn't enter her properly as she lay on her back and asked her to move on to her knees. He reached in his back pocket for a condom. He hated himself for being so careful, so prepared. The sex was over in seconds. She gasped and reached for him. He recoiled. He rolled down the condom quickly and threw it through the window; he used to ponder on what kind of person did such a thoughtless thing, knowing kids might find it.

★

Carey had to ask:

"Why do you think things have gone okay for you, and not for me?"

"I tell you one thing — it's got little to do with having talent. It's about finding a patron, someone who believes in you. The band were lucky because we found Rob Bailey and the rest kicked on from there, from that one person. Even there though, it's not what you think. I always assumed bands got signed because they had great tunes, but it's usually on some whimsical basis like the A and R bloke being gay and fancying the bass player or a budget they have to use up by a certain time or because some new band reminds him of a group he was into when he was fourteen and he's been looking for that same buzz he got from a monumental gig in Winchester or wherever by Stackridge or Savoy Brown in 1971. I would imagine publishing is much the same, except it's probably even harder to find that gate-keeper to success."

"Why's that?"

"Because I get the impression it's more of a stitch-up in terms of class. Ninety per cent of books are about poshos, aren't they? It's *their* history, not ours, that we read about again and again in all those so-called classics, going way back. And it's poshos that own the publishing companies and commission the books. In the music industry there's a tradition of hunting out rough-house kids and supporting them because people make money from it, it's a process that works."

★

Jenny was quiet as they drove back down, the lights of the town glistening like fluorescent sediment. He sensed she was disappointed. He had misread her.

"That meant a lot to me," she said.

"Did it?"

"It did."

"Why?"

"Because of something you said before."

He tracked back, unable to remember.

"What was that?"

"When you said you wanted me. No one's said that to me for a long time."

★

Carey immediately regretted his candour. Barrett, of all people. Why had he trusted him with his feelings when he was a collector of stories, and nothing more? And how could he expect him to relate to *his* story when it was the antithesis of his own? Any understanding Barrett had shown was a form of vanity: him reflecting on a sorrowful life that might have been his own if it had gone disastrously wrong. Got to get back to Barrett,

308

thought Carey—the subject, the protagonist, the theme of the book—and away from me.

"What about the drinking? Is it possible to gauge how much you drank on, say, a daily basis?" [He realised he was talking in the past tense, as if being in the hospital had allowed Barrett to leave his old self behind.]

"It depends on what you see as the cut-off point. I just drank and drank. With me, I can't accept that things have to end. I find it impossible to let go."

"What do you trace it to?"

"It's probably genetic, ultimately. My dad believed everything had to be lived in the moment and built around whatever mood he was in. Remember those Friday nights when he'd have us all dancing? He was boozed up then. I used to think how calm your mum and dad were, how easy it was to be around them. In our house it was mad."

★

A few days afterwards, Jenny phoned. She had found Carey's number in the telephone book. He didn't recognise her voice at first.

"Hello, it's me."

"Oh, hello."

"Have you missed me?"

He hadn't realised she was so forward; she seemed different on the phone.

"Er, yeah. What have you been up to?"

"You don't want to know! This week has been a nightmare at work, one thing after the other. I tell you, I could do with a night out."

"Right."

"Well, are you going to ask me out, or not?"

"Yeah, when?"

"Whenever."

"Saturday?"

"Done."

They arranged to meet outside a pub. She was waiting at the entrance when he arrived, wearing a white blouse and dark skirt, almost like a uniform. She smiled sweetly and he thought he'd done well for himself, just a few months after the breakdown of his marriage and out with a woman like this.

★

"It wasn't that mad."

"I think they were on their best behaviour when you visited. They thought you came from a sort of posh family. I remember your dad liked classical music and your mum used to do crosswords."

"Maybe it was because I was a bit pious."

"You weren't. You were really cool and dead funny, the one who'd have us all in stitches."

"Really? I never got that impression. I always felt like you thought I judged you, that I considered myself better than everyone else."

"No, you were one of us, but funnier. Everyone got on with you. I used to like it when it was just me and you going around because we sort of matched."

"Matched?"

"Our personalities were similar but different enough to complement one another. The only other person I've really felt that with was Al. I've met lots of people since but you were the only two where I've properly had that."

★

At the end of the evening, Jenny wanted to go to a club and carry on drinking. Carey said he was tired.

"Is everything all right?" she asked.

"Yeah, I'm just knackered."

He drove her home. As they approached her house she asked him to carry on driving. He parked in a side-street, a few hundred yards away.

"I want you to tell me what's wrong," she said.

"Nothing."

"There is, I can tell."

There was. In the pub she'd referred to him as 'wacky'. Funny or unusual, he could have lived with, but not wacky: how could she have got him so wrong? Her pulling funny faces, too. She had been talking about a work colleague when she announced, 'She's really good looking, not like me' before twisting her mouth, wrinkling her nose and going cross-eyed. When she did this, it was as if she was rubbing herself away, a kind of false modesty that Carey didn't believe in. He didn't mention it, but he hadn't liked her tracking down his phone number and the contrast of being scarily confident on the phone and then twinkly and demure when they met. And the sex just a few hours after meeting that first night: it was reasonably enjoyable and he liked her commitment to the moment but wasn't sure he wanted to be with someone so eager.

"Do you already know?" she asked.

"Know what?"

311

"That I'm married?"

He had two thoughts, one-two. The first was that he was going to get beaten up for shagging someone else's wife and the second, sheer relief: he had an out. She told him she'd married young. Her husband didn't pay her any attention and would rather go out with his mates. They didn't have sex any more. They planned to separate when she'd saved enough to put down on a place of her own. Carey reached for her hand. She gripped his tightly and smiled. He thought about driving somewhere out of the way again. She read his thoughts.

"I'd like more of what we had the other night," she whispered.

He didn't return to the moors but drove along a dirt road that played hopscotch with the motorway, dipping under bridges and skirting roundabouts. It was rutted by tractor tracks and hemmed in by thick hedgerows. The motorway, just a field away, hummed like a distant swarm of bluebottles. Eventually they came to quarries and deep gravel pits filled with water, where the lad from school had drowned.

Carey parked on a grassy verge. While they were kissing he reached down. She moved his hand away.

"That might not be a good idea," she said.

He presumed she was on her period.

She reached into his trousers. Afterwards, she held up her hand, spreading the fingers:

"Sticky!"

He passed her a tissue from his pocket. She was dreamy and sitting deep in the seat. He was determined to hide his urgency to get away.

"Look at the sky," she said.

It was streaked with patches of light and trails of silvery clouds. He remembered a line from a song. He sang it quietly:

"A billion stars are a moving sight, for all you out there hearing me tonight. It's just a trick of the light." It was one of Barrett's.

As he turned the key in the ignition he vowed this would be the last time he saw her: he was stringing her along, messing her about. He dropped her off at the bottom of her street. She didn't linger but quickly opened and closed the car door behind her. As she walked surefooted along the pavement, although the light was dim anyone could see she was pretty and held herself well. No-one would guess how much hurt and insecurity was inside her, he thought.

★

Carey wanted to talk more about Barrett's alcoholism. It would form a central theme of the book. He was thinking about his favourite works on the subject: *Leaving Las Vegas*, *The Lost Weekend*, *Under the Volcano*, *John Barleycorn*, *A Fan's Notes* — pages drenched in liquor.

"How do you view the drinking, now?" he asked.

"I let myself down. Real rock'n'roll, the thing I aspired to most, is about having lots of energy — being high on everything for what it is, not using anything to give it you falsely. I had everything except the one thing I had with people who knew me before I was famous — real friendships. You get nostalgic and the booze helps you dream yourself back there. When you're famous you have a choice. You can accept all the privileges, all the pats on the back, and walk around thinking you're great and that everyone else can fuck off. Or you can fight it and try and stay what you always were, being decent with people and constantly playing yourself down. The trouble is, if you do this it can actually stop you being successful and spoil it for you at the time. I could never make up my mind and opted out. I let myself sort of float through it, especially at the end."

*

There were two or three other nights when Carey got lucky. He'd walk the streets the next morning, an hour or so after dawn, smelling of beer and sweat and aftershave, his mouth dry and head aching. Every few steps he'd catch the scent of last night's woman about him.

He speculated on Lucy's whereabouts and imagined her life to be the converse of his. She might have moved to a run-down part of town but she was probably going to smart bars, whisked away by buffed-up chaps in check jackets and cream trousers. He imagined her with a doctor, dentist or a solicitor, someone from one of the formal professions. This was, he knew, his class thing again. He recognised that he was taut, still singing fusty homilies to the romantic notion of the working man. It wasn't envy of money or status, but the easy grace. The rich and the smooth had 'place', always had done, so there was no white noise going on. His head rang with it. And she had been able to reinvent herself too. All those things that had compromised her unhappiness could be ascribed to either him or their relationship. By virtue of her rejecting him, he was left to fester in their past, made responsible for it, while she claimed the newness for herself.

*

Another day had almost slipped by. No mention of the bottle.

"Shall we wrap up?" asked Carey.

"If you want."

"Same time tomorrow?"

"Probably."

"Probably?"

"Did you bring the stuff?"

"What's that?"

"You know."

"John, don't put me through this moral dilemma."

"Moral dilemma!" he scoffed.

Shaking his head, Carey turned and left.

★

Eventually Carey began to resent Lucy. It was her fault he had been thrown into hollow encounters with the lost souls he met in clubs and pubs. Her fault. All the thinking was futile too. He hadn't done anything wrong. It was the old routine: someone getting fed up with their partner or fed up with themselves and believing that changing them would make them fresh and new again.

Again, she contacted him unexpectedly, inviting him to a party at the house where she was living with the other girls. He assumed it was a kind of trial, her checking whether her feelings for him had changed or stayed the same.

When they met at the house he noticed she was wearing new clothes and different perfume. She had dyed her hair in streaks of watery gold and was more effusive than he remembered, smiling excessively, making pronounced eye contact.

The party was focused mainly in a large attic room. She

introduced him to people and he felt like a new boyfriend. He went along with the handshakes and hello,-nice-to-meet-you's. After a while he found himself by the window, looking down to the street. A kid was sitting on the edge of the pavement, scratching at the floor with a stone. She caught him staring:

"What are you thinking?"

"Nothing."

He was thinking what bullshit it was. Here they were in new clothes, back as they were when they had first met, nervous and excited, please and thank you; all of it fakery. He wasn't her new boyfriend, he was her old boyfriend. Every expression, turn of phrase and intonation of his voice was known to her like a story told over and over again.

"Have you been with anyone since we split up?" she asked.

"Not really."

"I think you're supposed to answer yes or no."

He didn't know what to say. Should he try to provoke jealously by telling her he had been with someone (with its attendant risk that she might be indifferent to his answer)? If he said he hadn't been with anyone, would he appear pitiful, as if he was still holding out for her? What did she want him to be? All guess-what?-I'm-over-it (maybe this would prompt her into wanting him back, the appeal of the indifferent) or still there — waiting, grieving, pining?

"I've had a kind of date with someone."

He was thinking of Jenny.

He didn't expect the next question.

"Is she good-looking?"

Interesting.

"Yeah, she's okay."

"What does she do?"

He wondered if she was asking these questions so she could

tell him about *her* new bloke. She was disingenuously empowering him, allowing him a brief triumph before torching him with information about the new man in her life.

'I've met someone too.'

She didn't say this but he heard it clearly in his head. He then imagined her smile and it wasn't condescending or designed to hurt, but a beaming, dazzling manifestation of both the love she felt for her new man and confirmation of Carey's new position as friend, his reduced status in her life. She changed the subject:

"A few of them are going for a drink while the party warms up. Let's tag along."

In the pub, they sat among a group of six or seven people. Carey hated that they knew about him and his situation but he knew nothing of them. He quickly learned that two of the blokes worked in advertising, supplying flyers to local businesses. He spoke to them but felt as if he was trying to ingratiate himself. Everyone told stories about mutual friends and laughed out loud. Lucy joined in. Carey noticed that she was staring directly at whoever was talking, turning to face them, nodding, smiling. It was as if she'd read a book on social etiquette or self-help, making people feel as if they were the centre of the world. She tried at first to explain who the various people were being mentioned, but then gave up; the effort was slowing down the chitchat.

The drink had no affect on Carey, his anxiety was fixed. It was late when they finally left. Most said they would give the party a miss now and began phoning for taxis. The street was different than before, quieter, the air clearer.

"I hope the party's still going strong," she whispered.

Carey looked at his watch: gone midnight.

★

It was night time. The three other patients in the side ward were asleep. Pain suddenly criss-crossed Barrett's upper body. When it eased off, he pressed his chest with the heel of his hand. He spat into a tissue. The phlegm was reddish-brown. Someone had told him years before that if it was more brown than red, it was old blood. He guessed it had been on his chest for a few days, lodged there from when he fell down the steps.

★

Only a handful of people were left at the party. A couple were sitting together in the lounge, locked into a conversation, and others were in the kitchen. Lucy turned to Carey:

"I knew we should have come back sooner."

"I thought you were enjoying it at the pub."

She didn't answer.

They went upstairs; she had agreed earlier that he could camp on her bedroom floor. She sat at the dressing table. He watched as she removed her ear-rings, tilting her head and stroking the ear lobes to loosen the fastener. He went to get his overnight bag from the car. Climbing back up the stairs, he swung it over his shoulder. It collided with a large ornament on the window sill, a bust of an African woman, causing it to topple and shatter.

"What was that?" she shouted from the bedroom.

"I've had an accident."

"I might have known."

"What do you mean?"

She pushed past him and he went into the bedroom. He could hear her cursing as she brushed up the pieces. When she came in the room again he had stripped off and got into her bed. She undressed and climbed in too. He reached across and held her tightly. He began crying, soft sobs that developed into spasms of grief. She stroked his forehead, making soothing noises. He stopped crying and listened as she fell into a rhythmic breathing pattern, the light wafts of air causing her lips to tremble. She moaned and shuffled to her side, her face close to the wall. Carey turned on to his back and stared around the room which was partially lit by a streetlight outside the window. The tears dried and he felt the skin on his cheeks tingling where salt had worked into pores. There were other people in other bedrooms and Lucy was just inches away but he felt more alone than ever before. He liked the feeling, with it came an exhilarating sense of strength. He wasn't what she'd said he was: an accident waiting to happen. He was strong. Quietly, he got up and dressed, and left for home.

*

Barrett coughed again and drew up more phlegm. Once more he spat into a tissue: red, bright red. He could see this even in the dimmed light. He felt a surge of panic. This was it. His time come. Internal injuries, bleeding to death. He imagined that all the vodka over all the years had burned away the lining, until, shaken by the fall, the various tubes and vessels inside him had burst. He leaned over and felt for one of the grey cardboard sick-catchers beneath; he'd joked to the nurses earlier in the day that they were industrial-issue kiss-me-quick hats. No joking now, just the serious business of being gravely ill.

*

Carey got through. Night on night he came home to an unchanged house. He formed the habit of turning on the lights quickly, and the television or radio, filling it with voices. The place smelled damp. He wondered if he was imagining this; it was difficult to know without anyone to ask. Every item of furniture told the story of him and her, their marriage — shopping trips they'd made, loading the car or waiting in for the delivery men a few days later; sitting together on the settee; eating meals at the table; passing books or magazines to one another — a finger pointing to the relevant passage, some great piece of writing or a new insight.

He shopped for one, eating make-do, post-break-up meals: grated cheese on pasta, tomatoes on toast, cereals at teatime. He suffered constant broken sleep. He returned to his book and record fairs. He volunteered for night-jobs at the paper. He told himself he was a good person, a strong person, and that he didn't deserve this. All his life he'd only ever had little truths about himself and they were painful enough, but now he'd had a truth-slab toppled on to him: not good enough, spurned, unloved. No wonder his chest was tight. When his well-meaning friends told him it could be worse or that no one had actually died, he thought (but didn't say) that it might have been better if someone had. Her death would have at least spared him the rejection and the knowledge that her life continued without him, with someone else.

Concentrating hard, he thought of all the things he had disliked about her: the numerous male friends, many of whom misinterpreted her effervescence for flirting — were they right all along?; her female friends — self-absorbed, gossipy; her playing with her hair; her occasional indifference to his feelings, followed by the insinuation that he was over-sensitive or, worse, that he was sulking (which he was, anyone would have done);

her full and busy life; her willingness to see all sides, notably when the counter-opinion was to his own; her laugh, a decibel too loud; her silences, perceived (by him) as enigmatic while his own were plain and empty air.

It was, in truth, a list that didn't come easy. He recognised that much of it was a disclosure of his own weaknesses and insecurities, conjoined to his depth of feeling for her. He got through.

★

Barrett buzzed for the nurse. When she arrived he was lying down again, sweat pouring from him.

"Have you got a fever?"

"I think I've had some kind of panic attack."

She looked in the bowl.

"There's blood in there," said Barrett.

"I can see."

"Am I going to be okay?"

★

Almost two years after she had left, Carey received a phone call from her.

"Dave?"

"Yes."

"It's me."

"Hello."

"How's things?"

"Not bad."

"Still at the paper?"

"Yeah."

"Everything okay there?"

"As it ever was."

"Good."

Get to the point, woman.

"I've got something to tell you."

"Go on."

"I'm seeing someone else."

"Oh. Anyone I know?"

This was a joke, really.

"It is actually."

"Who?"

"John Barrett."

"You're joking."

"No, we met at a gig a few weeks ago and we've been together since."

"Well you're one of a number then, aren't you?"

"What do you mean?"

"It's in the paper every week that he's bedding someone different."

"Dave, don't be facetious."

"I'm not being facetious. He's supposed to have had seventeen thousand women, hasn't he? Something like that."

"Well he's not having them any more. He's happy with one."

"Good for you."

"Please, don't be sarcastic. I didn't have to make this call."

"Nice one."

"Nice one, what?"

"I suppose I should wish you all the best."

"You don't have to."

"I won't, then."

"That's your prerogative."

"Are you sure you got together a few weeks ago and not, let me see now, two years back?"

"I promise."

"I bet you do."

"What do you mean by that?"

"Nothing."

"Do you think I've been seeing him all this time?"

"People don't usually leave without someone else to go to. There's usually someone tapping gently at the back door. What did you tell me—you wanted to *find* yourself?"

"Well I did."

"That's okay, then. I hope you liked what you found."

"I did actually."

"Fine."

"Look, Dave, I'm making this call because I respect you. John and me want to be straight with you."

"So it was his idea, was it? Got a guilty conscience, has he? Why didn't *he* ring, then?"

"He's in the States."

"And I'm down the road tomorrow interviewing a couple celebrating their golden wedding. Funny how life turns out, isn't it?" He'd made this up; he'd not done a golden wedding for years.

"Don't be like that."

"No, it's spiteful of me, isn't it?"

"It is actually."

"I'm so sorry."

"Please."

"Okay, what do you want me to say?"

"Nothing. I just wanted you to know what has happened."

"Well I know now, don't I?"

"I suppose so."

"Dave, I still care about you."

"That's nice."

"Just because you leave someone doesn't mean you stop thinking about them."

"Right."

"I can see I'm wasting my time. I'm going now."

"Goodbye."

★

The nurse looked into the bowl.

"Most of this is old blood," she said. "Probably from the accident."

"That's what I was thinking."

"We'll have to make the doctor aware though because there's some fresh stuff too."

"Is that serious?"

"It depends."

"Will I have to see someone straight away?"

"If you bring up any more we'll get the duty doctor to see you, otherwise we'll monitor you through the night. Try and sleep if you can."

★

Carey didn't believe her. He remembered the regular trips to London and how, at the time, thinking it was odd attending A and R meetings for a band that wasn't formally signed to the label. She was sometimes disappointed too when she hadn't seen

Barrett, complaining a little too earnestly that he didn't have time for his old friends any more and doubting whether he'd played the tapes she'd sent of local bands.

Secretly (though it flattered him too, annoyingly), he was surprised Barrett had fallen for her. Once he had become famous, Carey imagined Barrett to hover above the earth, no longer part of it properly—one fixed point—but forever moving and so quickly that he didn't alight on people and places long enough to form a proper bond. She was too real, too substantial a person to be part of his world.

He told friends that he hoped Barrett never referred to her as Lucy; he wanted it to remain a term of endearment exclusive to their relationship. You had to have known her from young, to have seen the childhood photographs, spent time (hour upon hour) with her—on the canal bank, weekends in Ambleside, chatting with her parents after shepherd's pie and soporific TV on a Sunday evening, to know her as Lucy. Then, and more so now, Judy was too formal, too austere. Barrett was welcome to Judy.

Carey hated them for a long while, wished them the worst. These people had driven him deep into loneliness, made him into someone else. Among his books he found a passage by Francis Bacon that offered most succour. He photocopied it at work, blowing it up to 36pt and fastening it to his bedroom wall: 'But little do we perceive what solitude is. And how far it extendeth. For a crowd is not company, and faces are but a gallery of pictures, and talk a tinkling cymbal, where there is no love.'

★

It was a cold morning, the sun watery in the sky. As he left the hotel lobby Carey blew out long trails of steam. He crossed the road and walked to the edge of the sea. He watched the waves, the lisping and bubbling, the swelling circles, the crashing against the pebbles and the gentle after-splash. Thinking of that time now—Lucy leaving him, its absolute misery—he despised Barrett all over again. He'd buy the bottle and nurse it to his lips if need be, drown him in vodka.

*

The healing began properly for Carey when Judy did the same to Barrett as she'd done to him. She left him for a lawyer working in the music industry: a 'suit', of all things. Carey read about it in the papers and later bought *Burning Blue* to collect up the details. His feelings towards him changed, mellowed. Retrospectively, he also admired their resolve. If he had met someone he would have dallied, no matter how strong the love, too afraid of hurting others and dropping a bomb on his own life. His hostility to Judy subsided too. No malice had been intended by either of them; it was love. If they had kept it hidden from him for those two years, wasn't this because they didn't want to hurt him and saw it as the most compassionate way to get through the business?

And he had met other women since, some of whom had fallen in love with him, and he'd seen the qualities they shared, the things that made them different than men. They were impulsive, open-hearted, trusting, dreaming. Any ruthlessness, the kind Judy had shown, was a by-product of this and nothing vindictive.

On some days this rationale failed catastrophically and he

hated them so much that it felt a pleasure to hold something so pure.

Carey remembered the postcard Barrett had sent him from Brighton soon after signing the record deal. It had formed the first stab of regret — had he done the right thing? On it, Barrett had written how sunny it was and said they had been larking around, chucking their socks into the sea ('No socks please — we're British!'). Carey recalled his reaction: he hoped they wouldn't forget him and continued to send these cheery notes from wherever they were. And then another thought, almost simultaneously: he didn't want them rubbing it in like this, gloating about how great their lives were.

He bought the vodka.

Barrett had been moved to a room on his own. He was asleep. The nurse said Carey should pull up a chair and wait. After a few minutes, during which time he deliberately rustled a newspaper, Barrett woke up.

"Oh, hello," he said, sitting up. "Could you pass me some water?"

His hands shook as he put the plastic cup to his mouth.

"I've been like this since the fall."

"I've got you a bottle ..." said Carey.

"Good."

" ... But I'm not giving it to you."

"Why not?"

"For the reasons I told you yesterday."

"How come you've brought it, then?"

"I changed my mind."

"When?"

"When I sat down two minutes ago."

"What happened?"

"You did. I saw you lying there."

"So?"

"You looked like a kid."

"I look shit."

"John, we go way back."

"I know that."

"Well trust me on this."

"Don't make it like this; all sentimental, talking about trust, setting up a test of loyalty."

"What do you mean?"

"You know, the playing on your conscience bit. Why don't you *trust* me?"

"Lots of reasons."

"Let's have them."

"Stuff from years ago."

"Like what?"

"You know."

"I don't, tell me."

Carey was tired of this cryptic game.

"Stuff like going off with my wife."

"Dave, that was a lifetime ago."

"Well it never goes away for me, not properly."

"I'm sorry about that."

"Being sorry doesn't help."

"It's all I can be."

"Why did you do it?"

"You don't *mean* to do things like that."

"Oh, come on. You had free will. You could have stopped yourself. Don't just say it happened."

"You're right, I could have done nothing but that would have meant there were two of us unhappy for the rest of our lives, me and Judy. And it wouldn't have been fair on you, either. You would have been with someone who wanted to be with someone else. You deserve more than that."

"Don't patronise me."

"I'm not patronising you. I'm speaking honestly."

"How could I compete with you?"

"It wasn't like that."

"Of course it was. I'm sure you played it all humble, telling her about your troubled life with your mam and dad or whatever, but it's always there with people like you, you can't help yourself."

"What's always there?"

"Laying on the bullshit. I bet you got the old guitar out, turned on the charm and dropped the tickets to America in her lap, inviting her to the studio or the next gig."

"Dave, she fell in love with me and I fell in love with her. It happens. Women I've loved have gone off with someone else. Life is about how you respond to these things."

"What was it she saw in you that she didn't see in me?"

"It's not that simple. It's a million things that make you stop loving someone or not loving them as much as you used to or as much as you think you should. She told me you'd grown apart, that you were interested in different things."

"We were both into the music."

"It's attitudes that change, how you see things that crop up every day and then the big issues, how you react. Dave, you know all these things. Let go of the anger."

"If you had the chance to go back, would you still do it?"

"Yes, probably. Those years we had together were special and I believe it was meant to be. She was fated to come into both our lives and move on."

329

"I hate all that written-in-the-stars rubbish."

"I do, but I can't explain it any other way."

"She left you in the end, though."

"I knew she would."

"Why?"

"She'd done me. She needed a new mystery to solve, someone else supremely confident but massively insecure to become enthralled by. Look, get things in perspective. There are other good women out there. Perhaps you're bitter because you haven't found anyone you feel the same way about."

"And you have?"

"I think I have, yes, in Esther. She's a lot younger than me, I know that. But she's incredibly strong. I've got a fight on there though. She's planning to leave me."

"Is she?"

"She more or less said so yesterday. She's had enough — you can't blame her."

"What you going to do?"

"Work at it, I suppose."

They fell quiet for a second.

"Not everyone's like you ..." said Carey finally. "... able to transfer their affection so easily to someone else. Some people only feel that way once."

"Do you see yourself like that?"

"I think so."

"Maybe you just like that idea. You and me have always had that martyrdom thing. We imagine ourselves as the most committed, the most loyal, all that do-or-die stuff."

"You've been lucky having an outlet for your emotions, being able to write lyrics and have people listen to you. With me, it has stayed inside, never got out. You wouldn't believe how sad I was when she left. Not sad, that isn't a strong enough word. I was devastated. It wouldn't go away. I ended up crying at my parents', like a kid."

"I had a good idea what you were going through, actually. She used to tell me. She saw you a few times afterwards, didn't she? She thought by keeping in touch and seeing you now and again she was helping you along."

"Like weaning me off?"

"I suppose so."

"It worked but not in the way she probably imagined. It made me hate her; seeing how hard she was trying to be indifferent and making sure I got the point. It took her finishing me to see a side of her I didn't like and that made losing her easier to take. I thought there was an arrogance about her."

"Judy's problem is that she's never been left by anyone. Until she is, she'll always miss out on the humility that comes with it."

"And the fatalism."

"Yeah, that too. It's no bad thing if it's moderated."

As he spoke, Barrett reached across to a drawer in the bedside cabinet and pulled out a tatty photograph. It was him, Carey and Fisher in the Barretts' back garden when they were about seventeen.

"I've had it in my wallet for years. Do you remember that day?"

"Yeah, your dad kept moaning at us, asking us to stop gabbing and do something worthwhile with our lives, like mowing the lawn."

"Dave ..."

"Yes?"

"I think I might be pretty badly ill. I've been bringing up blood."

"Really?"

Barrett nodded.

331

"It might not be that serious," said Carey.

"I'm waiting to have a few tests and for the doctor to examine me."

Carey looked into Barrett's face. The whites of his eyes were like melted butter. He kept thinking that this wasn't supposed to happen: how had they got from there to here? He wanted to hug him, put his arm around his shoulders at least, but he was afraid of the intimacy.

Reaching into the plastic bag at his feet, Carey took out the bottle and handed it over. He wondered if Barrett was going to knock it back greedily.

"Give me a lift, will you?" said Barrett, rising from the bed.

He offered his forearm and Carey took it with his palms tensed and facing upwards. Barrett forced his weight against him and manoeuvred so he was sitting on the edge of the bed.

"Now the hard bit."

He put out a toe gingerly as if looking for a footing on a cliff face. He found the linoleum and transferred the weight to his feet. Walking away from the bed, he put his hand on his lower back, rubbing gently. The bottle was in his other hand. He stopped when he reached the window and looked out.

"It's not a bad day, is it?" he said.

"A bit chilly but okay."

"The sun's trying to shine."

He placed the bottle under a pile of clothes at the bottom of a small cupboard and turned to shuffle back to the bed.

"Are you going to drink that later?" asked Carey.

"No. It's like I said, a kind of insurance policy."

Carey believed him.

POMONA BOOKS

Pomona is a wholly independent publisher dedicated to bringing before the public the work of prodigiously talented writers. Tell your friends. Our books can be purchased on-line at:

www.pomonauk.com

*

Pomona Backlist:

FOOTNOTE*
Boff Whalley
ISBN 1-904590-00-4

*Footnote** is clever, funny and irreverent—a story about a boy from the red-brick clichés of smalltown England reconciling Mormonism and punk rock, industrial courtesy and political insurrection.

He finds a guitar, anarchism and art terrorism and, after years (and years and years) of earnest, determined, honest-to-goodness slogging, his pop group† makes it big; that's BIG with a megaphone actually. They write a song that has the whole world singing and, funnily enough, it's an admirable summary of a life well lived — about getting knocked down and getting back up again.

Meanwhile, there's a whole world still happening: authentic lives carefully drawn, emotional but not sentimental and always with a writer's eye for detail. *Footnote* is not another plodding rock memoir but a compassionate, critical and sometimes cynical account of a life steeped in pop culture, lower division football and putting the world to rights.

---

* See page 293 of Boff Whalley's book.
† Boff Whalley is a member of Chumbawamba.

RULE OF NIGHT
Trevor Hoyle

ISBN 1-904590-01-2

If the Sixties were swinging, the Seventies were the hangover — darker, nastier, uglier — especially if you lived on a council estate in the north of England.

Rule of Night was first published in 1975 and has since become a cult classic. It pre-dates the current vogue for 'hard men' and 'football hoolie' books by 25 years.

It is, however, much more than this. Trevor Hoyle creates a chillingly detailed world, where teenagers prowl rainy fluorescent-lit streets dressed as their *Clockwork Orange* anti-heroes. The backdrop is provided by Ford Cortinas, Players No.6, the factory, the relentless struggle to maintain hope.

Hoyle, who has since been published by John Calder (home to Samuel Beckett and William S. Burroughs), has added a fascinating afterword to his original book which has been out of print and highly sought-after for many years.

*

THE FAN
Hunter Davies

ISBN 1-904590-02-0

Hunter Davies is one of Britain's most acclaimed writers and journalists. He has written over 30 books, among them modern classics, *The Beatles* and *A Walk Around The Lakes*. *The Glory Game*, published in 1972, is a benchmark work on football and is still in print today.

The Fan is a collection of very personal, unusual pieces about his life as a supporter. He observes football in its sovereignty of the late 1900s and early 2000s and tackles the big topics of the day: Beckham's haircuts, high finance, the price of pies, the size of match day programmes, the enormous wages, the influence of Sky TV, England's numerous managers.

Along the way, he also lets us into his home life, in London and the Lake District, his family, his work, his tortoise, his poorly knee (caused by too much Sunday football).

Originally published in the *New Statesman* magazine, *The Fan* catches Davies at his very best and most amusing. It will appeal to supporters of any age, sex and loyalties.

LOVE SONGS
Crass
ISBN 1-904590-03-9

> *Our love of life is total,*
> *everything we do is an expression of that.*
> *Everything that we write is a love song.*
> – Penny Rimbaud, *Yes, Sir, I Will*

CRASS: a rural collective based in Essex, formed in 1977 of a diverse and eclectic group of individuals who operated for several years using music, art, literature and film as vehicles to share information and ideas. They also wanted to change the world.

This is a collection of words spanning those seven short years; a book of shock slogans and mindless token tantrums. An anthology of passionate love songs that sought to inspire a generation, and succeeded.

*

SUM TOTAL
Ray Gosling
ISBN 1-904590-05-5

Sum Total is a lost masterpiece of British literature, a restless, hungry riposte to America's finest Beat writers.

Written in 1961 when he was just 21, Gosling's itchy 'sort of' autobiography is a startlingly original take on the England of the early Sixties: rock-'n'roll, trains, dead-end jobs, drizzle, hitchhiking, jukebox cafés, trudging through hometown streets.

All the time he remains gloriously indulgent, disillusioned yet hopeful, tired but desperate for every new day.

Although now famous for hundreds of television and radio documentaries, in *Sum Total* Gosling reveals himself as a writer years ahead of his time, presenting a skew-whiff, arch and droll view of the world, both inside and out.

He has added a typically idiosyncratic and lengthy preface to the original text.

DIARY OF A HYPERDREAMER
Bill Nelson

ISBN 1-904590-06-3

Bill Nelson is one of Britain's most respected creative forces. He came to prominence in the Seventies with Be Bop Deluxe and later Red Noise. He has collaborated with like-minds such as Yellow Magic Orchestra, David Sylvian, Harold Budd and Roger Eno and still releases a prolific amount of new music.

Diary of a Hyperdreamer is his day-by-day journal in which he ponders on life, art and the nation. His unique perspective is fed by a career creating and producing music, photography, painting and video.

Written from his home in a hamlet in north Yorkshire, he also includes engaging details of his family life, regular musings on mortality, along with reflections on his childhood and former life as a globe-trotting 'pop star.'

*

THE PRICE OF COAL
Barry Hines

ISBN 1-904590-08-x

Barry Hines is a master craftsman. while he is rightly celebrated for his classic, *A Kestrel for a Knave* (later filmed as *Kes*), his other work is equally powerful.

The Price of Coal is an uncompromising depiction of life at a colliery where beer, snooker, cricket and time spent on the allotment is the only respite from clawing coal from the earth.

A royal visit prompts the introduction of soft soap to the toilets, grass seeds scattered on the slag heap, and lashings of white paint across the site.

But when disaster strikes the superficial is forgotten as men fight for their lives in the darkness underneath collapsing seams of coal.

As ever, Hines proves himself an exemplary storyteller with a discerning eye for detail and when bolder, gaudier writing is long forgotten, his stays in the mind and nourishes it.

He has written a new foreword to the original text which was first published in 1979 and later adapted for television as two linked plays, directed by Ken Loach in the acclaimed *Play for Today* series.

LOOKS & SMILES
Barry Hines
ISBN 1-904590-09-8

Looks and Smiles is a lost bulletin from the early-Eighties when the sun felt to have set permanently on hope and optimism. Unemployment was rampant, especially in the north where traditional industries were laid waste by Margaret Thatcher and her government.

Set amid this gloom, *Looks and Smiles* is an under-stated love affair between unemployed school-leaver Mick and Karen who works in a town centre shoe shop. They both want little more from life than a decent chance.

As ever, Hines proves himself an exemplary storyteller with a discerning eye for detail. He never resorts to sentimentality, and hope, however slender, flickers always.

The book was originally published in 1981 and later made into a film by Ken Loach.

*

KICKED INTO TOUCH (PLUS EXTRA-TIME)
Fred Eyre
ISBN 1-904590-12-8

Fred Eyre's sporting life began full of promise when he became Manchester City's first ever apprentice. He never made their first team. In fact, he seldom made anyone's first team. Injuries played a part but limited talent was the greater curse. As he plummeted down the leagues he had something few footballers possess: a stud-sharp memory and an ability to write humorously about the sport he loves.

Originally published in 1981, *Kicked Into Touch* has become an enigma —selling more than a million copies yet still retaining cult status within the sport and among fans. This new version has been completely revised, extended and updated with a new set of photographs included.

It is set to reach a new generation of football fans looking for an antidote to the glib reportage of a sport lost to show business.

MEAN WITH MONEY
Hunter Davies

ISBN 1-904590-13-6

At last, a book about money that tells it straight: put it under the bed. All of it. Sure, it makes for easy access to burglars but better them than the felons passing themselves off as financial advisors or acting as foot-soldiers for organisations with words like union, mutual, trust, alliance, equitable or assurance in their name.

Mean With Money, inspired by Hunter Davies' well-loved column in *The Sunday Times*, is wilfully short on practical advice but offers instead good humour and much-needed empathy as we face the corporate horror of high-handed and indifferent financial institutions.

Davies, one of Britain's most celebrated writers, also looks at ingenious ways to save money (cut your own hair, for starters) and what to do with it when it arrives. Along the way, he reveals details of his regular visits to McDonald's (it's free to use their toilets), the eccentric old ladies who staff his local Oxfam shop and the swim that cost him £333.

Famous for seminal works on The Beatles, football, and subjects as diverse as lottery winners and walking disused railway tracks, Davies is, once more, on top form. Go get 'em Hunt.

*

ZONE OF THE INTERIOR
Clancy Sigal

ISBN 1-904590-10-1

'The book they dared not print', zone of the interior isa lost classic of zonked-out, high-as-a-kite Sixties literature. It tells the story of Sid Bell, an American political fugitive in London, who falls under the spell of Dr. Willie Last (partly modelled on the radical 'anti-psychiatrist' RD Laing). This unlikely duo feast on LSD, mescaline, psilocybin and psycho-babble, believing that only by self-injecting themselves with schizophrenia will they become true existentialist guerrillas. Their 'purple haze' odyssey takes them into the eye of the hurricane — mental hospitals, secure units for the violent, the Harley Street cabal of the 'Sacred 7' and semi-derelict churches that come complete with an underground tank for the woman convinced she's a fish. Sigal's approach is richly sardonic and anti-establishment, of both right and left, in a jazz-influenced free-form prose, comic and serious, myth-puncturing and elegiac. Along the way Sigal, now an established Hollywood screen-writer, makes the case for a revolutionary period of mental health nursing whose task is as yet undone.

THE ARMS OF THE INFINITE
Christopher Barker

ISBN 1-904590-04-7

Christopher Barker is the son of the cult writer elizabeth Smart (*By Grand Central Station I Sat Down and Wept*) and the notorious poet, George Barker.

The Arms of the Infinite takes the reader inside the minds of both parents and, from their first fateful meeting and subsequent elopement, Barker candidly reveals their obsessive, passionate and volatile love affair.

He writes evocatively of his unconventional upbringing with his siblings in a shack in Ireland and, later, a rambling, falling-down house in Essex. Interesting and charismatic figures from the literary and art worlds are regular visitors and the book is full of fascinating cameos and anecdotes.

Barker is himself a gifted writer. An early draft of his memoir formed a cover story for the literary magazine, *Granta*.

*

THE SECOND HALF
Hunter Davies

ISBN 1-904590-14-4

The Second Half is another collection of personal pieces from the New Statesman covering the past three domestic seasons; the Euro Championship of 2004; and the 2006 World Cup when he unexpectedly became Wayne Rooney's top buddy.

'When a player gets sent off shouldn't we fans get some of our money back?' ponders Davies in one piece. 'I just wish he'd shave his stupid face,' he berates José Mourhino in another. And, goooaaal!, Hunt rumbles Sven early doors: 'He's a spare swede at a veggie gathering. What is the point of him?' he writes two years before England's World Cup debacle.

As ever, his outlook is fiercely that of the fan—disgruntled, bewildered and passionate—wondering what the players do with all that money, all those girls, and why match programmes are 'full of adverts or arse-licks for sponsors.'

And, finally, why did Peter Crouch? Because he saw Darren
Bent, of course.

BELIEVE IN THE SIGN
Mark Hodkinson

ISBN 1-904590-17-9

Believe in the Sign is about a damp corner of England where nothing much but everything happens. It is a 'sort of' memoir of a normal, average boy who would have grown up happily average and normal but for a dark and perverse passion: the seductive lure of masochistic devotion to a no-hope, near-derelict football club.

But it isn't all joyously uplifting. Swimming through the murk is a swarm of snapshots that bring growing up in the 1970s and 1980s into startling focus. Mad kids and sad kids and good kids from broken homes; teenage wrecking parties; pub brawls; long existential marches along the motorway banking; the baiting of Elton John and a club chairman caught playing 'away from home.'

Then Death bumps into Life. A girl is abducted and the town becomes a cave, the light sucked out. Meanwhile in the sunny shine outside, the future is afoot: cotton mills close down and supermarkets invade; school-leavers evolve into YOP-fodder and everyone's mum is holding Tupperware parties to get the down-payment on a colour telly.

Variously serious and funny, steely-eyed and tender, Hodkinson plumbs the depths but isn't afraid of the shallows. Dip a toe.

THE NOT DEAD
Simon Armitage
ISBN 978-1-904-59018-7

"*The Not Dead* is uniquely impressive. In transmuting the stories of particular soldiers into the lyrical music of Simon Armitage's poems, something exceptional is achieved: the painful truth of lives damaged beyond help is made meaningful for the rest of us. We can only catch our breath and read them again and again."
– Joan Bakewell

THIS ARTISTIC LIFE
Barry Hines

ISBN 978-1-904590-22-4

An anthology of essays and stories by Barry Hines, the author of the much-celebrated *A Kestrel for a Knave*, better known as *Kes*.

Many of the pieces were written at the same time as this seminal novel and have never been published before.

They cover Hines' love of sport along with his reflections on his home town of Hoyland Common, near Barnsley, both its landscape and the colourful characters that people it.

THE RICHARD MATTHEWMAN STORIES
Ian McMillan & Martyn Wiley

ISBN 978-1-904590-21-7

For a Yorkshireman who has spent half a lifetime in his native pit village, moving south is a mixed blessing and it is where Richard Matthewman's memories begin as he looks back with affection, humour, and no small measure of exasperation at 42 summers — and bitter winters. From boyhood through adolescence to marriage and a family, his stories are filled with a rich gallery of characters — the relations, friends and village notables of a vital community filled with life and incident but as brittle and unmistakably northern as the coal seams on which it was built.

Ian McMillan is a highly regarded poet, writer and performer from Barnsley. His work has led to extensive writing for Radio 1, 2, 3, 4 and Five Live as well as Yorkshire Television and BBC's *Newsnight Late Review*. He was recently profiled on the *South Bank Show*.

The Richard Matthewman Stories were originally aired as a popular series on Radio 4. Co-author Martyn Wiley died in 1994.